I0818320

THE MERCY OF LIONS

THE MERCY OF LIONS

The Renaissance Trilogy - Book I

HENRY VYNER-BROOKS

Henry Vyner-Brooks

CONTENTS

DRAMATIS PERSONAE

(**Fictional Characters** are marked with an asterisk *)

RHODES:

- ***Fra Hugh de Erpingham** - Knight of Rhodes and amateur painter. poet & philosopher
- **Emery d'Ambroise** - Grandmaster of Rhodes
- **Guy de Blanchefort**, Prior of Auvergne
- ***Fra Marcantonio Vendramin,** the knight who has disappeared
- **Guy Borel Valdiviessa e Maldonato,** Knight of the Langue of Castille
- ***Wilfred Carter,** manservant to Hugh de Erpingham
- ***Pico,** Orphan, Wilfred's helper

ROME - **Papal Curia:**

- **Pope Julius II** – Giuliano della Rovere, the Warrior Pope
- **Giuliano Leno** – Papal Chamberlain
- **Angelo Colocci** – Papal Secretary
- **Sigismondo de Conti** – Private papal Secretary
- **Johannes Burchard & Paris di Grassis** –Papal Masters of Ceremony
- **Donato Bramante** – Military Engineer and Papal Architect for the new St. Peters

- **Agostino Chigi** – Banker, Treasurer and Notary of the Apostolic Camera, richest man in Rome
- **Cardinal Ippolito d'Este** –Archbishop of Milan and brother to the Duke of Ferrara.
- **Cardinal Adriano de Cornetto**–former Papal chamberlain and Papal Nuncio to England & Scotland, owner of Villa Giraud

ROME - Other Cardinals:

- **Cardinal Casanova** – a Borgia stooge and former Papal Chamberlain under Pius III
- **Pietro Gamboa** - Bishop of Carinola, the pope's confessor
- **Cardinal Serra**
- **Cardinal Francesco Borgia** – former Pope's cousin
- **Cardinal Giovanni Castelar**
- **Cardinal de Loris** of Constantinople.
- **Cardinal Riario** – Pope Julius's cousin

ROME - Florentines in Rome:

- ***Giovanni Battista** – Prior of Rome for the knights of Rhodes
- **Giuliano de Sangallo** – Sculptor, Architect, friend of Pope and Michelangelo
- **Michelangelo di Buonarotti** – Sculptor, reluctant painter.
- **Pietro Torrigiano** – the Sculptor who broke Michelangelo's nose
- **Michelangelo's co-painters** – Granacci (Florentine painter), Tedesco, Buggiardini, Donnino, and Sangallo's nephew Sebastiano.
- **Cardinal Giovanni de Medici** – Future Pope Leo X
- **Alfonsa Orsini** – Giovanni de Medici's sister-in-law

ROME - Others in Rome:

- **Pietro Bembo** – Poet, literary scholar
- **Raphael di Santi**– Painter from Urbino
- **Duchess Elizabetta Montefeltro** of Urbino

TURKS:

- **Sultan Bayazid II** – Sultan of the Ottoman Empire
- **Kurkut Chelebi** – *The Lord Chonochiari,* son of Sultan Bayazid II
- **Kemal Beg** – unfortunate friend and envoy of Kurkut Cheleb
- ***Filcher** – English horse thief and galley slave

ISLAND OF ISCHIA:

- **Duchess Constanza D'Avalos** – Duchess of Francavilla, la Gioconda, the laughing lady
- **Vittoria Colonna** – poetess, daughter of Frabrizio, Grand Constable of Naples, and granddaughter of the illustrious Duke Frederico de Montefeltro of Urbino

- **Sannazaro, Paolo Giovio, Tansillo and Bernardo Tasso** – Poets at court

BRACCIANO
- **Madonna Felice Orsini** - (nee. De Cupis) The Pope's daughter, business woman
- **Duke Gian Giordano Orsini** – Felice's husband, Warlord allied to the French
- **Madonna Claudette Colett**e – Felice's lady in waiting
- **Lady Emilia Pia** – lady in waiting and sister-in-law to the Duchess of Urbino

ORVIETO
- **Lucca Signorelli of Cortona** (not present) fresco painter who finished off Fra Angelico's work and created scenes from the reign of Antichrist and the judgement
- **Gian Paolo Baglioni** – Lord of Perugia, ally of Pandolfo Petrucci

KONSTANZ
- ***Brother Santfrid** – Benedictine host on the monastic island of Reichenau
- **Maximilian I** - Holy Roman Emperor
- **Cardinal Georges d'Amboise** – First minister of France & Papal Legate, brother to Hugh's magister
- **Martin Luther** – Augustinian canon.

SAN GIMIGNANO
- **Paolo Cortesi** – Former apostolic secretary & author of *De Cardinalatu*, 'The Cardinal'

FLORENCE
- **Nicolo Machiavelli** - Civil servant, Secretary of the Council of Ten
- **Francesco Guicciardini,** diplomat, historian and law tutor at the Florence studio
- **Michelotto *or Don Michelle*** - Bargello for Florence's civic militia, and former friend of Cesare Borgia
- **Sandro Botticelli** - Painter

MILAN
- **Leonardo da Vinci** – military engineer and *il maestro pittore* (master painter)
- **Francesco Melzi & Sallai** - Leonardo's apprentices
- **Charles II d'Amboise** – French Governor of Milan, nephew of Hugh's magister
- **Thomas Cromwell** – Cockney mercenary, victualer, fixer.

SIENNA
- **Pandolfo Petrucci** - Tyrant of Siena
- **Cardinal Alfonso Petrucci** - Pandolfo's 18-year-old son

ASSISI

- ***Fra Francesco i Bisognoso** – Franciscan Friar who runs the leper colony
- ***Fra Paolo Todesco** – Francesco's assistant

THE DECEASED & manner of death:

- **Rodrigo Borgia** – Pope Alexander VI (poisoned)
- **Cesare Borgia** – The former pope's son and Duke Valentino of Romagna (slain)
- **Francesco Todeschini Piccolomini** – Pope Pius III (murdered)
- **Cardinal Casanova** – Papal Chamberlain under Pius III (ill health)
- **Magister Pierre d'Aubusson** – Grand Master of the Knights of Rhodes (bitterness & old age)
- **Guidobaldo da Montefeltro** – Duke of Urbino, husband of Elizabetta Gonzaga (aged 36, gout, ill health)
- **Pico di Mirandola** – Count of Mirandola, poet, scholar (aged 31, Arsenic poisoning)
- **Polition** – Latinist, scholar (poisoned with arsenic on the same day as the above.)
- **Lorenzo de Medici** – Il Magnifico (aged 43, at peace listening to the Gospels)
- **Ficino** – Platonist scholar, reluctant tutor to the House of Medici. (Aged 65)
- **Francesco Petrarca** – (Petrarch) Priest, poet, early Christian humanist. (Aged 69)
- **Dante Alighieri** – Poet of the Vita Nuova and the Divina Comedia (aged 56, Malaria)
- **Walafrid Strabo and Herman the Lame** – part of the Carolingian Renaissance at Reichenau
- **Pinturicchio** – frescoed the Borgia's papal apartments (aged 59)
- **Guillaume de Guileville** – author of the *Pilgrimage of the Soul* (aged about 60)
- **Jacopone da Todi** – Ultra-ascetic Franciscan poet (aged 76, broken health)
- **Francesco della Rivere** – Pope Sixtus IV (aged 70, 'declining' health)

ACKNOWLEDGEMENTS

THE RENAISSANCE TRILOGY

Book I. **The Mercy of Lions** (1503-1509)
Book II. **The Shadow of Cain** (1509-1510)
Book III. **The Heretic** (1536-1539)

I must be frank, the most demoralising aspect of book writing for me has been penning these acknowledgements year on year, and realising that I have done so little to repay the kindness of so many.

I once read of a man trapped in a coma, who could hear everything going on around his hospital bed but could do nothing to communicate - not so much as a finger twitch or an eyelash flicker. I am that man. I feel conscious of so much help, yet I am unable to adequately respond or reciprocate. That poor man in the coma was fortunate enough to have a wife who wouldn't let the doctors turn off the ventilator. She kept believing he would come through it and, after 28 years, he did.

So, in the same vein, I want to first acknowledge the loving support of my wife, Ruth. I am writing this in the 25th year of a marriage, over half of which has been spent writing. She has kept my proverbial ventilator switched on long after professionals and concerned family members counselled that I give up and get a proper job. She never wavered in wisdom or encouragement, even when there was precious little of either to be found in the manuscript or the author. She proof read and edited numerous drafts, often late at night after long days teaching. What can a man do to repay such sacrifice? No wonder the Christians coined the term 'grace' to sum up the situation *viz a viz* salvation. You just have to accept what is offered so freely, and then live in the light of it.

For fourteen years, the author John Steinbeck signed letters to his literary agent as from 'your unprofitable client.' That is about the length of time I have been hoping to repay my agent Pieter Kwant for his encouragement and mentorship. I was hoping by now to have made him and Elria enough money so that they could have a place nearer us int he Lakes, and so that we could take long walks together (nowhere in particular) and talk about many things. Alas! But perhaps this is what eternity is for.

Many thanks also goes to general editor Leanne Hardy, who worked with so much skill on books I & II. I am very grateful. Thanks also goes to Lion's then commissioning editor Tony Collins who, in a moment of either absent mindedness or divine inspiration, suggested I consider writing a sequel to *The Heretic*. A sequel, set at the settling of the New World seemed too much a stretch to me, so I have answered the request with two prequels instead.

There are many friends and family, colleagues and even a few literary critics that have encouraged me in the *Renaissance Trilogy* project. I will not mention all your names, but I will mention my eldest daughter Abigail, who edited an early draft and also came with me for a research trip throughout the the Italian ducal courts in 2016. Sitting on the steps of *Santa Spirito* in Florence, eating Pizza and sketching together as people milled around the piazza and night fell, will always be a treasured memory of very happy of times. (And well earned after visiting 27 of the city's cultural attractions on our 72 hour city pass!)

My final thanks is to the reader, for their investment of time. May it enrich and reward you as much as it did the author.

HISTORICAL NOTE

I once read that the greatest tragedy expressed in gothic literature is almost always misunderstood. It is *not* so much that vampires are condemned to a derivative existence of eternal predation and self-loathing. It is *not* even that they are powerless against the deterministic urges that lead them to kill the things they so often love. Their greatest tragedy is, in fact, that they can never see themselves in a mirror. This novel cannot help but be a mirror, however imperfect and partial.

It is set at one of those moments in history which make the writer's job so much easier. So many characters and events in High Renaissance Italy are at such polar extremes of good and evil that the writer is likely to be accused of sensation when all the time he or she is merely repeating the historical record. For example, the infamies of the Borgias and their associates are almost impossible exaggerate. With the exception of the initial plot about the gold shipment (which I invented), I have had to do little but recount these villains as they actually were. The details of Pope Alexander's final illness and death are reconstructed fairly accurately from contemporary sources. The manner of burial, as recounted in Johannes Burchard's diary, are eye-witness accounts given verbatim. In fact, the reader might almost always assume that any sensational or lurid detail about historical figures in these novels is literally – and regrettably – true. Frankly some of it you could not make up, or even want to. They portray human nature in its worst possible light. Having said all that, in Book II *The Shadow of Cain*, I attempt to portray the Borgia siblings Lucretia and Cesare with greater sympathy.

It is not just the characters, but also the times themselves that are extraordinary. The Ottoman threat was then a pressing reality, and I cannot recall inventing anything with regard to the Sultan, the various naval skirmishes, the debacle involving Kurkut, or the preparations of the Sultan's armada at Gallipoli and Constantinople. These strategic threats from the east were clear and present dangers to western European powers mired in selfish national squabbles – here is nothing new. It is unclear to me to what extent the knights of Rhodes really were 'the shield of Christendom' at that moment in history, but they and Venice were certainly something very nearly like it.

Hugh de Erpingham and Marc Antonio Vendramin are fictional, but everyone else associated with the knights has kept their real name. Hugh's grandmaster was one of nine sons of the noble house of d'Amboise, and his siblings were ubiquitous throughout the French polity at this time – not least his brother George, who was the first minister of France, and who we will meet in books I and II. The war with Venice and the various battles, dates and commanders are portrayed accurately as well. Innovations in artillery made these wars particularly horrific and shameful at a time of supposed cultural elevation. In that regard, we may assume the effects on the European psyche and Christian conscience were something similar to World War I.

Even though this era is tantalising in many respects, it was primarily the cultural and intellectual shifts occurring in early modernity that captured my attention and drew me in. This epoch was one of the great hinges of western civilisation, and I sought to understand the epistemological revolution taking place then, which in many ways has made us who we are today. In High Renaissance Italy, we find the seeds of the Enlightenment in germination and dispersal. We are the full flower of those seeds; some would say even the cut and wilting flowers.

To help navigate this sea change, we have the help of many of the actual gatekeepers of that cultural development. Firstly, we have the historical Neoplatonist poet and literary critic Pietro Bembo. He plays a large part in Books I & II, and so naturally, has been heavily fictionalised. He makes a useful and lively foil for Hugh's melancholy and metaphysical speculations and an explainer of Italian literary and intellectual culture. Though not a premier culture shaper himself, Bembo would one day become a cardinal and even a knight of Rhodes. His Neoplatonist work *Gli Asolani* secured him great fame at the time when he meets our fictional protagonist, Hugh. Bembo's formative years in Venice and Florence open up tensions regarding his ultimate allegiances.

Shelley claimed, the poets are 'the unacknowledged legislators of mankind', and this was never truer than at this time, as also for artists, sculptors, architects, historians and fledgling political philosophers. A new spirit was abroad in Italy. The humble but dignified craftsmen and women of a former age were experiencing an elevation as the new high priests of culture. Their legacy is still among us and the results of their elevation within the culture have been very mixed.

In Book I. we meet three men (Cortesi, Castiglione, and Machiavelli) whose books *The Cardinal, The Courtier*, and *The Prince* were very influential in the courts of northern Europe –Cardinal Wolsey and Henry VIII to name but two influential recipients and transmitters. Wolsey wouldn't have been the man he was, nor built Hampton Court as he did, without Cortesi. And Henry would not have acted quite as he did without the influence of Machiavelli's *The Prince*, which was given him by Thomas Cromwell. Among the five books always at the bedside of Emperor Maximilian were Erasmus' *Handbook of the Christian Soldier*, Castiglione's *The Courtier*, and Machiavelli's *The Prince*.

In many ways the deceased are, if anything, more influential than the living in this volume. Perhaps they always are? Dante, Petrarch, Francis of Assisi, Savonarola, and Thomas Aquinas, for example, had a profound effect on later generations - even our own. These, along with other sources more ancient, were my delight to rediscover and share with the reader. Their cosmology, their sense of drive and purpose, their wrestling with ultimate questions that are still debated among us, was for me deeply enriching. A reader might judge them wrong at certain points, but you could never say they were poor, cowardly or inhumane.

In this volume, we also meet Michelangelo, Sangallo, Botticelli, Leonardo da Vinci, Raphael and Bramante (the latter two suffer somewhat unjustly under my pen). In terms of art history, these are the *bright suns among* (some other) *small stars* who are also mentioned, and each of them have their part to play. Their chief patron, the quite extraordinary 'Warrior Pope,' Julius II, is portrayed as I found him in the historical record. He is, like most of us, a mass of contradictions, and a man in an almost frantic hurry to establish his legacy. There may not have been another man alive who could have bullied Michelangelo to fresco the Sistine Chapel ceiling, so we owe some great debt to his patronage at least. That ceiling came at the expense of the prior commission for his own tomb, which still though only very partially complete, can be seen at San Pietro in Vincola, Rome. *The Pope's Daughter*, Felice, who has been given an excellent biography by Caroline Murphy, is shown much as she was – a remarkably tender, brave and enterprising woman. And so is the Poetess Vittoria Colonna, though I have taken the liberty of using some of her later poetry chronologically earlier in these novels as a salvific bulwark to Hugh's existential despair. Emilia Pia, who also appears in books I & II, was doubtless Shakespeare's model behind Beatrice in *Much Ado About Nothing*. (To continue the theme, I have made Bembo into her Benedict.)

The presence of the artists, sculptors and architects were, for me, part of the attraction of writing the book. Having first written Book III, I knew that I could not undertake a historical novel again without having a strong desire to immerse myself in the particular era. The Renaissance was for me such an era, for I had fallen under its spell long ago as a teenager when studying the history of art and architecture for A-level. *Oh blessed time!* I remember, as an aspiring lead singer and guitarist in a heavy metal band, coming alive during those lectures, watching Kenneth Clarke's *Civilisation* documentaries with a group of five others. I was pierced by the sweet beauty of those works of art with a longing or homesickness that is hard to describe. (I believe the Germans call it *Sehnsucht*, and C. S. Lewis called it 'joy' after the Romantic's term 'mystical joy'.) However it is to be described, I've always felt that I was aesthetically born again in Renaissance Italy, and so this book is as much a debt of justice to those artists as anything else.

There are also cameo appearances by our own Thomas Cromwell, who was finding his way about Italy as a mercenary and merchant at this time. We also meet a young Martin Luther in Konstanz, whose perspective I construct from his own writings. He had travelled to Rome by then and his chance meeting with Hugh and the prophecy of Jan Huss – which as far as I know is genuine – made a fitting reference to the religious tsunami about to break on Europe.

I have admitted above that my treatment of the architect Bramante and artist Raphael were not as generous as perhaps they deserved. The medium of historical fiction makes certain demands on a writer that must be acknowledged. However, other historical characters, who are represented as particularly depraved, actually were. Pandolfo Petrucci, the tyrant of Siena, probably was indeed the man behind the poisoning of Pius III's leg bandages. His various confederates were odious beyond words and I have made nothing up that cannot be easily found in the grimmest prose in any history book of the era. His son Alfonso who, contrary to this novel wasn't made a cardinal until 1511, was an equally pernicious schemer. He was eventually arrested and strangled in 1517 for plotting to assassinate the Medici Pope, Leo X.

It should go without saying, but in these days, one cannot assume it, that many viewpoints in this novel are expressed through the jaundiced perspective of Hugh and the cynicism of characters like Bembo. On occasions certain groups, like the Renaissance humanists or the Dominicans for example, are treated by them with unjust censure. This is the age of Bocaccio and Machiavelli; an age of cynicism and wit. They would have been right at home with Twitter. If they offend - and they often offend me - then please have patience. These novels do not intend to portray late modern people (like you or me) in doublets and hose. The Sisyphean task I have so imperfectly undertaken in these novels, was to recreate medieval-minded people on the cusp of modernity, simultaneously beginning to experience the new paradigm at different points and in different degrees.

My only hope in this trilogy, which has taken almost a decade to produce, is that, by letting those people speak to us as they would, we might begin to see ourselves as we should – as we in fact are. Here again is the great value of history. It is often an obscure mirror and even more often interpreted through besmirched spectacles. Yet, nevertheless, it is all we have. Churchill believed only those who reached back far into the past could in any way see the future. I suppose that is how Churchill, rather than others of greater intellect and ability, was able to understand his own times and save his island nation. We may not be tasked as Churchill was, yet we still owe a debt to our ancestors to heed them, and to our descendants, to transmit that central challenge that comes down to us through the great western tradition. It was written above the entrance to the oracle at Delphi, 'Know thyself'; and by the psalmist 'What is so special about humanity?'; and by suffering Job 'Why was I born? How can I be pure? Will I be conscious after death?' Such deep and searching questions! They are almost written through every book we read and many more we don't. The desire to know and be known, to have someone untangle the riddle that is us.

At times I have been, like Buddha and Confucius, straining after those ultimate answers. But more often I am Herod, Pilate or Judas, standing before the One who returns all my deepest questions with yet another; *'Who do you say that I am?'*

Those latter three all turned away, like vampires from a mirror. In this book, I have sought, through the eyes of my wounded protagonist, to see and to keep on seeing, however grim, however glorious.

'For with thee is the fountain of life: in thy light shall we see light.' Psalm 36 v.9

Henry Vyner-Brooks, Loweswater, 2022

THE JOURNEYS OF HUGH DE ERPINGHAM 1508-1509

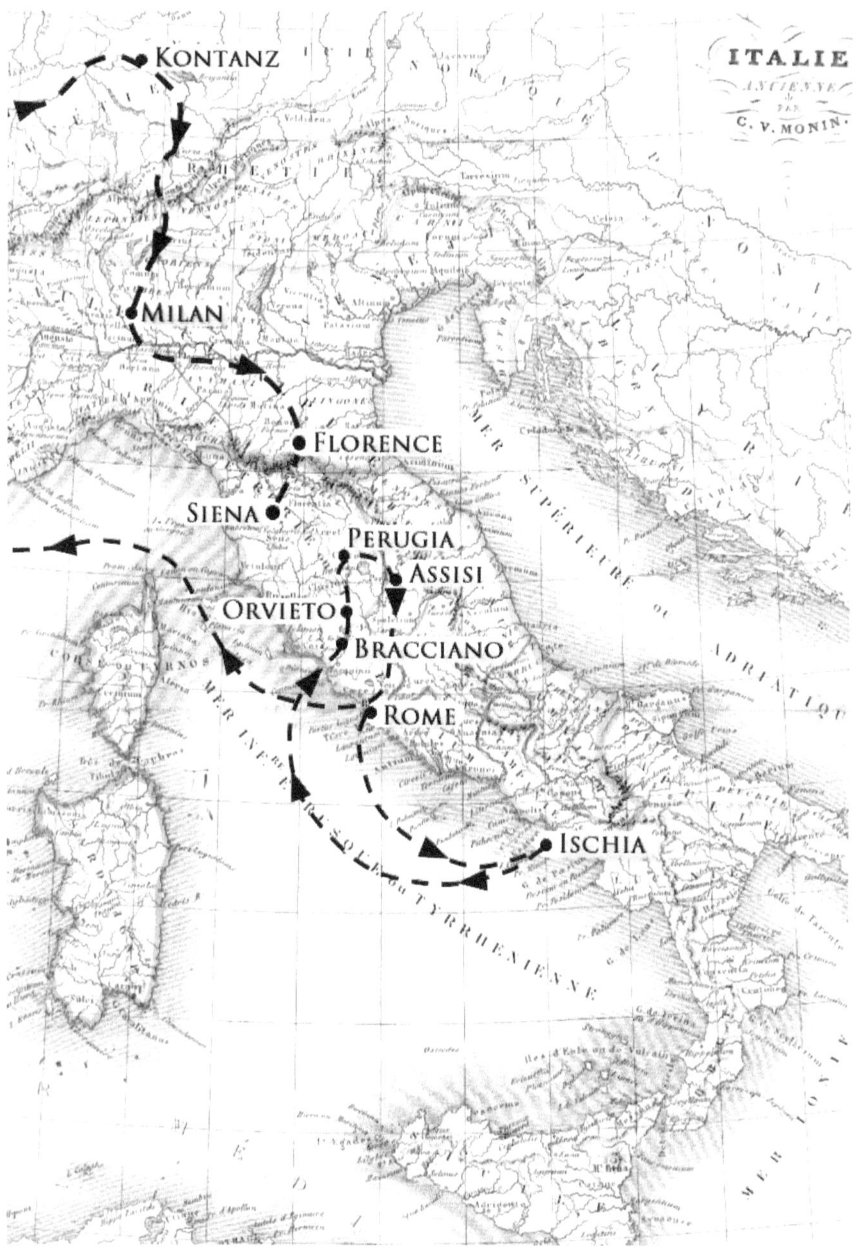

PROLOGUE

COMETH THE HOUR

THURSDAY, SEPTEMBER 2ND, 1508, OSTIA HARBOUR

The evening tide ebbs. Sicilian seamen sing as they offload cargo. Their dulcet tones echo comfortably off the carracks, merchantmen, galleys and galliots, many from the papal fleet. The air is full of the creak of hulls, the rattle of pulleys, the smell of fish, wood, rope, brine, sewerage.

The older sailors sit on the quayside like a Greek chorus; retired mariners who have come to watch passengers disembark from far and near—Genoa, Arragon, England, the Low Countries—at Ostia harbor, centre of the world.

Turned out by their wives with a little tavern money, these old boys drift like flotsam onto the quay around the time of the Vespers bell. They come to inspect the set of sails, trim of rigging, and condition of the hulls. Usually, they come to criticise these *Cretini Pigri*, these young *bastardi,* who strut about the wharf counting-houses like peacocks. They come to bemoan the fast-changing world, and join other aged Romans, from Pliny to the present, in their disquiet about the future. *Tempora Mutantor!* It is always easier to blame the next generation for the state of the world, easier than the alternative.

Usually they do all these things, but not this evening. For this evening they are looking intently at a lean, tanned man in black coming down the gangplank of a goke that started life as a Turkish man-of-war. His hair and beard are trimmed but unkempt from the journey; brown, but bleached by the sun in the parts still visible below the brim of his beret.

'He must be a Spaniard,' one old man mutters. 'They are all white moors, cruel as the devil,' and the others agree. But then, as the man steps onto the quayside, they catch sight of the large white cross on his cape, and again, the smaller one on his doublet.

'Maybe a hero from the siege?'

'*Santa Maria*, a knight of Rhodes!' They cross themselves as if choreographed and perhaps would have knelt too if he had come near enough. Anyone would, who had spent an uncertain lifetime close reefed in wicked seas among the Turks and Barbary corsairs.

'Too young.'

It is thirty years since the great siege. They all remember that well. They had nigh held their breath when they heard that Rhodes—the last crusader stronghold—might fall to the Turks. Any deckhand worth his salt on any merchantman from Antwerp to Athens could tell you who held the balance of power in the eastern Mediterranean. A sailor's life was never certain at the best of times, but it wouldn't be worth a shipwright's shaving east of Athens if Rhodes fell. But by some miracle the knights had beaten back the infidels, and legends and heroes had been made in the process. But this knight is too young to have been there. *What is he, thirty - maybe less?*

All musings of bygone days are rudely interrupted as a well-fleshed manservant follows his master off the gangplank, shouting in English at the Sicilian cargo handlers. He points from the trunks to the knight, and although no one can understand what he is saying, they recognize the name Erpingham amongst the dark oaths.

'Could this be the great Hugh Erpingham?' The old sailors mutter. 'The one who returned from the dead? *Dio mio.*'

Meanwhile on the quayside:

'You all right, master?' The manservant approaches the knight, wiping a broad and beaded brow, and looking back every now and then toward the Sicilians stevedores who are piling the luggage into a cart. 'Thought they would have your trunk in the drink the way they were handling that crane.' When he gets no response, he turns back to see his master's thousand-yard stare, and hands that twitch involuntarily. The manservant gently holds one of the knight's wrists, looking round to make sure no one can see, saying tenderly, 'Come on, Hugh. You're all right, lad. We're here now. I'll go get us all somewhere to stay.'

Hugh Erpingham begins to blink rapidly and then lets out a pent-up breath as he comes round. 'What? Yes. Thank you, Wilf.'

'Do anything else for you?' Wilf says, exhaling with relief.

'No.' Hugh shakes his head and half attempts a smile. Even now his eyes are the two great gashes that reveal a torn soul. 'But Wilf, give a few coins to the Sicilians, and to those old boys on the quay. Tell them they can drink our health.' He knows they are probably being watched anyway, so it is best to create a little stir in the hen house – see if there is a fox hiding in there.

Wilf shakes his head but goes to it. The old men raise the coins toward Hugh in thanks, and he touches his beret. When Wilf returns, he says, 'Those old dogs wanted to know who you are so they can toast you. Told'em like. Just hope that's all right with you. I know we're here on tricky business.' Hugh nods absently and Wilf goes back to swearing at the stevedores.

Told them who I am? I barely know myself anymore. I am the man with no country, no city, a refugee from the collapse of chivalry. I am the fallen man who is conscious that he has lost the ability to love, the man who has arrived in hell before his time. I am the man whose back became the hull upon which many waves broke. Fluctuamus, sed non submersi; tossed but not sunk. That is who I am. Sin is the only part of theology I have proved or perhaps can be proved. I am the sinner, who cannot forget and who will not be forgiven.

A half-written letter to his mother in England is scrunched tightly in his right hand. It reads like a suicide note. He cannot finish it, and it will never be sent in any case. The last lines display a fig leaf of scholarship to cover an ocean of pain. He unfolds it and glances at them with a great stab piercing his chest.

> ...and so much for my sorrows, Mater. Lucretius' stoic virtue of *apetheia* – what, I think, Epicurus called *ataraxia*: to observe one's trouble as if 'from a fortress of indifference' -- appear now to be law more easily applied to a neighbour than oneself. But I cannot write of philosophy now, for in truth I am sick of it, sick of all things – even painting and poetry.
>
> Keep my sisters in remembrance of me. Tell them to pray oft for me here. I have hope that God will hear them at least. And spare thyself no rest but to dissuade my brother Cecil from joining the knights. Let him take another path, a peaceful one as befits his nature and station. I pray heaven, lady, that you will have more profit in him than in me. Adieu.

He stuffs it back in his scrip with disgust.

My mother. Did ever a man have such a sweet, wise, understanding mother? What have I done? She said I should stay in Norfolk. A man never knows he is happy, only when he was. What can I tell her now? That she was right? That I am lost to her, lost to all the world, to myself even? I have built a rampart between us all. I can never be myself again after what I have done.

Hugh takes a backward glance at the ship – his last link with Rhodes, the place where he had wanted to hide. *What in the name of Saint Michael and all the angels am I doing here?* Another good question. He turns toward the Via Roma like Christ setting his face toward Jerusalem.

He has come to raise hell, and he knows that there will be hell to pay for it.

Part I - KNIGHTS ERRANT

Five Years earlier

18TH AUGUST 1503 - TUESDAY AFTERNOON. PAPAL APARTMENTS, ROME

'Cesare, Cesare!' Michelotto shakes his friend roughly from the drenched sheets where he is lying half delirious with fever. 'Cesare, wake up; the pope is dead.'

The young Borgia comes to with a jolt. 'What?'

'Your father is dead. Burchard has just now come from the apartments. The cardinals sent – '

'When? How long ago?' Cesare is suddenly his lupine self—Duke Valentino, bastard, murderer, syphilitic whoremonger, ex-cardinal, condotierro, antichrist, etcetera. He grabs Michelotto's sleeve, jerking it violently as he speaks in the Catalonian tongue. 'When, damn you?'

'Just now.'

Cesare releases an embittered moan. 'Take half the men; get over there; there's still time. They'll not catch me with my trousers' down and arse in a bucket. We must salvage what we can from this mess. Cardinal Casanova has the key. Stick a knife to his throat, dangle him from the window by his parts if you have to; just get that key and bring me everything you can. We must have it all today.'

It is a sign of the times, but mercenaries won't lay waste republics and pillage dukedoms just to make the world a better place anymore. They march on ducats, on rapine.

The echo of boots, the rustle of sheets, the milky stench of a sick-man's bed. Don Michelotto is gone, and behind him forty retainers, their colours of quartered red and yellow, emblazoned with the name 'Cesare'. A tad gaudy, but Cesare Borgia has learnt to paint with broad brush strokes as it is all the mob understand. There will be no trouble. If Don Michelotto's face isn't enough to get access to the papal treasury, then his men will be. They are known and feared. Some are from his original Spanish infantry, some Gascons, and, outside in the yard, the dreaded *Stradiotes,* Albanian light cavalry who gained their spurs fighting the Ottomans in the Balkans. They are hard bastards, not gentlemen. The duke has always attracted the most celebrated mercenaries, like the Swiss, for his lightning campaigns of terror in the Romagna and Marches. He always lets them indulge liberally in the rights of conquest. So, in return they obey orders, and then some. That is why there'll be no trouble.

Cesare strains without success to attain an upright position; but he who made all Italy tremble, sinks back into his feather pillow. His father is dead. Rodrigo Borgia, Pope Alexander VI, is no more. *This is not convenient. It puts pay to our plans. The plan, the great plan; me as gonfalonere of the papal army, me as pope and emperor – the sacred and temporal powers suffused. We'd have taught Domition a thing or two.*

The Orsini family have heard of Cesare's illness and are on their way back to Rome. The Vitellis will exploit this. *Scheming bastards. Must send letters to the prefects in the Romagna to let them know all is well, and recall the troops from Perugia.*

Memories. A legion of ghosts.

Two weeks before, the pope and Cesare took dinner at Cardinal Adriano's Villa Giraud, a lusty pile designed by Bramante. A crippling fever struck six days later. Rome was alight with gossip. Poison. Canterella or eternity powder? Some even say the pope had intended to poison the cardinal for his ready cash and acres but got the cups mixed up. Who can you believe in this web of villains?

Cesare winces, holds his breath, groans, mind and body going in different directions. *I'll beat this.* He exhales. Each breath is like raising a mountain. He does not suspect the cardinal. The cardinal is the pope's secretary, confidant, favourite, and nearest thing to a friend Lucifer had or could have. The method. Canterella? A fungal poison, an effortless way to send your enemies to the underworld ahead of you. But Canterella's effects manifest in two days, not six. The Borgias know their poison. Cardinal Adriano took sick of this same fever on the fifth. It is what his people claim anyway, and who's to say? It is the common complaint that Rome is plagued with miasmic vapours. The three had sat out too late in a season when ague in its most malignant form is rife. Now they are paying for it – or in his father's case, *had* paid.

Memories.

On the fifteenth they had taken thirteen ounces of blood from the pontiff, to supervene a tertiary ague. On the sixteenth, he was given medicine. The pope did not ask after his son, nor the son after his father.

Some idiot physician had the duke lowered into a vat of iced water, causing his whole skin to peel off as if he had been a snake – which of course he was. He turned delirious shortly after that, but today he is stronger than he has been. Yet he feels a powerful delirium taking him away to sleep.

Silver whispers slither within the silk sheets and echo on smooth marble.

Cesare awakes with a start. They are whispering at the door about him. *I will beat this. My father, Alexander VI, is no more.* Still, he can scarce believe it. A great force has been arrested on the earth, has ceased to be. *God, what dread timing is this?* The myriad occupants of the wasps' nest thrum with metaphysical contemplation. He tries to blink away the confusion. Dante leers at him from the end of his bed, laurels and all. 'I passed through hell because there was no way past the lean, she-wolf of avarice. Virgil was my guide. I will be yours.' Cesare twists and turns in his sheets. *I have beaten fever before. I will beat this.*

When he looks again, the Florentine prophet is quoting Isaiah at him. *Shit, that's all I need.* 'The realm of the dead below is all astir to meet you at your coming; it rouses the spirits of the departed to greet you, all those who were leaders in the world; it makes them rise from their thrones, all those who were kings over the nations. They will all respond, they will say to you, "You also have become weak, as we are; you have become like us." All your pomp has been brought down to the grave, along with the noise of your harps; maggots are spread out beneath you and worms cover you.'

Cesare resists it. *I won't die you bastard, and I won't go mad, and certainly not plagued by more damned Florentines; cowards who cursed me for cutting their grain to feed my horses when I besieged them. Yes, yes, I also hung farmers up until they told me where their money was hidden. And yes, Vittelozzo violated women and boys and took a great number to Rome on pack animals to sell. But that is war for you. Don't look at me like that. Wars are not won by sonnets and sweet talk. There are no laurels for the second man to the spoils. I brought sistemazione, order.*

Cesare cries out as the gut-wrenching pain furrows his inwards like a plough. He'll fight this. *Father is dead; he is no more; a great force has been arrested*. Dante is not smiling now. 'Abandon hope all ye who enter.' Sleep.

18TH AUGUST. 40 MINUTES LATER

'It is done. We have all secure.' Michelotto drags a mottled sleeve across his broad forehead. Thirsty work, securing the Borgia spoil.

'Thank God.' In his bed, Cesare lets out a long breath, gazing toward the half-opened shutters, then quickly back to his first lieutenant, university friend and countryman. 'Thank God. Who was there? Did they give over without a fight?'

'Like capons on market day. We had no problems.' He rolls off the names of those present in the pope's bedchamber, the tedious list of hangers on, leeches of every grade of scarlet, black, and purple. Of course, there was Johannes Burchard, Papal Master of Ceremonies, who hangs around everything like a vapour, his pale, flaccid face like a cushion bearing the impress of the last man who sat on it. There is little about melancholy that he doesn't know, and little about anything else that he does. Behind him was Don Pietro Gamboa, the Bishop of Carinola, the pope's confessor who veritably worshipped the quicksand he walked in. He still held his golden oil flask, unbelieving in the face of death and walking in small circuits about the room like a somnambulist. Extreme unction had not healed the over-fleshed devil who lay in state under purple sheets. Behind Gamboa, whispering in a small antechamber between the rooms as if the cadaver might hear them, were the other five cardinals: Serra, Francesco Borgia, Giovanni Castelar, Casanova and de Loris of Constantinople. As Michelotto finishes his litany, Cesare's ears prick up.

'Casanova was there. Good.' Cesare speaks without opening his eyes, his throat parched, a tide of white residue about his lips.

'Oh yes, he was there all right.' Michelotto smiles inwardly with apparent satisfaction. He had walked straight to the antechamber, grabbed a fistful of the papal chamberlain's ear and led him into the recessed alcove where the window shutters were open. 'I stuck a knife to his throat, showed him the view, reminded him about our Aragonese friend, and he gave the key over without any fuss.'

Aragonese friend? This reference is richly suggestive and Cesare almost manages a smile in remembrance. Alfonso of Aragon was married to Cesare's sister Lucrezia for a few years. The alliance needed to be dissolved somewhat hastily, so Cesare had Michelotto stab him in the arms, legs and face, then throw him from the window. Say what you will about the Aragonese, they have staying power. Alfonso survived the ordeal. And so, while he was recovering, Michelotto strangled him in his bed with a lyre string, and threw him out of an even higher window, just to make sure. By the end, Alfonso was so mutilated that Cesare ordered a closed casket funeral and banned Lucrezia from attending. It is something they still jest about: 'The Icarus of Aragon', a little light mirth between friends.

'How much, at an estimate?' Cesare's eyes are wide now, hungry as a whore, imagining Michelotto entering the locked chamber behind the pontiff's bed, the dull clank of gold tiaras and plate, the clink of ducats, and that pebbly rattle of pearls.

'Two caskets with a hundred thousand ducats a piece, and other monies, say about three hundred thousand in all I'd guess. It will keep us in metal for a while.'

Cesare, the wasps crowding in, says 'Good. Get it weighed yourself; account for it all personally. Three hundred thousand. The old fox wasn't lying then.'

'My lord?'

'That money is just the beginning. I asked him for funds to cover the back pay of the Swiss and Gascons in Perugia. He kept delaying. Said he had a hundred thousand laid by but needed it, but that he was expecting any day the largest shipment of gold yet from the New World.'

'So, he did lie.'

'Oh yes, about the coffers here, yes of course. What would you expect? But he did not lie about *the shipment*, and more importantly, at least now we know he didn't have it here already. We should send someone reliable to watch the port at Cittevechia with two hundred *stradiotes* tomorrow. Everything rests on that gold. Everything.'

Later Cesare sends Michelotto across to the Vatican to wring all the information he can from Cardinal Casanova, and then use 'such means as are necessary' to persuade him never to mention it to anyone else. That is easily done. Michelotto shows Casanova his lyre string and linchpin, whispering tenderly about how easily you can near depart a man's head from his trunk with it, explaining the science of levers. His lyre string has become something of a calling card, a signature piece for his handiwork. Among those who know, or who have the nerve to mention his name, he is known as 'the strangler'.

4 HOURS LATER, AFTER VESPERS

'In the vice-chancellor's name I ordered Giovanni Caroli, the messenger, on pain of losing his office, to go with his fellow messengers to inform all the clergy in Rome, secular priests and monks alike, that they must assemble early next morning at five o'clock in the papal palace for the funeral procession from the Sistine Chapel to the Basilica of St. Peter. Two hundred tapers were prepared for those who would assemble for the pope's funeral...'

From the diary of Johannes Burchard, 'At the Court of the Borgia'

Burchard needn't bother with threats; the clergy, like everyone else, will come for the spectacle, or to make sure the pope is actually dead. You can never trust these Spaniards, and he never seemed the dying sort. Those who really are indisposed? They will write to say how much they approve of the news. You literally had to stand in line to hate a man like Rodriguez Borgia, Pope Alexander VI. The vices of honest men were his virtues.

2PM, AFTER LUNCH

'After dining, the cardinals appointed for the task and with the aid of the Chamber clergy made an inventory of the valuables and the more precious moveable goods that had belonged to Alexander. They found the crown and two precious tiaras, all the rings which the pope wore for Mass, the credence-vessels for his use in celebrating and enough indeed to fill eight coffers. Amongst all these things were the golden vessels from the recess of the apartment adjoining the pope's bedroom about which Don Michelotto had known nothing, as well as a small cypress box, covered in strong cloth and containing precious stones and rings to the value of about twenty-five thousand ducats. There were also found many documents, the oaths of the cardinals, the bull for the investiture of the King of Naples, and a great number of other bulls...' From the diary of Johannes Burchard, *'At the Court of the Borgia'*

4PM, AFTER DIVIDING THE SPOILS

'In the meantime, the body of the pope had remained for a long time, as I have described, between the railings of the high altar. During that period, the four wax candles next to it burned right down, and the complexion of the dead man became increasingly foul and black. Already by four o'clock on that afternoon when I saw the corpse, again, its face had changed to the color of mulberry or the blackest cloth and it was covered in blue-black spots. The nose was swollen, the mouth distended where the tongue was doubled over, and the lips seemed to fill everything. The appearance of the face then was far more horrifying than anything that had ever been seen or reported before. Later after five o'clock, the body was carried to the Chapel of Santa Maria della Febbre and placed in its coffin next to the wall in a corner by the altar. Six laborers or porters, making blasphemous jokes about the pope or in contempt of his corpse, together with two master carpenters, performed this task. The carpenters had made the coffin too narrow and short, and so they placed the pope's miter at his side, rolled his body up in an old carpet, and pummeled and pushed it into the coffin with their fists. No wax tapers or lights were used, and no priests or any other persons attended to his body.' From the diary of Johannes Burchard, *'At the Court of the Borgia'*

'Of course, all Spaniards are great horsemen but I have heard tell that when the pope rode, he actually became part of the horse. Mind, they didn't say which part.' Pall bearers are all comedians. *Sic transit gloria mundi.* Their headman chides them that they should not speak ill of the dead, only good. They reply, 'the Spanish whoremonger is dead, *good*.' These things, and much else besides, Cesare hears from the lips of Michelotto. Someone has recast John Scotus' ditty about the bishop of Rheims and scratched it on the casket. *'Hic jacet Alexandrus, cleptes vehementer avarus, Hoc solum gessit nobile: quod periit.* Here lies Alexander, crook. But savage greed aside, he did one noble thing; he died. They say it was one of Cardinal Riario's people. Cesare makes a mental note. Revenge is a dish best served cold.

Focusing all his cunning now on the shipment of gold, he suppresses the shudder that runs between his shoulder blades. When Alexander the Great died, they slew his brother, wife and son. 'Not if I kill them first,' he mutters but then hears again the voice of Dante whose apparition is now leering again at him from the end of the bed. More Isaiah: 'All the kings of the nations lie in state, each in his own tomb. But you are cast out of your tomb like a rejected branch; you are covered with the slain, with those pierced by the sword, those who descend to the stones of the pit. Like a corpse trampled underfoot, you will not join them in burial, for you have destroyed your land and killed your people.'

Tuscan dog! Damn him, damn them all. I refuse to die.

23RD AUGUST, 1503. FOUR DAYS LATER

Venice, the great whore who trades on many waters, has made peace with the Turks. The necessities of trade must circumvent all other considerations. Without Venetian support the knights of Rhodes are exposed in the *mâchoires de la Turk,* the jaws of the Turk. On Saturday August 23rd a squadron of Turkish Corsairs from the port of Makri on the Turkish mainland attack and ravage the Rhodian countryside and villages. Collateral.

27TH AUGUST, 1503. FOUR DAYS LATER AND 1,000 MILES AWAY

By Wednesday, Prior Guy de Blanchefort is spitting feathers. The Prior of Auvergne, knight, zealot and acting grandmaster of the Knights of Rhodes, appoints captains for three galleys in the city. There will be blood. De Blanchefort, claw mad for battle, barks orders at a meeting of the general chapter. He'll have these infidel scum brought back in chains for his galleys; he'll teach even these Asiatic barbarians a lesson in cruelty they'll never forget.

'Flay the bastards! I want a hundred of them including the godless spawn of their nobility in our dungeons before winter.'

The *Petronilla, Victoriosa*, and *Catherineta* break harbour the next day, chasing Turkish corsairs toward Makri. They outrun them before the mainland is reached. Eight Turkish ships are sunk, and two captured with much spoil. One Rhodian galley is lost, but it is an undoubted victory to cheer the knights through the long, storm-tossed winter. And among the stories that do the rounds among their priories, and echo back in various shades in the courts of Europe, are the valorous deeds of one twenty-two-year-old English knight who had been conspicuous at all points of danger during the engagement.

It is the beginning of the legend of Hugh de Erpingham.

22ND SEPTEMBER, 1503. 30 DAYS LATER IN ROME

The peaceable Sienese Cardinal Francesco Piccolomini is elected Pope Pius III, a compromise candidate between warring devils: anything but another Borgia or della Rovere. The new pope confirms Cesare Borgia as gonfaloniere of the papal forces. Michelotto torches the Orsini palace at Monte Giordano, Rome. Payback for years of opposition. Twenty-six days later the new pope is dead, the bandages for his leg ulcers poisoned. The hideous screams of his passing, haunt the papal palace for weeks; to those that heard them, longer still. Fourteen days later, Cardinal Guiliano della Rovere is crowned pope. Anyone but another bloody Spaniard, they said, but you've got to watch where that sort of logic gets you.

Taking his name from the Roman dictator, Julius II – The Warrior Pope – has old scores to settle. Cesare and Michelotto are outmaneuvered, betrayed by friends and imprisoned separately. *Mene Mene Tekel Upharsin.*

APRIL 19TH, 1504. ROME. SIX MONTHS LATER

Early Tuesday morning before sun up, Cesare escapes the hitherto impregnable Castel Sant Angelo, leaving Michelotto still in chains. He flees by horse and boat to Naples where he, the arch-betrayer, is double crossed by his allies into the hands of Ferdinand II of Aragon and thence transferred to Spain. During that long hot summer this Duke Valentino *san terre* escapes from two castles, crosses three territories and is finally welcomed by Jean III of Navarre, only too pleased to have an experienced *condotierro* like Cesare to help him against Castile.

JUNE 17TH, 1504. MEHMED STRAITS, OFF RHODES

A glorious Monday, azure seas, winds strong from the west. A fine day for sailing, piracy, and man-stealing. It is the day that will finally give the Turks their wafer-thin pretext for war.

A carrack commanded by the Knights of Rhodes is hunting a goke flying the sultan's colours in the Mehmet Straits. They capture Kemal Beg, friend and envoy of Kurkut Chelebi, son of Sultan Bayazid II. Kemal's employer, also known as the Lord Chonochiari, will be royally insulted by the loss. The Turks, as a rule, have never taken a broad view of this sort of thing, unless they are doing it themselves. Kemal meanwhile is taken as a slave to Rhodes, but drowns a week later while trying to escape. Idiot.

The newly arrived Grandmaster Emery d'Amboise observes the corpse on the wharf with incredulity bordering on rage.

'Are you sure it's him?' Someone asks in a hopeful moment.

'Oh yes, you can always tell a Turkish envoy,' d'Amboise says with a long sigh, and then turns back with his escort toward the palace to finish his dinner. 'But you can't tell them much.'

The letters from Laodicea soon arrive, written in Greek and garnished liberally with oaths, culminating in a final threat that if nothing is done speedily, the matter will be raised with the Lord Chonochiari. As if by way of final blow, the letter concludes, 'and who will save you then from the wrath of my master?'

The magister, to his credit, takes it all with great equanimity and an almost stoic humour, for there was in the whole situation something that smacked of a mummer's farce. He writes back expressing regret at Kemal Beg's death and telling Kurkut that the warders have been given the lash in public for their laxity in guarding the esteemed guest. He wants to add something ironic about Kemal obviously needing to be guarded assiduously, 'being such a danger to himself and his servants', but he doubts that Kurkut has any serious capacity for irony.

'By St. Louis,' D'Amboise exclaims in a moment of rare jollity, 'what other culture could have produced such a scutcheon as Kurkut and not seen the joke! Beards and tombs of his ancestors, my hairy arse! Bring me some wine, Giles. I need it to finish this letter.'

He drains his goblet, then starts by listing complaints against the continued attacks by Cortogoli and his companion corsairs and of devastations made by the Turks in the area around the castle of St. Peter, Halicarnassus. He finishes, 'Most illustrious sir, your style is awful, but we are sure it is not the worst thing about you. Don't write that,' he tells the scribe. 'Pompous ass. *Merde*. Don't write that either. God, I don't want to finish my days as a sarcastic old fart, but these Turkish bastards don't make it easy.'

He takes a long draft of wine, sniffs, then says, 'All right, I'm ready now, write: Most illustrious sir, we are good and peaceful friends of the Lord Chonochiari, and of your own most illustrious lordship, and we are always ready to do everything that is just and honest and due to good friends. To this purpose, we are on this island, by order of the most serene Christian princes, from whom we have favor and help because we are their sons; and except for them we know no other superior, and to God and then to them we have to answer for our affairs, and we hope in God that while we do justice, his aid will not fail us. Yours etcetera.'

The letter makes little impact. Decisions have already been taken. A storm is brewing. A new fleet commissioned by the Sultan is being built at the arsenals of Constantinople and Gallipoli.

JULY 28TH, 1506. KOS

From right under the Sultan's very nose, in the waters between Kos and the Turkish mainland, the Hospitaliers capture seven Egyptian ships. Conspicuous in the action again is Hugh de Erpingham, outnumbered three to one and yet slaying his foe. Or was it six to one? The deeds of valour swell with the telling.

MARCH 4TH, 1507. HARBOUR IN CRETE

Before the seas are even fit for travel, a lightly armed galliot filled with knights captures a large merchant ship of Alexandria called the *Gran Nave Mogarbina* that had wintered in Crete en route to Tunis. No canon was fired; no blood spilled; the infidels just woke up one morning at the wrong end of a certain Englishman's blade. His men had already secured the hold and bound the soldiery before ever the captain called for his piss pot. The great prize is taken back to Rhodes, loaded with a huge cargo of spices, cloths, and carpets, and travelers for whose ransom the Egyptians will pay heavily. Business is good.

MARCH 11TH, 1507. OUTSIDE VIANNA CASTLE, NAVARRE.

On a wet Monday morning, the son of Pope Alexander VI, Cesare Borgia, and his light horse are giving chase to a band of knights that flee from his siege of Viana Castle in Navarre. He rushes ahead of his men, is isolated, ambushed, speared fatally and falls to the wet earth. The last thing he does on earth? Vomit his breakfast. The last thing he sees? His enemy stripping him of his finery. They seize his black silk doublet offset with gold collar of the order of Saint Michael, granted by Louis XII. They even take his underclothes and the leather mask that covers half of his syphilitic face. He is left lying naked in the mud and drizzle, a red clay tile covering his parts. He had dressed that morning to take a citadel, not to die. His plans fail with his breath; yet one more force has ceased in the earth.

Dante, who has followed him all the way from Rome to haunt his waking thoughts, is now dressed in the white of a Roman judge and breathes into Cesare's last corporeal moment. 'How you have fallen from heaven, morning star, son of the dawn! You have been cast down to the earth, you who once laid low the nations!

But you are brought down to the realm of the dead, to the depths of the pit. Those who see you stare at you, they ponder your fate: "Is this the man who shook the earth and made kingdoms tremble, the man who made the world a wilderness, who overthrew its cities and would not let his captives go home? Let the offspring of the wicked never be mentioned again. Prepare a place to slaughter his children, for the sins of their fathers; they are not to rise to inherit the land and cover the earth with their cities.'

Cesare blinks mud away and strains to see the exiled poet walk away in the direction of Castile. After six steps he turns casually, hands on hips. 'I have passed this way before. Once on the shores of *purgatorio* I saw Manfred, and he told me that he had hope of receiving repentance, even though he was excommunicated as his father Emperor Federick had been. He asked me to tell his daughter Constanza, of the house of Sicily and Aragon that he had hope, so I did. But whom shall I tell of you?'

'My sister Lucrezia,' he gasps, reaching out his hand with a final effort. 'Spirit, fiend, whatever you are, tell my sister.' But the poet makes no response.

On the same day over a thousand miles away, a galliot belonging to the knights of Rhodes is captured off the Carpathian straights, and all hands put to the oars and the lash.

For sixteen months Hugh de Erpingham will wish he had never been born.

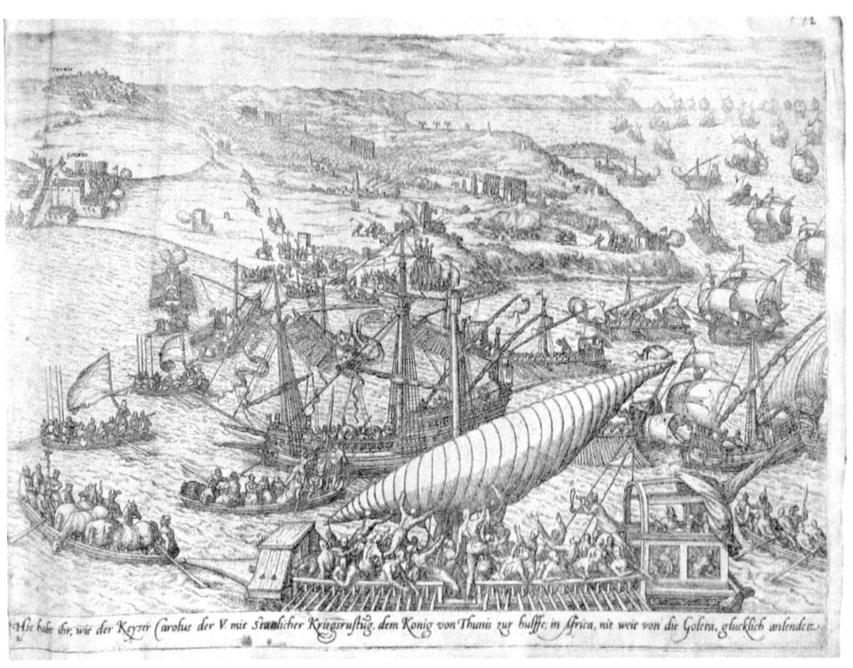

SEVENTEEN MONTHS LATER

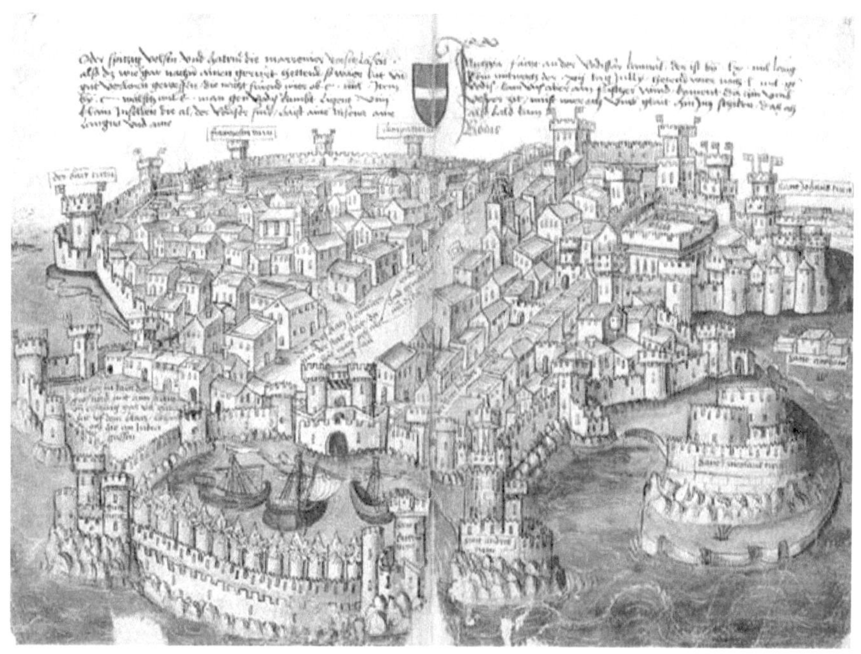

TUESDAY, 3RD AUGUST, 1508. THE GRAND MASTER'S PALACE, RHODES.

Fra Hugh Erpingham is ushered with reverence toward the dining room of Emery D'Amboise, *Magnus Magister* himself. It is a great honour. The Grand Master, or Prince of Rhodes, is the ruler of a sovereign state with possessions from the Iberian Peninsula to Scandinavia. The knights mint their own money and conduct diplomatic relations with the other states of Christendom and the heathen.

Hugh waits in an ante chamber with a flagged floor, vaulted stone ceiling, and tapestries on two walls that absorb the low whispers of ministers, chaplains, castellans, sergeants, servants and ambassadors who mill their particular grist in the corridors and on the grand staircase. He removes his beret and observes the Magister d'Amboise's coat of arms above the door: white crosses on a red background, two quadrants of red and yellow banding.

The magister himself is more an able manager than tactician, chosen because of connections where it matters. And, when you live in the jaws of the Turk, connections are everything. His father, Pierre d'Amboise, was Seigneur de Chaumont and chamberlain to Charles VII and Louis XI, and ambassador at Rome. Of his nine brothers, four are bishops. The eldest, Charles, is governor of the Île-de-France, Champagne and Burgundy, and councilor of Louis XI. Even more illustrious is Georges, cardinal and prime minister of France. Connections, though, are like soap; the more you use them the less you have. France is powerful now, but foul of the polity in Rome. So, the magister sits at his post, which he has occupied four years now, and waits to see who will be best placed to help them when his nemesis Sultan Bayazid II has enough strength to rid himself of this thorn called Rhodes embedded into his tender parts.

In the anteroom, Hugh can hear cutlery scraping the plates, low voices agreeing on some quiet business. He smells fish, onions, dish-water, saddle leather, and cinnamon. He instinctively scoops to pick up the crumbs of bread from the floor. The servant turns as he feverishly stuffs the crumbs into his mouth with three fingers. Their eyes meet. *Shit*. He comes to himself, and the servant turns back to the door, embarrassed. Still hollow from his resurrection, Hugh examines his bony fingers and the scars on his wrists. The shame. He sits slowly and stares helplessly toward the window.

That thousand-yard stare.

He can walk past a field of standing grain, but only see broken stalks; a street of houses, but only the cracks, the woodworm, the rot. Peopled solitude. He's the doctor who no longer discerns health, only disease; a watchman who only sees a world on fire. He looks at his right hand once more, then slowly bites his knuckle to fight back the tears, to stop his hull from breaking up, from the abyss.

He will beat this, these ghosts, these memories. But the more he pushes them down, the more they come.

MEMORIES OF HELL

One. . . Two . . . Pull.
The rest of your life stretches before you.
One. . . Two . . . Pull.

Skin burnt to your bones, back riven with scars, ploughed like an autumn field. One. . . Two . . . Pull. 'The small sound of Time's drum in the heart,' as our latest poet Hawes has put it. The oars glide in azure waters, which have become the 'foul waters of corruption in the moat around King Hart's castle.'

One. . . Two . . . Pull.

Labouring through waters he does not know, to ports along the Lycian coast that he never sees. The hull of this Turkish goke is the very bowels of the earth. He lives in darkness, the third, maybe fourth, circle of the Inferno where he pays with blood for the blood he has shed.

One. . . Two . . . Pull.

Harbours without names, voices without interpretation, life without meaning, pain without end. Just counting the strokes: One. . . Two . . . Pull.

At first, he cannot believe it is actually happening to him, disarmed, rough handled, spat at. They break his nose, flatten it across his face. He was returning to Rhodes for his greatest triumph yet. How could this have happened, unscripted, inscrutable? He'd always imagined that suffering for the faith would be something noble, a cell with straw, a shaft of light, a decent library, quiet for meditation.

This is not noble.

Over a hundred men, naked, rancid, infested, emaciated, chained, two to an oar in the stifling twilight. Air so hot you can hardly breathe it without scorching your lungs. They, the skeletal others, recognise that look in the new prisoner's eyes as he enters the hull, the horror mixed with hope, that this somehow will not be forever. It is not his destiny; he will be ransomed. Most remember that feeling, just. You keep it for the first two or three weeks, and after that you forget. One. . . Two . . . Pull.

His first rowing partner is already dying when they are chained together, possibly a Venetian. He can only mumble insanely for they have cut his tongue out and made him eat it. Madness, starvation, infestation. The man's ebbing strength gets them both the lash hour on hour in that first hideous week. The first time they open your back is the worst, for the nerves are all intact; the feeling is all there.

Pashur loves to see the virgin white back of a Christian devil, a perk of the job. He loves to show his skill with the purgative lash, knows how long to wait between strokes, where a bent back will stretch most, how to savour the opening of each new channel, every last infidel scream.

The Venetian dies after eight days, his last words for his mother, barely discernible. His passing is a mixed blessing; Hugh's new rowing partner is stronger but vile in all other respects. A new form of humiliation: to be chained to the foul mouth of a fellow countryman, but a commoner. A new form of torture to hear about England through the soiled filter of a fallen wretch's worm-eaten gums. Filcher, a nickname perhaps for the man is a horse thief, has been at these oars longer than any other.

His opening words are enough. 'Well, my lord knight, how do you like our vapours; wounds, blood, puss – like your woman's worst monthlies. You'll get used to it, you will. I knew a whore in Ravenna once, and I don't mind telling you...' etcetera. On and on, and then to finish he divulges the secrets of his longevity at the oars: 'Rats, gentle knight,' he says, always without any shred of deference for the great chain of being. 'Rats is what keeps men alive here.' He shows Hugh how he uses his bare feet to kill them and bring them near enough to his hands to grab them. 'You's gotta get 'em hard on the skulls master. Not pussy footin' or they'll bite you and make your feet rot, or worse.'

Hugh will not sink to it. He will be rescued. He is a knight. *This is not his story.*

But then Filcher takes even greater delight in telling him, 'Not 'ere you won't be, gentle sir. This here is one of Cortogoli's corsair ships. He won't be telling the Sultan what he's been up to. Works better for him to keep his spoils and forget his dues.'

After ten days at sea Hugh, weakened by the swill he is fed, succumbs to the desire for flesh. His first efforts at rat catching are ill executed. His legs are not as long as Filcher's, and he is bitten twice in the process. But desperation is his only mother now, hunger his father. In the end, he pins one turgid creature down in the bilge waters wriggling like an eel until it drowns. It takes him half the night to raise it on the hull wall to where he can finally take hold of it, and the rest of the night to pick at it amidst his hidden tears.

All the while Filcher intersperses his taunts at how long it has taken to catch, with discourses on the best parts to eat. In the end Hugh gladly gives him the tail, feet, skull and pelt just to shut him up. But when he has finished chewing through the hair, and crunching bone, tooth and nail, Filcher edges his buttocks backward to defecate into the bilge.

And in between his straining, for he is dehydrated like them all, he says, 'Now, you being an educated man will have an answer for this. The rats eat our shite, drink our blood, and we eat them and drink theirs. You and me's both. Now what's all that about then, eh? I'll tell you, it's a great *circle* of being, not a chain after all.' He farts, then eases himself forward, laughs, nudges and finishes with, 'Ain't we a pair, me and you, sitting here in our birthday suits. Ain't so different after all.'

Hugh makes no reply. He's thinking though, and almost praying, 'God knows I have been humbled as much as any man, learned my lesson. There is no further a man can fall.'

He is wrong. One. . . Two . . . Pull.

This is day ten.

There are four hundred and seventy-six still to go.

One. . . Two . . . Pull.

UNHOLY ORDERS

The magister's door opens. Satisfied bankers enter the antechamber from the dining room, among them representatives from the Medici, Fuger, Stozzi, Noveschi, Tornabuoni and Pitti branches. Their eyes on him are not well intentioned, he thinks, but they pass without comment. Liabilities like this Englishman present a real hazard to stability in an already volatile trading environment. One of them looks like he'll say something but merely grunts. He will not let the sight of Hugh keep him from his work – *the* work.

Magister D'Amboise asks, 'Is Fra Hugh there? Good. Then send him in.'

Hugh walks unsteadily into the great dining hall, which doubles as a trophy room – good place for impressing the guests. The walls are hung with various banners, statuary, shields and coats of arms, devices of many European nations. The ceiling is twice the height of the antechamber and coffered in reddish timbers, darkened by soot, tallow, and wax, as are the walls - at least, where you can see them, past the pageantry. Spoil is something everyone can understand; it gives the bankers confidence that they are all after the same thing. How wrong can you be? Fanatics like Hugh spoil trade, while the spoils of trade more often spoil everything else. Two granite pillars with sixth-century capitals divide the room, and in the far corner is a fireplace, with two more doors on the right-hand wall, and three windows facing south and west across the harbour.

At a table near one of these windows sits the magister himself, a thick bearded man of seventy-three, with a slightly hooked nose and eyes that never look quite at you. In fact, it is hard to imagine a man who puts less effort into facial expressions when he talks. It is altogether as if he had rented his face on long lease, and had grown so accustomed to living there that he couldn't conceive of moving out.

Hugh kisses the magister's ring. 'Please,' the man's voice is thick, honeyed, as he motions Hugh to join him at the table now being cleared by the servants.

Hugh sits down carefully, noting the crumbs on the unwiped table, fish bones with flesh on, skulls, shriveled eyes, all left. His lips are pursed as saliva floods his mouth. He takes a long breath. *I will beat this*. Every time he sees food all his humors rush about his body. He breaks out in a sweat of fear, and then behind the fear, the voice, the condemnation, the knowing of his great animal sins. His damnation.

The Magister speaks in French. 'I am to congratulate you on your victory last week. The ship you captured was, well, she was a great prize. You...er.' He pauses, moving a spoon this way and that with the tip of his index finger over the polished wood. 'You showed great endeavour I am told.' He adds with an enquiring inflection, 'Almost reckless of life itself.' He laughs gently, making a point. 'And there were many slain, I am told, many by your sword, and some even – ' he lets their eyes meet. 'After the surrender was sounded.'

Hugh is stern, defensive. 'They were all armed men.' *The crumbs.* He's eaten but a half hour since, yet still the scavenger-dog impulse persists.

'Yes, I'm sure they were, but you see our position, *non?'* D'Amboise turns the corners of his mouth down in that particular manner of his countrymen, and then raises his hands slightly in a half-hearted appeal. 'Men of rank, Hugh. It's not just the ransom, you understand. There is etiquette. Our position here is a balance.' A pause. And once more into the silence, the smirk, the shrug. The French don't have a word for shrug. Some things can be so ubiquitous that they are hidden in plain sight.

Hugh sniffs, looks defensively to the table. *The crumbs.* He is conscious that his fingers are quivering. *Shit.*

'They were armed, and I was engaged – ' He cannot finish the sentence. *The crumbs. Starvation.*

'Yes, I understand.' The magister's silence accuses as Hugh's own conscience recalls glimpses. He was not sure how it happened: the red mist, the overwhelming rage. His whole difficulty before that point was trying to find some way to emote, any way to respond normally again after his captivity. He has been so numb since his ransom, so emotionless, so aching with the melancholy of absence. But now vengeance speaks and rage arises. He is at once both exhilarated and disgusted. The disgust stems less from the act, and more from the exhilaration at being temporarily freed from his prison. Hugh wets his mouth. 'May I go now?'

'Pardon?'

'I want to go.'

'Where?'

'To my, my – ' *The crumbs.* Clawing black fingers. Starvation.

'Hugh, we all understand that you have been through a difficult time.'

The hell he does! Abandoned to rot by your friends, to sink as Sophocles' exiled Philocetes, friendless, solitary, without a city, a corpse among the living. 'I am alright.' He blinks rapidly. *I will beat this.*

'That you seek redress.' That smirk again. 'Revenge even... But your duties are no place to exact private – '

'I am alright.' A hint of defiance.

'Really? Sleeping alright?' It's a low blow, but the magister is busy and needs to move on.

'Not always.' Screaming, bed soiling. They've moved Hugh to a cell away from the other knights at the English convent. The English Knights wouldn't complain, too loyal – too much in awe of him. *Everyone wants to be Hugh de Erpingham*, he muses, *Hugh de-bloody-Erpingham. I always wanted to be someone too. Should have been more specific.* But then he wakes up and remembers who he is, a tormented wraith that can still just remember being an Englishman, firstborn of his father, darling of his mother. He is Alexander, Oedipus, Icarus, risen high only to be cut down as an example, a pariah. He often wakes screaming in the small hours with fouled sheets, and the night warder roused from his house thinking the Turks have invaded. Word is out. It is potentially embarrassing for the English knights.

They don't know about the suicide attempt. It's a dark place to be when a twenty-seven-year-old man will let his neck feel the weight of his boots. Suicide is perhaps the only sincere form of self-criticism, but even at this he failed. The logic was impeccable; die while still a hero, or live as a monster. He only decides to stay living now in this hell to see if he can atone for his past, or perhaps a perverse Sisyphean curiosity to see how much more he can take.

Zeus lays down the law that we may suffer. 'Suffer into truth,' Aeschylus' Mycenaean chorus says. The old Greeks understood it. Their mythologies are shot through with the paradox of existence as men find it under the sun. The great archer Apollo is the giver of sunlight but also of justice and measurement. Sophocles would have us feel an ominous severity of judgment throughout Oedipus' reign. *Oedipus must not be allowed to rule in peace, and neither am I allowed to live in peace,* Hugh thinks. That is the truth, the whole bloody truth: we are trapped by our twin knowledge--that we have sinned, and that, if the universe is just, sin must be punished. *That is all I have learnt and am learning*. Augustine knew it. *Per molestias erudutio.* True education begins with affliction. My desire to be punished is greater than my enemies' ability or desire to punish me. *When it comes to battle, or even torture—yes, even torture—I will indulge in their complicity. It is the least I can do to atone.*

He shudders at the remembrance of the bed sheets squeezing the life from his throat – eyes bulging to bursting. By providence his man, Wilfred Carter, happened upon him, heard the stool being kicked away, was already suspicious.

He's a good man is Wilf – a good Norfolk boy. Ox-stubborn, constant, drinks like a German. Most servants would have pissed off to England at the first chance. But not Wilf. To this day I don't know what made him stay. God knows I don't.

There is a pause now, and in the silence, Hugh realises that he is not here to be congratulated for almost single-handedly taking a ship with sword and buckler. He stares straight ahead, tight-lipped.

'There is no need to look like that; this is not a disciplinary tribunal. We are just talking. For now.' D'Amboise finally surrenders his spoon to the last servant and waves him to leave them alone. When the doors are closed, the magister pushes his chair back and walks toward the window. 'I am sure you cannot be unaware that your reputation in Europe is something approaching canonization at the present time, not least because of your recent resurrection from the galleys. Your reputation among the knights, and the sergeants – well, I am sure I don't need to tell you of their esteem. Of course, some of the older knights from other inns are jealous, but the younger men idolize you, Hugh, as you must well know. This and other things are put at stake if you remain on Rhodes in your present state. Your prior has very grave concerns, and your confessor says you will not seek absolution, that there is some sin you will not talk of– '

'Magister, I cannot–'

'Don't interrupt me. You have had more than the required three caravans—engagements that have brought glory to the order, your inn and yourself. You need a change, and I have work for you in Italy– '

'But Magister, surely– '

'I said don't interrupt. We are an order, not a bloody republic. You will report to the Grand Priory at Rome as my particular ambassador to the papal court.'

Hugh sets his jaw. *An ambassador?* Passing the winter on tittle-tattle at the papal palace, waiting in corridors with gossips, men of letters and clerics in their Bruges silks and small eyes. *An ambassador!* An honest man paid to tell lies in another country.

D'Amboise evidently chooses not to see his expression. 'This is for work very delicate and multifarious. Work you are uniquely qualified for as it happens. As you know we have fared ill under the Borgia pope, but now we must have indulgences for the relief of Rhodes. As you yourself have seen, Sultan Bayazid is preparing arsenals in Gallipoli and Constantinople. We must have support from the Italian city-states; we must have armaments, pledges of support. Pope Julius is sympathetic. He will open the doors for you to the various courts of southern Europe. You will do well for the order, I am sure.'

D'Amboise turns a fatherly eye toward the disconsolate knight, indicating with a small hand gesture that he is now free to respond – with gratitude and obedience.

'May...may I inquire, Magister, as to why I am particularly *suited* for this–' choose your words carefully '– honour?'

'Why, isn't it obvious? You –the poet, artist, soldier of the cross – you were made for this. You have caste; you speak the language; you have – as we say – *la Gloire*; and – now what do they call it? Ah yes – you have *spretzeturra:* ease and elegance, or at least you used to have and we are verily assured you will again, and, as you know, these things that matter to the Italians. And of course, you're English and not French.'

At this point D'Amboise modestly examines his cuffs. 'With my own brother at the head of an army occupying the Duchy of Milan, it is best not to rub it in. *Non?* An Englishman is what is required. England is popular at court. Your king Henry has already pledged twenty-thousand ducats for the defence of Rhodes. As you know, he wishes to come on crusade in person. The pope approves his zeal as he does anyone with a bit of fight in him – which is incidentally why he'll like you too. So, you see, Erpingham, you are amply suited on those points alone, but—' He pauses, looking toward the doors. 'There is yet one more reason. I need a discreet man who can handle himself in a tight corner.' Again, the look towards the doors. 'Please, come to the window and let me tell you the whole matter.'

His interest now piqued, Hugh walks to the deeply recessed windows and sits in a seat opposite his master. From there he can see the northern ramparts, towers, bulwarks of the city right down to the port where the sails of the windmills flutter on the harbour walls, as do the masts and flags of fifty or so ships. Today, unusually, the winds blow the wave crests west, back to Europe.

'As fine a sight as Christendom boasts,' the magister says, following Hugh's eyes. 'But it is only a fool who thinks we can go on like this forever without a serious investment in ships and armaments. It is money we need, Hugh, and not just twenty thousand ducats. Real money, and God may have brought that within our grasp. What I tell you now is in strictest confidence.'

Hugh was interested. 'Magister?'

'What do you know of Fra Marcantonio Vendramin?'

Who had not heard of him? He was the nearest thing a lusty Norfolk boy could have to an ideal, idol even. Fra Marcantonio, son of Doge Andrea Vendramin, master naval tactician, hero of the Great Siege of Mehmet. He was the pattern, the gold standard, the very ensign of the order. Hugh clears his throat as if to discourse on a sacred matter. 'Of course, he was the most decorated knight under Magister D'Aubusson. Sent as our ambassador to Pius III, he died in Italy.'

'Yes. First in the camp, and then first in the forum. Hugh, think on that. He was the consummate courtier, as you shall be, and more importantly, he was a great friend of Pius III, that unfortunate Piccolomini pope who died too soon.' D'Amboise pauses, places a deliberate forefinger over his lips, then takes it away again. 'But he did not die. That much was a necessary fiction to protect our reputation.'

'Magister?'

'He disappeared, Hugh—disappeared with perhaps enough gold to buy half of Asia and Cathay, too.'

'Fra Marcantonio betrayed the order for gold?'

'I know, I know. But he was a Venetian no matter what else he was. I never met the man myself, but the evidence speaks plainly enough.'

'But how... I mean, where was this gold from? How do we know this is true?'

'*Sotto voce,* Hugh, *sotto voce*. This place has ears. You are one of only a handful that know what I am about to say, and I'm trusting your upmost discretion.' The magister shoots Hugh a long, searching look until Hugh feels he should say something to avoid embarrassment.

'Do not worry, Magister. I am like the sundial; *sine sole sileo* – where there is no sun, I am silent.' *And there's been no sun, moon or stars above me for more days than I can count.*

'Very good. You understand then, so I will tell you.' The magister rubs both hands up and down his silk hose as if ironing out creases. Eventually he restarts in a conspiratorial whisper. 'The thing is, there was a shipment of gold from the New World that should have made Cittavechia just after the death of the Borgia pope. Borgia, in an uncharacteristic pious gesture, lavished a former shipload on the ceiling of Santa Maria Maggiore.' He chuckled. 'How he must have wished he could cash that in a few months later when he really needed funds. Anyway, few knew of this new shipment. Cardinal Casanova, the chamberlain, did, and he was sure Cesare Borgia knew, too, for he sent his light horse and some infantry to watch the port. The ship was provisioned at Cadiz on its return, then again at Cagliari on Sardinia–'

D'Amboise breaks off, as if remembering or calculating something, then resumes. 'Twenty-four hours later, it was boarded at night by a smaller vessel, we think, held for seven hours over four barrels of gun powder while the cargo was transferred. Reports vary. Some say they had a small army, some that there may have been only four corsairs.

The leader was very bold. He would have blown them all sky high; that much they all believed. They took the captain hostage and set him adrift when they were beyond the guns. They were last seen heading south toward Naples.'

'But Marcantonio Vendramin?'

'Don't be impatient. I am getting to that. Casanova knew more that he let on at the time, but a year later he was dying a penitent, as all good cardinals do, and he wanted to clear his conscience. He wrote to my predecessor telling him that Pope Pius was much vexed that Cesare would get this gold. For sure, the new pope had borrowed money from Cesare for the papal coronation, but he was a good man, and wanted an end to the excesses of the Borgias that had so stained the papacy. Cesare was already confirmed at *Gonfaloniere* of the Papal Forces. If armed with unlimited wealth, he would have been unstoppable.'

'I see.' Hugh knew that Pius III was a great friend of the arts, a man of broad and humane sympathy.

'Casanova reports, and I think he had no reason to perjure himself in the matter, that Pope Pius sent Vendramin to intercept the ship and bring the gold to Piombino, a Sienese port loyal to their Piccolomini pope. Of course, the pope was acting on the advice of Marcantonio Vendramin. He trusted him entirely. Who wouldn't? His credentials were impeccable, but he was the most cunning of all men and, as I say, a Venetian. They would sell their own sisters into the trade for the sniff of coin.'

'And this light ship?'

'Disappeared.' Again, the hands, the shrug, the smirk. 'The pope was murdered a week later. Fra Marcantonio was never seen again.'

'The crew?'

'Three men have made some sort of claim in the last five years, two to be crew members, a third a navigator.'

'You sent someone to interview these sailors?'

'Not quick enough. Someone got to them first. They are no longer with us. The third – this navigator – only divulged his identity as a bargaining chip. The galliot he was on was captured by Barbarossa off Algiers, and he used the information to get himself ransomed.'

Hugh shudders. *Memories.* The chaffing of the irons, the sounds of the lash, the creaking of the hull, the smell of pustulous humanity, filth, death, flies, rats, fleas, and big, fat lice, gorging themselves. All these, claw his mind back in an instant to that inferno of torment. 'And who ransomed him?'

'We did, or at least will. The *Petronilla* is sailing to treat with the corsairs as we speak. They will deliver him to the priory in Rome under strict guard. He has promised that the information is of great value for us, but of course we are not the only interested party. These matters seem to have mercurial wings of their own, Hugh. You will meet this navigator in Rome, find out what you can and pursue the information wherever it leads. Understand?'

'Yes.' Hugh nods, seeing now why he was really chosen: to be polite, speak with urbanity and yet have a plan to kill everyone who gets in the way.

The magister grips his arm suddenly. 'Find Marcantonio, wherever he's hiding out, and find that gold. I cannot but think God has hidden it for such a time as this, to help us here. So, I say bring it back, save Rhodes, we are the shield of Europe. This is your commission.'

'And Fra Marcantonio?'

The magister tilts his head slightly (his mercy) but then shakes his head gravely and briefly, eyes unmoved. Justice.

'I see.'

'It is best for him and for our name that his sins be forgotten.'

Hugh swallows hard, a dread tingling down to his loins. 'We have sworn only to fight against the infidel.'

'He is no Christian to have done this thing, Hugh. Whatever he has become, he is certainly no son of the church. You can be assured of that and carry out your duty, *pro fide*.'

For the faith? Joseph and Mary. Trophy hunting and assassination were probably not foremost in our founder's minds when they chose that motto for the order. 'Master,' Hugh says, nodding instinctively as if he were still a galley slave, then regrets it. He needs some time to think, to breathe.

'Resolve this matter, Hugh, and it will be a great feather in your cap.'

Hugh nods again, thinking, *Aye, and perhaps a white one at that.*

The magister stands and stretches his left leg. Gout. 'You depart next week on the Feast of Saint Lawrence, on the *Catherineta*. I want you to deliver this personally to the pontiff.'

He walks back toward the table to retrieve his folio of papers. He holds up a sealed letter. 'It is information that he will find most useful. Venice, that great whore, has allowed Turkish munitions on board one of her own ships. They have taken the cargo from Constantinople to Valona on the Dalmatian coast. When the European princes hear of this infamy, Venice's days will be numbered.'

Simmering, Hugh rises and walks to the table to receive the letter. The magister does not release it, and when their eyes meet, he says, 'You are in Italy on the gravest matter. Your public commission will gain you access to the great courts of that country, and there you will meet with every form of vice and wanton licentiousness, lasciviousness and so forth. Do not be distracted, my son. Do not be entangled in civilian affairs; be doughty, steadfast, a servant of God. We must have that gold for the defence of Rhodes, and thereby Europe too; Christendom may well depend on it.'

Enough pieties. Just give me the bloody letter. Hugh snatches it. If God won't do his own dirty work, I'll find this man myself, damn him – the only man I've found to look up to in this shithole – and slit his throat. I'll bring back enough gold to hang every Turkish sultan with the innards of every vizier. *Pro Fide* indeed. He bows stiffly and then exits, passing Guy de Blanchefort, Prior of Auvergne in the corridor without even a salute.

The prior, that one-eyed, battle-hardened zealot enters without knocking. 'Am I to take it that you have indeed commissioned the Englishman on the matter of great delicacy against my advice?' He has only two expressions, irritation and indigestion. Today it is the former.

D'Amboise, who does have indigestion, looks up wearily. ‘Guy, not now, I must – '

But *now* is always the right time for the prior who, as usual, looks as if his clothes have been thrown on with a pitchfork. 'I've just seen him in the corridor. He's not fit for sentry duty, much less a diplomatic mission.'

'I'm sure he can pass on our message about Venice – '

'Pass a message? He can't pass wind without getting into a knife fight.’

‘A kind word and a knife in Italy will usually get you more than a kind word.’

‘Do you want a blood bath on your hands in Italy like we had last week on that ship? Because that is what you will get. I've seen his eyes. He was born under a malignant star—Mars, I am told.'

'Mars! Guy *please* – '

'Mars produces wars, Magister, aye, *wars!'* There is nothing the prior would like better, in fact, if only their armaments were not so depleted.

The grandmaster is easing himself back into the dining room chair, brooding. His jowls and lips quiver slightly with mirth. He is unrattled. '*Infortuna Minor* produces warriors too, Guy. Don't forget that.'

'Aye, and martyrs, and if the Englishman blows up anywhere public like Rome? Saint Louis and Denis, Emery! Think of that. When Caligula made his horse consul, at least it couldn’t say anything particularly stupid, but this man could be like Samson, bringing the house down on us – have our critics shut us down, like they did the Templars.'

But the magister is already speaking over him having not finished his last point. ‘I have a feeling about that boy. I can’t escape it every time I meet him. So young, so much potential, Guy. So much, yet I cannot fathom whether providence shall use all that power for good or ill. It is hard to make predictions, you understand, especially about the future.’ D’Amboise ironical smile is not returned by the prior, so he continues decisively. ‘What I do know is that he’ll be there to do more than smooth the silks of cardinals. We need a man who will *make* a way if he can't find one.'

De Blanchefort, not ameliorated, says, 'Fine, fine, but you play a fast game – '

D'Amboise immediately slams his fist on the table. 'What, and they do not? The pontiff? These bloody cardinals? These petty tyrants and *condotierri*? I'll not release any more sane and saintly knights on this errand. There is dirty work to be done, Guy. Dirty work. And by God, we need someone to do it. We'll fight fire with fire, plough with the devil if we must, but we will succeed. Do you hear me? We will succeed. There is too much at stake.' The magister pauses for a moment, then adds with slightly less heat, 'Erpingham will go forth as Pallas went forth from the mind of Jove, an idea fully formed and armed for judgment.'

CHILDHOOD MEMORIES

Hugh hears none of this as he descends the main staircase. *Dear God, how could it have come to this?* Before the question has issued from his mind, or the sigh has left his lips, a conversation he had with his mother long ago insinuates itself before him. He was only six or seven, and she was tucking him in to bed. Usually it was Wilf's wife Sally, but tonight it was her, because tonight he was affrighted. It had been no ordinary day.

'Mater.'

'Yes dearest.'

'Do all men grow beards?'

'Yes, dear. Why do you ask?'

'I don't want a beard.'

Pause. Wise, loving expression.

'Your father loves you very much, Hughey.'

'Then why is he always angry with me?'

'Your father is angry sometimes with you because he wishes great things for you.'

'But he is always angry, Mother. Not just with me. He is always shouting at the men, at Wilf, at you.'

Pause.

'Hughey dearest, when you are older you will understand that your father has lost almost everything he and your ancestors worked for.'

'Because the king took our lands after the great battle.'

'That is right, dear. He, that is, we, have lost very much, and your father carries the weight of it. We all need to be patient with him and obey him. And pray.'

'Don't cry, Mother. I can be good for father.'

'I know you can, dear, and if you are kind and good as you are now, I shall always be proud of you.'

'He said I should not cry at the execution, and I did not.'

'Your father is a magistrate, dear, and one day you will be, too, when you are older.'

'I don't want to be older. I want to be here with you and Katey and Wilf and the dogs.'

'Oh, dearest child. The world is not as it should be.'

More wise and loving looks, now accompanied with a caressing of the forehead and hair. She understands him relentlessly. A mother not only gives life at the birthing stool but also longs to give it, ripe on a plate, at every point of life, now and forever. 'It is important for the people of Norwich and the shire to see that the king's justice is in firm hands.'

'He did not look like such a wicked man. But he must be, for he would not believe the sacrament. Said he despised it.' Already burning at the waist, the heretic Peke had spat blood at Doctors Hearne, Spragwell and Reading when they prodded him with white rods and tempted him with forty days indulgence if he recanted.

'I am sorry for Master Peke and for his family, but you can see, dearest, that bad ideas can cause much harm if they are allowed to spread.'

'The fire would not spread fast enough. Father said the faggots were damp. He would not die for ever such a long time. He cried out very much. Baron Curzon and John Audley used their swords to cut branches to make the fire stronger, but still he cried out for a long time. I wanted to help them but father would not let me.'

'Mercy is a noble impulse, Hugh, and it was right for Baron Curzon to show it. But you and your father represented the king's justice, and that is a solemn duty, too. Do you understand that?'

'Yes, Mama.' *I understand that ideas are a threat to the king, the church, the home; that men die slowly with damp wood and that they smell like roasted pork. And that when beards catch alight, they burn the face black and split the lips.*

Yes, Hugh remembers as he pauses at the bottom of the stairs in the magister's palace. To be the king's justice is a terrible job for a mortal man. How much more to be God's justice, as d'Amboise wants me to be in Italy.

ONE HOUR LATER, RHODES HARBOUR

The afternoon heat is so strong that even the lizards hide from it in the shady crevices. Hugh walks back toward the Inn of England. He is halfway down the Street of the Knights, ignoring the fragrances of cardamom and some incense he cannot quite place, something vaguely eastern, repellant. He passes the New Hospital then finds himself going through Saint Paul's Gate on the harbour and strolling by the windmills to the end of the great quay, where once the mighty Colossus of ancient times straddled the outer gates. He sits on the monumental plinth, resting his fingers against the very base of the structure. So large a foundation, yet incapable of resisting the earthquake that took it away over a millennium ago. *What is solid on this earth?* The greatest bronze work of Chares of Lindos, wonder of the world, reduced to scrap metal for an Egyptian salvage dealer.

Hugh observes the ramparts, bastions, towers, and gates of his own city, ships of his own chosen harbour. Behind those walls lie the mass of bankers, philosophers, artisans, mercenaries, merchants, and knights that make up the mightiest and loveliest city in the Mediterranean Sea, gateway for art, culture, ideas, and trade from the east to west and vice versa. What a broad foundation this city has. And yet shall we know what earthquakes may come to her? A wise man might guess they will come. Pindar says that when the world was divided, it was the sea god Helios who first chose Rhodes, and after him all manner of Greeks, Romans and Byzantines, each as soon as their turn came. But each faded as their star was eclipsed and yet another arose to replace it.

And now it is we, the Knights of Saint John, the smallest of all sovereign states. Are we too relics of a former era, like these quiet stones? Are we to be eclipsed by Islam? God granted us Rhodes for a thousand years, but the quality of our piety and devotion do not bind him to favour us. Fifty-eight castles are already lost throughout these holy lands. Hints maybe?

11TH AUGUST, 1508

Less than a week later, Hugh is standing on that same quayside. Wilf is seeing his trunk onto the *Catherineta*. The Order has given his servant new clothes of serge and chamblet – blends of silk, wool and linen. The English knights will not be shown up at the papal court. Hugh smiles inwardly; it is his same battered trunk that mounts the gangplank. You can dress up someone like Wilf, but he's still a Norfolk boy when all's done.

Wilf is happy to be away from the island. He has no love of foreigners or foreign places. Italy is a step nearer England though he doubts he'll see his homeland anytime soon. He volunteered for this job after his wife Sally and child were carried off with the sweating sickness. A Carter has served the Erpinghams since the great Sir Thomas Erpingham of Agincourt fame. But the Erpinghams remained faithful to Crookback Dicken at Bosworth (though he was no crookback) and had the bulk of their estates attainted. That was just after young Hugh was born, when Wilf was fifteen or thereabouts. He remembers taking news to Lord Erpingham that his firstborn was a son, and though he'd never say it, he's always held a special affection for Hugh since then.

He's a big man, Wilf is, not tall, but broad of shoulder and deep of chest. The ease of Rhodian life has left him a bit paunchy, but he's a good cook and handy with the pikestaff – and not bad even with the two-hander his grandfather used against the French. His sandy hair tinged with ginger is tight cropped and curly, his nose flattened slightly from the tavern brawling of his younger days, and wherever he goes he cannot help making unfavourable comparisons between foreign things, or foreigners (all of whom he calls 'dagos') and his native Norfolk, land of bountiful crops and good ale.

Hugh sees him looking uneasily from the top of the gangplank, waving and shouting at the top of his voluble voice, 'I'll stay with our stuff in the hold, master. Make sure none of these dagos get their thieving hands on it.' He wears his xenophobia like a livery.

At Wilf's side is Pico, a fatherless boy of twelve. His mother is a whore of Italian extraction who prevailed on Wilf to take him when she heard they were bound for her native land. What she gave Wilf in return, Hugh has not asked. Hugh has reasoned that having the boy along will be easier than having Wilf learn the language for the many times he'll need it, and the boy seems keen to learn. Pico is short, perhaps from his Rhodian father – if he was an islander – for they are all stocky and short here, a condensed humanity.

Pico slips along behind Wilf as if the man is an immortal god. He knows Wilf has near enough saved his life. Poverty doesn't usually grant the likes of him time to grow old. A boy like him should have been out of the home and apprenticed to a chandler, glazier, shipwright, wainwright, cooper, skinner, or glover even. Even the girl Hildegard was living as an anchorite at eight, Bede an oblate at seven. What business does a boy have hanging round his mother when he's twelve? He hasn't plucked up the courage to look at Hugh's eyes yet, much less address him. Pico and Wilf both have new black woolens and white hose for their new stations; they look almost respectable.

It is already mid-morning and that same westerly is blowing, warm, beguiling, unfaithful. It comes across the Arabian Desert, raising tall clouds miles high. They call her the Hamscene. Hugh has said one or two numb farewells, and, now that it comes to leaving, feels nothing at all. This place, this near celestial place, was once his all-consuming thought—to be here, to fight for the cross, defend Christendom. *Pro fide*. But now he does not recognize that twenty-two-year-old stripling. All that naivety, optimism, swagger, obdurate pride – that one died in the hull of a Turkish goke while the oil of youth was still on him. And so too did the phantom which is *his* Rhodes. How could so much high intention become so lowly a thing as mere piracy? He casts a glance to the base of the fallen Colossus. His dreams are not the only ones to have died in the sea.

His eye catches sight of Pico and thinks he sees himself at that age.

MORE MEMORIES.

Another bedtime conversation with his mother surfaces in his mind. His voice and body had begun to change, and the certainty of adulthood was one step closer. She came to his room to make sure the rush light was extinguished, and they sat awhile, talking about the world that lay beyond Norfolk, England even. His father's friend Sir Geoffrey de Hastings had visited, and they had discussed Sultan Mehmet's siege of Rhodes, the valour of Grandmaster d'Aubusson and of the great Cavalliere Vendramin. It was not the first Hugh had heard of these events or these people, but certainly it was the first time he realized that they were real, and connected to his world in some way. Years before he had been shaken by the burning of the heretic Peke, and the possibility of discord within Norfolk. Now he saw that there was discord in the world and possibly war in heaven too.

'Would the Mohammedans rule the whole world if they could?'

'Hughey, what a thought, and right before bed too! Now say your prayers and let us have this light out.'

'But would they?'

'Yes, I dare say they would if there was no one to stop them. But there are the knights on Rhodes, and besides, God would not let it happen.'

'But the knights have lost Jerusalem and sixty cities. Sir Geoffrey said so.'

'The knights are few and brave, and the Turks are numerous as locusts. But good will always triumph in the end. More will join them.'

'I will join them, Mother. Then they will not come to England and make you, Maude or Katey slaves as they do there.'

'What a child you are, Hugh! Join the knights indeed! Your duty is to be here, tend the estate, marry well, and make me comfortable in my old age when I have no teeth and my eyes are dim. Give me many grandchildren to dote on, and at least one heir to carry the title. Join the knights! Now let me have a kiss, and a *Pater Noster*, and hear no more about it.'

He kissed her. He remembers the softness of her cheek, and that her face had been, as it always seemed to be, beautiful with love. He still cannot smell thyme without remembering her. But nor can he forget his terrible resolve that tore the family apart. What good was a name, a family, wealth and advancement when all of that – all they held dear – hung by a thread a thousand miles away?

He would become a knight.

THE PRESENT

Returning to the present on the quayside on Rhodes, Hugh is about to take a last stroll to the foundations of the Colossus. Nothing had worked out as he dreamed. But even as the thought gnaws at his imagination, he hears the clatter of hooves. A small cavalcade passes the Pauline Gate. The banners and ensigns of Auvergne flutter, rising and falling to the canter of de Blanchefort's retainers. He is there at the centre, scowling like a man disturbed from his breakfast. Today's expression of choice: indigestion.

He calls a halt thirty yards before the galley as the carters and merchants are thick about the gangs and cranes. 'Fra Erpingham, Fra Erpingham.' A retainer scuttles past the trolleys and barrels, to where Hugh is standing. 'The prior will speak to you.' He adds, with a nervous twitch that shows he had been too long in de Blanchefort's employ, 'Err, now if you please, sir.'

Hugh follows to where the prior stands on the far side of the quay, looking across the bay to the fisherman drying their nets. De Blanchefort glances sharply to see them approach but then looks straight ahead across the bay again, all the while tapping his riding boots on the stones as though drumming up the words from the earth. Hugh is barely within earshot when the old goat starts a monologue directed seaward.

'I don't mind saying that I was against your being sent to Italy- nay, advised strongly against it. Great lot of good it did.' Hands on hips, more chewing of the gums, more shuffling of the boots, more flickering of fingers against thumbs.

Hugh draws alongside him. The old soldier turns slightly and observes him narrowly through his good eye. Did he remember the young man fresh from Cambridge who had come to Rhodes when he himself was acting Grandmaster before d'Amboise arrived?

'The magister has had his say, and I'll have mine. I know we've not seen eye to eye these last years, but I hope you'll hear me. After Mehmet lifted the siege, I was a mess, inside here.' He taps his head. 'We all were after the euphoria died down. It took a long time for the humors to balance again. The physics and older knights said that I would be right again in time. Of course, I didn't believe them. But they were right. That's the point. But until then I was not good to be around. Perhaps I'm still not. And you certainly aren't. But time is a healer, at least it is if you live long enough. You must rest where you can, find pleasure again in the small things, seek the counsel of a good confessor.'

He is silent for a few moments. It is over twenty-eight years since the Great Siege. He would have been Erpingham's age back then. Hugh says nothing. He can't hear consolation; it does not enter where he is.

The prior sniffs and starts to fiddle with the buckle on his belt. 'You're set among wolves, Erpingham. Those Italians do not have honour. A canker has corrupted them. It's all power and money with them now. They'll be expecting you, like they were the last fellow we sent. You watch that scarred back of yours. Don't trust anyone, not even the pope. In fact, especially not the pope. He's waited a long time to get where he is, outlived and outsmarted the Borgias. Do not underestimate him. He has big plans, and big plans cost money. He'll know all about us, what we're really about. The man's a dragon. And before you say that your patron saint is Saint George, you'd better remember that this is Italy we're talking about, and that you'd be better with a decent sword than a patron saint. So - ' Again the prior lingers and fidgets. 'So here you are. Take my Colhona.'

He unstraps and passes the carrack sword to Hugh without ceremony. 'Go on, take it.'

Hugh takes it obediently and without a word. The sword and hilt are heavy, but well balanced. The blade is black – for night work – and the name Colhona or 'big balls' refers to the two large protective rings on the guard terminals. He thumbs them. They are sharpened. *A little singular, but I suppose they would give extra cutting edges up close.*

'I know, not a gentleman's weapon, but that won't matter where you're headed. Served me well through many official engagements. And others. And through the Great Siege, too. Get it right, and you can use those rings to snap your enemy's blade. Double bladed, as good for cutting as it is for thrusting. You can punch your way out of most corners with this if you've a mind to. Damn good sword. Can't think why the Portuguese didn't make more of it. You never see them these days except with their traders.'

The prior turns to face Hugh for the first time. 'I know what the magister has told you. But remember that Vendramin, whatever he has become, was once a great man, and a friend, too.' He sniffs awkwardly. 'Well, a friend to many here. Have respect, do not use this blade against him if you can avoid it.'

De Blanchfort looks back toward the sea, then at his boots. He coughs slightly to clear his throat. 'Do not humiliate him or make him suffer. Anyway, there it is. If you survive, you can give it back to me. And if you don't, have your man send it back. And remember, you carry our name with you in Rome where your conduct could make or break this order. Make a sow's ear of things for us, and it's me who'll be after you, never mind the pope. Now, on your way.'

THE CROSSING, EIGHT DAYS LATER, IN THE LEE OF CRETE.

It is the second watch of the night and Wilf holds his master's wrists amidst the shrieks. Hugh is fighting his way out of another nightmare.

'It's all right, master; it's all right. Just a dream.' Wilf takes Hugh in his bear-like arms for the hundredth time. 'Just a dream, lad.'

Hugh takes sharp breaths as he gazes about the small cabin illumined grey by a full moon. He feels his groin and his cot's straw mattress, wet with urine. Smells it. *Just a dream*. He breathes out, this time shuddering almost into sobs. *Just a dream. Thank God.* Every creak of the hull or of Pico's hammock takes him back. It can even happen when he is awake. Sounds, yes, but also smells, like the smell of pitch used on the hull, or of a cankerous sore. There is no end to it. Once he was a prisoner to one oar, one chain, one ship. Now he is a prisoner everywhere and at all times.

'At least you weren't trying to strangle me this time. Here, use my cot, I'll fetch more straw.'

'Yes, I will. Thank you.' Again, the shuddering exhalation of breath.

'Don't distress yourself, master. You'll be well soon.'

Pause. 'Yes.' Then finally, 'Fetch some clean hose too, will you.'

It is on nights like these that Wilf gets him talking about the old days in Norfolk, the village of Erpingham, the family, the servants, the farm, what they'll be up to this time of year. Then the town of Aylesham, the Boleyns of Blickling, the city of Norwich, the pirates of Yarmouth, the Tucket fayre, the smell of sheep, of herring, of hops and good Norfolk ale. He thinks this will help Hugh. In truth, he doesn't know what else to do. Most times Hugh will give one- or two-word contributions. When he was very young, he used to think Wilf the cleverest and wittiest person in the world, always forthcoming with opinions on adult subjects like fly-tying, trap-setting, uncouth jokes, beer and cider. Wilf framed the whole world with mirth and irreverence. But Hugh soon came to despise him in equal measure. He had himself grown and gone up to Cambridge. When good taste becomes self-aware, it is a fall of sorts, perhaps a great fall, but in those days for Hugh to be in the same room as Wilf, subject to his coarse ignorance, forced to hear one more crude joke; it was sheer torture for the prig he had become. When Hugh left for Rhodes, his father charged Wilf to go with him. Hugh was sure it was part punishment. As it turned out they had got along tolerably, tossed as they were into an unfamiliar and dangerous world. And now here they were, still miles from home; another a long voyage, another long year.

Hugh takes the cool cotton chemise from Wilf. 'Thank you.' He wants to add, *and I don't know why you stick around when I know you miss your home*, but he is no good at saying things like that.

But Wilf, in a rare moment of perception, seems to answer the moment anyway by saying something he often has said on the rare occasion he was thanked. 'Oh, that's all right, master. Promised his lordship your father, I did. I said, "Aye, my lord, I'll do for him among the dagos and infidels, as my own father did for yours while he drew breath." That was what I said, and that's what I's doing. And we'll get by. Yes, we will.'

His lordship, my father.

MEMORIES OF HIS FATHER

How did I become cruel? My father was cruel and I swore I would never become like him. Gelert, daft old hound was like a big brother to me. We'd grown up together under tables, in the fields. I can still feel his warm breath on my face, my eyelids; his moist muzzle, his coarse grey fur. I rode as a child on his back. When I was ill, he slept next to my bed. He would never bite me if I pulled his tail, not ever. He was young then and so was I – our springtime of life. Then he was old, and lame in the hindquarters. Poor Gelert. He only bit Katey the once. She jumped on him when he was asleep by the fire. He was probably hunting in his sleep. He was not lame in his dreams. Yet for one bite, Father covered his head and ran him through. I swore I would never forgive him that, never be anything like him. Never cruel, I swore, never cruel. God help me, that is what I swore as a twelve-year-old – more than half a lifetime ago.

MIDNIGHT THURSDAY, SEPTEMBER 2ND, 1508, OSTIA

Signor M,

You will forgive, I am sure, the lack of formality in address when you remember that at our meeting on the feast of Saint Francis Caracciola, we agreed (because of the infamy of the present times) that anonymity would serve our purposes best, if these letters should fall into the pernicious hands of others.

I write tonight with news that the hospitalier has finally arrived from Rhodes. It is, as you rightly suspected, Sir Hugh de Erpingham, though I confess, not as tall as one might have thought from all the tales and songs that have bored our ears of recent years. If anything, he appears shy, which is surely a sign of pride out of its depth. And like all the English, he is ill favoured of visage. In his case it is a countenance subdued from his sojourn with the corsairs – or mayhap 'tis true what they say; that celebrity is indeed a mask which doth but canker the face. I do not think he will give us any trouble. I will follow him tomorrow to Rome and take what opportunities I can. Please send news of this to our esteemed benefactor in Siena. Time has rewarded his patience. The game begins in earnest.

I have attached a list of my expenses and copies of previous statements of account; I hope these meet with your approval and early response. Please send further orders, if any, and your remittance to our people in Rome.

Your obedient servant etcetera.

Part II: THE ETERNAL CITY

MID-MORNING, 6TH SEPTEMBER, 1508. DESCENDING THE AVENTINE HILL, ROME

The shithole: Rome. The Venetian ambassador calls it the 'sewer of the world' – which is rich coming from him.

A thousand years ago, she was home to half a million people, now only maybe seventy thousand. Five percent of the men are priests. Fifteen percent of the women are prostitutes. The select *cortegiane onesti*, with their dyed blonde hair, sit in loggias on unwashed silk cushions, reciting well-rehearsed extracts from Bocaccio's *Decameron*. The more numerous *cortegiane di candela* ply their wares in the bathhouses and down the narrow lanes near the Arch of Janus called the Bordeletto – places licensed for trade by the papacy. But whichever type they start out as, these inamoratas invariably end up, along with a good many of their former clients, languishing under the *Ponte Sisto.* Or if they have played the game well, they might be confined to the hospital of *San Girocomo degli Incurabili* to have their French disease treated with *lignum vitae*, a foul medicine made from some tree of the New World.

Maybe a half to two thirds of every building he's seen is ruin—crumbling, infested ruination. Goats clamber over mountains of rubble to eat the vines growing from carved and cracked masonry. Herds of cattle feed among antique domes, columns and porticos, all of such scale that they were once thought to have been built by giants or the gods. But now wrecking crews break them for building stone, and burn the marble slabs and columns for their lime content. Hundreds of families live pell-mell in the gaping dome of Pompey's theatre. Everywhere your horse must tread on dead and dying goats, cats, dogs, rats. He would have the *Maestro di Strada* strung up for allowing such squalor in Christendom's premiere city. It wouldn't be tolerated on Rhodes.

Hugh casts his eye right to the once vast Circus Maximus, now a field for herders and their stock. When the crumbling empire turned en masse to the crucified God, they forgot their circuses and built churches and cathedrals instead. *No one has built a sporting stadium now for over a thousand years*, Hugh muses. These new Romans race their *palios* and play their *calcio* on city streets with verve but don't enshrine them in separate sacral spaces as their pagan forbearers did. His mind is brought suddenly back to the street he is descending when his mare whinnies and nearly bucks as a rat scuttles out the backend of a dog's carcass and shoots across their path.

TEN MINUTES LATER. SIGNOR DIAMANTE'S DENTATORE AND BARBER SURGEON'S SHOP, VIA GIULIA, ROME

Hugh bypasses the queue of customers at Senior Diamante's – the man should change his name. No one dare mutter. Queuing is not in the Italian psyche anyway. As he sees it, courtesy is the virtue exercised between knights and ladies in twelfth century Provence, not among mercantile arrivistes in a crumbling dung heap like Rome.

Diamante hasn't seen him. He is sponging down a jowly wine bibber with a few less rotten teeth than when he came in, and trying to sell him a miniature of Saint Apolonia, patron saint of toothache, and as much physic as he thinks the man can cough up for – when he's finished coughing generally. Blooded rasps, files, spatulas and pliers lie on the bench, along with the extracted black teeth.

'Now then, mix wild mint and pepper – we have some ready mixed if you would like – and rinse with wine daily. Or for a few *scudi* more, I have some physic – a very highly recommended one that I mix myself – of sal ammoniac with rock salt and saccharin alum. Rub the powder in daily with a red cloth and you'll feel the benefit.' Diamante coughs modestly while the man computes how much he's prepared to pay never to have to come back here again. 'Uh, we have the cloth too. Price is on the bottle, just here.'

'Ah, welcome, welcome, most illustrious knight.' Diamante bends like a hoop. 'Hair or teeth, lordship?'

Hugh observes the blood-stained tools on the bench and feels something close to elation that those teeth left him by nature and the Turks are not giving him problems. He nods to the shears. 'Hair, beard.' He is being taken to seek an audience from the pontiff that afternoon. A neater beard will help him feel more focused. He has much on his mind. He is being followed already; two men with military bearing are now in the alley outside. He holds a drawn basilard dagger under his cape. Anyone tries anything in here and he'll make them regret it.

'*Va Bene*, and how would your lordship like his hair cut? *Almain, Hispaniola?*'

'In silence, signor.' Hugh removes his beret. Things are not according to plan. The *Petronilla* has not arrived with this newly ransomed navigator. He must think and plan. It is something he used to do without blinking, but now the threads will not stay joined in his mind. He must go over each detail like a child forming letters.

NOON, 6TH SEPTEMBER, 1508

An hour later, just after the angelus bell, he is back down river on the Aventine, where the Grand Priory of the Knights of Rhodes sits proud on a sharp rise above the Tiber. The Grand Priory of Rome is a collection of travertine and limestone villas, bottegas, and other outbuildings, all roofed in warm pantiles and all built onto the church of Santa Maria. Originally one of the finest abbeys in Rome, Santa Maria de Aventine was built in the tenth century by a Benedictine, Odo of Cluny, in hopes of spreading monastic reform in Rome. A tad optimistic. Now she seems, with her single nave and ramshackle pantile roof, a very small affair compared to the craze for vast new basilicas.

The Templars had been given the site in the twelfth century, and, when they were suppressed by Leo V's bull *Ad Providam*, the property devolved on the Knights of St John. 'Smells better up here, I can tell you.' The sprightly Grand Prior Giovanni Battista had told Hugh the day before. 'We still have the old priory in the forum of Augustus, but it's as low lying, miasmic, plague ridden a place as Rome has yet produced. Up here, we're on the edge of the city. Better vapours altogether.'

This afternoon Hugh is sitting alone on the terrace in the shade of hedges clipped in the form of cones and balls. The garden still has bougainvillea in flower, and other plants that are unfamiliar to him, but the first sharpness of autumn has touched this exposed place, and the trees are turning. Some leaves are orange and red. Blood red. Hugh nurses the letter which he will deliver that afternoon to the Warrior Pope. It is a weighty letter that will mean war. Thousands will die. He is Mars, the bringer of war.

From the terrace gardens, he looks down the steep banks to the slate-grey broiling hurrying mass of the Tiber. More red-rooved houses, barns, and hovels line the edges of the river in various states of decay. Even now and even from up here, he can see the devastation of the great flood, a decade back. One of the largest houses forty feet up the bank still has a huge, uprooted ash tree enmeshed in the roof. People fled to the hills from the dank remains of their city only to be brought lower by plague.

The aged gardener, who sees an opportunity for a rest, approaches with weary steps. He removes his cap. ‘Signor is looking at the devastation of our flood.’ He points a willowed finger up stream to the island. 'I remember it like yesterday, I do, and I will never forget; one hundred and fifty bodies a day were brought to that island for week after week. Many said—Fra Savonarola for one—that it was punishment for the sins of the Borgia pope, but it came worst on the poor. That is all I know. Terrible, terrible.'

He rakes some more lemon leaves and then leans on the rake, nodding to the north at a church roof. ‘That is the church of Santa Sabina, oldest in Rome now Saint Peter’s is a ruin. Do you know, brother, a gentleman who knows about antiquities says that the carving on the church doors is the oldest image of the crucifixion. One of them anyway. I said to him, for he was sitting where you sit now, I said, but what about the Christians of the east? How can you know that they do not have older images? He said that the Turks have destroyed all their images. So, I said, a curse on all Saracens and heathen. That is what I said. The poor will inherit the earth.’ When Hugh does not engage him, he tips his cap again and shuffles off, raking every now and again and looking toward the upper windows of the palace.

Hugh has kept to himself mostly, the last four days, eaten in his room away from the other brothers. Prior Giovanni Battista interviewed him at length on his second day. Hugh is thinking about this when, like a premonition, he looks to see him on the terrace approaching with lithe, bow-legged steps that belie his age. Hugh has asked if he is approaching seventy. He said he is— but from the other side. He is a Florentine by birth and inclination, with a narrow face, tight trimmed mustachio and goatee. He doesn't approve of Rome, Romans, or Livorno fish stew. Or, of course, Spaniards or French, unless they are professed knights of the order.

'Not prejudiced, Hugh my boy,’ he said in a lengthy discourse on the manners of the nations. ‘Not prejudiced; despise them all equally.' His smile shows that he doesn't mean it; it’s just for effect.

‘Good day to you, Prior.’ Hugh stands.

'Don't know why you're looking west, Hugh. The fairest prospect in Rome is north—the road to Florence.' He is a sparkle of a man, who wears his responsibilities lightly. Hugh envies him, but warms to him, too.

He smiles at the older man. 'I am told that you will accompany me to see His Holiness this afternoon.'

'My boy, I wouldn't let you go alone your first time. Are you nervous?' He motions with elegant fingers for Hugh to sit back down, while he himself walks nearer the edge of the terrace, facing away.

'Should I be?' Hugh says. *It'll take a lot of pope to scare me.*

'Perhaps.' Battista lingers. 'He has his moments, his *terribilitá*? I do not think the English have this word.' A glance round and the swish of his black silk gown reveals both sword and dagger. *'Terribilitá*?'

'A short fuse?' Hugh, the master gunner, is thinking of his own father.

'Ah, exactly so. You must not speak unless he speaks to you. If he does not like your conversation or your answer, he will speak over you, and you should be silent at once. Failing that – '

'And if a man wishes to make his point?'

'I wouldn't.' He smiles, fatherly. 'He will ring his bell, talk to someone else, punch you or beat you with a rod if he really likes you.'

'And if he doesn't?'

'Ah, I will show you the Castel Angelo on our ride in. There are many places in the bowels of that fortress where brave men will never be heard. But do not misunderstand me. The pope is in many ways a very great and just man, just impatient – strong thumbs but weak fingers, perhaps all thumbs. You know the type; autocrats are all the same, men are all the same. He was a cardinal at not much more than your age, and yet still wore the red beret before the election, causing a scandal. But that is Julius. He wanted the papal tiara twenty years ago, so he's making up for lost time. He even kept his first name in the Latinized form which is unheard of. And rather bad form.'

'So, he is forward.'

'Forward? Indeed, he is. He hasn't invaded anywhere in two years, which in this day and age is an attainment in moderation, but beware any man in search of a legacy. Makes them do unseemly things. You know, in ancient times they used to say that Caesar and Pompey were very much alike, especially Pompey. Have you heard that before?'

Hugh nods as the old man smiles wryly.

'Yes. Well, I think we could say the same for Caesar and Julius. Certainly, he'll be remembered as a Caesar, one way or the other.'

'He fears assassination?'

'This is Rome, my boy; if you want a friend, you get a dog.'

2PM, 6TH SEPTEMBER, 1508.

Two hours later, Hugh, accompanied by the Grand Prior Battista and his affinity, all well mounted, moves at a steady pace up the Via Guila, a broad street named after Pope Julius, who had ordered the tenements and crumbing villas cleared to make way for something more befitting the memory of his pontificate. It cuts a bit of the bend between the Ponte Sisto and Ponte Sant'Angelo, but not much. The prior is enjoying pointing out things here and there that might interest the newcomer. The numerous icons of Saint Anthony and Saint Sebastian are to ward off the men and women who empty their bladders – and worse – on the street. The veiled women are the married ones; the others are the other sort. *Lenzuoli*, good faces bad. Many of the beggars claim to be friars and monks, which might be true, though it is hard to say. Hugh nods.

'I hear you've been down here already today for a haircut.' Prior Battista rides with one hand on his hip, glancing every now and again at his ward.

Hugh returns the old man's impish smile. 'Ah, so it was your men tailing me.' *He doesn't trust me.*

'While you are here, under my roof, I need to know where you are. It is not safe for you to go out alone.'

'I can look after myself.'

'You misunderstand Rome, Hugh. It is not like Rhodes, Florence or, I suppose, London. You look around at these ruins, not the ancient ones, these recent ones, and you imagine that a foreign army laid waste the city, but you're wrong. This is what they did to themselves—the big families, the old patricians, the Colonnas and Orsinis. To get to your barber this morning, you crossed two lines in an ancient war without knowing it. In the days of my grandfather, the Savellis held the Aventine, the Frangipane held the Palatine, the Colonnas held the Quirinale and the Orsini held the Esquiline Hill.'

Hugh's mind whirls as he follows Battista's finger across the rooftops.

'At the Sant'Angelo bridge and the areas north of there, and just across the river in Trastevere, you meet the knives and pikes of a pack of Normannis, Tebaldis, Pierleones, Papareschi and God knows what else. Between them they reduced the city to rubble. The Romans live for their vendettas, couldn't forgive even if you paid them, so it just went on and on until the canker destroyed them and their city. The only old names left were ones like the Orsini, della Rovere, and Colonna, who had abundant lands in the *campagna*.'

Couldn't forgive or be forgiven... Just went on and on. Hugh gives way to the justice of the thought, yet still shudders under it. Canker destroyed them.

He changes tack. 'When did they start to rebuild?'

'Not until the reign of Martin V, a Colonna pope. That was in my grandfather's day. What you're seeing is a hundred years of that rebuilding. Tells you how bad it must have been. But it goes on apace—the porticos dismantled, streets repaved, compulsory purchase of derelict properties in prominent locations. Even the old basilica of Saint Peter is now coming down to make way for Signor Bramante's colossal monstrosity, though don't say I said so. The *Maestro de Ruinante* is the pope's current favourite and chief adviser in all matters of civil and military engineering. He's never wrong, and he never forgets an insult, *or* fails to exploit the weaknesses of his enemies and his friends to his own advantage. He's powerful right now, so if he is there, just nod and agree with whatever he says.'

'I can see there is much to learn about life in Rome.' Hugh says this absentmindedly, for he is at that moment looking up and squinting to see men frescoing the upper stories of a newly renovated villa with scenes from the *Iliad*. The sight, sounds and smell of the honest lime putty, well-aged quick lime bubbling in the water, the scraping of trowels and the artists and their quiet work, ignite for just the briefest millisecond, something of a spark inside him. It slips through all his defences, the hardness of every protective covering, and for that moment the memory of his *forgetting* is apparent, but then it is gone again. The smell reminds him of times when he had been happy. Or perhaps free from guilt.

'What's that you said, my boy?'

'I said that I have much to learn about life in Rome.'

'Indeed, our crusade and Bramante's plans to immortalise himself in stone are in some ways in conflict. There was a time when princes, beggars, young and old were content to renounce their enmities and work in silence and anonymity to build the great cathedrals of Europe, at least so says Archbishop Hugo of Rouen about Chartres. But not now. For now, eternal life is not good enough for these men who must be known for a few centuries as the builder of this or that in stone. So, as I say, tread carefully. Let me answer if you are uncertain. We cannot have him turn the pontiff's ear away from the larger issue either for his vanity or petty domestic issues. If the Turks are left unchecked, this new Saint Peter's will make a nice sister mosque to Haggia Sophia in Constantinople.'

2.30PM, ST. PETERS

Their cavalcade is approaching the new Saint Peter's twenty minutes later. Even from the Ponte Sant'Angelo, they can see the plumes of marble dust course eastward across the auburn rooftops toward them.

'Dio Mio! You can taste it from here!' Battista reaches for a napkin to cover his nostrils and mouth. 'You know, Hugh, when the pope's uncle, Sixtus, was pontiff, he heard a divine voice, so I'm told, that his nephew would one day be pope, and that he would rebuild the fourth century basilica into a new temple of Solomon, embodying the greatness of the present and the future. I confess that I cannot see why they should now paint on such a vast canvas when a smaller one would have displayed their faults just as well.'

Hugh adopts the same mood of cynicism as they turn left off the bridge and start the rise toward the building site. He is from an old English family, conservatism comes naturally. Bramante's army of two and a half thousand men are busy attaching cables to the columns on the south ambulatory of the old basilica. With a protest of groans and great cracks, and a hideous grinding, crushing, rushing and cataract of stone, of timber, of tile, ancient walls and pillars fall. Each new plume rises like the dying breath of a great man not ready to meet oblivion. Great monuments from the days of Boethius and wall tombs once viewed, read, and touched by Gregory, Augustine, and Ambrose fall among the rubble, sacrificed to Lucretian progress, smashed in a thousand fragments on the still-more-fragmented mosaic floors. Swarms of carters and labourers descend on the mounds that were once sacred memories. Like almost everyone else, they are clearing away what they have broken. The poor on the periphery of the rubble mounds pick through them for anything they can sell, timber for building or cooking, tiles for reuse, bones to be boiled for glue or burnt for paint. And so, this termite workforce digs like the new *Humanista* dig, as Dante, Petrarch and Boccaccio dug, downwards, *ad fontes,* back to the antique pavement. But even this they have damaged beyond use by their haste to erect some grander monument to their own honour. These antique remnants shall be used as Dante used them—re-sized and refitted to build a new system in which men will be better, more virtuous. For the great supporting columns inside the new Saint Peter's will be, so they say, hollow, and filled with the debris of the old. It is apt. It is poetic even—the atoms of Democritus gathered, garnered and furthered by the dignity of a new age. Hugh tastes the sepulchral dust on his ascent from the river toward the papal palace and between his teeth he grinds old Christendom, fine as dust. The Borgia tower rises against the pitted skyline of papal apartments, the center of the hive. Hugh imagines the Borgia pope and his infamous son plotting up there, lusting after the gold, only to be outwitted by Vendramin.

Hugh glances at the half-covered remnants of the old entrance steps to St. Peter's. Ramps and carts ascend on rubble, and whores tempt the masons with all their charms. Charlemagne ascended those steps on his knees after the siege of Pavia in Lombardy. A long, long time ago.

Leaving his mount at the stable yard, Hugh sees many statues from the old basilica, stored in crates, or under canvas, some in stables, or half in. Among them is one he has wanted to see since he first heard of it from the provost of his university. He dreamed of making some vague pilgrimage or embassage to Rome and kneeling before it in the half-lit holiness of a poignant feast day, of having some revelation that would transport him, change the course of his life. Yet here it is, nine years old, the *Pieta* of Michelangelo. He has never seen anything like it. The marble is stained with green mould where the courtyard roof has shed its own tears. Yet even here, part covered as it is and surrounded by the bustle and profane shouting of workmen, Hugh feels that same shudder from the center of his chest he felt half an hour before when he smelt the fresh *intonaco* on the Via Guilia, a suppressed hunger, a faint but undying ache in his inner most being, that recollection that he has forgotten something. He closes his eyes momentarily to gather his wits. The day is turning out strange. There is no time to walk over to the statue, or for any further introspection; the group is moving on. He has work to do.

Inside the papal palace, the marble cools his skin. He pinches the demolition dust from his nostrils and immediately smells the odors of mop water, incense, and the fust of aging tapestries. Hugh and the grand prior are delayed behind a long queue of suppliants, dignitaries, and merchants who spill out of an antechamber, along the corridor and down the stairs: French perfumers and glove makers, Teutonic bakers,

Spanish booksellers, Lombard carpenters from the Campo del Marzio, Greek copyists, German typographers, Portuguese trunk makers from the Via dei Baullari, goldsmiths of around San Giorgio. Whoever they are, wherever they have been employed in the vast papal enterprise, sooner or later they end up at the door of Papal Chamberlain Giuliano Leno, invoices, chits or promissory notes in hand, irritated, apprehensive.

'Don't worry, Hugh,' Battista says as his retainers clear a way through for them. 'They're not for the pope, only for Leno. Nothing much comes in or out of the Vatican, or happens anywhere else for that matter, unless he sanctions it. He's been with Julius a long time, and he's a power here as Julius himself was when his uncle was Pope Sixtus.'

They get free of the press in the corridor and eventually arrive at the newer part of the palace, though even here the tapers have marked the walls and ceilings. 'You, there,' the prior's chief captain says quietly but with the authority of a man who is only used to one answer. 'Fetch Colocci. Tell him we're here.'

'Angelo Colocci is the papal secretary, a helpful fellow.' Prior Battista leans in and speaks more confidentially as various clerics and ambassadors mill in the broad marble corridor. 'He will announce us. You will walk slightly to my right and a step behind. We bow on one knee together. Do not you speak or look him in the eye unless bidden.'

Colocci appears in a flurry of satin, tall with a horse shaped head, pigeon chest and slight hunch. He gives Hugh the barest nod when introduced, too busy for pleasantries.

'Well then, Angelo, who's in today?'

'The usual crowd: Cardinal Giovanni de Medici in the Parrot room, but also his grasping sister-in-law Alfonsa Orsini, come looking for more incomes from benefices and cardinal's hats for her spawn. Just look straight ahead, and I'll try to rush you through so you don't have to talk to them.'

And then, while Colocci catches a servant to give instructions over the afternoon dispatches, the prior whispers to Hugh. 'The pope keeps his friends close, and his enemies closer, in order to get them away from those who haven't made up their minds yet.'

Colocci turns back from the servant and says to Hugh, 'Have you got this letter then?'

'Yes,' Hugh says.

Colocci is matter of fact. 'I'll take it.'

'I may only hand it to His Holiness.' Hugh doesn't look at Battista.

'Hugh!' The prior is ruffled.

But Colocci is as quick. 'Suit yourself.' His eyes say something quite different as he leads them from the corridor – where the remainder of the prior's affinity stay – and into the first room of the pope's apartments.

'Apartmento Borgia.' The prior points to where Julius has defaced the Borgia insignia of Apis the bull god above the pediment of each door.' But you will see as we go through that no harm has come to the frescoes of Pinturichio, even though they bear the image of Alexander VI and his daughter Lucrezia.'

Colocci, whispers back, 'His Holiness is a great lover of the arts, none greater. Paris de Grassis would have had the apartments chipped back to the brick, but His Holiness would not see the frescoes destroyed. Even so, please don't mention the Borgia pope, the Borgia tower *etcetera*, or any such thing in his hearing. He cannot abide these dark apartments or the wickedness of their former occupants. Indeed, he had Alexander's remains exhumed and sent back to Spain. The sooner His Holiness can get upstairs to the new apartments, the better for all of us. That's what the noise is, by the way; they're laying the floors today.' He turns to halt their progress into the last anteroom before they reach the papal throne, whispering, 'And Bramante is in, too, with the poet Pietro Bembo, so you're forewarned.'

They enter the first room, now off the heavy blue-green glazed tiles and onto oriental carpets. Hugh cannot help but catch glimpses: one cardinal, four other men and one woman, *no threat*; gold ceilings, gaudy; Pinturicchio's murals of landscaped gardens, rich greens and blues, all blurs; views from the windows of gardens, orange trees, pines, river, Ponte Mario. *Possible escape route.*

Colocci hurries them on, one hand held out slightly as if he leads them with an invisible thread. They pass through another room, very similar to the last. This time Hugh does not bother to observe the ceiling or window views, but rather follows the prior's fingers to the fresco on the far-right wall where Pinturicchio has painted the Emperor Maxentius' dispute with Catherine, with various Asiatic and Frankish looking soldiers and courtiers in attendance. Prior Battista whispers, 'Nice family portrait: Alexander VI and his daughter Lucrezia. Cesare is that Turk, there. And see the inscription above the arch of Constantine?'

Hugh looks, and there under a finely observed arch surmounted by the Borgia bull god Apis, is the Latin inscription 'bringer of culture and peace'. The prior cannot resist the quip. 'Can't accuse them of not having a sense of humour.'

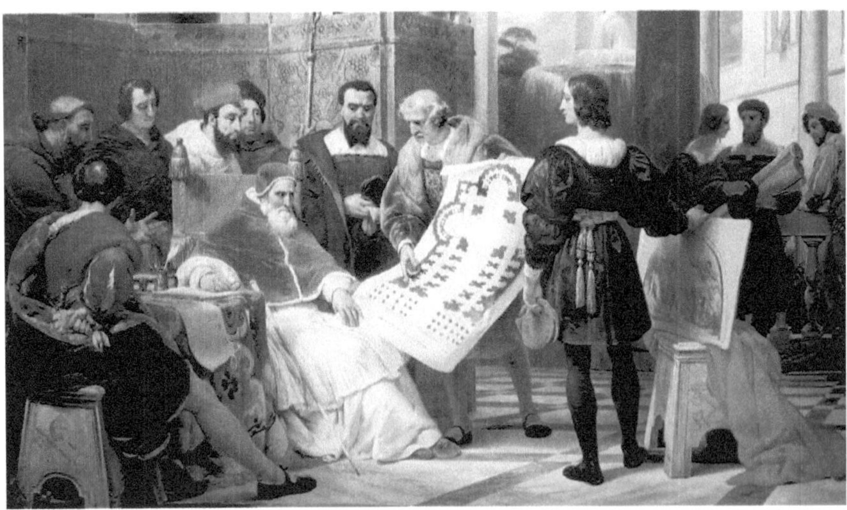

Hugh smiles, but is really looking at the depiction of Lucrezia: blonde, beautiful, slender hips, and shallow bosom. He has hardly processed her face and body when he passes through another door into the throne room itself. Hugh stands dutifully just behind the prior's right shoulder, and from this place takes stock: twenty men, half clerics, none visibly armed. The room is double length with exits behind him and opposite, doors unguarded. Everything is a trap; everyone an enemy. When the demons take hold of his mind you only have to look at him askance to get your nose broken. He is feeling a slight nausea in the front of his head and cold sweat down his back.

While they wait to be announced, Prior Battista whispers, 'The man just behind the pope is Sigismondo de Conti, the other secretary, the private one.' The prior straightens up but then leans in and whispers again. 'A man like Julius needs two; he's quite capable of dictating two brevies at once. Seen him do it myself. And he has two masters of ceremonies as well. That older fellow, Johannes Burchard, has been here forever. The other is Paris di Grassis. That is him with the red beret. I think he'd like it to be a cardinal's red cap one day. So, remember: it is "messer" for a doctor or canon, "don" for a monk, "padre" for a friar.'

The throne is against the right-hand wall, gold with purple silk cushioning and luxuriant silk canopy spangled with gold and silver embroidery, bordered by various kinds of damasks and tassels. Tapestries and silk hangings billow and shift in the afternoon breeze. About the pope, on tables or propped against chairs are an assembly of presents that have been donated that day and as yet have nowhere to go: wood carvings, arabesques on marble and sandstone, marquetry, portraits in wax, goldsmith's work and jewelry. Hugh lets his eyes wander again. Stools are ubiquitous here, but no one is seated, not even the pope, who instead pours over a table looking at the plans spread by Signor Donato Bramante. The papal architect looks up to see who has come. His keen blue eyes range from under a considerable forehead, crowned with curly grey hair in full retreat.

'Thank you, Prior,' Hugh snaps back, trying to fight the rising panic. 'I think I have learnt that much.'

He surveys the knots of bishops and clerics who have come on various issues. But these Hugh pays little attention to, for it is the poet, translator, literary critic and scholar Pietro Bembo, standing disinterestedly at Bramante's shoulder, who cuts the most interesting figure. High forehead, aquiline nose, hair swept back and eyes dark as ripe olives that peer back at him momentarily across the room. What intensity and intelligence in that face? It's like running a forefinger over a razor, thinking you're being ever so careful only to cut yourself. Bembo looks into Hugh, exuding the air of a man who finds himself endlessly fascinating.

And then in the next second, Colocci has done his whispering and the Holy Father of Christendom is himself at last making eye contact. A deep brow draws back momentarily, and his mercurial brown eyes take in the Hospitalier. 'Here already? I want to speak to them, but I haven't got time now.' And then louder, but still to Colocci: 'The Hospitaliers are welcome, but I cannot see them now. They will deliver the letter and arrange a convenient time with my secretary.'

The prior whispers, 'Bow, and for God's sake smile.'

Hugh obliges stiffly, but the pope is not looking, for now he whispers into Colocci's ear and then is straight back to Bramante. 'All I was saying, Donato, was that my tomb may look cramped in this corner, there should be more space about it. For example, do we need these piers here? Could we do without them, make this one bigger instead?'

Colocci walks over with a lupine air of triumph. He holds out his hand, but Hugh, having looked up, now walks straight past him and heads toward the pope. There is a gasp from Colocci and Battista and a general dimming of the ambient sound everywhere else. The Bishop of Basle whispers, '*Ha le palle di ottone.*'

Balls of brass, indeed, Hugh thinks, as he approaches Christ's vicar uninvited. A cardinal moves aside leaving Hugh just enough space on which to kneel and present his letter to Julius.

'What's this? The letter?' The pope, for once, is taken back.

'By your courtesy, holiness. My orders only permit me to hand it to Your Holiness.' Hugh is not looking up as he speaks, but his voice is firm.

Julius looks at Bramante. 'I wonder, Donato, whether all Hospitaliers obey their orders with such impudence?'

'I always fulfill my commissions.' Hugh glances up to see that Julius is not reaching for letter, so he places it carefully on the table, rises, takes one step back, bows with finesse, adding without a shred of defiance. 'Your Holiness.'

While Hugh is processing backwards from the pope's presence, head bowed, Bramante cannot resist answering the rhetorical question. 'The answer, Holiness, is that if they did, we'd have less trouble with the Turks than we do in the papal throne room.'

'Eh, what's that?' The pope is turning to see Pietro Bembo shake his head.

'I think Maestro Bramante is too quick to disparage the service of Your Holiness's loyal knights. I am sure I should not have the fortitude to live in the jaws of the Turk, much less approach Your Holiness uninvited! This knight's fidelity and assiduity should be rewarded, not disparaged.'

Julius puffs his cheeks for a moment, then grunts. 'Well, what d'you say to that, knight?'

Hugh glances at Bembo, something of the danger now making him feel alive again. 'Holiness, we are the Knights of Rhodes. We only live to protect you from, well, from people like us.'

Julius' leonine glower turns immediately into something approaching a smile. 'And a wit, too. It is well answered, is it not, Bembo? Bramante?'

'Well indeed,' Bembo says. Bramante smiles, although he always looks like he is trying to void something unnaturally large from his bowels.

The pope sprinkles the air with the fingers of his left hand as if in absolution. 'Very well, very well. But come now. Back to these drawings or we shall never be finished.'

He does not look again to Hugh, who now stands with the prior by the door. Colocci is again at the pope's elbow. The pope breaks off for a moment to whisper something in his ear. This Hugh sees as the prior takes him by the arm back into the doorway of the Parrot room.

'Well, what was that supposed to be?' Prior Battista is exasperated but still whispering. Hugh lingers and so the prior continues, 'After everything I said, you approach uninvited? If it were not for Bembo, we could all be in serious trouble.'

At this moment Colocci appears in the doorway, and the prior turns to smiles again. 'Angelo.'

'You'll have to teach your friend some manners.'

Hugh winds his neck out. 'You have something to say, you can say it to me.'

'Hugh!' Battista can see the quiet equilibrium of papal contacts evaporating.

'Very well, Erpingham, I'll spell it out. You may be a big noise on that windswept island you come from, but here you're nobody, and nobodies that make a nuisance of themselves don't last long.'

Hugh lets the demons speak and dares heaven. 'Well, Angelo, I'm still here.' He hates these ponces, these bishop's catamites, brown-nosed *maninos*, eunuchs.

Colocci, too used to being right, and too used to having all things his way within these chambers, stoops to prod Hugh's shoulder. 'You play a fast game, my English friend.'

'And so do you, secretary. Touch me with that finger again and I'll break it.'

The prior is now in full remonstration with Hugh, but Colocci merely straightens up and smiles. He's seen this sort before. Prior Battista says that they ought to go – not a bad idea under the circumstances. Hugh is still resolute, eyes bloodshot, a great vein throbbing in his neck. He'd like nothing better than to kick this dandy's knees from under him and ram his fat nose into the marble fireplace. It has taken less than half a minute for Colocci to become the sole object of hate and anger in Hugh's universe. His knuckles are white with a rising rage, the Medici cardinal and the Orsini Contessa peer at them from across the room, expecting a scene. This is Rome; these things are *not* unknown! But the prior manages to subdue Hugh with a stern but fatherly look, and make their apologies.

After a moment's stand-off Colocci says what he really came to say. 'Think nothing of it, Giovanni, but I suggest you keep working on his manners for, notwithstanding, His Holiness would like to entertain him this evening.' Giovanni Battista is starting to accept when Colocci says, 'No, dear Prior, just him.'

'Where?'

'The Castel Sant'Angelo, of course, after Vespers.' In this mode, when he smiles, Colocci looks like something that would eat its young. 'And, Erpingham, don't be late.'

THE SISTINE CHAPEL

On their way from the Borgia apartments – neither man is saying much – Hugh sees a fracas in the marble hallway at the bottom of a flight of stairs. A handful of young men, some dusty, others with hands darkened with charcoal or paint, are approaching and arguing amongst themselves as they walk. Prior Battista explains that he knows the man at their head, a fellow Florentine called Granacci, from a good family, a painter who had studied with Ghirlandaio and also at Lorenzo de Medici's sculpture garden. The others he has met but could not name their families - Tedesco, Buggiardini, Donnino, and the architect Sangallo's nephew Sebastiano - but they were of the same artisan mould, and all good Florentine boys.

'Messr Granacci, whatever is the matter, why this noise?'

'Grand Prior, how fortunate to see you, maybe you can help, for this will turn out to be the shame of Florence if it cannot be resolved.' The young man stops but does not bow to the prior, for he is in evident distress, as are those about him. Hugh stands behind Battista, almost unnoticed by the artists. From his inner disposition, which ranges from terror to rage, he envies them for their ability to emote so strongly over an issue which will probably be about nothing at all.

The prior raises a calming hand toward Granacci. 'But whatever can you mean? Florence?'

'Prior, Buonarotti has lost his mind. He has called us all down here to help him with the ceiling in Sixtus' chapel, and now he throws us all out a week later, shouting like a lunatic and swearing he will do the whole thing on his own.'

The prior leans forward to hear Granacci over the din of the others who are talking feverishly amongst themselves. 'But what has brought this on? You and Michelangelo are old friends, countrymen.'

'Oh, it is simple. He said our work is not good enough for him. Now that he is in Rome and has an international reputation, his old friends are not good enough. Of course, I don't think that's the reason. He cannot take the pressure. Such a huge job, and you know what a perfectionist he is.' Granacci casts an anxious glance toward Hugh, then takes the prior's arm and looks at him earnestly. 'We were on our way to see the chamberlain, but if you would speak to Michelangelo – I'm sure he would listen to you – then we will delay, in order that our city does not come into disrepute among the Roman *cognoscenti*.'

'Well, I will see what I can do, but I...er –

'Oh, thank you, Prior, how fortunate to have met you when we did.'

Battista, now forgetting all that had gone before, takes Hugh down the corridor toward the Sistine Chapel. Florentine honour is at stake.

'Have you been to the pope's chapel before? Not much of a place, designed by the Architect Sangallo, a Florentine, of course.'

'Of course.'

'Exactly. It was for Julius' Uncle Sixtus, to be part of a fortified citadel. It has crenulations, but no lower windows. It's very dark below really. The only bright part will be this ceiling, that is, if Michelangelo doesn't kill himself finishing it.'

The chapel door is shut but not locked. The prior turns to Hugh. 'Hugh, I know that *you* know a bit about fresco painting, and a fair bit about melancholy too. Keep your wits about you. See if you can think of anything helpful.' He's about to go through the door but hangs back to add, 'Best not to say anything to him directly. He's touchy, well... like you.'

The two men step onto the cool marble floors and peer down to the far end of the chapel where high up, the scaffold is braced just below the level of the clerestory windows. The chapel is divided midway by Mino da Fiesole's ornate marble screen, and beyond that, in the gloom, lie the doings of Michelangelo's now-disbanded *bottega*: pails of water, tubs of brushes, pestles full of pigments still to grind, open bags of ground marble dust and *pozzolano* (a volcanic tufa dust), small sacks of colour, cartoons rolled up and propped against the wall, bundles of sketches, bags of plaster, sand, and lime. Above all these, high in the vault spreads the vast expanse of ceiling waiting to be frescoed.

To his right and left Hugh sees the deep blues of Perugino's wall frescos, a heavenly blue. Again, he feels the ache. Everywhere is a thin layer of dust, the sort that gets right in your nose and dries your throat, and in everything the honest damp vapours of the wet *intonaco*. The two men pass the screen before they catch sight of a man, whom Hugh takes by his dress to be a grinder, sitting on his haunches, head in hands, a book discarded at his side on the bench. It's a Bible, Niccolo Malermi's Italian translation. It lies open at a page of woodcuts from the apocryphal book of Maccabees. Alongside are life sketch studies Michelangelo has been making for one of his ceiling medallions. Hugh squints to see both. It is none other than Judas Maccabee —who else? — the warrior priest who ushered in a new golden age at Jerusalem. It seems everyone is on a legacy project for the pontiff these days.

The prior tries a cheerful approach. 'Where is the great master of frescoes?' Getting no response from the ragged man, he approaches more softly. '*Caro*, what is the matter?'

The man raises his baleful head, eyes red with tears. Mid-thirties Hugh guesses, another careworn face grown old before it's time. There's a tell-tale line on the bridge of a decidedly bent nose—broken badly and set worse. He is not tall, perhaps even shorter than Hugh, about five foot four, broad shoulders, square knuckles, and square forehead, which protrudes beyond his nose. Beyond the far doorway to their left, Hugh makes out two other figures, young lads, probably servants. But no sign of the great man himself.

The prior, directly in front of Hugh, crouches stiffly to lay a hand on the young man. '*Caro Mio!* Your friend Granacci says you sent him away, sent them all away. It is a joke, no? A misunderstanding?'

Hugh stares again. It's him, the ragged man.

The *Maestro della Bottega* drags a dusty knuckle over his nose, sniffs, shakes his head, blinking rapidly. Hugh sees a man as close to the edge as himself.

Michelangelo speaks in a husky voice. 'It was a mistake to bring them down. Their work is not good enough. I regret it. They do not understand.'

'Understand what?'

'The seriousness of this commission, my position here, how I am set up to fail by Bramante. He wants me out and his pet from Urbino, Raphaello, to be the court painter. He has already suggested I only do half the commission and give the rest to this untried, beardless arsehole from the Marches.'

'Bramante? Are you sure?'

'Oh yes, all his idea. Put it in the pope's mind when I was quite happy working on his tomb. More than enough work there for ten years.' Michelangelo throws up his hands. 'And now this place will be *my* tomb. I shall have to do it all myself, and it will take me many years, years away from marble. I'm no fresco painter. Haven't done one since I was sixteen at Ghirlandaio's studio. I have marble-hunger, Prior. I know that you cannot understand that, but I'm a sculptor. I would be happy even to be a mere *scapellino,* not even a sculptor, if only to be left alone with the marble. This—' He points to the vault. 'This will kill me, and bring me to disgrace.'

And Florence too, the prior is thinking, but he does not say so. 'And you are sure that you cannot work with Granacci on this commission?'

Michelangelo shakes his head woefully. There is no point arm-twisting him when his mind is made.

'And would it help you cope better if I smoothed it over with them, made sure Giuliano Leno pays them off with no questions asked, no fuss with His Holiness?'

Michelangelo's face brightens almost immediately. 'Would you?'

'Of course. His Holiness need not know. He'll just have to wait a little longer, that's all.'

'Patience is not chief amongst his virtues.' Michelangelo wipes his nose again, and looks up at the vault. 'He wanted three thousand ducats for twelve apostles with *customary decorations!* Can you imagine painting *customary decorations?* And as for twelve apostles, I ignored him. If I was going to be made to give up two years of my life to work with paint, I'd give the world something more than apostles. I'd give them the whole drama of creation like they'd never seen it – for the glory of God, Prior.'

'But of course. And you persuaded him?'

'He came round eventually, but he didn't like my coloured sketches; wanted my patriarchs decorated in gold. So, I told him, "But Holy Father, in those days men of God did not dress in gold, but despised wealth." He didn't like it, but he may as well know. No one else will stand up to him. All tell him what he wants to hear.'

'Yes, yes, quite so, but I would advise caution. His *terribilita,* you know –

'Oh, I know. He hit me once, when I demanded the money he owed me.'

'Yes, Michelangelo. All Rome knows you stormed off back to Florence, and that the pope sent men after you with an apology.'

'Hardly an apology.' Michelangelo traces what looks like a foot in the dust on a crate. 'I'm sure they had leg irons if I'd refused to return.'

'Well, that's my point; you should not push things too far.'

During the conversation Hugh spots Michelangelo's young servant boy approaching from the west doorway of the chapel. Hugh summons him with a gesture and walks toward the dividing screen. The lad joins Hugh and each observes the other. 'You're his servant?' The lad nods. Hugh sees under the apron that his clothes are the workaday sort, much darned but clean. 'What's your name?'

'Michi.' The boy wipes his hands on his apron, and then rubs them together like he was preparing to bake bread.

'Well, Michi, your master looks like shite. Are you feeding him?'

The lad glowers. 'I look after him best I can. I'm a good cook, a good servant. Ask anyone.'

'Is he sleeping well?' No answer. 'So, he isn't.'

'I never said that.'

'Didn't have to, but look, if a man doesn't sleep, it sets his humors out. So, get him a sleeping draft tonight from the apothecary.'

The lad's proud defiance is now replaced with a shameful look that Hugh is surprised to see in someone of his station. Michi shakes his head. 'With what? The pope only pays for completed work, and now after today and the master being as he is –

Hugh takes a few scudi from his purse. 'Take this. Get some and slip it in his wine tonight. It's what my man does for me when he thinks I'm not looking! No sleep makes a bad master; that I *do* know.'

The lad smiles and slips the coin into his belt.

JOURNEY BACK TO THE GRAND PRIORY

The knights' cavalcade passes back on the other side of the river bordering the Trastevere section of the city under the shade of the verdant Monte Gianicolo, called 'the Golden Mountain' in ancient times, because of its yellow sand. Prior Battista has been lost in thought until this point, but now he sits more upright in his saddle, like a man free once more to breathe the air. He gestures magnanimously to his right at the houses that sit under the protection of the Gianicolo Hill. 'Little Florence, they call it. You'll find a different side to Rome here, Hugh.'

Let me guess, Hugh thinks, then accidentally thinks out loud. 'Full of Florentines.'

'Quite. Fine palaces, streets washed daily, cobbles repaired, houses only let to Florentines, fines for anyone who lets their house or frontage look like a Roman lived there. I tell you the truth, in little Florence the letters SPQR stand for *Sono Porci, Questi Romani*!' The prior chuckles. 'Well, it's true; they are pigs, most of them, and at least here you can walk the streets without tripping over a dead body.' He points out the houses he knows: bankers, merchants, noble families. Rucellai, Tournabuoni, Strozzi, Pazzi, Altoviti, Bracci, Olivieri, Ranfredini, Calvalcanti. 'And that big pile we passed back there, the Palazzo Farnesina, is the one they're building for Agostino Chigi, banker and treasurer to Julius. You'll meet him tonight. Try to befriend him. He's the richest man in Rome; could be useful.' He glances at Hugh apprehensively. 'Or at least don't get into a fight with him.'

GRAND PRIORY - PREPARING TO FACE THE LIONS

'Pheasants love their feathers, master.' Wilf's attempt at humour.

'Cock pheasants, you mean.' Hugh shakes his weary head, glances from his bed, where everything he needs and does not need is spread out. He looks back toward the window, which faces across the terrace garden and down to the river. 'I'm not wearing the bloody thing in my beret and that's final. Look like a bishop's catamite.'

Wilf, seeing his master is tense, places the feather back in the box and returns quickly to lacing him into his doublet. It's a rich burgundy, lightly overstitched with gold thread at the seams, shoulders and neck. It's about as brash as you could get a man like Hugh to wear, but even then, he'll look positively conservative in Rome. The tailor back on Rhodes wanted him to have slashed sleeves. 'Oh, yes indeed, sir, they are quite the thing now in the European courts', he'd said. 'A chance for your lordship to exhibit some of our fine silk chemises.' Hugh replied that he was an Englishman, as if it were enough of an explanation, and gave him one of those stares that let the tailor know the conversation was over.

Wilf adeptly threads the doublet together, all the time trying not to breathe too heavily as he's been at the bottle. When he has finished, he stands back. 'Tell you what, sir, you look every part the prince in this. Don't think I ever saw you so finely clad. If your father could see you –'

'Yes, all right, Wilf, enough. That, and the drink. Pass me my weapons - I want those two boot knives as well, and the lock picks.'

'Expecting trouble?'

He does not answer. In truth, he hardly knows. He'll probably get there and be the only one with a blade. The prior is not happy to let him go alone. Wilf fumbles about in the chest and eventually finds the boot knives. He turns a worried eye toward his master, now drumming nervous fingers on the window ledge. If there were room enough in his bedchamber, he'd be pacing up and down it right now. Hugh is twisting to make sure he has enough space to move.

'Right, then. Some iron for your boots, and here's your basilard. Gave it a bit of a polish. The brass pommel will go nicely with the gold thread in your doublet.' No answer. It's not even the sort of thing someone like Wilf would naturally say, only he remembers it was how his master would think and talk, or at least *used* to.

Hugh lets Wilf insert the knives into his boots but shakes his head at the basilard. 'No. Get me the Italian one.'

Wilf is unfazed. He knows what this means because in the days when they used to talk, Hugh would explain all his thinking behind his choice of arms. Hugh would only ask for this particular dagger if he felt he might be asked to relinquish his sword. 'I see. Sensible precaution, master. Sort of dirty trick these dagos would pull I suppose. Ought to let me come with you. Watch your back.'

No reply.

He starts digging in the trunk, and he soon finds the knife, about eighteen inches long, wound steel wire around the handle, pommel like a large acorn, and an unusual three-part guard, each curling downwards with the same acorn-like bauble as the pommel, though smaller. The design is effective in securing your opponent's blade, in much the same way as his carrack sword does, with a twist of the hand. The bulbous ends stop the opponent from sliding his blade out laterally. Hugh has mastered it, but does not carry it often because the third part of the guard, which protrudes away from the body, always catches on his clothes or gloves.

When he is finally shod, Wilf hands him his gloves and cloak. 'I would have a word about the lad Pico if you have a moment, sir. It's just that –'

'I don't. Get me my beret, will you?'

CASTEL SANT'ANGELO

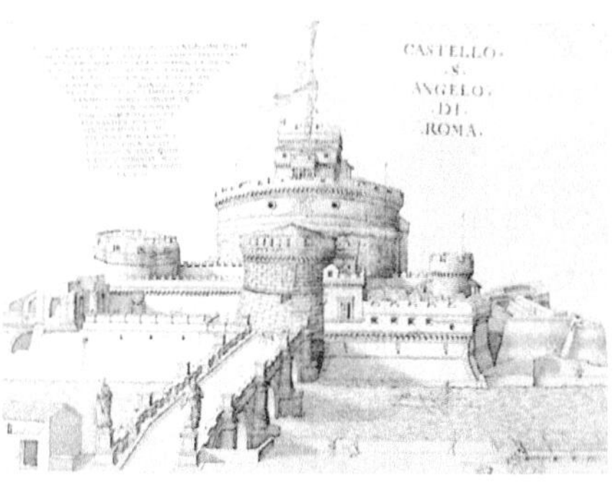

It's a monster of a building, Hadrian's old cylindrical mausoleum-turned-fortress. Hugh is late, having dragged his escort around the entire perimeter so he can make mental notes. They will miss their share of the dinner in the servants' yard at the base of the citadel. Hugh doesn't care. He enters from the riverside, passing the outer defensive wall and, after leaving his horse and escort, is led into the bowels of the building by the pope's own Corsican bodyguard. This entrance is large enough to drive a cart through, with high domed ceiling and an alcove at the far end that probably had some statue of Apollo in it at one time. It is more guard-room, than guest entrance. The pope and his coterie will come by foot down the protected passage from the Vatican. The captain takes one look at Hugh, asks for his sword and assigns three men to escort him; one in front, two behind. He doesn't want this one wandering about. Hugh is marking each of them: who has keys, who looks like they can handle themselves, their weapons – who to take first if it came to a scuffle. He is led up a shallow, curving passage, which runs around the cylinder. He marks each opening, but he knows he's getting far off the ground. To his left will be the dungeons, he guesses. Vents in the floor carry the unmistakable smell of human filth. *Poor wretches, would to God that I knew nothing of your sufferings. Down there, chained in pitch darkness, it's not that you see nothing, for by God's oath, that would be a release. No, down there in the darkness you see everything. You see it, and the darkness stares back at you.* His stomach tightens at the thought. He fights back the ghosts, doubles his grip on the Italian dagger under his cloak, tries to control his breathing, the thumping beats of his heart, and a rising heat in his body that almost makes his legs tremble. And then the thought: *no one will wall me up alive in here; I'll kill myself first.* It repeats itself, round and round, with a force of its own in his mind as they process round and round, and up and up inside the mausoleum.

They eventually turn left up a steeper incline, passing straight up to an outer terrace. The change of direction helps him break the cycle of thought, and the appearance of the evening sky gives him hope. The courtyard is small, and to his surprise he is relieved to see the papal secretary Angelo Colocci on a further terrace, holding a glass of wine and talking with another finely dressed man. The lead guard turns to him, saying in French, 'They're just up there, sir. Enjoy your dinner.'

'Fra Erpingham.' Colocci is all bonhomie, and perhaps feeling safer in the presence of a third party. 'Whatever is the matter, man? Your face looks like a smacked arse. Was it a hard walk up? Come, let me introduce you to the ambassador.'

THE AMBASSADOR'S AMBASSADOR

Before Hugh can answer the stranger removes his voluminous black velvet beret. His cloak slips back, revealing his rather superior broken sleeves, and he bows. 'Fra Hugh Erpingham, a great honour to meet you. I am Baldasarre Castiglione, Courtier of Urbino.'

'Tosh, too modest, too modest,' Colocci says. 'Playwright, poet, the ambassador's ambassador, advisor of nobility, a man of Mantua, famed eloquence and loquaciousness.'

'Please, Antonio, please,' Castiglione demurs. 'As I am sure Fra Erpingham knows by now, an ambassador is a man who usually thinks twice before saying nothing.'

'See what I mean?' Colocci says with an envious grin. '*Il est l'homme.* And what was the one you told me that day out of your little pocket book? Ah yes: an ambassador is a man who always remembers a lady's birthday but not her age. I confess I have used that one myself.'

Hugh uses the moment to observe the round, honest face beneath the beard, and the exact and measured gesture of his new acquaintance. He then reciprocates the bow. 'Pleased to make your acquaintance, signor. I have heard many good things of your city, your master's family.'

'And I have heard of *your* exploits, too, and of your commission to gather support against the infidel. You should not neglect to come to

Urbino, and you can see for yourself that she is indeed a beacon of light, learning, virtue and beauty among the thousands of Italy, and our new university.' He gestures as if everyone should know about it, and Hugh nods approvingly. Frederico de Montefeltro was a personal hero of Hugh's, first in camp and the forum, and also a humane man of letters. Erasmus had said his copies of the Patristics alone were worth the visit. The duke built the hill town into a magnificent citadel. The palace, so Hugh had heard, was itself a wonder, and he'd yearned to study there instead of Cambridge.

'This I should be honoured to do, signor, and also become familiar with your work. It has been a long time.' Hugh pauses as he is taken with an unexpected rush of emotion. 'I must apologise. My humors are quite out tonight.' He checks that the sleeves of his linen chemise are still covering his wrists, and glances to the side momentarily before re-stating rather too firmly. 'It has been too long since I had the leisure, that is, the pleasure to indulge my old passion for literature. If the world were different, I would trade this active life for one of contemplation readily.'

'Yes, I'm sure we all would,' Colocci says without emotion, smiling as if he had just evicted a widow. 'But if you would excuse me gentlemen, I must leave you to the pleasure of contemplation, while I attend to some pressing matters before we dine. Excuse me.'

The three bow, and Colocci departs toward a colonnaded upper terrace where the bulk of the guests, men and women mingle. For a moment the two men stare out over the city, observing the swallows darting about the battlements and passing through the air down, far down, toward the Tiber, glistening in oranges and pinks.

Castiglione talks of the death of his master, Duke Guidobaldo, the sickly son of Frederico; the great virtues of Guidobaldo's widow, Elizabetta; and how his eclogue 'Tirsi,' published the previous year, had tried in pastoral allegory to show the many excellences of court life in Urbino. 'I flatter myself that the work is favourably compared with Poliziano and even Virgil.' He quickly demurs with an apologetic cough, obviously regretting being so self-referential. Humility is often sacrificed when the world seems unwilling to acknowledge true genius. He changes the subject by asking Hugh how he finds Rome and his new role as courtier.

'Old habits die hard. I have been at sea for what seems like so many years, I scarce remember my manners these days.'

'Nonsense man, the ideal courtier must always be first a soldier, otherwise our courts will be filled with that despicable eunuch class that infected Rome of old, and now is happily a scourge of the Sultan's court.' Castiglione tries to find Hugh's eyes, which have wandered after the swallows. 'You must take heart. I have heard of your troubles. Indeed, we gave you up for dead. Your survival was nothing short of miraculous. God looks after his own.'

'Aye, and the devil too, signor.' Hugh places a shaky hand on the battlements and inwardly shudders. 'It was no miracle.'

'Yes, well, I admit I know little of the depredations of the Turks, but those days are behind you now. The past, as they say, is no more. We cannot go there.'

Hugh looks up, gazing at the round, simple face of the ambassador. *How can he know? How can anyone know who is not already dead? To believe a man can move through life like a ship leaving each port behind is a convenient fiction.* At this present moment he feels that his whole being is still immersed in the past, with just the barest tip of his head above the waves left to breathe.

'I pray you are right, signor, and I thank you, but I'm afraid my captivity has left me less fit for society.'

'My friend, you may, or at least I hope you may, be at home at our courts.' Castiglione speaks all of sudden with a spontaneous and unaffected tenderness. 'To be fallen, wounded in battle is no disgrace. These Romans trace their ancestry to Hector, not Achilles. No one ever claimed to be descended from *that* invincible man. If a Christian knight is anything, anything at all, *caro*, he is the wounded man, his back against the wall as Hector's was against Troy, and there is no shame in the isolation.'

The words almost breach Hugh's outer defences. But he is spared having to think, feel or answer by the approach of a slender figure on the steps.

THE POET'S POET

'Ah, Signor Bembo,' Castiglione confides to Hugh. 'Now if you want to talk literature, then he's your man, but don't get him started on Petrarch if you want to get your dinner. Or breakfast.' As Pietro Bembo gets closer, Castiglione whispers, 'As we say in Urbino, there is no poet but Petrarch, and Bembo is his prophet!'

'What are you whispering over there, Baldasarre? I hope it is about me. Is he boring you, signor?'

'Pietro *mio*, how could you think such a thing? Come, meet the scourge of the Sultan, Fra Hugh Erpingham.'

'Yes, we met this afternoon. He made quite an impression.' The men bow with grace, removing their berets with urbanity, though each closely observes the other as they do so. Bembo, perhaps early forties, reveals his near bald crown and greying hair when he lowers his long neck. 'And all that I said I meant, sir. You have my entire admiration and thanks for your work on Rhodes.'

'As you have mine,' Hugh says. 'Your *Asolani* has brought me much diversion.' He would have said comfort, but that would not be true.

'Tush, tush. Mine is adequate only, bearable to my ears now only when sung with a female voice to a lute. What *I* say to any man so unfortunate to be born beyond our shores is, learn Italian in the Tuscan dialect as *quick* as you can so you can read Petrarch – *somma poeta* – as *soon* as you can.'

Castiglione gives Hugh a knowing smile, but Bembo carries on notwithstanding,

'Don't let Castiglione put you off, my friend. In his case it is professional jealousy. Petrarch is the one to follow. He carries the torch, and I don't mind saying it.'

Their following parlance ranges from the politics of the Levant, to the virtues of Dante, Boccaccio and Petrarch, of whom the latter naturally wins Bembo's vote as the stylistic model. Hugh notes that whenever he or Castiglione talk, Bembo's eyes dart about, though perhaps not in an intended impoliteness, but rather because he seems able to absorb what people say without diverting too many resources to the task. This is proved to Hugh's mind by Bembo's following questions, which show that he has heard not only what was intended and emphasized, but also what was left out.

Compared to Castiglione, Bembo is not personable, social, warm. It seems that Bembo 'the poet of feeling' has become subsumed by Bembo 'the literary critic', that conversation has in some part become, not so much about the warmth of social interaction, but rather the rapid and efficient transmission of information. The mentioning of Petrarch, leads Bembo to bemoan the lack of progress that he is making on his new work, the *Prose della Volgar Lingua*. 'But how can I make progress when I am summoned hither and thither by dukes and popes. A man's life is never his own. But,' he says, his eyes now aflame, 'when it is finished, I will have proved our Italian fathers, like Petrarch, to have used their words, their craft, their rhyme, rhythm, sounds, consonants, vowels *etcetera* to produce the most perfect work in Europe. That is my hope at least, and then I shall be all the freer to attend the whims of the mighty.'

At this point Bembo breaks off suddenly. 'But here I am talking of my own small afflictions in front of a man who, well, I am ashamed, Fra Hugh, truly ashamed. Ah, I see they are calling us into the banqueting hall. And there is Agostino Chigi, with whom I would very much like to speak before we sit. Would you excuse me?' He bounds back up the steps and embraces the richest man in Rome as if he were a brother, and at once they fall into conversation.

Castiglione leads Hugh toward the steps. 'He is a brilliant man. A touch eccentric perhaps. Awful saddle-style, rides bolt upright like a Venetian – which I've tried to tell him about. He's better on further acquaintance you'll find. He's been a great help to me at any rate.'

Once on the upper terrace Castiglione explains, 'This is all quite new. Julius himself got Sangallo to create this loggia facing the river, and the banqueting hall—' He points to the backs of several guests disappearing up the steps and through a large doorway '—is really very fine, and quite correct of him to entertain here rather than in the Vatican as the Borgia pope did. Orgies after Vespers. There was no one quite like Alexander VI, except perhaps the devil. Julius wants to dissociate himself as much from that dark time as possible, and quite right, too. Shall we go?'

The ceremonial staff bangs twice on the glazed tile floor of the banquet hall for the last guests to enter.

PROSEIGUIRE L'IMPRESA CONTRA TURKI

'Signora et Patrona, Signor Baldassare Castiglione, Ambassador from Urbino and Fra Hugh de Erpingham, Knight of the Sovereign Order of Rhodes.' Paris de Grassis, in crimson and yellow silks, delights in his role as joint master of papal ceremonies by rolling his 'Rs' when announcing the *'Cavillieri di Rhodi'*. The hall is not enormous, perhaps forty by twenty feet, walls and ceiling richly frescoed and gilded, with additional wall hangings, though Hugh is not observing these, but rather the fifty or so people who have fallen almost silent, and are now looking in his direction. For once it isn't his demons talking.

'They're not looking at me; that's for sure,' Castiglione murmurs in Hugh's direction. 'Fancy they'd never imagined Hector rising from the dead. You should take heart, my friend. The looks of admiration certainly outweigh the jealous, particularly among the fairer sex.'

But Hugh hears little, overcome by the smell of food and the rush of humours. He clenches a white knuckle and swallows the saliva and some rising bile. Through the blur of watering eyes, he espies Bramante and his coterie in the window to the left, the man's elephantine head and bug-eyes angle with malevolent interest at the object of so much attention. Two long tables run the length of the room, and one other is laid parallel to the back wall. It is from here that Pope Julius now turns from his conversation with his brother Giovanni, Lord of Senegallia and two cardinals, to face the newcomers.

'Erpingham, but this is the man who came to my apartment this afternoon, with the letter.' The pontiff loosens his embroidered velvet sleeve as if by freeing his wrists he will better be able to apprehend the illusive vision of chivalric virtue that the Italians, more than any other people, begrudgingly associate with the non-Italian – Erpingham. 'Why did no one tell me it was he, Colocci?'

The secretary steps out from another group near Bramante. 'Holiness, but I did.'

'You said the knights had come, nothing about this man whom you knew I wanted to meet.'

'Pardon me, I certainly intended to say *the* knight.' Colocci bows, but Julius does not notice, for he is now beckoning Hugh with partially outstretched arms and small, impatient twitches of the mid fingers.

'Come forward, my son. Let me see you.' Hugh passes the onlookers and approaches the Warrior Pope, who is clad in a thick, red damask robe in the style of an Almain fur houppleande – too thick for what has turned out to be a warm evening, but he obviously wants to show it off. The man is enormous, probably a whole foot taller than Hugh. Even from here Hugh can see Julius' leonine stare, and rugged, square hands spreading like tentacles over the table cloth in anticipation. He is distracted momentarily as he catches the tail end of a whisper from some gossip to his left. "More knights after indulgences for the relief of Rhodes, I suppose."

He takes his bow, and then also the invitation to kiss the pontiff's ring – of which there are three to choose from. He goes for the middle one, taking hold of the pontiff's hand gently, and kissing the air near one of the largest emeralds he's ever seen. It is something of a frozen moment in his own mind, the smell of old vellum, ink and wax about the fingers, the nauseating sight of sliced venison, done rare from crimson to pink, on the table behind, and everywhere the tittering of the Roman *cognoscenti*.

Virgin table clothes, and venison.

Credenza covers, pink and red flesh of strangled meat.

White linen napkins in the shape of pure doves to wipe away the fruit of slaughter.

Stop it. Stop it, damn you!

Hugh's spiraling thoughts are broken when all at once Julius closes a vice-like grip on his hand, and then continues to clamp it firmly within his. Hugh looks up and sees beyond the beard of the first bearded pope, the eyes of an old man reaching out, searching for something he'd lost long ago, as if they two had been twins. 'You have come a long way. I am glad you are here. My own father was a sailor, you know, near Genoa. Might have been my profession, too, if not for other things. I used to run cargoes of onions with him down the Ligurian coast. I am told that your endeavours equal that of the great Calabrian admiral who won such honours for the Aragonese.'

He speaks louder so almost everyone can hear. 'I wish to God that more of my own people had half the courage and endeavour of this Englishman. He brings me word that Sultan Byazid is preparing arsenals at Constantinople and Gallipoli. That's right! By the immortal gods! And that the whore Venice is complicit with them, trading behind our backs with these accursed infidels. The sons of Saint Mark must be punished; I will see to that. Is Girolamo Donato here?' He finally releases Hugh's hand and scowls across the room.

Colocci says, 'The Venetian ambassador is absent, Holiness.' He waits for the intended titter of amusement to die down; Donato is famously scatty and very un-Venetian.

'What!' growls Julius.

'He begged leave to work on his music, Holiness.'

Julius, hands on hips, bellows, 'I bet he did! I'll give them music when my canon gets to their blessed *Serenissima*, and we'll dance madrigals together, by Saint Michael we will. Then we'll see who has the right to appoint bishops. Then we'll see who can shield villains like the Bentivoglios from my wrath. Then we'll see who keeps the city of Faenza. By God, by the immortal gods, they'll wish they had returned it when my ambassador Edigio da Viterbo demanded it of them in my name. I will not rest until they are stripped of their possessions and reduced to being the peasant fishermen they once were.'

As the news of Venice's duplicity creates its own ripples about the room, the pope engages Hugh directly in a way that shows he has played out the conversation many times in his head. 'There is nothing I would like to do more than continue our enterprise against the Turks, but I cannot commence while my own house is in such disarray. We need a Franco-German peace. It cannot be done in any other way if states like Florence will shun their duty to the church by remaining neutral. So, we must have the Germans and the French together on our side – even though France's many treacheries must be answered in some way. Soon enough, soon enough.' At this the pope's voice trails away, his thoughts seeming to wander to some recess of his own mind and secret purposes. Hugh sees his lips muttering, and just hears the words, '*Vederò, si averò sì grossi li coglioni come ha il re di Franza*'; let's see if I have balls as big as those of France. Suddenly his eyes ignite with a new fire, and he barks out, 'But that is later. First things must be first. So, you see, we can only make progress slowly. Your King Henry is a man after my own heart. He has pledged arms and sent twenty thousand ducats as his *Cruciata* tax. My legate Cardinal Adriano de Cornetto tells me Henry is keen to go in person, as am I, if I were not so mired in the north. Is that not right, Cardinal Adriano?'

A slender and alabaster-faced man with dark hair flecked with silver, and eyes keen as a hawk, bows in acquiescence. 'Indeed, he did, Holiness. And as you can see from our young friend here, the English are not wont to make garrulous claims. They are men of action and courtesy.' Hugh thinks the man seems to eye him with an unnatural interest, and a smile that too easily overspreads the face in between sentences. 'Indeed, Holiness, who could but say that it may not even be your own person that calls forth such fidelity and sacrifice. For was it not this same king who offered only eleven guineas when Pope Innocent made a similar appeal? And later on, Holiness, in the days of your most unworthy predecessor, was it not this king whose court pleaded penury and passed the burden of twelve thousand pounds onto the See of Canterbury.

Nay, I say it is your Holiness who has called forth this virtue from England. As sayeth Hosea, *the Lion has roared, who will not tremble?'*

Hugh, unused to a foreigner speaking thus of his race, eyes the cardinal closely. *Those beady eyes are looking at me. I warrant he is after something more than silk and lampreys.*

The smooth cardinal is interrupted by the pope, who thumps the table. 'That's right, and would to God my own countrymen were as zealous as these English - that they would hear my voice when I call. Would to God that the other princes of Europe might cease fighting amongst themselves, and abide by my rule.' His voice is now raised, his face hardened with a dragon's resentment, and he doesn't care which ambassador takes the most offence. 'But no! They must have it their own way, and where is my *Cruciata* tax from the dukes of Savoy, Spain, France, Hungary, Poland? Have we seen one cent, one obulus, one dime, ducat, denarius, except from the English king? Is there no other realm that shares my wrath against *Christi nomines hostes,* these enemies of Christ?'

In the awkward silence that follows, Julius turns his baleful blue eyes back on Hugh. The peripheral wisps of white eyebrow quiver slightly, as if his whole face were alive and pulsating with purpose, energy, intent. His nostrils take in and give out two breaths of air, then he speaks to Hugh in a solemn and deliberate tone. 'Tell Grand Master d'Amboise from me that he is no whit less a man than his illustrious predecessor Pierre d'Aubusson, and also this: when the time comes for this anti-christ to raise its head against us, that he will find my support every bit as firm as my uncle, Pope Sixtus' support was for d'Aubusson. He'll get the tithes he is due from the ecclesiastics, even if I have to wring it out of them myself with these two hands.' The pope brandishes fists as gnarled as olive wood and shakes them violently before continuing. 'But above all, tell him to take heart, for Byazid is old, unwarlike, pre-occupied with the king of Persia. He wants his epitaph to be that he took Rhodes, but he'll be long dead before his fleet sails. He'll likely die even before then at the blade of some pretender from the wrong side of the blanket as is the manner of these Turks.' The Pope now turns introspective in his soliloquy allowing people to hear, or at least think that they are hearing, his conclusions. 'No, these infidels will wait a while longer I fancy. They'll leave us time to chastise these sons of Saint Mark.'

He pauses to raise a green glass goblet to his lips. His mind must be connecting loose threads: Sons of Saint Mark and money, for he'll need at least a thousand ducats a day to run the campaign from his Bolognese headquarters. Before taking a draft of his fine ruby claret, Julius pauses long enough to say quietly, 'Any news from *your* wayward Venetian son, Vendramin?'

Hugh feels a smarting sensation in his cheeks, and then a cold, tingly shiver pass through his body at the name. When he speaks his voice is weak, dry. 'He is reported dead, Holiness.'

Julius maintains a steady stare as he takes his draft, and then he leans forward to whisper. 'I do not believe that, nor do you. So, I will confide in you, knight, for remember, you have taken an oath to me alone when you made your vows on Rhodes. I want to treat with this knight errant, offer him amnesty. Of course, there are certain things I want in exchange for this, which he will understand: the recovery of stolen goods *et cetera*, but as long as he knows that we have all sinned, that there is forgiveness within the skirts of the church—very broad skirts—and that he has my word, no harm will come to him.'

'I can assure Your Holiness, that I have not a clue –' Partially true, but Hugh is interrupted.

'And I believe you. Only remember that you are *my* servant, that we work for the same goal, and besides, who knows what fresh things tomorrow's tide will bring in?' Julius maintains the same affable tone, but something of the forced smile now ebbs from his lips. 'For example, I heard only today that one of your fleet, the *Petronilla*, made harbour at Ostia this afternoon. She was queen of Aragon and Castile, you know. Petronilla. Married off to a Ramon of Barcelona when she was only one. Spaniards have no scruples about these things. But come, signor, don't look so offended. It is time to dine and enjoy the *dolce vita*, for who knows what trouble the morrow will bring?'

Raising his voice, he concludes his remarks about the new crusade. 'This soldier of Christ will depart on his tour of the provinces with my blessing. May every door be open to him, and may the sight of him, be enough to shame us into action. I will send my own people to assist him, my own vintners to supply him, my own galleys to tran sport him, if need be, until he has fanned into flames the zeal of Christendom.'

DINNER WITH LA SIGNORA D'ORSINI

'Well done, Hugh. Looks like you have the pope's support.' Castiglione leads him to his chair as quail eggs are brought in by harassed lads in the papal livery. No one is looking now; they've had their gape at the spectacle. Now they are hungry and dinner is late.

'A man couldn't ask for more,' Hugh replies, hoping his sarcasm does not spill too much into his words. *What a mess. Attended round Italy with Julius' spies and henchmen? As if I didn't have enough to deal with. But at least the* Petronilla *is here. I'll be able to talk to this navigator unless some-one else gets to him first. Perhaps I should ride to Ostia tonight, inter-view him. How did we not know before the pope's people? We should have landed him privily down the coast and brought him up by mule.*

Hugh's thoughts are cut short by Castiglione, who wants to seat him next to someone special. 'Signora Felice, is the pope's daughter – though not openly, you understand. She is an exceptional, devout and capable woman, a great lover of the arts and good books, like her father.' He points to a corner table, where a beautiful woman with thick, black hair is staring out of the long south window. 'Of late I have been some-thing of a confidant to her. Poor woman has suffered the bereavement of a child, but I know she wants to meet you most especially. I have saved us seats.' Hugh notices first that she is beautiful and then also the evening light reflecting on her necklace.

'A lavish piety.' Hugh points Castiglione toward her *crocette*, a diamond studded cross, which she is fingering absentmindedly.

'It was given her by her father. Worth over seven hundred ducats. She has others like it and has always been a believer in portable chattels, for her life has been an uncertain one. It looks well does it not? Perhaps you think it overstated? Do not be harsh or quick. Roman women used, by local custom you know, to be covered from head to toe with a *lenzuolo*. They have come along way.'

'How do I address her?'

'Ah yes, very correct of you. She was widowed when young, but recently married to Duke Gian Giordano d'Orsini, an eccentric widower, *condotierro*, much her senior. You address her as Signora d'Orsini, unless she invites you to use her first name on another occasion.'

She rises to meet him, bowing gracefully, and he to her. He guesses her to be just younger than himself, though with that smooth, olive skin he finds it is hard to tell. These Latin women can look like they are in the first flower of womanhood, when their northern European counterparts are well down the hill. Felice's lips and cheeks are full, girlish even, but her deep brown eyes, though full of a warm intelligence and sensibility, betray somewhat of that sorrow Castiglione has mentioned, and perhaps also that special sadness of an unhappy or unequal marriage. A woman unloved shows it oftenest in a weariness of the eye. They lack a certain shine. 'As a house untenanted is a soul uncherished,' his own mother had once said to him, *and she whereof she spake*. He has known women like this, seen them satiate that natural craving in flirtation, adultery, in business, wine, or in wolfish dedication to their children. But he immediately senses that he has not ever met a woman like this. They take their seats, feeling hidden amidst the bustle and babble of the meal.

'Well, signor, I am honored to share a table with you. It must be a relief to be away from the perils of the sea.' For a moment he cannot answer, only grin like an idiot. *Is she teasing me? I cannot tell. How well the black velvet, silk brocade and pearls go with her hair.* She wears these, and a white silk hat in the style of the Spanish as her husband is an honorary member of the Aragonese nobility, a mixed blessing.

While Hugh is still finding his tongue, Castiglione exclaims, 'The perils of the sea! The Signora has her own tales on that score. When Rodriguez Borgia became pope, the Signora was forced to flee by ship from Cittevechia to Liguria, or thereabouts, with the Borgias sending ships after her, no doubt thinking she'd make a fine hostage. Isn't that true?'

Felice blushes. 'I saw other ships and perhaps fancied them to be in pursuit. I am not so sure now. I was only a girl, but—' Her face comes alight with a dramatic inclination. 'I do remember determining not to be taken alive by them, but rather throw myself overboard.' The tops of her cheeks show a rose hue. 'Too many Frankish and Provencal books with tragic heroines!'

She had meant these remarks to lighten the tone and deflect praise. But the thought of a noble Roman death before capture strikes some deeper chord in Hugh, and he remarks almost instantly, 'No, I think it a good resolution.' And then at once he sees how much he has revealed, and backtracks. 'But, of course, our lives, that is to say, our bodies, our futures are not ours to do with as we please.'

'Spoken like a soldier,' Castiglione says.

'Like a Christian,' Felice adds.

But Hugh feels only a pang of conscience. *Spoken like a hypocrite.*

Seeing his unease, Felice says, 'You must visit Bracciano on this grand tour of yours, stay at the castle. My husband would certainly wish to meet you. No doubt he will drill you for information on the latest in munitions and siege-works. You would be very welcome, though I do not know how long we could entertain all my father's entourage. I wonder how many he will send with you.'

'I hope not too many.' Hugh sees that Castiglione is talking to the banker on his left.

'Why, signor, you sound as if you disdain my father's patronage. It is not found easily you know, not even by those close to him.'

'Not at all, Signora. I am merely unused to such attentions.'

'*Such* attentions?'

'From the pope.' Hugh hazards a glance toward the top table only to see Julius looking straight at him. 'I am used to watching my own back.'

'Ah, well I know how that feels. For over twenty years I was the unacknowledged daughter of a near-outlawed cardinal. I was raised here in Rome. My mother married Bernardo de Cupis, a good man, and we lived in the Piazza Navona. I was very happy there, though I received no attention from my real father. Yes, I was happy there.' She looks pensively at her quail eggs, and Hugh catches a guilty glance above the dimples in her cheeks.

'And then?'

'*And then*, the Borgias.'

'Ah, and how old were you then?'

'Just eleven. Taken from our happy home, shipped to Savona, to the censure and ostracism of my Della Rovere relatives. They are hard people. I was just a child. I missed my brother Gian Domenico and sister Francesca.' She smiles into her glass. 'Half brother and sister, I should say. We are still close. I know we shouldn't complain about our portion in life. There are always those who are so much worse off right at our gate. I do understand all that, but nevertheless they were some dark years in Savona. I cannot pretend otherwise.' She gives him another dimpled smile. 'Though it was there that I first began to know my father. He built his palace there. Palaces and public works are something he believes in, you know. If you ask him about it, he will tell you at length that it was Bernardo Rucellai who told him to invest not in progeny but in magnificent buildings, which would endure longer than flesh and blood.'

'He told you that?' *Under that hard exterior really does beat a heart of stone.*

'Sympathy is a woman's gift, signor, but my father is not without feeling. In many ways he has shown his care for me.' She gestures to his plate, tells him to try his quail, before continuing. 'And it was there, at the palace that I began to see that I could be of some use. I was able to help—negotiate with traders, plead the cause of the poor. I have a head for the accounts, and it took my mind off other things.'

'Your relatives?'

'No, well, yes, that and my husband. I was married at fourteen. Tomasso was a local merchant, not a bad man, but I was very young in many ways. My father settled a small dowry on me, but did not attend the nuptials, nor could my mother. I was on my own, as we women often are. That was ten years ago this month. Where were you ten years ago?'

'Me? Going up to Cambridge, with dog Latin and even less Greek!' Hugh glances at his hands. He will not contemplate the young idealist he destroyed, certainly not when the words of this woman seem to act on his scarred soul like a balm. He dismisses his own past with a small gesture of the hand while taking a draft of the wine; and encouraging her to continue.

'What's to tell? Tomasso suddenly died of a distemper two years later. I was able to live modestly as a widow, freed at last from the control of my cousins in Savona. Then the Borgia pope died. My father was elected and sent papal galleys at full sail to bring me back to Ostia and Rome.'

'A happy ending?'

'A story, like all stories, grows in the telling, Fra Erpingham.' Her lips purse into a tight, cautious smile. 'My father decided my independence and my devotion to books was not as useful as it might be; I was to be married. *He* settled on Jacopo Apiano of Piombino, a loathsome man. It was not his great age—we women are not so fussy as you men suppose—but his legendary infidelities that made me defy my father's wishes.'

'I see.'

'They had left him with the French disease. Even Lucrezia Borgia refused to marry him! My father was adamant, settled forty thousand ducats on me. But he's not the only one in the family with a strong will. This battle between the generations is at least a battle we have a chance to fight on both sides.' She looks down at her napkin demurely, then looks up, nodding toward Castiglione, who is still engrossed with the banker. 'I can smile about it now, but Baldasarre will tell you that I have been a willful daughter.' She laughs quietly. 'I think Father and I understand each other better now. Besides, I have given him a granddaughter, Julia, by my lord, the Duke of the Orsini. One day my father may meet her.' She looks once more to her fingers, and speaks almost vacantly. 'But you men want sons and grandsons, don't you? I had a son this summer, Julio, but he did not survive.' In the dreadful silence that follows, her stare intensifies upon the hands that could not save him.

Hugh says how sorry he is, but she does not hear. He knows that place. Her eyes glisten, and she says, with a smile that is the involuntary diversion of her grief. 'You know, we do so much to protect ourselves from these troubles, but then death comes, and we are as powerless as babes. Little babes.'

'Yes, I know it.' For a moment they are both silent, an ocean of grief three feet wide across the table, isolating them each in their own continent of pain. And then he says it, no more premeditated than his comment about the noble Roman death. It just comes out, called forth almost. 'Do you blame God?'

'No.' She waits for him to look up. 'Though I did. For weeks. But all the time I knew I was wrong to. You?'

He has scarce got over her answer, when this fore-frontal assault on his particular bastion catches him off guard. He was a fool to start the conversation. 'Me?'

'A year and half on a Turkish galley? Did you not ever rail at God as Jeremiah did? I know I would have done, but you English are so reserved.'

His eyes return quickly to the plate, and he shakes his head slightly. 'I blame myself,' he mumbles.

'Oh come, I cannot believe you a saint, as well as a famed knight. That would really be too much.'

‘Pardon me, but I cannot speak of it, Signora, and I’m certainly no saint. Rest assured on that point.’ He stuffs his trembling hands under the table, trying in vain to pull the sleeves over the sweating, scarred wrists.

‘Even saints have a past.’ She reaches a hand across the ocean to touch his arm. ‘I should know, my father is the pope.’

NEXT MORNING 8AM, 7TH SEPTEMBER, 1508.

‘What’s he like?’ Hugh has just approached Prior Battista in the cloister near the guest quarters. The navigator has arrived from Ostia.

‘What do you think?’ the prior snaps. ‘He’s a mess, like you were, I suppose.’ The prior is wearing full harness–breastplate, bucklers, cross hilts. Everyone is, apart from the servants. The morning fogs are still settled on the city. The smell of olive wood burning is faint but pleasant, as are the sounds of distant church bells, calling for the morning office.

‘Trouble?’ Hugh says, observing the knights guarding a guest room twenty yards away.

‘Prowlers last night, and the cavalcade was followed from Ostia. I don’t like it; this is not a castle.’ The prior glances across the cloister, as if expecting imminent attack. ‘And why were you so late last night? What did Julius want with you?’

‘Show me off, I think,’ Hugh observes. ‘He’s keen to help us.’

'I bet he is.' The prior leaves off his vigil for a moment to rest his right hand on the pommel of his sword, and lean against the stone colonnade. 'He didn't make you promise him anything, did he?'

'No, but he's pledged to have me escorted by his people around Italy, show support and so forth.'

The prior's face falls, with many of his tense facial lines dropping like snapped kindling. 'I knew he'd be onto us. Don't trust his daughter either. Yes, I know you spent most of the night in conversation with her. Beware of her, and the Orsini, particularly her husband, the duke. Even Cesare Borgia steered clear of him. Duke Gian Giordano Orsini is too unpredictable.'

Hugh doesn't take him on. 'Julius is meeting his *Maestro di Ruinante* at the Domus Aurea this morning. He wants to show me inside the grottos; wants my opinion on the frescoes. He's worried about water damage.'

'Are you sure that's wise?'

Hugh has heard that Nero's subterranean villa is partially collapsed. It is no doubt dark and poorly lit. 'I confess, Prior, that I am more than a little curious to see them—frescoes preserved from the time of the Caesars.'

'He's trying to win you over. Be warned, Hugh.' The prior wags his bony finger. Then he draws close. 'He'll be after information that he thinks you've got from our new guest.' He gestures down the corridor to the navigator's room. 'Mark my words. After he has what he wants from you, he will spit you out like Nero did his friends. You know, I suppose, what he said to his old tutor Seneca? *Amicitia nostra dissoluta est*, our friendship is dissolved, which was code for "Go home run a hot bath and find a razor to open your veins."'

'Have no fear on that account. I'll not be sharing it with anyone else.' *Not even you, my dear Prior*, he thinks. 'Who has talked to him so far?'

'No one. There were strict instructions. He's all yours.'

The guards let him past, and Hugh knocks gently on the oak door before entering. He closes it and makes sure it is locked again. Hugh adjusts his eyes to the gloom. The blind is drawn, leaving the room in an orange half-light. A curtain separates the bedchamber from the rest of the room. It is half closed so that the bed is hidden.

'Signor Gabriel?' He approaches the bed for he can hear rustling and mute murmurs. He pulls back the curtain to reveal the navigator, gagged, and near throttled by a tall, masked man in gentlemen's clothes. Another binding rope lies on the bed, as yet unused. Hugh is about to draw his knife when he feels a blow to his head and then sees the ceiling move in front of his eyes. He staggers back toward the door, unable to cry out for the singing pain reverberating in his ears and throughout his skull. A second blow sends him to his knees, then his hands.

Darkness shrouds his mind.

Hushed voices. Throbbing pain at the back of his head. Two blows. *How long have I been out?* Cold earthen tiles under his cheek, that and sticky saliva. He opens his right eye slightly and focuses on two leather pantoffle shoes approaching him. *The ankles under those hoses are thin enough, not a big man, perhaps a burglar, but not a mercenary. Quick.* Hugh does a roll call through his muscles and, in an instant, readies his right leg.

Now. Do it. Go.

He shins the assassin as hard as he can with his boot. It buys him an extra second in which he springs up, wheels round and parries a further cudgeled blow with his left arm. It stings like hell, but better there than on his temple. Besides, it will be the last shot the fellow will get. He is masked like the Saracens mask their Janissaries, a black turban around the face. But he's no Moor, and he's no match for Hugh either. Hugh pulls him close and then squarely head-butts the turbaned face three times until it is considerably flatter, and wet with blood.

Hugh holds his dagger to the man's throat, and sees that the other assassin has already done the same to the navigator. Hugh is panting, baring his teeth, blood running down his forehead into his mouth. He observes the other assassin for moment: lean, cool, not showing signs of tension. The navigator's eyes are white with terror, his mouth covered by the other's glove. Hugh's victim is still conscious and able to stand. Hugh kicks him behind the knees, dropping him into the execution position. 'Touch my navigator with that knife and it will be the last thing you do.'

'I will not harm him if you let us leave.' The assassin tugs at his victim, his voice calm. 'A gentlemen's agreement if you will: I release the navigator, you release my man.' Hugh is not expert enough to detect the dialect, but even through the head covering, there is something chillingly dispassionate and considered in the man's voice.

Hugh starts to release his hand, the other reciprocates. Hugh moves to the side; the masked man lets the navigator fall back to his bed. Each man's eyes are locked on the other in the gloom. But no sooner is the navigator slightly beyond the reach of the other's blade, than Hugh, in one motion, grabs his prisoner by the hair and drives his dagger through his neck, just behind the windpipe. 'I'm no gentleman.'

The blade severs the jugular vein, which issues a great fountain of bright blood, spraying ten feet across the room and covering the wall and wardrobe. It all happens in the faintest blink of an eye, and in the next, Hugh, who does not appear to have even taken his eyes off the real threat, raises the same dagger and throws it at the intruder. The assassin lurches toward the window, avoiding the dagger. Before Hugh can negotiate the bed to catch him, the man is through the window and in the street. It was a considerable jump, but he mounts his horse unharmed.

Hugh does not give further chase for he calculates his chances are slim, and besides, another plan is already forming in his mind.

He steps away from the window, and faces the still white-eyed navigator. The window light reveals a man in his mid-thirties, with a drawn, narrow face, unkempt hair and beard, and a yellowish tinge to what is visible of his face and eyes. 'Congratulations, Signor Gabriel, I have just found a man who will give up his own life so that you can disappear.'

'What?' The navigator, still in his small clothes, ashen white with shock and trembling in the shoulders, looks with incomprehension. 'Who?' What do you mean?'

'Him.' Hugh points to the twitching carcass as he might have pointed at a piece of fruit or a book.

'You, you, you killed him.'

'Yes. I don't have many talents, but that is one of them.' Hugh moves round the bed and uses his hands to block the man's nose and mouth. The breaths are getting shorter, but they may not have long before they are disturbed. 'I'm sure he'd have done the same to me. Now help me undress him before the blood gets in his doublet and hose.'

'But, why, I don't understand –'

'Because you're going to wear these clothes, and climb out of the window, the sooner the better. No one here knows what you look like, and this fellow won't look like anyone in particular now I've rearranged his face.'

'But his chemise is soaked in blood.'

'Haven't you got your own?' *You'd think he'd be more worried about faking his own death.*

'Don't have anything. Just these and a wool jacket.'

'Don't worry. Put his doublet on then.'

The navigator's eyes and hands tremble. 'What...' He still seems stupefied by shock.

'Do it now,' Hugh hisses, shoving the doublet at his chest. He checks the door behind him. Nothing. Hugh uses his foot to stop the dying man's leg chaffing on the boards as it convulses either with the final passing of life, or else in rigor mortis. 'When you're changed, climb down from the balcony and then wait in the hay market at the end of the street. My man will find you there and bring you what you need. Now quick.'

MID-MORNING, BATHS ON THE *VIA DE PASTINI*, ROME. 7TH SEPTEMBER, 1508

In the end it is Hugh who goes to meet the navigator, with Wilf and Pico in tow.

They are all armed; even Pico has a concealed knife, which makes him grin from ear to ear. It seems to be in their blood, these Italians. It feels a relief just to be beyond the priory walls. All hell broke loose when

Hugh was found, seemingly unconscious in the guest chamber. He'd set the scene, cleaned his blade, wiped his head, told them he'd been surprised and overcome, which was true, and that the assassin escaped. Almost true.

Prior Battista appears suspicious, but the corpse is undeniable, and so are the bruises on Hugh's head and arm. The navigator was delivered by men from the *Petronilla* at night. No one could seriously identify him. Besides, they expected trouble, and this fits their worst fears: a corpse and no information. The place looks like a charnel house, and they fall for it. Hugh will clean up Signor Gabriel and get him down to Signor Diamante's for a shave and haircut, then import him back as one of his own affinity. Thus, the man can melt away in plain sight. It will fool everyone perhaps, everyone apart from the assassin – whoever he is – and his employers, whoever they are. But at least that narrows the field.

They find Gabriel at the Haymarket and take him to the baths on the Via de Pastini, after a visit to Signor Diamante's. When they are alone in the changing area, Gabriel is clean-shaven, sitting in his hose and shirt, head in hands, looking considerably younger, but still yellow about the face.

'Some of your emperors thought the people most needed *panem et circenses*, bread and circuses. Others realized they were far more in need of a good bath, as were you, my friend. You look better for it. How do you feel?' Hugh's attempts at humour and even small talk appear as forced as they are. Through the doorway, quietly guarded by Wilf and Pico, Hugh can see and hear the doings of the baths: old men perambulating in their towels as if they were senators, young men coming from the saunas, others queuing for the massage room, some swimming, some playing ball games, some doing business. The navigator does not answer straight away. That thousand-yard stare. Hugh recognises that much.

Eventually he says, 'When they exchanged me, I thought it was all over, but you knights treated me like a prisoner, too: chains, guards, no barber, and now this.' He's referring to being throttled in his bed.

Hugh tries not to empathise. 'I'm sorry for it. Any ideas who they were?'

'No, but not Vendramin, thank God. They used to say you'd never hear him when he came for you.'

'Really.' The man should have been a dramatist. 'Did you tell them anything?'

'No, but I would have. Don't mind anyone knowing it.' He seems to shrink into himself as he speaks, hands across his stomach. 'I've had enough pain for one lifetime.'

Hugh stops pacing like a caged lion and takes a seat. 'Look, if it helps, I know what it is to be a guest of the Barbary Corsairs.'

'You? Ah, I did notice your wrists.'

'Sixteen months.'

'You survived for sixteen months?' Gabriel grins and rocks slightly on the bench. He's not well. 'How? The painter Fra Fillipo Lippi was captured off Ancona by corsairs belonging to Abdul Maumen. He, too, was put to the oars of a Barbary slave galley, but eventually painted his way back to Naples and freedom. I say he must have been a good painter. How did you do it?'

'Just did,' Hugh, says officiously. 'Now, I need to ask you some questions.'

'Does your back ever recover?'

Hugh floored. 'What?'

'Did yours?'

'No.' Hugh feels the tears coming, so says quietly, 'No, mine is still hard as saddle leather. You were brave to enter the *caldarium* pool as you did, with people looking. I could not do it.'

'And yet you'll take on assassins two to one?'

'Ah, that's nothing,' Hugh says seriously. 'Just me warming up.'

But Gabriel cuts him dead. 'You didn't have to kill that man, did you?' It's not a question.

'What are you, a priest?' Hugh's blue eyes harden. 'I make it a policy not to face my enemies twice if I can help it, particularly ones with cudgels, blades and garroting wire. Frankly, I'd have expected a bit more gratitude from you.'

'Forgive me, signor.' Gabriel casts his eyes back down. 'I am a navigator, not a soldier, and I've seen enough blood for two lifetimes.'

'Yes, well, we all wish the world different, signor.' *Not least the smell of sweat, damp and black mould that thrives in these plebeian baths.*

'And ourselves too, no doubt.' A wary look from Signor Gabriel shows he, too, knows a thing or two about the depravity of human nature.

'No doubt, signor.' Hugh is thinking more about others today. 'But we must talk to you about Vendramin.'

'Vendramin, yes. I'll tell you about Vendramin. It's what I'm here for, what you paid for, though I suppose it'll do you no good.' Gabriel becomes animated with a barely suppressed terror, looking straight ahead at the mosaic floor and jabbering his words like a man at the gibbet. His head is tilted and shakes slightly as he goes on, with a speech he's rehearsed. 'Yes, I'll tell you all I know: where we sunk the ship, where we lodged, how we parted and the bloody oath we all took, an oath which I am now going to break, and that only because I was too much a coward to die in the hull of a Turkish goke.'

'No one will blame you for saving yourself from that.'

'Won't they? This worthless, purged neck? God forgive me, for Vendramin surely will not.'

'So, he is alive then.'

'The devil never dies, signor. You should know that. And if the world thinks he's dead, it is only because he wishes it so. If I am still alive today, it is because he has allowed it. Perhaps he waits for me to break my oath, then he will descend on me.'

'You need not fear while you are with me.'

'You cannot protect me, and besides—' He looks straight into Hugh's eyes. 'You should be more worried about yourself. He'll know all about you 'fore you ever set foot in Italy; count on it. And don't think just because you're a noble knight that you'll escape him. You won't. He'll know why they've sent you, too – even I can see that.'

'What's that supposed to mean?'

'Come Fra Hugh, even if I had not seen you at work in my chamber this morning, your eyes would tell me all I'd need to know. They don't send men like you to negotiate.'

'Looks can deceive.' *He's got pluck this fellow. I wasn't in half as lucid a state when they rescued me.*

'Eyes don't deceive, signor. They're windows of the soul. Yours are like his—Vendramin's: cold, unfeeling, eyes that have seen what they should not. There's no need to look at me like that. I'm only telling you because I like you, 'cause you saved my life, 'cause maybe there's hope for you. I wouldn't have spoken so freely with him, great Neptune! Those eyes of his! It was like looking into hell. It wasn't just me either; all the men said the same. Big burly sailors, necks like capstans who weren't afraid of anything on land or sea wouldn't say boo in his presence. They said he could see the future, that he had a hairy devil at his back and that's why he was always ten steps ahead of his enemies.'

'Enough of this mummery. I don't need to hear wives' tales, signor.' Hugh stands and walks toward the door to make sure no one is near, then returns speaking fast but quietly. 'I'm looking for a cunning old man who was foolish enough to disappear with someone else's gold. Now tell me where you sunk this ship, and let me see if I can make him and the gold reappear. I agree that he will have some advantages in this game, but I'm a cunning little bastard, too, when I put my mind to things, and who knows? Maybe *Fortuna* will smile on us for once. So, for the last time, tell me everything you know without the theatricals.'

'Very well, I will honour my side of the bargain I made with the knights, even as I break mine to Vendramin, so help me God.' Gabriel's sinewy shoulders lose definition for a moment and slump in resignation as he relaxes. 'There were just six of us, him included. He hired us to take him to Caligara on Sardinia. They didn't need me really, but Marius – the boat's owner and captain – was a good friend. And the money was so good, and of course we all knew who he was, believed all the stories about him. Jesu, we were young men, Fra Erpingham. To sail with him would be something to tell our grandchildren.'

'Didn't you think it strange he was on his own?'

'No. I suppose you think we're thick. But no, we didn't. Too busy pinching ourselves. Of course, we didn't know what he was like or what we'd really got ourselves into, or we'd never have been so stupid. He made us load his cargo that night. It was barrels of some oily tar. In truth I don't know to this day what it was, but it smelt of pine and brimstone.' He breathes deeply and shudders, 'smells of death. And there was three barrels of the black powder too. You know, gunpowder. Anyway, we had just loaded up when it happened.'

'What?' Hugh says this with an air of distraction, for his mind is now being pulled in two directions. Barrels of pitch that smell of pine resin and Hades? He had read of that before in old books. Some said fire that could burn on water was a myth, but ancient Greek naval dominance of the eastern Mediterranean was certainly no myth. It was such a closely guarded state secret that it disappeared from the arts of men. 'Tell me, Gabriel, what happened?

'Borgia's men—hundreds of 'em—arrived at the port, swarmed the wharf.' For a moment the navigator's eyes drift in memory, shaking his head as if he distrusts even what he sees in his mind's eye.

'Go on. How many?'

'Two hundred probably, light horse, and infantry. We were surrounded, and he was just one man. They knew he was there. Their captain came down to the boat with six officers, all armed and very pleased with themselves. Come to arrest him. Duke Valentino's orders. Well! He handed me his cloak and cap, stepped onto the quay, told them that he would give them one chance to surrender, and after that no quarter. Of course, they laughed, but not for long. He cut them to ribbons with just one sword—six of them like it was nothing. And then he walks down the quay, the captain's severed head in his left hand, comes within fifty yards of the mounted troop and says something to them. He was a hundred yards away by now and it wasn't clear, but they start to make a charge, and then it happens.'

'What happens?'

'The entire cavalcade bursts into flames. Saw it with my own eyes. Two hundred horses and men consumed. Maybe more.'

'Come now. Your eyes deceived you. It was gunpowder or some such.' But even as he is saying this, Hugh is biting his bottom lip. Surely this is the fabled Greek Fire? Could this devil Vendramin be in possession of such a diabolic weapon? Hugh feels a terrible shudder in his torso. *Is this the weapon that God will give the knights of Rhodes – a stone to slay their Turkish Goliath?*

'I know gunpowder. This was sorcery, and I don't care what you say. He just looked at them, and they burned. Great columns of smoke filled the sky and choked the moon. And him? He walks back, gives the captain back his head, cleans his blade then asks for his cloak. Marius says he doesn't want to go if it's all the same, and Vendramin just looks at him and says that his only chance of seeing his home again is to do exactly what he's told, and that went for the rest of us.'

'So, you went.'

'Aye, we went, more fool us. All the way to Sardinia. There we tailed this ship as she left Caligari, pretended to be in distress, then attached ourselves to her, held her to ransom with the gunpowder. We didn't say much, but Vendramin told them who he was and said how he'd rather us all die than let Borgia get a single ingot to tyrannize Italy.'

'And the captain believed him.'

'We all believed him, standing there with his flint over the open barrel with that look of his. He wasn't bluffing; we all knew it. Their captain stayed with him in our boat while the crates were transferred. No one said anything; no one tried anything. It was all the same to them. They weren't going to die for it. We took their captain and set him adrift the next day.'

'Where were you headed?'

'Naples, so he said at first, but we didn't make it that far. After we passed the Island of Ischia, he made us sail into the sunken volcanic craters two miles to the southwest on the Procida Archipelago. He had us blindfolded for that last part of the journey, and I don't know how much the others understood about our location, but you can't hide things like that from a man who's been a navigator about those parts. Besides, there was a part of me that wanted to know, fool that I was.'

'Good. Now be very exact in what you say, signor, and sketch me a map on this, as much as you can guess.' Hugh hands him some sharp charcoal and thick paper which he unfolds on the bench.

Gabriel takes them up. 'It is very simple. The islet of Vivara is really the northern wall of the outlying crater. We passed the southern point here.' The navigator adds the words *Punta di Mezzgiomo* at the end of the crescent-shaped islet attached to a larger island marked *Isola di Procida*. 'The cliffs all along this stretch are precipitous, and just about here—' He rests the point of the charcoal on the line of the cliff, leaving a discernable mark. 'There's a cave, not easily visible because of an outcrop of rocks in front, but just big enough for us to maneuver our boat in with the mast down. Dark and deep, it is, like an antechamber of the underworld. He must have known about the place beforehand and chosen Marius' boat accordingly. They certainly train you knights well. He took us in during the small hours, without lanterns, never so much as touched the sides.'

'And the crates?' Hugh is almost sure the man is telling the truth, but he is aware he is hearing what he wants to hear and so maintains a skeptical edge.

'Made us cast them overboard in the cave.'

'How many? How deep?'

'Forty-eight crates. It was deep. Five, maybe ten fathoms, but I cannot be sure because it was just before dawn, and the light was bad.'

'And then?'

'He put the choices before us along with more than double the ducats we'd originally agreed.'

'The choices?'

'Take the money with an oath of silence, enjoy the good life. *The dolceur de vivre*, he called it, as if he was a Frenchie.'

'Or?'

'Or fight him then and there for the rest. Well, we weren't up for doing that having seen him at work on the wharf. Besides, at this point we thought he was saving it for that good Pope Pius. We had no idea that the poor pope was about to be murdered and that Vendramin intended to steal it all for himself.'

'Yes, yes, so none of you had the balls to fight him. What else?'

'What?' Gabriel's mind is locked momentarily back on that dreadful morning when he made a bargain with Lucifer.

'The third choice. You said he gave you three.'

'It was more like a prophecy. He said we could take the money, but then betray the oath, and die for it. I can still see him, standing at the stern, looking us up and down. It makes me shudder even now. It was like he cursed us. He said that none of us would ever come back to the cave, but that all would break the oath and die for it. He said that he wouldn't kill us now because we'd not known what we were getting into, but that once we took the oath and the double money – which was really six or seven times what the work had been worth – that we would be bound to him, and that he'd hold us to our word. And that is how it worked out. Marius and the others talked and died, in unspeakable ways.'

'And why are you so sure it was him?'

'Because I saw the way he looked at us. Eyes don't lie, signor, as I said to you, and I think he must have eyes everywhere. It's the devil. Marius told me about the others. Two went to Cesare Borgia, one to you knights, another to Julius, but they were all found dead. Marius went to your lot, not for the money, but for protection from Vendramin, but it did him no good. They found him flayed and crucified on his own mast. We'd have been all right if only we'd kept quiet, but once one talked, it opened up the hornets' nest. And now there is just me left.'

'And me.' *The Reaper is welcome to my carcass anytime.* Hugh folds the map and puts it in his scrip. 'Where did you separate after the cave?'

'Well, we took the oath. He left the money in the stern, told the others to put their blindfolds on until midday, all except me. I think he guessed I knew where we were. He said I'd steer them north. And that was it, he stepped off the boat and bid us farewell. "Until next time," he said. That was it. We went north.'

'You left him there in the cave?'

'That's right. No provisions neither.'

'How far back did it go?'

'Don't know; too dark. And there was no way up the rocks either, before you ask.'

'I see.' Hugh's cogs are going. *The man had help, local help. From the Island of Procida or maybe Ischia. That's why Vendramin could wait in the cave without provisions.* Hugh pinches the end of his nose as he does when he's thinking hard. It's not a great plan, but if you were thinking on the hop, it would do. But it does mean he has accomplices, other eyes in the area.

Hugh broods a while longer, then says, 'Thank you for this. The information may not be new, but I consider you have discharged your part of the deal. For the time being I suggest you wear our livery, and stay close to Wilf, Pico, and me. Word will be out that you're dead, and with the work of Signor Diamante's razor I cannot see anyone recognising you. So, get dressed or we'll be late.'

'For what?'

'Lunch and other diversions with the pope.'

LETTER 2 – DATED 7TH SEPTEMBER, 1508

Signor M.,

This epistle comes to you on the very wings of Fortuna herself. We have, even in the short time since my last writing, seen such strange changes in our circumstance, that I cannot but conclude it so. Your men were unable to intercept the navigator coming up from the port to Rome, and I myself was also foiled in a more subtle attempt to extract a confession from him this very morning at the Grand Priory. We got in easily enough thanks to your contact there, but the man Erpingham disturbed us, made short work of that wiry young thief you sent, leaving me to get away with my life but nothing more. The knights have put word out that the navigator is slain, but that is a ruse either by them or Erpingham himself.

As I say, I am not without resource, and you need not lose faith in my ability to satisfy your demands; for, as of yesterday, I am appointed by His Holiness to be part of Fra Erpingham's escort around the Magna Curia, and thence northward toward you and, no doubt, to our illustrious friends across the border in Siena. So, you see, there is no need for alarm, or to send further people to accomplish your bidding. Wherever Erpingham goes, I will go. Whatever he sees, I will see. Whatever he knows, I will make it my business to know also, and of course, report back to you. The man is not so quick or bright as he fancies, and he is not, I fancy, altogether immune from female charm either, which may yet prove useful. So, there is every reason for confidence. Every day brings us closer one way or another.

Pardon me, signor, but I now see that in my haste to deliver the news as succinctly as possible I have failed to remember that my noble assistant who perished today was in fact a member of your own household, a nephew I think he told me? Forgive this oversight. It was out of my power to save his life, and you may be assured that the act will be avenged when expedient, or if you prefer, I could lead him to you in good time.

Again, may I mention my account and shortage of funds? I realize that even now your letter to our bank will probably be crossing my last reminder. If by any chance you have not yet returned it, then a similar endorsement to the bankers in Naples, and not Rome, will suffice.

Most grievous apologies for the length of this letter, but I do write in much haste and would have been briefer if I had more time.

Until I have the pleasure etcetera.

LUNCH, 7TH SEPTEMBER, 1508. THE DOMUS AUREA, OPPIAN HILL, ROME

It is not a long journey to their next appointment, but nevertheless, they are late. Wilf has been teaching horsemanship to Pico who still rides, as Wilf delicately termed it, like someone with a pike up his arse.

'Look at me,' Wilf says, cantering along the edge of the Circus Maximus like a buffoon. 'See how my body responds to the rise and fall of the saddle.' Pico and Gabriel burst out laughing, followed closely by Hugh, who cannot remember when he last did so. It is not so much at his joke, or Wilf turning this way and that asking what was said, but more the sight of Pico nearly falling off his own meagre mount, tears of sheer joy and innocence in his face. Wilf was indeed a fine horseman in his leaner youth, and even now there is little he does not know about riding and horse doctoring. He looks at his master laughing and for a moment appears content to be the butt of any number of jokes.

The day has grown very warm by the time they dismount at the Oppian Hill. Wilf's knock-kneed palfrey gives an almost audible sigh of relief when he dismounts. Pico's falling black curls only vaguely mask his amusement. The black woollen doublet Hugh wears is making him hot under the collar as he walks the short distance from the track, where he has left Wilf and Pico with the horses, to where the papal party has gathered. Gabriel, loosely dressed in Wilf's servant's livery, accompanies Hugh, walking demurely behind, eyes down as instructed.

Hugh mingles at the back of the crowd of courtiers, ambassadors and hangers on, wishing he could loosen his doublet at the neck, and inwardly cursing Wilf for lacing it from the top to bottom. The ground is uneven, and he manages to find a small rock to stand on, from which he sees that all are listening to a man standing next to His Holiness. The speaker shares the papal parasol with the pope and the Duke of Senegallia. Behind them are the works of yet more excavations, though nothing on the scale of the St. Peter's works. Hugh counts only fifteen or sixteen men, going into and coming out of a hole in the ground like ants, carrying buckets and building materials. Behind that, stretching up the uneven Oppian Hill are the apses, domes and bulwarks of various buildings that one can only guess at. They lack any marble cladding, just thin red bricks baked, as Hugh imagines, without straw by some poor slaves for a forgotten pharaoh. He checks that Gabriel is close, looks about for any threats, and seeing none, focuses on the speaker, a man with a lean face, large hooked nose and skin hanging from his cheeks in a manner that would immediately remind anyone of a tortoise.

The man points to the left and speaks in the Toscana dialect. *Good God, not more Florentines! They're like frogs here. Can there be many left in Tuscany?*

The man's voice carries well. 'We found the sculpture under a vineyard just over there, against the city wall, two years ago. I was sure from the first look of it that we had found none other than the Laocoon by the great Phidias, mentioned by Pliny. We dug around it, made sketches for His Holiness, then had some lunch.'

Amidst the titter, Julius gestures to the speaker, whom Hugh now perceives to be sculptor and architect Guiliano da Sangallo, and the old man bows and gestures for the small crowd of thirty to follow.

As Hugh looks for someone to explain to him what exactly is going on, he feels a gentle hand on his sleeve. 'Cavaliere Erpingham, *caro*!' It is Baldasarre Castiglione, the ambassador of Urbino.

'Signor, good day to you.' Hugh bows. 'Pray, where are we going?'

'Do you not know?' The ambassador looks pleased to be privy to the secret. 'Ah, I see you do not. Let me enlighten you, for it really is a treat. We are standing on the ruins of Nero's great golden palace, the *Domus Aurea*.'

'Fine, but where are *they* going?' Not at all at ease, Hugh points to the procession of cardinals and other worthies descending steeply into a hole in the side of the hill, as if it were some macabre retelling of the *Comedia*.

'Oh, they've been chipping away at this place for decades. Julius' palace is just round the corner at Vincola. He had men up here all the time, obsessed with what treasures might be left undiscovered. Some years back, one of the men disappeared into the earth, dropped straight into chambers with frescoes and marble features from as far away as Egypt. It created quite a sensation. Half the artists in Italy have been down here to sketch the swirling motifs, which they call *grotesques* after this grotto, and now they're *de rigeur*. Julius is using them all over the papal apartments. The ducal palace at Urbino is awash with them in a modest fashion, of course.'

'Of course,' Hugh adds.

'They are mainly carved in light marble relief in the door reveals and pediments and around fireplaces, that sort of thing. The effect is not unpleasant. I'm surprised you haven't got them in Rhodes.'

'We've been busy.' He doesn't mean to sound sharp, but he can feel his bile rising at the thought of the dark and maybe confined spaces.

The Swiss Guard, armed with nasty looking halberds, are evenly spaced in the corridor and at the entrances. Hugh suddenly remembers the last man he killed with one of those things—a young Turk, not much more than a lad. It was on that ship a few weeks back when he lost control. The lad's eyes cast about wildly as his guts emptied on the deck. Hugh hears Gabriel's words: You didn't have to kill him, did you? In his mind's eye his mother gives him one of those enquiring looks that she was famous for. *The shadow of Cain*. He puts his own words into her mouth. 'What have they done to you?' It is easy to deflect blame. He would rather blame them, whoever they are, for what he has become, than take the blame on himself.

'Busy? Yes, well I suppose you have. Let us join the others and not keep His Holiness waiting.'

Hugh feels the oak props as they enter the grotto. Gabriel is close behind, and behind them, yet more men and women. Castiglione mistakes Hugh's backward glance. 'Signora Felice is not here today. I believe she is using her time to secure grain contracts with her father's chamberlain, but she was most complimentary about your conversation last night. Your manners did not disappoint.'

Conversation and manners, he thinks, that's the easy part. 'Her husband is a most fortunate man.'

'Indeed, he is. Now mind your head here; the ceiling is low.'

When he straightens again, Hugh sees he has entered another world. Like some portal between his own modern time and that lost world of antiquity, this torch-lit hallway, perhaps forty feet long, with its broken plaster and fractured ceiling, seems to span the ages. He has stepped back into a ghost world of the Caesars, with a second Julius, torch in hand, at the head as they go deeper and deeper. In the welcome cool of that darkness, Hugh can smell the mouldering plaster, plaster laid down fifteen hundred years ago. It is almost too much to take in. Partly collapsed passages lead off left and right, and the torches of the servants lining it obscure the extent of the damage. Hugh imagines all sorts of mischief hiding in those dark recesses. He feels Gabriel at his back, holding the hem of his doublet to steady himself and keep close. All the while the ambassador is talking about the artists who have been here to make studies, cartoons: Pinturichio, Udine, even Raphael, whom he points out just ahead of them, talking to none other than Pietro Bembo. They pass to the end of the corridor. Some of the frescoed detail becomes visible around the door reveals as the light from the larger entrance spills out.

They enter a vast octagonal room, perhaps fifty feet across. Sunlight pours from an ocule in the ceiling. The guests take seats at tables.

Behind them the alcoves on five sides are variously filled with tables, food, wines, and servants in the papal livery.

'The domed ceiling is pumice stone concrete. Can you believe our ancestors?' Castiglione marvels. 'They were so accomplished in the art of building, and this was built a half-century or more before the Pantheon. Extraordinary!'

Hugh nods, pausing in the entrance to gape at the scale. He is standing on the same red and white marble pavement walked by Nero, Valerian, Domition, Gallerius, Titus, Vespasian, Hadrian. The papal master of ceremonies, Johannes Burchard, scuttles about the tables arranging everyone with an expression of a man used to having guests do everything to upset his plans. Hugh imagines he is rarely disappointed. Burchard hurries over, speaking without greeting between heavy breaths. 'Good, Signor Erpingham. His Holiness wishes you to sit at meat with him. Your man will have to wait outside.' Burchard gestures dismissively to Gabriel before turning to Castiglione. 'Ambassador, I have put you with our friends from Mantua. Signor, this way please.'

Hugh turns to Gabriel. 'Don't hang around down here. Rejoin the others with the horses. Wilf will look after you.'

Gabriel looks back at him with some mix of fear and resignation. His watery twitching eye, and weak involuntary smile belie a fatalist who knew from the first it would happen this way. The whole event and all happenings lead inevitably to their separation; nothing can keep him from the all-seeing eye of *Fortuna*, the long fingers of fate – from Vendramin.

Hugh takes one last look at him as Gabriel disappears into the gloom of the long corridor. *Shit.* All the hairs on the back of his neck stand up and a cold sensation runs from the top to the bottom of his spine. For two hours he felt he had taken back the game, had been in control, one step ahead. Now, however irrational, it feels instinctively that that was an illusion. It is more than a little disquieting to imagine yourself suddenly on a cross, and perhaps worst of all, not even to know who it is who holds the nails and who the hammer. All this because servants are not permitted into a dining room? He tries to shake the stupidity of the foreboding from his mind, but he cannot.

Burchard draws a chair out for him next to the pontiff's left elbow, saying with the air of an executioner inviting a noble to lay down his head, 'Just here, if you please.'

Julius doesn't see Hugh at first. He is raising his torch like a sword and talking to a young courtier clad in the black silks of a Spaniard. 'I was told, you know, that Alfonso El Benigno of Aragon took his father's sword at his own coronation, that he kissed the cross, strapped it on and then drew the blade. Like this,' Julius raises his torch higher and at an angle so that pitch drips onto the ground and very nearly onto the young courtier's doublet.

Burchard materialises in a worried series of gestures and remonstrations trying in vain to disarm the pontiff. 'Get away you imbecile. Get away,' Julius barks at Burchard before turning back to the Spaniard. 'Alfonso did it thus three times. Yes, three times: once to defy the enemies of the Holy Catholic church, once to defend orphans, wards and widows; and once more to maintain justice all his life. I like that. By all the saints, I do. Ah, the knight is here. He is welcome.' He relinquishes the torch and beckons Hugh closer.

The pope holds forth his hand, and Hugh bends once more to kiss the ring. Julius, now ignoring the young courtier as if he had never been there, gives vague gestures toward Sangallo, his own brother Giovanni, and two ambassadors from the Low Countries, whose pale faces are flushed red with the heat, or the wine, or perhaps both. He introduces Hugh as 'the great knight of Rhodes, come in the flesh to Italy to call to arms true sons of the church against the infernal Turks' et cetera et cetera. All the while, Hugh can taste on his lips the fragrance of citrus from the soap Julius has washed with. He is conscious again of the saliva filling his mouth as the cheeses are delivered to the table, and an almost irresistible urge to grab them—three of them! —and stash them in his doublet.

Julius asks Hugh what he thinks of Nero's palace but before he can answer, the pope continues speaking, partly to Hugh and partly for the top table guests. 'We judge Nero by Christian standards to our disgrace. He was a pagan and a man of great sensibility. His early reign was golden. He banished the secret trials of Claudius, as I have done with regard to the enormities of the Borgia. Furthermore, he issued many pardons and held working dinners for poets and musicians, as I have. And he built with magnificent vision, as I have too.'

'You say nothing of his excesses, Holiness?' The voice comes from Hugh's left. He turns to see Cardinal Adriano arriving late. 'His Holiness must beware this modern fetish in scholarship that would scarce let any corpse go undissected.' He kisses the proffered ring of the pontiff and makes a meagre apology.

Hugh observes him closely. There is ease and wit here. You can see it in the eyes and the creases. A man who has known greater offices than legate, he was once apostolic secretary to the Borgia pope. He was there the night the pope and Cesare were poisoned, or got malaria. Not an easy thing to sup with the devil and the antichrist and then live to tell the tale. He survived well enough, and looks well enough on it.

Julius takes back his hand and the papal ring abruptly. 'Excesses? Well yes, we cannot deny or overlook them. *Non Aliud* was Philip the Good's motto, I think; enough but not too much.' But then the pope raises a forbearing hand in a good-natured gesture, looking at his other guests, particularly his brother. For once he is not in crusading mode, but alive with a warmth of enthusiasm about his aesthetic tastes in palaces, pictures, sculptures, churches. As Cardinal Adriano takes his seat down the table from Hugh and out of view, the pope casts an eye toward the ceiling dome.

'Poor Nero, I say,' Julius mutters. 'He was full of inordinate desire to hear his own praise, to have public approval for his own mediocre singing, poetry and lyre playing. The vices of youth. He was only seventeen when he assumed the purple, you know, and I, seventy. He thought he was something that he was not, and he let his love of the arts consume too much of his energy when he should have been stabilising his political affairs. He had grand plans, as do we all, but no money because the legions were not involved in conquest. It is a paradox of any golden age among princes that tax revenues alone will not enable them to achieve the higher goals.'

At this Julius lays white, bony fingers around Hugh's wrist, just as he is reaching for his goblet to stop the servant overfilling it with Pucino Vino. Hugh feels the grip suddenly tighten, and the embroidery on his cotton sleeve dig uncomfortably into his wrist wounds. Julius turns and speaks intentionally to him, looking at him eye to eye. 'For higher goals, like say, a holy crusade, a prince would need substantial resources. You understand that, *mio cavalliere, no?*'

Hugh hesitates. A firm shake of his wrist, elicits an affirmative response, and almost immediately the old man's eyes rekindle with amiability as he returns to discoursing about the past. He pats Hugh's wrist as if he expects it to remain there until bid otherwise. 'Nero's public gymnasium, his elevation of the poor, of Greek culture and the arts, yes, even his exempting of the Greeks from further taxes because of their cultural contribution, may have been excessive, as you said Fra Hugh, but I say –'

'Pardon me, Holiness.' Hugh says. 'I was thinking more that he let Rome burn for his ambition, and let Christians burn in pitch for his garden parties, and that he kicked his pregnant wife to death.'

Looks shoot about the table. Sangallo almost chokes on his olive, but the pope's corpulent brother, the Lord of Senegallia, is much amused. 'Yes Julius, the man speaks aright. They say Sabina was his true love, after he murdered the other one. And that there is a madness or malignant star that causes men to destroy the thing they love most.'

'Very well, both of you. We'll agree to say what I was saying at the beginning, that Nero was not a saint, but an artist who happened also to be emperor, and that the greatness of that office broke his mind.' Once more turning to Hugh and fixing him with his firmest stare, he adds, 'The dead do not write their own history, Fra Hugh. We judge them by their best self, their best actions, by what they leave us in stone, stucco and—' He waits to give added emphasis. '—and in verse—which is why I have chosen amongst others to send the poet Bembo with you when you tour Italy. This crusade will become something posterity will remember—the final submission of the infidels. You will need the finest pen in Italy to record the project from the beginning. There will be two cardinals: the archbishop of Milan and my secretary Angelo Colocci, who will accompany you on my behalf. He has already sent letters to the master of the papal galleys in Cittevechia. They are expecting you this week.'

'Your Holiness is very attentive,' Hugh says, trying hard not to speak between his teeth. 'And where would you suggest I sail?' How does he know I even want to take ship?

'South toward Naples, I would have thought.' He turns to his brother. 'Giovanni, stop hogging the cheeses. We're not in a siege you know. There's plenty for all.'

Lunch is, as it always is when you're in Italy and busy, an interminably long affair. Hugh finds himself sidelined from the conversation almost deliberately by Julius, who seems to want to punish him for countering him at the beginning of the meal. He looks about at the other guests sitting at respectable distances from the top table. He acknowledges a nod from Castiglione, Bembo, even Colocci with whom he will be spending rather more time than he had intended. The pope seems to have decided to oversee the details of his quest. *South to Naples!* Hugh broods about it, wanting desperately to contrive a way to check on the others. He casts his eye about the crumbling frescoes that remain in isolated patches about the brick and concrete walls. Some seem to cling to the walls by no more than the cobwebs. He fixes on one scene on the opposite wall where a painted colonnade stretches in sharp perspective away from him, the columns dusky red as if in evening light. A peacock rests on a wall in front, and the whole scene is framed by two fluted columns on plinths so expertly wrought that Hugh almost feels he could never pick up a paintbrush again.

After the third course – Julius is no glutton like his predecessor; three courses are sufficient for a light working lunch – Hugh notices a number of people getting up to excuse themselves. He waits a little longer, then does the same. Within two minutes he is above the surface and walking toward the hub of horses and servants, among them Wilf and Pico, but no Gabriel.

'Oh no! Where is he? I sent him back to you at the start of the meal.'

'We never saw him, master.' Wilf's face reflects the wide-eyed alarm on Hugh's. 'And we've a good view of the entrance and all.'

After using a few expressions not often heard in church, Hugh dashes back up the slope, and into the mouth of the labyrinth. The Swiss Guard watch suspiciously as he approaches but recognise him as the guest who has just left and let him past. In the dark hallway he pauses a moment to take stock and to let his eyes adjust. From the far doorway come the clink of cutlery, the tinkle of glass, and the affected laughter of women. *Think, think, you idiot. He came this way.* Hugh looks behind him at the steps he has just come down, and at the corridor filled with rubble and debris. *Not up there. Wilf would have seen him. So, between here and the banquet room.* He starts a slow walk down the hallway, looking carefully at the corridors that lead off. There are eight in all, and this time only two Swiss Guard in the entire area. Six of the corridors are choked with rubble from collapsed rooves, but two are not, for in them the darkness stretches away, with no rubble visible at all. The guards stand stoically over these entrances, either to stop guests wandering off, or something else perhaps? 'What's down there? My man servant is missing.'

'Not to enter. *Verboten.*' The guard is a hard case, over six feet, with a halberd, and a guttural mix of Italian with his native tongue.

Hugh looks opposite to the other corridor, also black as pitch, but no sooner has he done so, than he hears sounds like falling metal on stone. It is far distant down the first corridor, behind the big man. His first thought comes with a cold shudder: *Vendramin*. There seems to be only one way to turn and no time to negotiate. The guard starts to repeat 'Not to enter' when Hugh wheels on him without warning and uses his whole weight centered on one shoulder to charge and wind him before he can level the halberd. The guard is caught off balance and slams into the wall, giving Hugh time to stumble past him into the darkness. The echoes of the shouting guards behind give him a mental picture of what may be around him—a long corridor, but from the echo, not endless. The guards do not follow. They shout to each other in their own tongue. Perhaps they need permission? Or are afraid? *He* certainly is. Will he face Vendramin in the next minute, the next moment? He stumbles further and deeper, one hand on the side of the wall and one in front, clutching his dagger.

Sometimes he senses damp plastered walls, sometimes the rough brick; sometimes he smells the mould, the mortar, sometimes the foul stench of rotting flesh. *Can devils see in the dark? Are they watching now, ready to take me away?* The voices behind have faded. Hugh slows down, straining above his own thumping heart to hear anything else. He senses a movement of air, and as he waits, he hears the low murmur of voices, the scuffle of feet. He moves on more quietly now, until after another minute, he comes to a dead end. His right hand passes a collapsed doorway, but it is blocked with rubble, so he feels his way to the left, finding a corresponding doorway. It is not blocked. No sooner is he through, than he hears the same sounds but louder. Shapes appear, more archways further on, and a source of light. *Steady now. Breathe slower. Careful.*

His chemise sticks to his back; an acrid scent rises from between the stitching of his doublet, his hard heart thumps relentlessly on the walls of his rib cage. He advances on the balls of his feet, swifter now. Broken mosaic crunches on the floor. He moves faster toward the doorway, toward the light. Grey walls, another room beyond, dust, a ray of sunlight. A ladder, two men, no, three men, one on the ladder, another about to ascend with a sack—small but bulging with irregular shaped objects.

Hugh pauses in the darkness, out of sight and sound. The third man, the one at the bottom of the ladder with his back to him, turns almost instinctively and faces the darkness. He has a long riding cloak and is hooded, his back now to the light. His hands are on his hips, feet spread confidently.

'And who are you, man in the shadows?' The voice is deep, searching, penetrating. The words scorch the air like gunpowder. The insinuation lingers long inside Hugh's mind. He finds himself approaching, though he gives his feet no command. He stops in the twilight just before the doorway.

'Fra Erpingham, knight of Rhodes.'

Hugh reaches across to the hilt of his carrack black sword, feeling the steel glide silently from the wool lining of the scabbard. His eyes are steady on the hooded man, and then for a crystal moment as he advances, the light catches bright on his own blade, revealing a streak of light steel mottled only by the tiny flecks of lanolin from the lining. Hugh takes a careful and steady breath, inhaling the comforting smell of oil residue from the sharpening. 'And who, signor, are you?'

'Who do you think I am?'

'The traitor, Vendramin.'

'Really? I am flattered. But I will tell you now that I am not the man you're looking for.' He does not move. It is uncanny. Is his blade already drawn under the cape? The second man continues up the ladder.

Hugh steps into the doorway. 'Where is my navigator?'

'*Your* navigator?'

'What have you done with him?'

'What do you care?'

'What have you done with him?'

'Set him free.'

'Then he is dead.'

'A man who lives in fear is nine tenths dead already.'

'Murderer.'

'As regards that sin, I am as you, Fra Erpingham.'

'Quite so.' Hugh, now inside the room and only ten feet from the man, takes his guard; right leg thrown back, blade low and to the left, basilard dagger covering it. 'Arm yourself, signor, or I will run you through where you stand.'

'It is not your destiny to die today.' The words are crisp and confident, and the man's silhouette is heron-still, erect, unflinching. 'Put up your sword. We know what you seek, and you shall have it anon, only do not abandon your life now by obstructing us here.'

Hugh hears the creaking of a crossbow ratchet. *Unmistakable. I've walked right into it. Idiot.* He glances up, where the second man has now disappeared above ground into blazing light. He looks back to a further room beyond, as dark as the one he has come from. He, or they, could be anywhere.

The man is conversational, philosophical almost. 'They say you never hear the bolt that has your name on it, but I suspect that is untrue. Now please go back the way you came.'

'You are Vendramin, aren't you?'

'I am a phantom, young man, and nothing more.'

'Tell me by what art did you killed Borgia's light cavalry at Citevechia?'

'Why?'

'Because the soldiers of Christ need every advantage against the infidel menace. Because only a monster, a devil from hell would keep such arts from God's elect.'

'You seek arts that would destroy you and the very things for which you fight. You are young, signor, but not so young perhaps that you cannot know yourself. That is why I tell you this.'

'And yet you used them to kill your enemies?'

'They were warned, defiance was given.' The shadowy figure places a riding boot on the first rung. 'And as you know, the devil always keeps his promises. Adieu, until we meet again.'

Hugh tries not to blink, and fails. 'I could–could still finish you now, even with a bolt in my chest.'

'Perhaps, but then you would never know, would you?' His air is matter of fact. 'And you'd never find what you are looking for. Besides,' he says as he begins to mount the ladder himself. 'You cannot really kill a man who has already died once in this world. We will meet again soon enough. *Adieu*.'

9TH SEPTEMBER, THE APOSTOLIC CAMERA, ROME.

A sharp morning light glints off the Tuscan marble in the window stone tracery. Hugh gazes with exasperation about the high shelves crammed with musty manuscripts, affidavits, contracts, and mortgage papers as he tries for the last time to state his position before grabbing the throat of the idiot in front of him.

Through clenched teeth he says, 'His Holiness told me that the papers would be ready today, so we could make the evening tide.' Hugh has little time for these little notaries with their small eyes and pinched faces. *The law*, as his father ruefully put it, *is as old as that other oldest profession in the world, and worse by far—the only one that has made crime pay*. That was when the bulk of the Erpingham estates were attaindered after Bosworth, by the Tudor usurper, otherwise referred to among the family as "that Welsh bastard." Hugh has had mercifully little to do with lawyers but has always preserved his father's prejudice as firstborn and inheritor *sans terre*. He is here to secure the financial help offered by the Holy See, and the black cloaked, crow-like creature before him does not seem to want to help, that is, until this moment when the god almighty of the banking world breezes into the vast office where they stand.

Agostino Chigi, indisputably the richest man in Rome, probably Europe for that matter, has not only the unenviable position of running a banking empire in every country except Cathay, but is also Papal Treasurer and Notary of the Apostolic Camera, appointed by Julius. Everyone of note owes him money, and for a man with over twenty thousand employees, he doesn't seem at all burdened. He lets an ermine-trimmed cloak fall from his shoulders to one of the fawning young men that orbit him like minor planets, hoping to become fixed stars in the *caelum ipsum*, the very Chigi heavens. The great families' send their sons to be enlisted in Chigi's commerce, some say corrupted in the service of Mamon. Once after a lavish banquet, he had an entire golden dinner service thrown from the terrace of his villa into the Tiber by his guests, or so it is reported. With many other tokens and allurements his insolence has corrupted both the mercantile *arrivistas* of Italy and some of the impecunious sons of her oldest families. He snaps his fingers and they part from about his person, like the Jordan River before the Ark of God. He points in Hugh's direction and starts to glide toward him.

'Signor, you are the knight, are you not?' Chigi is early forties, eyes piercing blue, hair ginger going white. He approaches in rhythmic steps with all the confidence of a man who assumes posterity's debt to him, paid with interest at six percent, of course.

'Fra Hugh Erpingham,' Hugh says, bowing with grace, an action not reciprocated.

'Of Rhodes. Yes, I have heard of you from Julius – uh, His Holiness. My man here is giving you what you need?'

'So far I have nothing.'

The small clerk shrinks visibly smaller at the desk where he stands. 'We have no notification from the secretary. We –'

'You have mine, man. See he has all he needs.' He speaks to Hugh. 'When you return to Rome anon, I should like to entertain you, hear these stories from the east. So exotic.'

'I fear that I would be a disappointment, signor.'

'I dare say it must go hard with a man to be the darling one moment and then forgotten the next.' Chigi says this with one long, disinterested breath, while scratching the side of his beard with a forefinger. 'But I have been ordered by certain ladies to *make* you appear, and we who are enrolled under the banners of love's law must comply. Eh, eh?'

'I am afraid my vocation leaves me ignorant of the old Order of Love, its solemn customs and usages.' Hugh slips in the word *old* to see whether Chigi is a man who can distinguish between his own lies, or if his conscience really does stop at his belt. To his surprise the older man's eyes light up with a new intensity, and when he finally does speak, it is not really just to Hugh, but for the benefit of all.

'It is, as someone wrote, "only the noblest heart that love deigns to enslave," signor.' Chigi speaks with an expansive gesture of the right hand. Those around him nod approvingly, urging him to drop more honey from his lips by their nods and smiles. 'A man should consider it high praise indeed to be selected for service to *Amor*, a god that respects neither gender nor vocation. You are still young, or perhaps not Love's man, but either way, you should not mock what you know not. We are none of us free men.' A general velvet murmur of approval comes from the acolytes in Chigi's train. Chigi: the self-made man who worships his creator. Hugh detests being patronized as much as he hates the falsity of the Provencal love poetry.

'If a wise man may overrule the stars even when the masses do not, then I think, signor, that we may be free of other less weighty matters also?' He tries to phrase it like a question, but the meaning is clear enough.

Chigi looks to the upper lights in a saint-like manner, and raises his right hand again, letting his thumb and forefinger flutter together as he summons the Bishop of Pavia back out of the the sixth century. 'How does Bishop Enodius have his Cupid reproach Venus? Ah yes: "we have lost our empire, Venus. Cold virginity possesses the world. Arise, shake off your sleep." And what does Venus reply?'

Two competing apprentices try to complete the lines, but Chigi ignores them. 'Venus says, "We shall be stronger for our rest. Let the nation learn that a goddess grows in power when no one thinks of her."' He smiles rather too broadly at Hugh. 'It may be a mistake to make too much of her, signor, but worse by far to make too little. We have spoken enough. I do not blame you in your current state, only be sure to report to my villa when you are next in town.'

And that was it. Chigi, the man of humane letters, leads his tittering entourage to another palatial chamber where he will ruthlessly execute his monopolies of the salt extraction in the Papal States, and his equally lucrative rights to the alum in Tolfa, Agnato and Ischia di Castro. So it is, with the rich. Whatever he professes, Chigi is assured that when it comes to money, all men are of the same religion.

11TH SEPTEMBER, 1508, BECALMED *EN ROUTE* TO THE ISLAND OF ISCHIA.

'No, no, my dear Castiglione, it is precisely the absence of moral effort in Aristotle's ideal man that is the sign of his virtue." Bembo speaks between mouthfuls of melon. "He abstains because he *likes* abstaining. It is not until men like Seneca and Statius came that we are aware, as the Greeks had *not* been, of a divided will, of a *Bellum Intestinum*'.

We. Interesting addition, Hugh thinks.

The man is a machine, and the ten others about the table, including Hugh, the grand prior, Colocci, Castiglione, the bishop, Archbishop Ippolito, another cardinal amongst others, are only too happy to let Bembo have the air space. For one thing, the melons they are eating are like sweet sunlight distilled in water, and for another, he's a hard man to match in matters of philosophy and literature, ancient or modern. In Hugh's case there is yet another reason. This internal war, this *bellum intestinum*, of which Bembo speaks – between a man's ideals and his inability to live up to them – has been the downfall of his whole world, perhaps Bembo's too.

They sit aft on the poop deck at a table under a canvas awning which only just lessens the effects of the blistering midday sun. The shade is as sweet as the melon, and Zephyrus has smiled on them with a gentle if intermittent breath. The papal galley has no rowers to take them on, so they will have to wait for a change in the weather. There are worse places to be stranded, and even Colocci wears something approaching a smile. He and the Grand Prior Battista have been thick as thieves since leaving Rome.

Bembo raises his glass to Julius before taking a long draft of Pucino Vino from His Holiness' private casks. 'I'll say this for the church, they don't drink vinegar. Our pontiff is, as dear Petrarch put it, one of our age's *Verum Nobiles*, truly noble men, not least because of his exquisite taste in the finer things of life. Now where was I? Oh, yes, the *Bellum Intestinum*.' His eyes widen at the word. 'This new state of mind can be studied equally well in Seneca, Paul, Epictetus, Marcus Aurellius and Tertullian. It is the awakening of a deeper view, a more Hebraic understanding of the human condition. "The life of every man is a soldier's service," wrote Epictetus, "long, and various." And Seneca: "we must all be soldiers, in a campaign where there is no intermission and no rest. " And Seneca again, rather reminiscent of St Paul, I think, "Let us conquer all things. For our prize is not a crown nor a palm, nor a herald calling silence to cry our name, but virtue, and strength of mind and peace."'

Bembo pauses only to breathe, and of course, to see who has already lost interest, which is nearly all apart from Hugh, whose ears have pricked up even more at the word *pace,* peace. For this again is not a subject of academic speculation for him. Bembo leans back on his chair, staring up into the awning. It is hard to live among mortals. 'Tertullian has no other language than the *Bellum Intestinum*. In one place, he has Patience laugh at the devil in a threatening way, and in *De Spectaculis* he writes, "If you must have gladiators, then behold Shamelessness hurled down by Chastity, Perfidy slain by Faith, and Cruelty crushed by Pity..."'

He is about to continue when Castiglione, who favours Aristotle anyway, raises a glass to stop his friend droning on. 'To the *Bellum Intestinum*,' he says.

At this remark, the Archbishop of Milan, Ippolito d'Este, brother of the Duke of Ferarra, who has up until this moment been in conversation with the prior, casts a reptilian eye across the table. The movement is sharp. A pale faced man, his alabaster-smooth cheeks and high forehead look like they have been worked over with a strigil every day of the forty or so years of his life. He eases back on his chair deliberately and says under his breath, but so that all can hear, 'Which our learned friend *should* know about, one way or another.'

Bembo looks straight ahead at the awning as if he hadn't heard, but Hugh hears, and it sets him thinking. There is a story here. Has Bembo been caught with his trousers down? Doesn't look the sort. In the briefest of lulls in the poet's monologue, while the capstans creak, something of a darkness passes over the whole gathering, which up until that moment has been equitable and convivial. In this new, heightened atmosphere Hugh feels instantly more at home.

Into that void Bembo pours yet more wasted words, discoursing on the heroic societies of antiquity and their concept of virtue, singling out Hugh for a favourable mention as he seems to be the only one listening. 'In the heroic society, morality and social structure are one and the same thing. They cannot be divorced, nor can a man theoretically detach himself or step outside the social structure, which we would say is a prerequisite to our modern human selfhood. The Homeric man and his actions are one. He has no hidden depths. He is not understood beyond anything his words, deeds, or suffering confer. I should think your Rhodes, Fra Hugh, is as near that sort of atmosphere as we could find anywhere today.'

Hugh raises his jaw to contemplate the proposition and finds himself agreeing. 'Yes, perhaps we are something of a relic in this modern age.' He smiles apologetically but then stops. There is nothing faintly amusing in any of this. 'When I am *there*, almost everything makes sense: the things we do and justify, the men we have become even. But when I am away –' He stares into his wine and puckers his lips.

'Away you are Odysseus adrift, eh? A stranger, landless, without a city, an invisible being.' When he glances up, Hugh sees Bembo observing him across the table with a deeper empathy than either his eyes or smile exhibit to the others. His next words are uncharacteristically unaffected in tone. 'I suspect that none here, except perhaps Castiglione, approaches sainthood. We all wander, as does Odysseus in uncertain waters with imperfect systems of navigation.'

Hugh, who has forgotten more about navigation than any of the others have ever read, cannot help but grimace. 'Yes, signor. But for all our smooth litigation at the judge's bench, we know the truth of what

Aristotle warned long ago, that the least deviation in the truth is later multiplied a thousand-fold.' It is not just Aristotle but also Gabriel the Navigator he can hear, accusing him in his inward parts. 'I am haunted sometimes that we, I mean, I, have become more like my enemy than I have become like Christ.'

'"We protect you from people like us." Isn't that what you said to His Holiness?' Bembo reaches across the table with the decanter. 'I liked the turn of phrase then, and I still like it. Have a drink. Yes, a drink! In this brief moment that we all have, between crisis with Venice and the catastrophe with the Sultan, let us at least enjoy a drink.'

'That bad, eh.' Hugh does not know what to say. He feels naked after his confession and almost on the brink of tears.

'Worse, probably. What do the Armenians say? *The past is terrible, the present is catastrophic. Thank God we don't have a future!* So come Fra Hugh, forget your dolorous introspection. I do not imagine God will damn a man of such sentiment or consequence. God, imagine how boring paradise would be.'

Hugh raises a hand to stop Bembo overfilling his glass. It is a comforting thought.

14TH SEPTEMBER - LA VIA PORTA, ISLAND OF ISCHIA

Blessed *Ponentina*, their word for a sea breeze. Eventually it rose up and blew them here. For a main harbor, it's not busy. The wharf has the usual mix of ostlers, carters and seaman, but not in any great quantity. In fact, there seem to be more relaxing in the mid-morning sun than actually working, as if some enchantment has befallen the island. It is a fair, warm westerly wind that has carried Hugh and his companions at last to this place. It still blows, reminding him of all the tidbits he gleaned about the place from Castiglione and Prior Battista. It is a fantasy island, they said, ruled over by a benign spirit called Constanza d'Avalos, Duchess of Francavilla, also known as *la Gioconda*, the laughing lady.

Bembo is in high spirits for the duchess is a woman of humane letters and has gathered about her court literary luminaries like Sannazaro, Paolo Giovio, Tansillo and Bernardo Tasso. They will all be waiting for him, no doubt, eager for the honey that drops from his mouth as dew falls on morning grass.

They are greeted by the castellan of the port and conveyed by horse the few miles to the Castello d'Avalos along the coast to the south. Hugh is not quite prepared for the vista that soon opens to him.

The prior, who rides at his right, notices Hugh's wide-eyed astonishment and comments, 'Welcome to the Hesperides, my friend.'

Hesperides indeed, Hugh thinks, for it is not just a castle but another island a short distance from the southern tip of the main island. And above the walls and bastions which crown the rocks, rise successive terraces of gardens and vineyards, limestone houses with pantile roofs, and domed churches, and finally a citadel on the summit. *If I had ever imagined a heavenly city – the Rhodes of my boyhood dreams,* Hugh muses, *then this is it.* How azure the water, how warm the stone, how stately her terraces and spires! He feels once more that inner yearning that surged beneath the surface in Rome. *Oh, sweet pang.* He would gladly wait by the side of the road to think on it all, but Prior Battista is talking about the illustrious family of which they will be guests.

'I last met the duchess in Rome shortly after she was widowed. She was twenty-three, young, vulnerable. I have not seen her since then, perhaps a quarter century ago. She did not remarry, but by my oath, she has made a great name for the d'Avalos dynasty, even though she has no children of her own. She is likened, so I am told, to Eleanora d'Arborea of Sardinia in her administration and fortitude.'

'Really,' Hugh says, shading his eyes from the sun and looking over the vista. 'It is as fair a citadel as a man could imagine. Even the antiquated ramparts have a charm that is hard to resist.'

'But they resisted the French three years back, and the duchess withstood them in a four-month siege that earned her the civil and military governance of the island. So, it is more than just sonnets and minarets up there, my boy; there is steel too.'

'As terrible as an army with banners!'

'Indeed, and I very much look forward to renewing the acquaintance.'

'You said you would tell me about the cardinals.'

'Yes, I did. My apologies, Hugh. I never quite shake the feeling that one is likely to be overheard on board a ship.' He tightens the reins on the horse and draws closer to Hugh. 'The young one is Alfonso, the son of Pandolfo Petrucci, the tyrant of Siena. I confess that I do not know the youth. It is so hard to keep up with all the new cardinals these days; they pop up everywhere and anywhere a pope needs ready funds. The other—Ippolito d'Este—is archbishop of Milan, a man whose pride it is better not to insult. It is well known that Cesare Borgia's cousin Angella favoured his brother Giulio over him. She repulsed Ippolito's advances by telling him that Giulio's eyes were worth more than his entire person, or something equally stupid. Anyway, the man sent assassins to remove Giulio's eyes – his own brother! – over a woman. That is the kind of man we're talking about. In fact, there are four brothers in that family. The other brother, Ferrante, sided with Giulio, and they formed a conspiracy against the duke and Ippolito but were discovered two years ago and now reside in the dungeon under the duke's dining room, or so they say. You couldn't accuse him of not being his brothers' keeper, at any rate.'

'Strange, I had heard he was a great patron of the arts.'

'Yes, indeed he is; they all are. What else is money for? Their uncle, Borso d'Este, paid ten Bolognese lire for a square *pede* of fresco. Got to admire a man like that; I'll have this much fresco and no more.' The prior's snigger degenerates into a hoarse cough. 'So, they invest in the arts and anything else that will establish the Ferrarese court with greatness as a musical and artistic centre. Their father, Ercole, only got the legitimation of the ducal title seven years ago when Alfonso married the pope's daughter Lucrezia, so they are still catching up. Ippolito is not beyond kidnapping musicians from other courts. I am serious. Do not cross him.'

There is something of an isthmus going toward the island, helped the rest of the way by a stone bridge. Men from the garrison, and the Arragonese castellan who attends them, are liveried with the D'Avalos crest, a castle tower on a blue background, surrounded by red and white banding.

Hugh glances down through the shallow waters as they pass to the citadel island, watching the fish scatter across the blue sandy bottom and under the mussel-encrusted rocks. On the bridge they pass a grey flock of waddling nuns from the Convent of Clarissa. Their mother superior is the only one who looks up. Having seen that the newcomers are not pirates and might even be respectable, she moves on. The cavalcade eventually passes into the welcome shadow of the northern battlements and through a well-appointed gate hung with studded oak doors. Spanish guards bark orders at each other as the important guests are offered litters for the arduous ascent to the citadel. The volcanic rock faces, rising as they do nearly a hundred feet straight up on this side of the island, are only assailable via an inclined tunnel cut out of the rock.

Hugh glances over to see Wilf scowling at the, what he calls, *dago porters* who are trying to help him with the luggage. The sound of braying mules masks any dark oaths coming from the beleaguered Englishman. Hugh smiles inwardly, takes one last look at how the lower walls are guarded, then starts walking with the others up the cobbled tunnel.

As the last drafts of salt and seaweed are replaced in his lungs by the damp and miasmic vapours of the tunnel, Hugh's stomach tightens. Anything dungeon-like puts him on edge and starts a rapid blinking in his left eye. He is brought to himself by a nudge from the litter of the young Cardinal Alfonso Petrucci, who is busy arranging the rings on his slender fingers. His red biretta was bought at great expense while he was still a youth. He is little more than that now; his black goatee is sparse like grass grown on saltmarsh. Petrucci moves the ringlets of black hair from his eyes, and chides the stout litter bearers for their clumsiness. 'You will pardon me, Fra Hugh. I would be safer walking than entrusting myself to these island oafs, but I must endure certain luxuries, if luxuries they be, on behalf of the church and my high office.'

'Indeed, monsignor, as the apostle says, "Each must bear his own burden." You and they.'

'Yes, indeed,' Cardinal Petrucci's face, lit as it is by tunnel lamps, glows with all the malice of an injured child. There are evidently no jokes where his own person is concerned. He flaps out his robes, recrosses his legs, and goes back to his rings. 'As must we all, *mio calvaliere*. As must we all.'

Hugh cannot tell whether he speaks with a tinge of irony or not, for his voice seems permanently affected by a theatrical edge, leaving even his gravest or angriest pronouncements sounding as if he is doing little more than acting a part. They have talked before, on the boat, and this has always seemed the case to Hugh. He dislikes Petrucci for it, and for the fact that he always interrupts what might otherwise be a useful conversation by diverting the flow towards himself, usually by means of worthless personal anecdotes. A man may lead a selfish life, like Bembo, and yet use that life to focus on a thousand other things which he can talk of. Even though both conditions might be damning to the soul, the self-absorbed man like Petrucci is surely a step lower. Hugh drops back slightly to let the litter pass. He's in no mood for this.

Parts of the tunnel are steep, and sometimes they are hampered by teams of boys collecting the horse and mule manure for the gardens. But the tunnel does not last more than a few minutes, and soon they appear in full daylight again on the main ramparts, where Hugh sees the garrison has its headquarters. A winding cobbled thoroughfare leads farther up to the lower town. Hugh breathes the air, now not only free from the miasmic vapours of the tunnel, but also fragranced by the many gardens and vineyards that cover the southern part of this small island where the ground is less steep.

Basil, lemon, mint and thyme are better than a pomander. He drinks the air deeply and is at once reminded of similar days, similar scents, as a child when he was happy.

Dante wrote that there was no greater sadness than happiness remembered. *But hope is also contained in that army of ghosts,* Hugh thinks.

They pass small churches, and then a larger one with a pantiled cupola dedicated to *San Giovan Giuseppe della Croce,* the patron saint of the island. At one corner in the road Hugh catches a glimpse of the Islands of Procida a few miles northeast. He wanders toward a parapet to stare across at them, an archipelago of green jewels in a sea of blue velvet. But his musings are less poetic today. He sees neither jewel nor velvet, only the last place where anyone saw Vendramin. *Is the Borgia gold there? Probably not, but there may be clues. And there may be clues here, too, if I ask the right questions, offer the right bribes, threaten the right person.*

His darker thoughts are interrupted by the chattering and subdued laughter of young women. Two maids appear from a door to his left. As it opens, he sees a well-ordered terraced garden overlooking the sea. The women, or girls – he finds it hard to tell – are dressed in simple dresses and running barefoot passed him, clutching lemon-mint, oregano and lavender. Their dark brown eyes are full of mischief and life, and one is very fair.

She addresses him, 'Sir knight, shield us for we are beset by a dragon!' Her diction does not match her dress, he thinks. The other girl sniggers. Hugh hears the voice of an older woman now, calling after her wards.

'Where are you? I will tell the duchess, I will, so help me I will – ' These breathless pants and threats fade as she mounts the steps toward the door. Hugh can see from where he stands it is an old nun.

Hugh lays a gentle hand on hers. 'Maiden, do not worry about this old woman, I will not betray you.' The fair maid seizes her friend's hand. 'Quick, behind that wall. Sir, we entrust ourselves to your protection. Pray do not tell.' They dart behind the wall. Hugh hears more giggling, and then the fair one rushes out, takes his arm and leads him away from the doorway where they cannot be seen. 'But do not fight this dragon on our account, sir, for she has devoured many a goodly knight, and I would not have it on my conscience that you died for us, seeing we are not yet acquainted. Sheaf thou thy sword, sir. Let her alone.' The girl is a consummate jocateur and seems to have complete confidence in her own ruse.

'Hah!' she says. 'Do not be fooled for oft she appears in the guise of an old woman. Take care not to arouse her for under this guise she is known as *la Bafana*, the vile crone who rides a broom stick to swap children's presents for coal at Epiphany. I must away for she is here.' And with that she was gone back to her cover.

The nun, her face pale as porridge, even after the exercise, leans on the door. 'You, sir! Have you seen two impudent young women pass this way?'

'I have, mother.'

'Well,' she snaps. 'Where are they now? And don't lie to me, young man, for I heard their voices. Making me mount those steps at my age. Wait until I get my hands on them!'

'All I say, mother, is that they have passed on.' He looks to the cobbled street where the procession is still passing. 'And so must I.'

'On the street without their slippers! Ooh, I'll teach them to run off! I'll fetch a birch rod, so help me God.'

'If you will excuse me.' Hugh bows and makes for the street, joining the rear near Wilf, who is busy keeping his eye on their baggage.

'Master?' Wilf looks over the sea.

'I'm going to need a boat for a day.'

'With crew?'

'No, just you and Pico.'

'I'll get down the harbour later when we've settled this gear.' Wilf gives a customary scowl in the direction of their things, and toward a 'dago' who might have a thieving eye on it, and then he turns back to Hugh. 'You gonna tell me what this is about then?'

'Tomorrow.'

EVENING, 14TH SEPTEMBER, 1508 – THE COURT OF LA GIRACONDA

'I beg your pardon, Signora.' Hugh's mind has wandered, inexcusably so considering the company.

He is sitting with Constanza D'Avalos, the queen of the place, at the top table in the great hall. He and Bembo sit where the cardinals by rights should be, on either side of her, but the duchess has her own way here. Convention seems not to count so high in this place. She had been talking about the artist Leonardo of Vinci, from near Florence. Will Hugh be visiting there or Milan? If so, could he get the portrait she was promised and paid for? He says he will do what he can, and then his mind drifts to the doves perched high on the open shutters. They coo and bob while servants flutter about the tables. Far beyond the bleached wood and rich damask curtains, far below the balcony, down through cliffs, hedges, vines, and bird's nests, the great sea swells about the island though only faintly heard.

His mind is taken with the tapestries celebrating the seven liberal arts, thinking of all the learning that he does not now use. There was a time when he could have had a different life as a scholar or a cleric or – God forbid – a lawyer even, but that that time has passed. His life has gone through a door that only opens one way. He cannot undo what he has done, what he has failed to do, what he has seen, what he has become. *Alea iacta est*, the die is cast.

'I said, signor, that I think we should move on to the oysters rather than wait any longer for my companion, Madonna Vittoria.' The duchess smiles warmly, the creases of her cheeks showing that it is a natural and well used expression. Her mouth and nose are small, her face round and firm. She wears black silks in the Spanish style, but lessened in severity by the white linen under-sleeves and large pearls. She is just shy of fifty, but no gray can be discerned in her dark brown hair. Hugh already approves of her taste and courtesy, but he is wary, too. Some instinct tells him that he is nearer Vendramin here.

Constanza sighs. 'We shall forgive her for she is young, but these oysters will not keep warm forever.'

She has barely finished speaking when the door opens and Madonna Vittoria and her maid breeze in. She is wearing a simple blue silk dress, over which fall her chestnut curls. There are no pearls, no jewels and there needn't be. It is none other than the girl he spoke to in the garden, bowing to the duchess, saying repentantly, '*Nostro delictissimo familare*, forgive me for I was at my studies and lost track of time.'

The duchess reaches forward. '*Soror amantissima*, finishing a chapter of a French prose romance no doubt! Dear friends, my companion Madonna Vittoria Colonna, daughter of Frabrizio, Grand Constable of Naples, and Granddaughter of the illustrious Duke Frederico de Montefeltro of Urbino.' After the introductions the duchess bids the girl sit next to Hugh. 'Fra Hugh Erpingham, the shield of Rhodes, so I am told.'

'I am inclined to believe it, for we met this afternoon, and he, good fellow that he is, shielded me from a fate worse than the Turks.' She turns her full impish smile on Hugh.

'Ah yes,' the duchess says, 'Sister Clemence told me of your escape today.'

'Oh, she pushes and pinches us like bread dough.'

The duchess speaks past her ward's theatricals. 'I hope, signor, you had no part in abetting an impressionable young woman to escape from her lessons in the use of herbs?'

Hugh is about to answer when Vittoria leans forward. 'Tush, I have had enough natural philosophy to last a lifetime, nay, two lifetimes.' And then speaking in a monotone, nasal voice, 'A powder mixed from the lavender flower, cinnamon and cloves, then mixed with water doth help the panting and passion of the heart, and prevaileth against giddiness, swimming or turning of the brain. Whereas lavender water on its own whether smelt or rubbed into the temples and forehead refresheth them stricken with catalepsy and migraines.'

'*And* the falling sickness, Signora,' Hugh adds.

'Oh, yes, the falling sickness too, of course. Men and their obsession with facts! I cannot live on just cold facts. God put us in the middle of a great story, surrounded by so many great stories, in any one of which I would gladly live rather than face Sister Clemence again.'

'You will forgive my young friend, Fra Hugh. I fear it is all my influence, for she came to us as quite a sensible young woman, but we have spoiled her on merry jests, chansons, love lyrics in *tersa rima* and the like. She will now hear of nothing but to be a poet herself.'

'Do not apologise, Duchess,' Hugh says. 'The more I have lived in this world, the more I wish that I could go back to the former days of my learning at Cambridge, where I would readily have become a poet myself.'

'Why, signor, you are full of surprises.' Vittoria pushes some loose ringlets behind her neck and reaches delicately for her water glass. 'Whatever happened to you to turn you away from such a noble enterprise?'

Hugh looks into his wine, deeply aware of the scarring of his wrists and the coarseness of his soul. There was a time before he shed blood, when he knew what it was to look forward to a good night's sleep. His digs, his university friends, John, James, and Andrew whom they called the apostles, and Henry, that cousin of the Northumberland Percys with his freckles and bad jokes; all of them talking nonsense half the night, full of verse and grand schemes and epics. He would trade the rest of his days on earth to be back there for just one evening, to pass Andrew's large cracked jug full of Norfolk ale about their table. *Whatever happened, she asks? Rhodes happened.* He puts the glass down and closes his eyes for a moment to stop the twitching in his left eye from getting a hold. *Rhodes happened.* The duchess comes to his aid, to say something, to fill the silence, but he does eventually speak.

'It is quite alright. Please, I am all right. Signora, you ask what happened, and I will tell you, and you must judge for yourself. Your esteemed benefactress will tell you, too, that this world is not as we would wish it. Somewhere in my career I came to the understanding that fine ideas, words and paintings were of only limited use against the evil arrayed against the church.'

Vittoria looks at him. 'So, you traded your pen for a sword.'

Hugh nods soberly.

Vittoria's face is crestfallen. 'And you say that you did, right? I pity you.'

'That was my decision.'

'That is not what I asked, signor.'

'I did not feel a man in my position could justify a private life while other good men were dying to protect Christendom. If I were to write or paint, at least I would do so with a sword in one hand and within sight of the enemy.' He feels pleased with that; it was well said, he thinks.

'And did you?'

'Vittoria?' The duchess raises an eyebrow.

'It is all right, Duchess. The answer is no. I did not do right, at least not as I had hoped.' Hugh pulls his sleeve forward, picks up his glass again, and pauses before taking a long draft. 'War was very different than I had been led to believe.' Hugh broods upon his wine. There are only so many times a man can tell himself, "This is the glorious stuff that Homer wrote about" before it sounds stale. There was great comradery at first, but not after he was ransomed.

In the pause that follows, the clink of crockery and the shifting of satin fades, and Hugh retreats into the dark recesses of his own memory.

When he eventually returns to the outer world, he notices that the duchess too has ghosts in her eyes. *Does she remember this hall when they were besieged by the French? Incessant noise, the bodies, the blood, the constant crying out of those in agony. Slow deaths. Innards spilled like tripe. Limbs. God, limbs and so much blood. I know of these things, but no woman should. The eyes white and quite alone in death. No one should see it.*

They make a strange threesome, seated there in their own worlds, amidst a throng of thirty guests, and it is the duchess who speaks first. 'I believe, Fra Hugh, that it is a holy war that you have come to discuss?'

'I have.'

'I find it indeed a great honour, that you should come here when we have so little compared our illustrious neighbours.'

'"The hills do not the lowly dales disdain," as the poet says.' Hugh smiles but is aware that he is coming across badly. 'Duchess, the Holy Father is, I am sure, no respecter of persons or size when it comes to a sacred obligation of crusade.'

Vittoria interjects, her eyes intense, eyebrows sharply furrowed, 'Sacred obligation! Indeed, signor, I cannot find that injunction in scripture. Only that we should love our enemies, turn the other cheek.'

'And so, we shall when we have removed their teeth and brought them to their knees before the cross.'

'As was done in Spain to Jews and Mohammedans! I fear that you place too much confidence in your sword – '

Hugh speaks over her as his ire rises. 'It is all the language they understand – '

She carries on over him. 'For I never in all my life heard of anyone giving their willing devotion to God at the point of a sword.'

'Perhaps.' Hugh spreads his fingers on the table like a good patrician. 'That may be because you are still very young.' He does not look at her, but rather down to his fingers, which he slowly withdraws. He is not prepared for such an assault.

'I am aware of my years, signor, but you forget that I am a general's daughter, and the man to whom I am fiancéd will, I have no doubt, win great honour for his family as a *condotierro* in the service of the emperor.'

'Indeed.' Hugh breaks in before she has finished. 'Christian nations deplete their own blood while the real enemy gathers strength.'

'France must be repulsed, sir.' Her use of the English *sir* brings Hugh up short. She sounds like his mother. 'I know you would not have her destroy wherever she wishes. I am not so naïve to believe that France will cease warmongering before Christ's return. But I do question whether we can use so blunt an instrument as a sword to draw infidels to the cross. But, as you say, I am young and have little experience in diplomacy.'

'As you say.' Hugh unsuccessfully tries to master his tone. 'As we speak, an Ottoman fleet is being built at the arsenals in Galipoli, a fleet I have seen with my own eyes. We cannot sit back and allow the insolence of the Turk to tear down a divided Christendom and everything our ancestors have worked towards for over a millennium.'

The duchess gives Vittoria a look, and she demurs, stroking out the creases at her knees and speaking with an obvious lack of feeling. 'Signor, I fear I have spoken about things which a woman could scarcely hope to grasp.'

Hugh raises an eyebrow.

The duchess interjects, 'And particularly one of such tender years. Really Vittoria, you would give Fra Hugh the impression that we on the island entertain thoughts contrary to the teaching and wisdom of the church, which I assure you, signor, is not the case.' The duchess takes a draft of wine, and glances around as if to make sure no one else had been listening. Colocci can be heard laughing, which always sounds like he is choking. Bembo is deep in conversation with Bernardo Tasso the poet, and Prior Battista is holding his own against the cardinals.

Hugh glances left to see the grand defiance still in Vittoria's eyes, then turns toward the duchess. 'I would never entertain such a thought against you, Signora, but while we are talking of entertaining, I wonder whether you would tell me all you can about Marcantonio Vendramin's visit.' He is taking a risk in saying this for he has no evidence until he registers the look in her eyes. They first narrow defensively, then feign innocent surprise. Hugh suddenly feels a pang of shame for obtaining this silent confession from a lady. He licks his lips guiltily, then says, 'You know, he was a personal hero of mine, the great Achilles of our Order. I feel very much that I walk in his footsteps on this tour and would learn all I can, for his disappearance has vexed us on Rhodes greatly.' He stops as she seems ready to speak.

'Ah yes, Fra Marcantonio, a knight respectable for his courage and amiable by his courtesy. Yes, we had the pleasure of his company on a number of occasions.'

'A regular visitor, would you say?'

'I would say not, more is the pity. This island is enchanted, as you know, and Zephyrus blows in one compass point as well as another – you cannot keep tabs on the gods.'

'When did you last see him?'

'Oh, I don't know. A long time ago.'

Hugh watches a slight watering in her eyes as she evades the question. 'He is a deep man, with a heavy heart and many questions. Much like you.'

He ignores the last comment. Seeing that she does not speak of Vendramin in the past tense, he says quietly to her, 'I know what it is to live on an island, out on a limb, away from help, and what unusual – perhaps unsought – alliances may be forged under those circumstances. If Fra Marcantonio is alive, if you know where I can find him, then – '

'Signor, believe me when I say that I cannot help you.'

'Cannot or will not, Duchess?' He senses a breach in her defences. 'Confide in me, I beg you. What are you afraid of?'

'You are quite right; I am afraid. Very much so.' The duchess looks at him with the faintest of smiles, the merest impression in the corner of the lips, and then looks down as if in shame. 'If I betrayed a man, my punishment might be harsh, but it would at least be finite. But there are powers beyond this world, signor, and there is punishment that does not end, that cannot end. So please, do not ask me again.'

Slightly stunned by the enigmatic response, Hugh says, 'I beg your pardon.' *Is she serious?*

They are interrupted by Bembo, who is remonstrating with Tasso. 'No, my friend, what Cato the younger said was that Caesar is the only man to try to overturn the republic while sober, but enough of this.' He turns to the duchess. 'My dear Signora, the mussels were magnificent, the cream and garlic sauce to die for. We jaded mariners offer profound thanks. And now your servants have so generously laid peppered bread, eels, mussels, wine, apricots, ricotta before our eyes! And we wait upon your word. May we permit the good cardinal – or the other one – to bless the next course before we die of hunger, while this Englishman keeps you all to himself?'

She grants the honour to Cardinal Petrucci, while Cardinal d'Este scowls amiably, and after he is done, Bembo leans across the table. 'My dear Hugh, what were you all so engrossed in that you held up our supper?'

'He was,' Duchess Constanza says, 'getting assurance of our support for the church's crusade against the Saracens.'

'Really?' Bembo seems surprised, but it is hard to tell whether his eyes are scrutinizing you or merely some other matter while he speaks to you.

'But of course, signor. It is good to know where all our loyalties lie.'

Bembo raises an eyebrow and stares darkly into his glass. 'Indeed.'

'It is rightly said,' Hugh says before turning back to Vittoria. 'My lady, may I serve you some eel?' She takes it with thanks, but he sees from her eyes that he is repellent to her. He finds colder comfort still in that he is probably more repellent to himself. He has killed; he has slain; he is the snake who cannot shed his skin. He remembers the blessings and curses uttered from the mountains in Deuteronomy. Two mountains, Ebal and Gerazim, two states of being in relation to God: blessed or cursed. He knows which he is, and would pray – if he had any hope – to find some small place between the two. A rock to crawl under. But he has no hope. The heavens are as brass and his stain remains insoluble.

FIRST LIGHT, 15TH SEPTEMBER, 1508 – ISOLA DI PROCIDA

'You've done well. She handles like a dream.' Hugh peers off the bow of the fishing skiff Wilf has rented on the quiet. The slate sea is choppy, and winds gust strong from the west. Hugh tastes the salt spray, then helps Pico secure the mainsail, trying to find the right way of explaining the English word for trim. '*Navigare. Bene, Pico*. Good. Keep straight, tight, full of wind. You understand? Tight?'

The lad grins, nose wrinkling. 'Sure, tight. I can do that, always tight. Si, si!'

Pico likes it when it is just the three of them, when he is near Hugh.

'Was your father a sailor? Did you sail with him?'

Pico shrugs. It's hard to know. The lad casts his eye vacantly back east. When you don't know your own father, you are always a long way from land.

Feeling sorry for the lad, Hugh says, 'Want to handle her?'

Pico's eyes widen with delight. He replaces Hugh at the tiller before another word is exchanged. An identical grin stays on his face for the next hour.

When Hugh is confident that Pico can weave them gently through the troughs and crests, he tussles his hair. '*Va bene, Pico, va bene.*' Hugh then looks across to the other person he has been neglecting. Wilf stoically examines some loose stitching on his shoe. Hugh decides to humour him. 'Been walking too much Wilf? You should put your feet up more.'

Wilf doesn't look up. 'All right, you gonna tell us what all this is about then?'

'If you like.'

'Aye, I do like. My bloody neck, ain't it.' Wilf's been waiting for an explanation for over a week.

Hugh takes no notice. 'We're not here seeking support for the crusade.'

'Well, I gathered that – '

'Then let me finish,' Hugh snaps. 'We're here to recover some stolen gold that will help finance Rhodes' defences and our victory.'

'Must be a lot of gold.'

'It is.'

'And that dago—the navigator?'

'The witness to where it was hidden. That day at the baths, the day he was taken, I made him draw this map.' Hugh shows the paper to Wilf. 'We are here, that is the headland, and this cross is where we will find a cave.'

Wilf, the cynic, smirks. 'X marks the spot.'

'Something like that, but I don't think it will be there now.'

'But if it is?'

'Then we commandeer a ship from somewhere to take us and it back to Rhodes.'

Wilf chuckles, but stops at his master's serious expression.

By sun up, they have rounded the headland and are scouring the cliffs on the inside of the vast, submerged volcanic crater. They have already passed it when Wilf glances back and sees a cave behind a barrage of outlying rocks that mostly hide it. Gabriel was right. Hugh takes the tiller and gets Wilf to attend the sails as they come about. He takes her in at what he thinks is the best angle, but even then, the hull scrapes the bottom. A wave lifts them and takes them over in the next second. Wilf takes the sail down, and Pico fends off the waiting rocks as the boat slips into the cave. The mast easily clears the roof and inside breaking waves and mischievous winds echo far back in the darkness. They secure the boat on iron rings already there.

'This is where they must have moored the boat,' Hugh says. He peers overboard to port. 'And this is where they must have tipped the cargo.'

The first rays of morning light penetrate the dark recesses of the cave, which is not so vast as the initial darkness made them think. For now, they see the whites of waves breaking fifty feet away on the smooth back walls. Hugh strips and without giving any direction to the others, dives into the sea. It is not too cold. He likes swimming. He feels clean in water.

He is finally here, so near. It is dark at first, and cold, in the green gloom of that cave. He descends down and down, and just when he thinks his ears will burst, he finds the bottom. There is just enough light to see by. Boulders, bones, skulls and iron debris but no barrels, no gold. He works methodically, coming up for air and cursing, then going down again, beyond the seaweed and algae, levels to that other sepulchral world known only to very few, and the dead.

He finds the hoops from one barrel and some iron nails, which at least give him the satisfaction of thinking something was there. Back on board, Wilf brings him a blanket and Pico produces some bread and cheese. They sit a while, Hugh not speaking, only thinking where this leaves them. He came for clues, not the gold. This he reminds himself over and over. He never really thought a man like Vendramin was so stupid as to leave the gold in one place for two years. Hugh casts his eye about the cave, remembering that Gabriel and the crew left Vendramin in the cave without transport. *Suppose he did not have help from the duchess? Suppose he climbed out and walked to the southern part of the island to seek help there in the villages?* Hugh, clutches his blanket, and hobbling barefoot on the jagged rocks, wanders to the edge of the cave and glances up. The rock faces are sheer, in some places overhanging. No one would attempt a route up there unless their life were threatened.

He comes back to Wilf. 'We'll search this cave. Fetch torches and get them lit.' Pico helps Hugh to change his loin cloth, which he calls a *brache*, and hands him his short drawers, breeches, shirt and sandals. Before the torches are lit, Pico is already scrambling far up to the right-hand side and shouting back that he has found a crevice like a chimney rising out of the inner cave. As Wilf arrives with the pitch torch, Hugh is positioning Pico to give him a lift up to the first ledge.

'Want Pico to come?' The lad tries his English.

'No, Pico stay with Wilf.' Hugh turns to Wilf. 'Torch.' After this the climbing is easy and well-worn too. Hugh follows the black smoke up, climbing with one hand and rarely having to swap hands. After what he guesses is a hundred to a hundred and fifty feet, rocks around him have dried faeces on them. The aperture of his chimney narrows to a round opening, and beyond that are the tiles of a roof.

The flies retreat from his flames but the stench is acrid. *Is it a genuine garderobe or just a disguised escape?* He thinks the latter seeing there is so little in the way of faeces left. He places the torch on a ledge where it can burn, and using both hands, reaches up to pull himself clear of the latrine. It is a struggle to do it without soiling his own breaches on the way up but once in the room he sees that the latrine is one of five. From the bucket and sponge, the robes hanging on a nearby peg, they are still in use.

He moves to a substantial olivewood door at the far end of the room and listens intently. Goats bleating, the bell of a cow, maybe two, and then also the voices of men. Is this a Neapolitan garrison outpost? Is it Vendramin's hideout?

Hugh is lightly armed, just his dagger. Not ideal. He is deliberating whether to open the door when he hears hurried footsteps coming, the crunch of gravel, the slapping of leather on stone. Hugh slips behind the door. It opens with speed, and Hugh grabs the man who steps in, pulling his head back and placing the basilard at the man's throat. The man releases a small shriek of terror. 'Keep quiet, or you're a dead man.' Hugh tightens his grip relentlessly.

The coarse material is the rustic habit of a Franciscan. The monk raises both hands. 'We have no money here, but you are welcome to our food. We, we, we turn none away.'

Hugh releases him and lets him turn so they may see each other face to face.

'What is this place?'

The Franciscan, whom Hugh guesses to be around forty, with a long nose, big ears and hound-dog eyes says, 'Just a house of poor brothers.'

'How many?'

'Of us?' He lowers his hands and assumes the look of a man who understands, empathises. 'Ten, sometimes more, though some are visiting from other houses.'

'Your name?' Hugh lowers the knife.

'Fra Paolo Todesco, of Assisi. And you, friend?'

'Doesn't matter.'

'Well then, where do you come from?' He gestures with open palms. 'Your accent is foreign to me. French? German perhaps?'

'What are you doing here, Paolo?'

'I came to relieve myself.' He smiles sheepishly.

'No, I mean why come down from Assisi?'

'Oh, to relieve the poor, and encourage the brothers. To see they have all they need, to preach, you know.'

'I see, and this tunnel from inside that last latrine, who uses it?'

'Oh, apart from you? That would be our escape route and hiding place in times of trouble. You know this place is awash with pirates.' Paolo looks toward the latrine, and sees the torch smoke rising. 'Did you come up this way from the cave?' He seems amused, but Hugh is not.

He grabs the man again and shoves him against the wall. 'Tell me where Marcantonio Vendramin is and you can keep your life.'

'Please, signor!' Paolo's droopy eyes grow wide with alarm. 'All Italy knows this name, but we know no more than anyone else. How could we?'

Hugh screws up his face and moves the knife closer. 'Tell me!' He must be sure.

'Please, signor, Vendramin is dead.' The monk is lying.

'Last chance.' But even now when the knife is pressing on the man's jugular vein, he will not yield. Hugh has done all he could to convince the man that he was in earnest, yet even now he does not yield. Either he isn't lying or else he fears Vendramin more than death.

Shit. I can't kill a friar. 'Very well.' Hugh forces the monk to show him about the complex, the chapel, the dormitories and outbuildings but finds nothing amiss. The other monks seem, if anything, even less likely to be pirates' accomplices. And Paolo, all the while, seems more concerned with Hugh's welfare than his own, introducing him always as, 'my foreign friend, who came out of the privy'. By the end, Hugh wants to give the man some sort of apology, and yet it nags him that he has been strung along at some point. At the privy door Fra Paolo asks, 'Will you go down the same way?'

'Is there another?'

'Alas no.' He smiles, the veins in his cheek visible as if he were a much older man. 'But tell me for what you are searching?'

'I told you: I look for Vendramin.'

'Really?'

'And something he stole that was once hidden in the cave below, and which he has moved in the last two years.'

'Oh, treasure then!'

'What of it?'

'We know nought of that sort of treasure, friend. We are wed to lady poverty. We have renounced this world's treasure for Christ's sake.' He opens his palms again, making vague gestures with his stubby fingers toward the sky. 'It is a strange thing that you come looking here of all places.'

'Few men are what they seem.'

'Ah, but then surely, some men are.' Paolo takes a step closer. 'Mind you, there is treasure in Assisi, my foreign friend. If you come there, many people find that for which they search.'

'I told you what I am searching for.'

Paolo seems not to hear. There is something of the absent saint about him, the mystic. Or a lunatic. 'We have freedom in Assisi.'

'What do you mean, freedom?' It is not phrased as a question, but more a cynical man's mockery of third-rate sophistry. Hugh is already walking away when he hears the friar at his back say, 'A free man would not have to ask.'

Enough of this. 'Good day to you, friar.'

'*Au revoir*, signor.' Paolo fumbles the Frankish pronunciation but it is not this that Hugh notices, but his eyes. *Why does he look at me like that?*

AFTER VESPERS, 15TH SEPTEMBER, 1508 – THE GREAT TERRACE, CASTELLO D'AVALOS

The guests perambulate variously in twos and threes along the flagged terrace outside the great hall.

Bembo and Cardinals Petrucci and d'Este are escorting Duchess Constanza as the gentlest and balmiest of breezes kisses her face and shudders her silks. The reddening sun lies low across the western seaboard, but the chill is not yet felt. Hugh leans on the warm stone balustrade with Castiglione. Both men gaze with silent contentment at their Greek wine and the dying ball of fire that warms their skin. The scent of bougainvillea, honeysuckle and lavender is so thick at this time of day that Hugh can almost taste it. Each plant gives its best to God before the dying of the light, before winter lays its fingers on them.

'You are not drinking your malmsey, Hugh,' Castiglione says. 'Not to your taste?'

'On the contrary, I am savouring it.' Hugh has been analysing his feelings about the failure of the morning's expedition. The clues have run dry. He must write to Rhodes, tell the grandmaster of it. And yet for all this, he does not feel crushed. And it is this, more than anything else that gives him pause. *Why not, I wonder?*

'Good. It is an acquired taste, and I confess we have little in the Marches.' He pauses for breath, takes a nervous sip, gives a small murmur of approval and delicately licks his lips. 'Your day was profitable? We missed you earlier.' The ambassador straightens a linen sleeve, and then brushes a mosquito from his hand.

They are interrupted from behind. It is Bembo. 'Indeed, my thoughts exactly, *maitre l'ambassador*. Had you been out wenching, Hugh, and forgot to wake up? I do hope not.'

'Signor Bembo, do not say such a thing,' the duchess remonstrates as she nears them. Hugh observes the redness in Bembo's cheek, the dilation of his pupils, the slight slurring of his voice.

Bembo gives a lavish gesture with his drained cup of sweet Greek wine. 'Do not think hard on him, my lady, for as you know, courtesy demands that the lover should serve all ladies.' Bembo pats her hand reassuringly, and Cardinal Petrucci cannot resist a snigger at the jest. Bembo then wags his finger at Hugh. 'All *ladies*, I say Hugh, but not all women, which I fancy is all you will find in the lower town.'

Cardinal d'Este, dressed head to toe in red silk, reveals his own reading and darker vices. 'Andreas Capellanus says that those unfortunate to fall in love with a peasant woman may *si locum inveneris opportum*, make use of *modica coactio*. For he says, how else shall we overcome the rigour of such creatures?'

At the look of disapproval on his hostess' face, Hugh bows and speaks quietly to the side, 'You both seem better informed than I on such matters, but let us desist for decency's sake.'

But whether through the strong wine or motives of his own, Bembo speaks all the louder. 'My dear Hugh, we can't all be as saintly as you.' His voice drops to a whisper, and he leers. 'Especially with so much *propter otia multa et abuntantiam ciborum.*'

'Signor Bembo, please desist. You make my guests blush with your forwardness.'

'My lady, I will, if only this rogue will tell us his secrets – disappearing at ungodly hours with his shady *confrères*.'

'Yes, yes, *Dio mio*, tell us all.' Cardinal Petrucci's eyes are aflame with a lupine delight, and Castiglione stares. 'All this intrigue and mystery you bring, signor. You know that His Holiness once said in my hearing that if Venice did not exist, we'd have to invent her. I think we could say the same about you. Knight, courtier, lover, poet, painter, philosopher, assassin – no one could accuse the English of idleness!'

Hugh examines his malmsey. 'Your Grace exaggerates my virtues.' And that is the truth.

'Aha, always with you English the *bon mot*, but I swear that you will either die on the gallows or of the French disease.'

Hugh contemplates for a moment how pleasant it would be to show this inflated bag of silk the quick way to the harbor. He glances toward the balcony. *I could have him over it while the snigger is still on his face*. Hugh subdues his evil genius in order to remember who this notorious profligate is. He's the son of Siena's *de facto* tyrant—not someone you want to get on the wrong side of.

'On the gallows or of the French disease!' Bembo chortles into his glass as he takes another draft.

'I think, Your Grace—' Hugh gives his Sicilian smile to the young cardinal, whilst trying to avoid the duchess's stare. 'That it rather depends on whether I embrace His Grace's principals or his mistress.'

While the cardinal's eyes nearly burst from their sockets, Bembo coughs up his wine and laughs loudly, arousing the attention of the others.

Castiglione watches attentively, and they are, at this moment, joined by the others: Madonna Vittoria who has been with her lady in waiting, and Colocci who up until now has been in deep conference at the far end of the terrace with the grand prior. They come like bees to honey, and it seems to Hugh as if each has been waiting for this moment.

'What is this?' Colocci says, the intensity of his inner eye betraying the disinterested tone of his voice. 'Have you found out where our knight errant was this morning, refusing the ladies the pleasure of his delightful company?'

'Ah, but *has* he denied the ladies?' Bembo draws Vitorria into the centre by an outstretched arm, and a look of mock horror. 'We suspect he has been entertaining the *donne perdute* of the darker alleys – *tout aux tavernes et aux filles* – taverns and girls.'

'Signor Bembo, you jest in bad taste, and it does you no credit!' Evidently Vittoria has not heard this sort of talk in the great hall before, and has none of her patroness's tact in dealing with men in high spirits.

Her eyes burn hot with righteous indignation. In fact, Hugh thinks, when angry, she has all the delicate fierceness of a thoroughbred, an indignant fineness of the nostril, and perhaps when she is a little older and more experienced, the possibility of excellent disdain.

Vittoria erupts. 'You must not sully the reputation of a man under the vow of celibacy, nor, nor, nor indeed, signor, sully the high regard we hold here in this fair court toward the mysteries, b-b-b-beauties of the conjugal state - that the marriage bed is undefiled, as syaeth the scriptures - with talk of what the disobedient do in darkness. Common decency, the teachings of the church.'

Her words burst on Bembo like a wave of pure, innocent impetuosity. For a moment he seems bewitched by the sight of a woman with so little artifice, and perhaps also because he is not used to being seriously challenged –or so much in the wrong. As she continues, he gathers his wits. But not enough of them to carry his jest with the whole party. In the dilemma of appearing witty or being right, he chooses the latter. He draws back from her, appealing to the audience. 'The teachings of the church, you say? The church's greatest divines say the act is as sinful inside marriage as outside. So what hope is there for us mortals?'

'It is not as you say, signor. It is simply not...'

'Oh, is that so? Gregory says that if man had not fallen, he would have procreated *sine carnis incentivo,* without the incentive of the flesh. Saint Victor says the act is *only* excusable because of the good ends it produces in childbearing, and Peter Lombard, well! Peter Lombard informs us that *omnis ardentior amator propriae uxoris adulter est.* Even passionate love of one's own wife is adultery! So where does that leave your pure bed sheets, Madonna, pray, where?'

After the brief pause, the duchess takes Signor Bembo's rigid arm. 'Come, signor, let us not deprive Venus of her mysteries on such a night.'

'He's wrong. I know he is.'

'Vittoria, that is enough. You will forgive her, signor. She is to be married shortly to my nephew, a match long intended and eagerly anticipated. We have been content on our small island with Ovidian hymns to Cupid. Let us not –

'He is wrong!' Vittoria's cheeks burn red, and her eyes water up, and none of her patroness's charmed conversation will call her away now from standing up against something she knows by intuition to be warped and wicked. Her eyes burn at Bembo as if he'd been the very devil. Constanza for a moment appears not to know how to ameliorate the situation.

Hugh speaks, so low at first that the duchess has to ask him to repeat it. 'I said, he is wrong. The lady has felt and spoken truly.'

The duchess's face loses its usual composure. 'Oh.'

Bembo glowers. 'Do the English care to enlighten us? You sir, the *homme serieux*, the melancholic. I suppose you know that the ancient physician Aristratus said long ago that all melancholia has its roots in sexual disfunction.'

'Pietro, *caro*,' the duchess intercedes, with growing alarm.

Bembo raises his hands in affected defence. 'Well, really. Are we to be lectured by him?'

But before he has finished, Hugh is already talking, fast but lucidly. 'Lombard is quoting a Pythagorean source, which was not classed as canonical last time I looked. And you quite misunderstand the Patristic sources, too, for they were at pains to tell us that the act itself is not sinful, only the submergence of the rational faculties to the passions. In fact, much later, even Albertus Magnus writes that he is sure that the pleasures of the marriage bed would have been greater in paradise.' At this he risks a glance at Vittoria who is staring wide-eyed at him, with two great tears running down her cheeks. 'And that our problem again is not too much passion, but too little reason.'

'No, no, no!' Bembo retrieves his arm from his hostess and uses a bony finger to stab his points into the air. 'Aquinas reasons that the act is evil itself, but that it must have been present before the fall, or why else would God have given such a creature as a helpmate for Adam when a man seemed so much more suitable.'

'Aquinas, though usually so succinct, is of no help here.'

'Oh really! Not only a knight, but now a theologian to criticize Aquinas!'

'I can assure you, a man under a vow like mine soon knows his enemy.'

'I hope,' Vittoria says with girlish coyness, 'that I am not your enemy, Fra Hugh.'

'By no means. I meant my own inordinate desire.'

'Ah, so you have the desire.' Bembo claps his hands. 'A mortal after all, and not merely a saint with a sword.'

Hugh ignores him, carrying on in the same even tone. 'Aquinas is too enamoured with Aristotle, who holds marriage to be a species of *amiticia,* of alliance or friendship. But again, even Aquinas uses the word *evil* not to denote sin but merely an evil by-product of the fall. If anything, the scholastics hold out for physical pleasure to the maximum with emotional disturbance at the minimum. Perhaps—' He gestures across the golden waters in the direction of Sorrento. '—not unlike the cold sensuality of your former emperor Tiberius over there on Capri.'

Vittoria's face lightens with hope. 'So, marriage is –'

'Honourable,' Hugh replies. 'And as the apostle says, *the marriage bed undefiled* as you most rightly quoted.' This for him is more hope than belief. As a refugee from the collapse of chivalry, he hopes beyond hope that there may be still one pure place left in the universe where the religious and amatory ideals are in perfect harmony.

But Bembo interrupts again. 'If your husband be a saint, otherwise you may count on his animal passions soiling more than just your Flemish bed linens.' These comments are so barbed that more than one intake of breath is heard on the balcony.

Even Castiglione's eyes and nostril flare in indignation, though, Hugh thinks, not with surprise. He knows more about his friend's poisoned cynicism than he lets on. Nevertheless, even he cries out, 'Pietro, *caro*!'

To which the other merely says, 'Well, all this fairy tale talk. It is as well she is prepared for the "honourable estate."'

Hugh, who would almost as readily flatten the man's nose, aims at his pride instead. 'Signor, once again you show that you might best confine your comments to fields of knowledge that you understand, like literature. You mistake the matter entirely again, for when the ancients talk of "the passions" they do not mean mere animal intoxication, but a corporeal change upon the appetite and affections that turn them into something other than they were. It is *these* that they cast as more or less wicked.'

'You are just picking at words. It means the same thing.'

'To a *certain person* perhaps it does, but not to them. Not to her.' He gestures to Vittoria with a small bow. 'And not to anyone who wishes to see the quarrel between the Provencal troubadours and the church made up.'

Castiglione takes Bembo by the arm in good humour. 'Come, Pietro. Away with this gloom, this, this, this darkness of humor. Explain to everyone that the quarrel has been mended by Dante, and let us have our dinner.'

Bembo bows with an ill-grace, and marks Hugh with an ugly stare. He almost looks like he would cry with some barely hidden rage. Hugh, however, is looking at the vision which is Vittoria, and thinking how easy it must have been to really believe in the Religion of Love, to serve the god Amor, as they did and still do in many places. As the French poet de Lorris said, *love is learned at a lady's eyes*. Could a pure creature like this teach him to love again? Looking at her—the smoothness of her neck, the light in her eyes, the way her throat moves when she swallows, how her mouth hangs innocently open to drink in each moment—he could almost remember the excesses of his Cambridge days when he oft quoted the errant knight Aucassin, 'I would follow all the sweet ladies and goodly knights down to hell than go to heaven without them.'

Hugh steals another look—her delicate fingers as she passes her glass to the servant, the nod of her head to the prior. *Quid est femina?* What is woman? The sages were right to ask it. Mordent Tacitus held them with a primitive awe, thought them uncanny, prophetic beings. Now, more than ever, Hugh feels something of the magic and wonder of womanhood, as it stands there before him in all the springtime of virginity. There is something here that calls forth greater things than Bembo or Boccaccio reckon on, calls forth the fullness of a man.

Dante painted Beatrice as a celestial signpost, looking on her as Saint Bernard looked on the Virgin, trembling before her, reproaching himself for his sins. Petrarch was less sure, wondering whether his *donna gentile*, Laura, was more a source of carnal temptation. But in the end even Petrarch sees her as a beatific ideal, rescuing him from his passions. Do women really have this saving power? *God knows, I need it, and could verily believe it tonight.*

Hugh leans on the balustrade and glances sideways, breathing deeply. The draft of wine always makes him introspect remorselessly. It is "The nature of desire," Aristotle said, "not to be satisfied." *But can I really believe the Creator of all appetites to be as Zeus, who kept Tantalus in a state of insatiate desire? Or two-faced as the Roman god Janus?* He turns away from them all toward the balustrade, the sea, the sunset, and then, out of a crack, a lone, green lizard waiting motionless, unblinking, wondering if he has been seen. Hugh wonders the same.

NEXT MORNING, ISCHIA

He sees her waiting at a window seat in a corridor adjacent to the *Piano Nobile,* the upper hall. It is how they do things here; deep recessed windows, a single stone seat on each side with a single carved pillar under each seat. Looking like Venus, with morning light falling like white gold about her head and shoulders, she makes a mockery of his vows again. *She doesn't mean to do it. Doesn't know she's doing it. Didn't position herself there to snare me. It's just not in her.*

But he knows it is in him, some weakness. The simple sage green cotton dress makes her look like a new-born dryad, yes, like a sapling in new leaf, dewy droplets glistening with light. *Saint Michael help me.* He passes on the far side of the corridor, head down. In her hand is a letter. *Probably from him. Bastard, I hate him.* She looks nervous. Hugh is aware of her looking at him. She stands.

‘Fra Hugh? Do not pass, I pray you.’

‘Madonna Vittoria. I trust you slept well.’

‘Quite refreshed,’ she answers quickly. ‘And you?’

‘You look it. What me? Yes, I slept better, thank you.’

They both start talking at once. She saying ‘I was minded to’ and he ‘I was just on my way to.’ Both beg pardon, bow again, then insist the other go first, twice. Eventually she laughs, draws an angelic wrist over her brow and says, ‘Very well.’ She pauses, gives another girlish laugh, then takes another deep breath. ‘You see I was waiting for you. Ah, you didn’t expect that, did you? Well, it is true. Furthermore, I have somewhat of a favour to ask of you.’

‘If it is in my power –

‘Oh, I believe it is. I am told you are a poet.’

‘Really?’

‘Signor Castiglione.’

‘Did he? I was once perhaps, but now I am an ill judge of verse.’

‘And Signor Bembo says your verse shows fine sentiment and judgement.’

‘Really? He said that?’

‘Yes, he spoke very highly of it at breakfast, the sonnets he’d seen, and of your person generally.’

‘You do surprise me, Madonna.’ Hugh maintains his face. *I thought he hated me. He should at any rate. Perhaps he is passing compliments intentionally second hand to flatter me into some compromise.*

‘Well, he does, though I did not tell them the reason for my questions.’

‘Which were?’

‘To ask for help crafting sonnets and other verse. I think I have a gift in that direction, for surely it is not toward algebra and arithmetic, and I needed someone that I might correspond with on occasion for tutelage – with my aunt’s permission, of course. At first, I asked the ambassador, but he said you would serve me better.’

‘Me? I am a soldier.’

'That is exactly what he said, and that is why he deferred in favour of you. He said that if I wanted to write – how did he put it, ah, yes – "verse sharpened by necessity" that would have the ear and garner the praise of my lord and husband-to-be, then you would be a better guide. It is why I did not trouble Signor Tasso and the others, though I love them all dearly as if they were my own uncles. And my dear brother Francesco and my father in Naples have no mind for it. But when I heard you defend virtue, uh, marriage, last night, I felt settled that you would be as honourable a guide as I could pray for. If, that is, you will consider it.'

'I really don't think –

'But I did hope you would.'

'You see, it is just –

'My aunt would censor all correspondence. It would be under her supervision. I know she wouldn't mind.'

'You haven't asked her yet?'

'Not exactly. Oh, please, say that you will consider it.'

'Very well, if your aunt allows, I will consider it. But only by request at her hand.' Which she won't give if she has any sense of propriety. 'You may address the correspondence to me through her.'

'Oh, thank you, signor, thank you.' Her hands are clasped to her breast. 'I hope I shall not prove a bore.' She starts to walk away and then swirls about so that her dress makes a swish, then a flap. 'I almost forgot my first sonnets.' She glides back over the marble floor on delicate toes and extends the papers.

Hugh hesitates. He knows only too well that offering your own verse to anyone is like giving away a piece of your heart, and he does not wish to cause hurt, but nothing is yet agreed. She offers it again, with a wide-eyed vulnerability and chest rising and falling in trepidation. 'It is in the *Petrarchismo* metre as favoured by Signor Bembo.'

Hugh bows. 'By your courtesy, Madonna, only with your aunt's approval, and only at her hand if it please you.'

She gasps, and holds the bundle back against her chest. 'Oh, but of course, forgive me.'

'For your honour,' Hugh proffers.

'Yes, of course, and yours too. I quite understand. Forgive me. We forget ourselves on this island where so many formalities have fallen by the wayside because people are so decent. It is all my aunt's doing. She has cast a spell over all of them. Even the men behave themselves here – most of them!'

LETTER TO RHODES, 23RD SEPTEMBER, 1508

Grandmaster,

I write from the kingdom of Naples, sending word briefly of my progress.

I have gained the favour of His Holiness and do currently tour to the courts south of Rome seeking alliances from dukes and princes who now, through my report, understand the plight of Christendom better. Even here King Ferdinand has offered certain ships, munitions and hands, as detailed in the attached inventory. (You will notice that it is signed by the Grand Constable Fabrizio Colonna's own hand, so you may depend it.)

Regarding the other matter, I was able to foil one plot to assassinate the navigator soon after his arrival and, fearing that we were betrayed from the inside, was able to remove him elsewhere. One assailant escaped me, the other I arrested, permanently. I later interviewed the navigator to my satisfaction, but he was taken from us that same day, possibly by Vendramin.

Our enemy seems unusually well informed, and exerts an almost universal fear on all who knew him. I have privily followed and verified the navigator's story, seeing in a cave on the island of Procida, evidence of the cargo's storage – but no contents. I have but one possible lead to follow up now, but will not commit to ink, for obvious reasons.

We head north next week, bypassing Ostia and Rome for Cittavechia, Bracciano (whose noble patroness, Signora d'Orsini, I have met), Viterbo, Bolsena, Orvieto, Perugia, San Giminato and perhaps even beyond the Magna Curia to Siena if there is time.

I will send further reports in due course. I am expected in Rome for the celebration of our Lord's birth, so send replies to the Grand Priory.

Pardon me. I am in haste to catch the tide for this.

Yours, et cetera.

LETTER TO FLORENCE, 24TH SEPTEMBER, 1508

Signor M,

I trust you are in health and that your work prospers in the finest of all cities, among the noblest citizens and the fairest dialect.

I write from Naples with news of the Englishman's progress. As I promised, he has been watched closely and all correspondence intercepted. We are now come from the Isle of Ischia and as suspected, he inspected the cave on the island of Procida. I would dispatch him forthwith, as you ask, for the murder of your nephew, only he claims, in a letter to his grandmaster, to have one last lead to follow up – though what this is we will wait to see.

We travel north soon, passing Siena in the next two months, so if you wish to meet me, or expedite matters towards him yourself, then you are welcome.

I visited the cell in the castile where they held Cesare after his betrayal. It is a pitiful, dark place. I pray to God that I will not disgrace myself in the avenging of his noble memory.

Again, at the risk of appearing tiresome I attach a list of my expenses. The bank here has yet to receive your authorisation. They were inflexible to the point of rudeness. It is possible that your letter has been lost or delayed, but either way I find myself taking out more loans at an unreasonable rate of interest which has been degrading for a man in my situation. I mention it only because I am sure you will take it into account when we meet.

Until I have the pleasure et cetera.

CITTEVECHIA, 30TH SEPTEMBER, 1508, LATE AFTERNOON

The great port is crowded with a forest of masts, ropes and canvas, all interspersed with the fluttering songs of a thousand silk banners, flags and pennons, trailing like smoke on a strong south-westerly breeze. Rigged and unrigged pinnaces cluster like shoals of herring around the great ships. The biggest of all are the galleys from the shipyards of Barcelona, Valencia, and Palma which are drawn from the great oak forests of Mountseny.

From the deck, Hugh looks over the passing hulls with admiration as they come into port. To think that it was from these oaks, in vessels like these, that legends like Ruggiero di Lauria and Pere de Moncada made their names. Even a hundred and fifty years ago, the great fleets of Aragon could put out for a year at a time.

The gulls cry above the general hubbub of the quayside, as carts appear to unload the baggage of the gentleman and church dignitaries. Hugh watches the port, considering his reduced options for finding Vendramin and the gold. He has decided on a course of reckless action, for he cannot seem to be ahead in cunning or enquiry, and he is so far from native soil, he cannot trust any network of allies to be reliable. What is left, but bold action? What is there to lose? He is no admirer of his own head in any case, but perhaps he can draw out his adversary. He cannot be everywhere at once, as Vendramin seems to be, but he can make his presence felt wherever he goes. He does not know by what means of supernatural terror Vendramin can subdue those who might otherwise have helped him, or by what devilry he burned up some of Borgia's cavalry at this harbour, but he has his own ways of getting to the bottom of things and making his presence felt.

Pico is at his side, his black woollens not so well appointed as they were when they left Rome, or Rhodes for that matter. He gazes about in wonder at the harbour as the wind whips his black curls this way and that.

'What is it?' Hugh asks.

'Wilf wants to know where we are to take the baggage.'

'Tell him to get the carter to take the necessaries for one night to that grand edifice to the left of the castle.'

'Eh?'

'That shithole with the sagging roof.'

A minute later Wilf is at his side. Hugh doesn't look at him and speaks with irritation. 'All right, are you?'

'Feel my oats, master, that I do.' Wilf rubs his neck and sees Hugh smiling. 'You wait, master. All right to laugh now, but one day you'll wake up with a stiff back and turkey's neck, up peeing half the neight and you'll wonder where the years went to.' He pauses before saying what he came for. 'Master, the cardinal's men have gone to the castile to ask for rooms. Would we not be better –

'Wilf, do as I ask and don't bother telling anyone else. It's just for one night.' He needs to stay apart tonight. He has work to do.

Hugh examines the wharf buildings on the quayside for it is hard to see any effects of the fire on the cobbles. Scorching can still be clearly seen in the masonry, sometimes a green tinge discernible at the edges. He draws close and smells it, detecting pitch, sulphur and maybe even quicklime, though of this he cannot be sure because of the lime mortar. Pico copies him and then wrinkles his nose in disgust. 'What is it?'

Hugh keeps his council.

Later that evening, Hugh is dressed in coarse woollens and asking questions at the hostelry bar, over which he is billeted. The landlord eyes his purse. 'Say that again?'

'I want to talk to people who saw what happened to Borgia's cavalry the night they were burned four years back.'

'Wouldn't know about that.'

'It was just outside your door'

'People don't like talking about it, especially to foreigners.'

'I want to talk about it.' Hugh grabs him by the apron strap. 'Now tell me who saw something.' The landlord's eye flits nervously in the direction of a table where three thick-bearded seamen nurse their wine. A moment later Hugh is standing over them. 'Evening.'

'What do you want?' The accent is thick Ligurian, the words slurred either through sloth or the drink. Broad shouldered with corded forearms, these men were born with leathered faces and ropes in hand.

'Information.' Hugh drops the purse on the table. 'The night of the fire when Duke Valentino's cavalry perished.'

'We don't know nothing about the fire, Vendramin, nothing.'

'I didn't mention Vendramin.' The last word scorches the air like a powder fuse and for a moment there is no breath. Then the flicker of the first man's eyelid. *The purse.* A nod of the other's head. They move. One reaches a hand across the table for the purse; the others start to deploy their gutting knives. Hugh skewers the thief's hand to the table with his basilard, kicks the second man clean off his stool, and jumps across the table to the third in a flurry of fists and elbows. Him dealt with, Hugh head-butts the screaming thief unconscious and retrieves his knife ready for the attack of the second man who by now is on his feet. Hugh leaves the purse on the table and walks steadily around it. He is breathing hard, and raises his bloody hand and dagger to the sailor. 'Tell me what I want to know.'

The other drinkers scatter from them. The two men circle each other so that the sailor comes near to the table. The purse. *Fool.* It is a moment Hugh planned. For the briefest moment the man glances to the money to measure his chances of reaching it, and when he looks back, Hugh is all over him brandishing a stool. He fells the man with blows to the face and chest.

When he comes to, the sailor is on the wharf tied to a barrel. It is night and the quayside deserted. His cheek is split, and his eyes only open enough to see Hugh standing over him. 'Where am I. Where are my shipmates?'

'Tell me your part with Vendramin in the murder of those soldiers, or you will join your shipmates in the drink.'

'You wouldn't.'

'Do I look like a man who'll stop?'

'I don't know anything.'

Hugh walks behind him to kick the barrel closer to the edge of the quay. 'Two hundred men and beasts died right here. What did you see?' Kick.

'I didn't see anything, I swear it.' Kick. Kick. The sailor's legs vainly flail, but Hugh drives him on. 'Please, please, I didn't, I didn't.' Kick.

'Didn't what?' Kick. He's two feet from the edge now. His boots are hanging over the thirty-foot drop into the sea. Two other barrels with ropes on bob between a merchant man, and a hefty Genoese carrack. 'Didn't what?' Kick.

'Didn't do anything.'

'But you helped him. You knew his name. So, what did he make you do?' Kick.

'Please don't, signor. He made us swear.' Kick. 'Said he would kill us if we told.'

'What? Worse than this?' Kick.

'He will find me.'

Hugh leans over to bring his face close. 'Good, then you can tell him that I am coming to cut his heart out. NOW TELL ME.' Hugh goes back for another kick but the man dissolves in tears and promises that he will tell all.

'He hired us to cover this whole area with a thick liquid from twenty barrels that he had in some wagons. He offered good money, no questions asked, but said we had to do it while he was in the hostel. I swear we did not know what the liquid was, signor, I swear it.'

'Describe it.'

'Black, thick, smelt of bitumen, pine, sulphur – like Hades, like Hell itself, signor. Signor?' He hears the clink of coin as the purse hits the cobbles, then Hugh's footsteps walking away. 'Signor?'

'Your friends are still inside, spend the money quickly, and don't forget to give Vendramin my message if you see him.'

LETTER FROM CITTEVECHIA TO RHODES

Most Esteemed Grandmaster,

What news do I enclose on the heels of my last dispatch, if that has indeed reached you? While in Cittevechia pursuing further information given by the navigator, I have happened upon news of great import for our situation. For I believe now that the man whom we seek has in his possession a weapon which on its own may do more to relieve us of the depredations of the Turks than many thousands of ducats. If you are unsure of that which I write, magister, then by all means consult the Prior de Blanchfort, for I know that he has made great searches for this weapon which has been lost since the fall of Constantinople.

These facts, as I'm sure you will see, increase the necessity of my commission and steel my resolve to bring the villain to justice for his double betrayal of us all, first, for the sake of filthy lucre, and second, that he withholds the means by which we all may yet be delivered from this monstrous fleet which Antichrist amasses for our downfall.

I have shared this information with Prior Battista, who sends his greetings.

On other matters, I attach my spending which has been minimal due to the generosity of my hosts, and also the benevolence of His Holiness who, I now understand, is planning a league which will include the French against the Venetians. I will write more of this when I winter in Rome and have ascertained for myself the new developments. Please send correspondence to the Grand Priory there.

I am, as ever, your most obedient servant, etcetera.

ROCCA D'ORSINI, BRACCIANO, 31ST SEPTEMBER, 1508

The fortress stands on a great plug of volcanic rock looking out over a circular lake, which itself is a volcanic crater a few miles in circumference. The emperor Nerva in the second century brought water from here to Rome, and under Pope Paul V in 1427, the aqueduct was restored to supply fresh water to the Aqua Paolo there.

'Lucrative rights are water rights,' Castiglione points out to Hugh and gestures across the lake. 'Everything we can see, and many more miles beyond that, are Orsini fiefs, a sizeable domain, though it has cost much to defend it. Trevignano, Isola, Galera et cetera.'

Colocci and the cardinals proceed at the forefront, talking loudly as they pass the outer town defences, large earthworks called *la Sentinella*. Castiglione leans towards Hugh as they cross the drawbridge. 'They were dug little over a decade ago when Cesare Borgia, then a cardinal, besieged the castle.'

'Did our host Gian Giordano defend it well?'

'He was away, in the employ of France, and his father in a Neapolitan prison where he died. So, the task fell to his sister and her husband, who by all accounts defended it well enough.'

'And they succeeded?'

'Yes, with help from other quarters, but yes, they did – even though the Borgias offered the defenders bribes to desist.'

'Typical of the Borgias?'

'Alas, *caro*, typical of Italian warfare. I cannot decide whether it is the old world or realism, or a new cynical spirit in our modern age—one without honour, without a conviction of what is right.' Castiglione sucks in his lip.

Hugh has his own thoughts but says rather, 'But they resisted successfully.' Castiglione looks about him as if to make sure they are not overheard by the dead, then says in a lower voice, 'Reinforcements arrived and pressed the attackers right up to Monte Mario, so much so that Cesare barely escaped with his life. He never came back for a second try, even many years later when he had a sizeable force. Once bitten and all that.'

They enter at the front of the fortress with the lake at their backs, weary from a long journey and expecting a good dinner. The duke himself greets them in a loose chemise, and unbuttoned velvet doublet. 'Welcome, welcome. You are right welcome.' Gian Giordano, the Orsini family head, is hard to weigh. He seems affable enough standing in the courtyard with his retainers – none chosen for their looks – and yet there is some madness about him in the eyes, something unaccountable.

Hugh notices it even in his attire, which seems to offend men like the prior and Castiglione more than anything else, the latter remarking quietly to Hugh, 'Even when he's in Rome, he looks like he's slept in his clothes, or just come in from hunting, or both.'

The duke is in his mid-fifties with a face heavily lined from a life of campaigns. He is surrounded by large hounds and eager to meet Hugh most of all so they can talk ramparts, siege works and munitions. Gian Giordano is an experienced *condotierro*, bear-like in form and manners.

He is a lover of the field more than the library, and fancies himself something of a wit, which might be more the result of nerves when not in the camp among his soldiers – soldiers are not discerning in this regard.

Prior Battista sidles up to Hugh before they enter. 'No one is quite sure whose side he is on, if, in fact, he is on anyone's side. At another point, when Borgia was laying waste castles left and right, he did not besiege Bracciano. Some say he feared Gian Giordano because he is so unstable, others that Borgia was honour bound *not* to attack because both of them had been made Knights of San Michelle by King Louis. In either case, you had best be on your guard. His alliance with France makes him unpopular with Julius, but he may be useful for our cause. Besides, alliances shift like water here. This is Italy my boy. You want a friend –

'I know. You told me: get a dog.'

They are presented in turn to the duke by Colocci, Hugh being last. But it is Hugh the duke wishes most to meet. As soon as they are introduced, he takes him by the arm like a brother and leads him toward the brick ramp leading to an upper courtyard where the walls are richly frescoed. All the while he chatters excitedly about the six bastions erected by his father and grandfather, apologising for *la Sentinella*. 'It was erected in haste in my absence, hmm, during the Borgia siege, you know, though my sister saw them off. It needs to be deeper, something I will see to. Have you seen the new angled bastions of Ferrara? The duke has over two hundred canon I am told! Collects them like chamber pots, oversees the castings even. Have you eaten? I expect you're famished after the ride. I know I am, by Jupiter, and I've only been drilling some new recruits.'

He takes the briefest pause for breath before gazing headlong at Hugh. '*Va Bene!* I have looked forward to meeting you, Fra Erpingham, to hear what news you bring from the east. How I wish sometimes that I had been at Rhodes, myself a brother knight to you, the simplicity and comradery, rather than the heavy duties I have born here for my family. I swear to you, that if it were not for my wife and estates manager, I would do nothing all day long but inspect grain receipts and sign olive oil contracts.'

'I have met the Signora.' Hugh slips in a comment during a brief lull. 'A very noble and capable lady.'

'Indeed, she is the complete opposite to her predecessor, God rest her, but the Arragonese are often sanguine, like me I suppose.' And with that he laughs, and slaps Hugh on the shoulder. 'No, Signora Felice is what we call in our language *prudentissima*. Do you have this word?'

'Yes, indeed.' Hugh glances at the two fresco cycles, and the duke tells him the upper cycle shows deeds from his father's life, the lower, a visit from Piero de Medici.

Their conversation moves onto horses. Would Hugh like to see a young stallion the duke has bred from an Italian warhorse and more slender French equine stock? Would he like to see the armoury? The duke's mind is everywhere, and before Hugh can even answer, he is being led past the guardhouse toward the steps leading down to the cellars.

Hugh makes sure his Portuguese carrack sword is loose in the scabbard, but he cannot imagine the duke capable of such a low trick. There is some cursing from the duke while a page lights the torch, but eventually they are walking along rows of arquebuses, iron pikes, light guns called falconets, German pikes, Brescia harquebuses, breastplates, crown pieces for horses, colophony, picks, ballasts and five huge shields ornamented with embossed roses, another Orsini motif. Some of their best artillery pieces and munitions are kept elsewhere.

The duke is all a fuss about the firearms, and wants Hugh's opinion – though without pausing long enough to get it. Apparently, the Spanish favour using pike and arquebus formations, which won them the battle at Cerignola a few years back. The duke's men don't like it—too much extra gear to carry, too much that can go wrong. 'And if it were too damp or some vile storm or some such? Well, of course, they'd be left holding their dicks in the breeze. But as commander I have to consider all sides. Crossbow bolts take craft and money to make, while the mass production of powder and shot is tipping the balance. It's hard, I admit.' On and on. His mind is like a bag of ferrets. 'Does d'Amboise put much stock in firearms? I know his brother well, and that old goat de Blanchfort. How is he by the way?'

Hugh says that they do have a goodly stock of firearms, though for his own taste, and because of the nature of his work at sea, he favours the English bow and crossbow. Although he admits as an afterthought that even the crossbow was held at one time to be a diabolical and most unknightly weapon.

The duke leads Hugh up the steps and back across the courtyard, this time rather apologetic that he has kept him from the others. The yard is awash with servants, and stewards shouting orders. 'The Signora and her ladies will be awaiting us no doubt in the great hall, excited to have such august company. My brother Carlos and his wife Porsche are expected to join us. They live just across the lake in Anguillara. You will like them, well, him at any rate. Women are a bloody mystery, my friend.'

The duke leaves him with an acne-ridden page, and Hugh bows with grace. He tells the lad that he is thirsty, and he is led to the courtyard well, made from coarse basalt rock and inscribed with the insignia of Saint James of Compostella. While the lad lowers the bucket, Hugh enquires after the coat of arms, but before the boy can answer Hugh hears a familiar, soft voice from behind him. 'The bears are for the Orsini. The other device is for Arragon, for my husband's previous wife, God rest her soul.'

'Signora Felice.' Hugh bows. She and her two ladies reciprocate. 'I am honoured to see you again.'

'On the contrary, it is we who are honoured to offer you hospitality. I trust you approve of your quarters?'

'In truth, Signora, I have not seen them yet for I have been entertained by your illustrious husband.'

'Treated to a tour of the stables and armouries?'

'Indeed, a most impressive stock, and a most courteous host.'

The page pours the water. Hugh takes the olive-wood cup from his hand and first offers it to the ladies. The others decline, but Felice takes a small draft then hands it back. 'You will find our water very sweet. It is prized in Rome.'

Without thinking, he rotates the cup and presses it to his lips, the coolness of the water only enhanced by the fragrance she has left. Rosewater and lemon balm. He notices something stronger in her on this second meeting, some determination, perhaps some of her father's *terribilitá*. 'It is sweet indeed. I am refreshed already.'

She brushes the pleats in her rich blue silk dress. 'Then would you permit us to escort you to your room ourselves?'

'I would be most honoured.'

'Good. May I present my lady in waiting Madonna Claudette Colette, and also Lady Emilia Pia, lady in waiting to the Duchess of Urbino.'

'Ladies, at your service.' Hugh bows again, this time examining the other women—Madonna Claudette's short, robust frame and profusion of blonde curls, and Emilia's sharp blue eyes and pert mouth framed by long, straight brown hair. *There's a story there, I warrant.*
He is invited to take Felice's hand, the other ladies falling in respectfully behind, and they process past fawning servants, into the castle and up the welcome cool of the grand staircase. 'I have ordered for you the rooms my father's uncle, Pope Sixtus, used when he came here during a time of plague in Rome. There is a study to the side, and though the ceilings are not so high, yet they are frescoed very finely, and the views, ah the views.' She turns and smiles. 'Well, you will judge for yourself.'

She leads him to the top of several flights within the tower and eventually into a modest suite of rooms frescoed with swags, grotesques and various depictions from antiquity's pantheon. Wilf and Pico leave the trunks to bow low.

'This was Pope Sixtus's library, and this—' She leads him into the bedroom further on '—is where he slept.' She walks across the uneven terracotta tiles toward the window. Pointing across the panorama of lakes and mountains, she says, 'These are the Sibillini Mountains. Soon we will see the snow on them.'

'Not too soon I hope.'

'You men detest it because it makes warring and besieging nigh impossible, but we depend on the winter rains for our land, our crops, the livelihoods of many thousands of our people.' She shoots him a smile with her full lips. She is not chiding today. 'Come, Fra Erpingham, I have put some books for you in your *studiolo* while you are with us.' She leads him back to the first room, and up some steps to the back. 'You will find it quiet here, for I think you should have quiet for prayer and study after all you have suffered. Here is Ariosto. I have marked canto XIV for you on the dignity of prayer, for I found it most pious.'

'I am greatly indebted to you, Signora. They are fine books.'

'They are printed by Manutius of Venice. I am sure you have heard of him. I have become too regular a customer for my husband's fancy, but I am afraid that if we do not lay-up treasure like this for our heirs then Lady Emilia will continue to scorn us as barbarians.' She glances behind her to see Emilia smiling coyly. 'For verily we have but a tenth of their treasures, manuscripts that go back, as did Lorenzo d'Medici's, to the Patristics.'

'I heard, Madonna,' Hugh says turning to Emilia, 'that Cesare Borgia took many of them.'

'Yes, indeed. The beast took them all and much booty, took them away up north to Imola. It was only when the Spaniard was finally subdued by His Holiness that my former master Duke Guidobaldo recovered them. My lady says that he wept when he found them mostly intact at the Imola Castle, though the compensation was never paid.'

'Two hundred thousand ducats, was it not?' Felice asks, as if she needed to.

'Indeed, a drop in the pale compared to what that monster and his father had hidden in their vaults.'

'Or,' Felice adds with a smile, 'what they had coming in their ships from the New World, eh, signor? But why stand we here when there is so much to prepare for the feasts tonight. Come ladies, let us leave this man to rest for my husband is a great dancer and will not expect less from his guests, even the cardinals if I know him.'

THAT EVENING, THE HALL OF THE TROPHIES

The great hall has a ceiling nearly thirty feet in height. Hugh gazes up at the richly painted beams, ceiling boards and friezes. The room is known as the Hall of the Trophies, so many are the mounted heads of boar, bear and deer, but this ancient baronial style is not to the liking of some of the guests. Hugh passes the first window seats and hears the Lady Emilia remarking quietly to Colocci that she had heard this whole area was once famous for its swine.

'It was once called *Porcianum.*' She looks up at a large boar. 'Indeed, one cannot but wonder whether we are surrounded by portraits of our host's ancestors.'

Hugh does not look back, but he hears Colocci's laugh, sounding something between a braying donkey and a drowning man.

Much encouraged, Lady Emilia continues. 'And at poor Felice's wedding, I tell no lie, signor, after shaming her with a vulgar Florentine kiss at the altar in front of all her guests, we were treated to a wedding feast at the burnt-out garret that passes for the Orsini palace in Rome where we had to eat cold meat with our bare hands!' Again, the laugh, saints deliver us.

As far as Hugh can see, the entrees pass without incident. But during the third course the duke's brother, Carlos, leans back on his chair, waving his fork and saying good-humouredly to a serving boy. 'Is *this* boar on the end of my fork, my boy?' At which point a few people can hear Lady Pia carping rather too loudly, 'Which end?' Most pretend not to hear, and Hugh notices that no one seems to have heard it at the top table either.

Later however, when the plates are being cleared at the top table, the Signor of Bracciano exposes himself in a boastful rant. Apparently, the explosion is occasioned because either he heard, or saw, or perhaps was told by a retainer that Cardinal d'Este spoke insolently about the layout and décor of the castle.

Gian Giordano stands, steadying himself with the arm of his great oak chair with one hand while brandishing his goblet with the other. He addresses his comments as if to his brother, though everyone understands they are directed elsewhere. 'Welcome honoured guests, and the rest. My wife and I say you are all right welcome. My brother Carlos, and his beautiful wife, Signora Porsche, extend you the same. We live in simple but honest style, do we not, brother? Our castles may not have the affectations of the latest fashions of Spain or France, nor have we built our bastions and ramparts *all'antica* as if we were one of these *arrivista* prelates who populate the Curia with naught to do but build themselves endless palaces. We are the Orsini! Our lineage illustrious, our conquests legendary. These are bastions that prevailed against the papal forces at the Battle of Soriano. These walls celebrate the honoured memory of our great father and grandfather.'

He gestures loosely to the fresco by Romano on the far wall of his father Gentil Virginio in triumphal procession as newly appointed gonfalonier of the Arragonese troops. On the long gallery that runs the length of the north wall, the lutists falter on their strings, wondering whether this is a planned speech and they should stop altogether. Felice rests her left hand on her husband's, in a vain gesture to attract his attention.

But he has not finished. 'By justice and force of arms we have defended and ruled our fiefs in Santo Polo, Isola, Campana, San Gregorio, Scrofano, Cantalupo, Canemorto, Montorio, Vicarello, and, and –

At this point he looks to his brother to remind him of the others, and in the interim, Prior Battista stands to amicably raise his glass. 'To our most generous host and his illustrious family.' The other guests reciprocate and a pacified duke finishes by saying once again how welcome they all are.

When they are seated, the prior remarks to Hugh, 'This, my boy, is how feuds are usually started. Sometimes I think we Italians should adopt the prohibitions of the infidels.'

'But then you taste a vintage like this one,' Hugh says.

The prior sniffs his glass. 'Burgundian *pinot gris*. Yes, it is rather fine, but wait till you taste the Pucino Vino and Frascati of Tuscany, sunlight distilled in water, then you will know God is smiling on you.'

Hugh smiles. *Now that would be something to know.*

They are both distracted by the duke and his brother who have broken into raucous song. In no time their retainers and friends are singing the old drinking songs of Burgundy where the duke has travelled often. Hugh watches Felice's suppressed nervousness, eyes on the table as her husband's rich baritone leads 'Chevalier de la Table Ronde' and then her fingers arrange and rearrange her cutlery as more join him for 'Boire un Petit Coup'. She eyes nervously at the condescending glances of the cardinals, and Hugh makes sure she sees he is not offended by the vulgarity, even when they reach a crescendo of sonic merriment with a third song.

'*Le Duc de Bordeaux ne boit qu' du Bourgogne,*
Mais l' Duc de Bourgogne, lui, ne boit que de l'eau…

The Duke of Bordeaux only drinks Bourgogne,
But the Duke of Bourgogne drinks water alone,
So, neither felt shame when they sought to exchange,
A glass of Bourgogne for the port of Bordeaux.

While the more inebriated guests descend into fits of laughter, Felice places a hand gently on her husband's fist, which hitherto had been pounding the table with verve. He wipes the sweat from his eye with his other hand then lays it gently on hers. He smiles and raises a goblet to his brother. 'Ah my dear, as Count Boso said at the Synod of Mantaille, *Dei Gratia id quo sum,* by God's grace, I am what I am, or something like that. To our illustrious ancestors, and our noble guests.'

The family raise their goblets to the guests, and heads tilt in respect. Peaches are being served to clear their palates between courses.

SIX HOURS LATER

It must be around the third watch of the night when a cry goes up from the watchman in the courtyard. Lights are called for. Hugh has been sleeping fitfully as he always does, so he is dressed and armed quickly, making his way down the stairs in bounds as if Vendramin himself has been spotted in some dark recess. He arrives in time to see the castellan, dressed in nothing but his nightshirt, torch in one hand, cross hilt in the other, interviewing the watch. 'Come on, spit it out, man.'

The watchman, ghostly white in the face and bleeding from a wound below the neck, trembles. 'Nero went off to sniff something out, but he didn't come back, so I's went to find him, and that's when I saw the man in the shadows making his way quiet as a cat to the tower stairs, the ones up to the papal chambers.'

'My chambers?' Hugh says, tucking the rest of his chemise in and glancing about the perimeter of arches and doorways. 'Who was it? Did he speak? Come, quickly now.'

'No, signor. I challenged him, but he was too quick for me. Strong too. He knocked me down and made off that way.'

'And you did not recognise him?' the castellan says.

'No. I took no torch for I wanted to sneak up on him, but oh!' The beleaguered watchman rubs his head. 'I'm nothing without my Nero for doing this job. Where is that dog?'

'Which way did he go?' Hugh asks, his stomach already beginning to tighten.

'That way, signor.' The watch points in the same direction as the assailant ran. 'But you mustn't trouble yourself being a guest, and all.'

'It is no trouble; I can assure you.' Hugh takes the torch and walks around the courtyard to an alley that leads past the kitchens and out to another yard. The blacked blade of de Blanchfort's carrack sword makes no show in the moonlight as he approaches the alley. Other servants appear behind him in the main yard, and from somewhere he hears Gian Giordano's voice bellowing orders, but in front all is quiet. Just the alleyway and a small pool of light in the courtyard beyond. He grips and re-grips the hilt as sweat greases his palms. The familiar drumming in his chest is reassuring. He can at least still feel a little fear, or excitement, in the chase. Perhaps he should not have bothered with the torch at all, but it's too late now. He wanders into the alley swishing the flame this way then that, testing the doors as he goes.

All are locked as they should be. He comes to the edge of the smaller cloistered yard, observing quickly the possible hiding places. The intruder has likely lured and killed the watchdog here to cover his escape. *One way to find out. Big breath. One. Two. Three.* Hugh bursts from the alleyway and darts around the cloister, again trying doors until he near trips headlong over the remains of the dog, lying in a pool of black blood in front of the corner door, inset into another bastion.

This door, too, is locked. Hugh makes a quick search, even sniffing the door for any sign of the assailant, but he detects nothing at all. He thumps the door in anger, then returns to examine the mastiff. Torn skin and blood encircle the beast's neck, as if someone had run a blade almost the entire way around. Hugh fights back the rising bile, but before he can think the problem through, he hears the others coming for him. A moment later a small party led by Gian Giordano arrive.

The duke's face glistens with sweat, the smell of wine still about him. 'Ah, Fra Hugh, which way did the intruder go?'

'No intruder, my lord.' Hugh straightens up and raises his torch to illumine the corner door. 'Where does this lead.'

'To the upper rooms, the guest apartments.'

Hugh straightens up and says, 'Then, as I say, my lord, not an intruder but a member or guest in your own house.'

The duke prods the dog with his foot. 'One who kills old Nero. A dark business. Any reason why someone would want to be getting to your rooms at such an hour? If it were a lady, I can imagine it, but a man and this...' He nudges the dog again with his foot.

'In truth, my lord, I cannot say, but if you will excuse me, I will return there and let your men clear things up here.' Hugh retreats with his thoughts, taking a detour to examine the door at the base of his own bastion. It is locked fast, but as he rattles it, an iron pick drops to the floor. As he stoops to pick this up, torch light glints on a shining coil—a lyre string made more reflective by a liquid sticky to his touch, Nero's blood.

THE CASTLE OF PALO, 1ST OCTOBER, 1508

The next morning Hugh sets Pico to linger near the bastion wall in case the killer comes to recover his tools. He also has Wilf escort him down to break his fast. They are armed, and Wilf is ebullient. 'Let them try it, master. Bloody dagos creeping about in the night! They'll get my bloody bodkin up their foreign arses if I catch them. Good bloody Norfolk steel's what they need.'

They reach the bottom of the stairs, and Wilf instinctively leads as they go around the corner. No one is in the corridor, and he whispers, 'Think they were after information about the gold?'

'No. He was coming to kill us in our beds. All of us, I suppose.'

'It's probably that Colocci. Looks like an evil swine, and he hates you.'

'Can you imagine him as a lock picking garrotting type?'

'Perhaps not.' Wilf sniffs, then scratches his behind. 'But who then?'

'We'll find out soon enough, I suppose.' Hugh cannot put the uncomfortable thought from his mind that Felice had arranged for his room to be apart and isolated from the other guests.

'You gonna tell'em about the lyre string?'

'No, we'll keep it close. See what comes.'

Felice rises to greet him in the Hall of Trophies, the other guests turn also, though Hugh consciously engages none of them with his eyes. Felice leads him to the seats in a window reveal where they can talk apart from the other guests. She appears not to have slept. Her eyes are ringed and weary, perhaps even with tears, though he is not sure.

'Signor, let me speak with you. We are appalled that someone came to rob your apartment last night. We are used to sieges from without but villains within? This is new.'

'Signora, I suspect that the villainy is not from within your house, and that it will pass with our leaving.'

'You have enemies in your party?'

'I accuse no one.'

'I see. It's your business, and I will not ask further, only be assured that it was I, and I alone, who insisted that you have the papal chamber apart from the other guests. But only out of motives of kindness.'

Hugh nods benevolently, for despite himself he cannot think ill of her when in her presence. 'It was most courteous of you, Signora, and I am, as ever, in your debt.'

'Good.' She joins her fingers on her lap in a kind of girlish satisfaction, turning a garnet ring this way and that and looking out at the clouds to the west. 'Then perhaps I can ask you a favour, seeing the weather will be fine today.'

'I am at your service.'

'My father made a gift to me recently and with it I have purchased a castle of my own on the coast at Palo, with good lands. But seeing it is on the coast I fear the attacks of the Barbary corsairs and other villains and would appreciate your eye on our seaward fortifications.'

'Would your husband mind?'

'I have already asked his advice, but he is always too busy, and today he is off with his falcons. Have you read Petrarch on nobility and hunting?' She leans in close before he can answer. 'In truth, signor, I wish to accomplish as much as I can without family help, for these Orsinis – not my husband, but his near kin – despise me, being so high born themselves, and me coming from the wrong side of the sheets, and so I must prove to them that I am their match, and more. Your prior and Signor Castiglione have agreed to come to, and we shall make a merry party.'

'Then I shall tell my man to prepare the horses for us. It will be my honour.'

In the courtyard Wilf and Pico steady the horses.

Prior Battista pretends to admire Hugh's destrier's flanks. 'I am sorry that your sleep was disturbed. Any idea what was going on?'

Hugh says, 'I wondered if my interview of the sailors in Cittevechia had the desired effect of drawing Vendramin out of the shadows. Do you think it was his work?'

'No, my boy. If he wanted you dead, you would be. It is not in his nature to fail at anything.'

The Signora rides well, aided by the saddle-horn which is the latest innovation in Italian saddlery. She bursts from the gates like a hind, her retainers and the two knights not far in the rear. The town's people cheer her, and soon their small cavalcade is cantering at a steady rate past fields of grain and barley, vineyards and olive groves. On the scrublands of lower slopes swine herders jostle with the boar-like pigs so popular in this part of Italy.

They make the coast for a late lunch. The Signora is all vital energy, moving between her castellan and estates manager in a magisterial flurry of orders, brevies to be written by her secretary Giulio, invoices, missives and receipts to be sent or settled, all interspersed with comments to Hugh, Castiglione and Prior Battista who follow her about with wonder and admiration.

'I've seen grain fluctuate from twenty ducats to just a few *scudi* a *rubbio* in the short time I've been selling, so having a stable client in the Vatican like our noble chamberlain Juliano Leno is sometimes more consoling than a good harvest. They know that here. We have an understanding between us.'

She has a passion for tapestries. She takes the party to a large hall with sea views, which she calls her Sala Neptune, and shows them a particularly fine work by a man she has employed from Brussels. 'Gilo di Brusela has, like all those masters of the Low Countries, a most exquisite hand. My Maestro di Tapeziro Nicolo Todesco, whom you met last night, found him for me. They work very hard, the northerners.'

She shows them other northern tapestries from the Flemish weavers. One depicts the life of Solomon, and another that of Saint Anthony – the latter not really the subject for lavish coverings. She is keen to point out all the soft furnishings that her father has given her, for these she cherishes above all and lists meticulously as if they were engraved on her very heart. 'These thirteen silk hangings, and those six large carpets and four smaller ones which I have used upstairs. And look at these four silk brocade cushions, he sent those also. Three more like them with purple velvet and brocade are in my *studiolo*, which I will show you anon.' She shows it with great relish, as if it were for her and should be for them, a crowning moment.

'Here, noble signors, is my *studiolo*, and I know, Baldasarre, it has not the fine marquetry of the dukes at Urbino, but I have something the Montefeltros do not have.'

She opens a cupboard with lattice doors in cherry wood, and moving aside copies of Jerome, Suetonius and Augustine, reaches for three large books bound in red satin with silver locks and clasps. 'This castle stands on the site of the villa of Pliny's uncle, and these are his last three volumes. When I sit here to read them, I can almost hear the great admiral bellowing below my window from his ship!' They are suitably impressed and express themselves as such.

After the tour Hugh is able to be of some help to the castellan. The lower bastions need reinforcing as the waves of preceding decades have taken their toll. His advice over artillery for the battlements is also duly noted. The upper walls are too thin, artillery has moved on apace in the previous decades; they must be strengthened as well.

Felice seems pleased to see her little kingdom-apart taking shape under her ever-watchful eye. They are brought slices of melon on a shady terrace, in full view of the vineyards. The prior and ambassador are away relieving themselves, and they are left alone for several minutes.

Hugh reclines on his chair and watches a bee fussing around his melon skin. 'I congratulate you, Signora, on a fine purchase. Your father is very generous.'

She tilts her head slightly as if to see whether he is teasing her. 'Monsieur, Papa Terrebilita can afford to be generous. Why, he settled forty thousand ducats on my half-sister not long ago.' She must have seen that he meant what he said, which he invariably did. 'Forgive me, that sounded bitter, when in truth I am not.'

'I am sure he does not love you less.'

'No, I am sure not, but she did marry where she was bid, whereas I refused his matches twice. If my dowry was small, it was my own doing, I suppose.'

'But this is compensation surely, such fair estates that simple Englishmen only dream off.'

'Indeed. I think he gave the gift because I suffered the death of a child. He would not have me looked down on by the other Orsini relations, or disinherited by my husband's first son Napoleone if I did not manage to produce any heirs. But enough of me. You talk of England and estates; are you ever homesick?'

'You should know better than to ask a man like me such a question, my lady. I am sworn to seek a heavenly country now and the defence of the church.'

'And how does your search progress?' There is such force in her chestnut eyes.

'In truth, poorly.' He's looking at his hands and can feel his eye starting to twitch.

She, too, looks down, closes her eyes and recites some well-worn lines. '"And none, O Lord, have perfect rest, for none are wholly free from sin; and they who fain would serve Thee best, are conscious most of sin within." There.'

'Your lines?'

'Verily I wish they were.'

'They are well said.'

'Comforting, consoling?' She smiles. 'Just a little?'

He pretends to ditch the weight which crushes his heart, and returns her smile. *If she only knew.*

After a pause she asks about his more temporal search. He says that he has found the nobility of the Magna Curia and Naples to be supportive to the cause, to which she answers, 'And your other search?'

'Signora?'

'I hear you seek a knight errant, and what he may have.'

'Tell me, Signora.' Hugh leans forward and raises his chin slightly. 'Do you ask this for yourself or has your father asked it?'

'I will not lie to you. His Holiness seeks the security and prosperity of all Christendom. It is a war on many fronts. You know that he supports you and the knights, only you must not incur his displeasure by removing from Italy property pertaining to the Curia.'

'You may tell His Holiness that the navigator gave me no information regarding the Borgia gold that has been fruitful. I am at this moment without any information regarding it.'

'If I may be frank, signor, a man without information, is hardly a man worth robbing. Someone went to much trouble last night to get to you.'

'If I too may be frank, Signora,' Hugh says, reaching into his doublet and placing the lyre string on the table. 'The man came to kill me, not to steal.'

Her face grows pale at the sight of the string. 'You found this?'

'In the grass at the base of the tower.' Hugh nudges it about on the table with his finger as he toys with various ideas. 'I inspected the ground below the guest apartments after we spoke this morning and saw signs of disturbance—broken grass, fresh earth.'

'I don't understand.'

'I have revised my opinion. I now believe the attacker was let in from without by one of my own party.'

'And you know who this is?'

'I must keep my suspicions to myself, but I cannot imagine that it is your father's men, unless they are working secretly for another party. Nor is it one from your own household, for the attacker used lock picks rather than a key. Besides—' He manages a smile, an impish raising of his left eyebrow. 'It would be better for a host to poison an English guest, for though we are hard to kill, we are terrific bleeders. Think of the mess!'

'You should not jest, Fra Hugh. A guest's safety is a point of honour for the Orsini. My husband is distressed for yours and his own honour's sake. If he finds out who it is, justice will be swift.'

'Then let the assassin pray that it is your husband catches him and not me,' Hugh murmurs absentmindedly. He glances across the field where, even at this distance, he can spot some broken stalks in the standing grain.

The prior and the ambassador are returning from the far side of the terrace. Felice says quickly, 'Fra Hugh, I do not doubt that you are a most capable man, but I would that you know this: others have made search for this man, this treasure, far longer than you. I am not speaking of honourable men like my father, but ones without principal. You speak of journeying north of here after you leave us. I say, beware Siena; do not trust the tyrant of that place, Pandolfo Petrucci.'

'The young cardinal's father? I have heard of him.'

'It was doubtless he who had had Pope Pius' leg bandages poisoned occasioning his cruel death.'

'But why? Pius was a Sienese Pope.'

'Do they need a reason? I don't know. Patrician rivalry. Or perhaps someone told him about the imminent arrival of the shipment from the New World. Either way he knows of it and has spies everywhere making enquiries. I would not even visit Siena if Petrucci knows or thinks he knows you have information.'

'What is that about Siena?' Castiglione has arrived back.

'Ah, my dear Baldasarre, what good ears you have. I was just saying that Fra Hugh need not visit there because the Sienese are obsessed with their own glory and would not contribute one *scudo* for a crusade.'

The ambassador sits down heavily on the bench. 'It is true, just as the Signora says, but it would not be prudent to show disrespect to them, particularly when Cardinal Petrucci is one of our party.'

'As ever, ambassador.' Felice smiles with easy grace. 'You school us with your prudence and impartiality.'

Hugh sees that she intends him to catch her eye. He knows what that means: beware Siena; beware the man who takes you there.

There is no more evidence of mischief during their sojourn at Bracciano, even though Wilf invites it with dares and mutters. Hugh watches Bembo, Castiglione, the cardinals, Colocci, even the grand prior for signs of duplicity, but he sees no change in any of their behaviour. The prior is as cheerful and informative as ever, Castiglione as amiable, Bembo as eager to display and dispense his knowledge, Colocci to hover and snipe, Cardinal Petrucci to preen and titter, Cardinal d'Este to vainly attempt purchases of tapestries from his host. Even the various retainers and servants seem indifferent.

They journey north and enjoy a few nights of begrudged hospitality in Viterbo with the de Vico family. They are entertained one evening in a large hall in the old papal palace that housed the infamous three-year conclave that elected Gregory X more than two centuries before.

It delights Bembo to be there. 'Three years! Can you imagine it? Eventually some enterprising prelate locked the cardinals in, reduced their rations and even had sections of the roof removed. They say that three of them died before a compromise was reached.'

While Hugh and the two Visconti gaze at the ceiling, which seems intact that evening, Bembo quips, 'Of course, the French were to blame for it. No wonder Petrarch thought them not much better than a horde of Scythians. They were to blame, just like now.'

The next day, after heavy rains, they are on very poor roads to Bolsena and from there to Orvieto.

EXTRACT FROM HUGH'S LETTER TO ISCHIA:

To the most serene Duchess of Frankavilla, and her illustrious ward, the lady Vittoria Colonna,

To you all, greetings from the noble town of Orvieto, where the rain has given us renewed thankfulness for dry lodgings and firm beds. Here I remember the land of my birth where rain is our portion the oftener.

I speak for the whole party when I say with what relish and wonder we now look back on our sojourn on your island. In truth, I have often prayed heaven that I may be fortunate enough to visit again without the indelicacies of duty pressing on my mind and conduct.

Regarding the lady Vittoria's poetry, I thank you, Duchess, for your acquiescence to this service and the honour that you bestow upon me in its regard. I pray that I should not be found wanting in diligence, nor rude in knowledge or sentiment – in short, that your ward may profit by what little I can bring. If it please you, I will consult with my traveling companion, Signor Bembo, on matters of form and taste, so that she may receive as deep a benefit as possible.

To the work Donna Vittoria gave me when we met last, let me now come without delay, and with comments general in nature. If this letter does prove beneficent, then it would be my greatest pleasure to receive more verse and make comments of a more particular nature.

You write, lady, of love and beauty which we are assured is a proper subject. Your youth and inexperience will prove a blessing or a curse depending on how you receive the current literature. For many have loved the form of beauty, but not the indwelling power of it. Ours is the age of gilt wood and highly polished brass, and many have mistaken the mere colour of gold for the true ring of it. The Provencal love lyrics were often a worse medicine than the original disease of loveless contractual marriages among the courts of those days. French gallantry is not love, nor sentiment true passion, nor passion lasting devotion. Mistake not sentiment for pathos; strive to express the things themselves as they appear to you, and not how they appear reflected in the art of others. To see truly, and to help others see what you see is the administration of love, and the whole province of the poet. It is, as I understand it, one of the excellencies of Dante. Signor Bembo and I are agreed on this point at least.

Signor Bembo made a comment in this regard, upon which I have reflected often. He said, as a man more used to Venice and the sea, he had not really appreciated trees to any degree when he was growing up. Fruit, almonds and plums came to him in crates at the Rialto. He was not ignorant of natural philosophy, but he did not see trees – that is, understand their value and position under heaven – until he saw the paintings of Giotto in Assisi. The artist, he would say, opened his eyes.

What is a tree? How may we justify a tree? To say it is merely a means of fruit for us, fodder for the beasts and fuel for the fire, is surely an error of category. Surely, we must say that a tree was made by God and needs no further justification. The thing itself, the tree, rather demands a response of thanks because God made it.

I hope I do not divert you from the subject by this analogy. Giotto helped Signor Bembo see trees. So, too, you may strive to help us understand the affections of the betrothed and the divine love of God by honest words and those of another.

We do honour in imitating the poets that have gone before as you do Petrarch. The terza rima, you have made good use of. Bembo agrees. Indeed, he says you may make the genius of Petrarch flower once more. Our tutors, our models, are like parents with their hand on ours to help us form the letters when we were, as it were, learning to write. But it is a false humility – nay, sometimes pride and sloth – that causes us to remain in that state too long. Think on these things, discuss them with your friends. Yes, a good but cultivated ear for verse, real pleasure in a fine phrase or a strong word well chosen, are all admirable. But as a soldier – for such you chose as a tutor – I prize truth, as does God. Affectation will not do for us. If we are surrounded and in peril, we must know the numbers of our enemy. If we are set upon by a galley, we must know it's guns, and the reputation of its admiral. We want reality and not rosewater. If you would win your fiancé's admiration and heart, then think on what I have said.

And if you trust not yourself with these gifts, graces, and acquirements at the present hour, then begin to trust the very things themselves, for they are the real and apparent. Speak of what you know and know well. And let God do them justice through your poetry.

In writing this I remember the signal shame of the Florentine sculptor Michelangelo when he allowed Milanese to pass off his sculpture of Cupid Asleep to Cardinal Riario for two hundred ducats, as if it were of antique provenance and only recently dug up. The story is well known, and I do not think I betray my admiration for Michelangelo by repeating it here. The subject and style were doubtless correct, but the layer of artifice added by Milanese brought out avarice in the seller and pride in the buyer. If Michelangelo had not been of so great a soul, he might well have set his entire career to making counterfeits for the sake of filthy lucre. And we would all have been doubly robbed; for we would not have seen the antique masters as they were, neither would we know the full powers of Michelangelo as he is, and we hope, shall continue to be in the time to come. So again, I say, trust in the subject and strive to express it truly and with grace, and God will aid you.

Nota Bene: the rain has not abated all day and I find myself with time to write down on the reverse side of this page, those verses where I believe you come closest to my advice above.

CAPELLA NUOVA, THE DUOMO, ORVIETO. 15TH OCTOBER, 1508

Orvieto sits proud and clean on the saddle of a precipitous, golden rock, like a queen on a stone mare. She has always been seen as a jewel among the papal possessions, jealously guarded, often fought over. The duomo presents its monumental façade to the Umbrian hills, forests and fields of stubble. As the cavalcade approaches, a shaft of late afternoon light makes the marble shine with an unnatural intensity. Hugh imagines it to be an omen. He is right.

They are billeted lavishly at the episcopal palace, but even here the party are fractious and weary with travel. They are all thinking of excuses to give Julius why, after the winter break, they might be excused from re-joining the tour next spring.

'Damn it, a man needs his own bed,' one says.

'We can't let our own estates go to rack and ruin because of a crusade that will probably never take to water,' says another.

Hugh hears all this from Wilf via Pico via the other servants. Servants always talk among their own; it is their way, their currency, their pardonable sin, their own outlet for pride. The winter rains will not come too soon for some. *Good*, Hugh thinks. *The sooner I am rid of them the better. If they found out what I was really after perhaps they wouldn't be so eager for their own beds. One or two of them surely know already. But who is anyone's guess. Perhaps they'll make their move on me before Perugia, our last stop before winter falls.*

They attend High Mass midmorning in the duomo, so the local bishop can show off his important guests. He appears pleased to see a number of red berettas, and hear the rustles of crimson silk at communion.

After mass Hugh is hunched in a corner of the new chapel to the south of the high altar. He has long wanted to come here, to see the Last Judgment ceiling frescos of the Dominican Fra Angelico, but now he is here he is as miserable as sin. He is not wearing finery to please the bishop but a punched black leather jerkin with a high collar. He has kept his weapons on him, which is not considered polite. He'd wear a steel harness if he could, dare his unseen enemies to come at him. But for now, the leather jerkin will do. He'd rather fight than think, that much he starts to understand, sitting here under the work of that pious Dominican. How can he coo over fresco techniques as if he has never done what he has done? How can he sit here, looking at Christ robed for judgement and think about *intonaco* and brushes? He draws his cape about him and shrinks. His sins. The horror of them. At times like this he wishes he could tear his own skin off.

He is brought back to the world of the living by the footsteps of Castiglione who is being escorted into the chapel by a local magistrate who evidently wishes to show off the wall and lunette mural by, what he loudly announces as the '*famosissimus pictor in tota Italia*.' The fresco work of Lucca Signorelli of Cortona is striking and extraordinary. He was brought in by the bishop less than a decade ago to finish off what Fra Angelico left undone in the chapel, and before the frescoes were dry his work had caused a sensation throughout Italy.

The magistrate gestures proudly through the voluminous folds of his black over gown. 'You will see, ambassador, that Signorelli has closely studied the classical form. None of those serpentine, pot-bellied slips that they paint up north. No, here are real men and women, with muscle, sinew.'

From where he sits, Hugh follows Castiglione's eye about the wall, until their eyes finally meet. 'What does our English friend think?' the man asks.

'I don't know. Is the artist a pious man?'

The magistrate replies, 'I am sure he is, signor.'

'Well.' Hugh does not look at him. 'They are too heroic for my taste, their muscles crammed full with walnuts. No sense of the shame of the fall about them.'

'Well, ambassador.' The magistrate billows out his sleeves, places his hands on his hips, and speaks past Hugh. 'That is what I mean about the backwardness of the northern countries. It is up to Italy to lead.'

Castiglione draws the man away to show him the cycle of the frescoes, probably to avoid any further unpleasantness. The magistrate, now joined by Bembo and the cardinals, points out the scenes from the Apocalypse, the last days, the end of the world. The scene to the left of the entrance depicts the preaching of Antichrist and the persecution of the church.

Hugh looks at the black knights who carry out Antichrist's orders and wonders if he were alive at the end of the world whether that would be him, maiming and killing in the name of God when all the time he was acting for the dark side. Would he even notice the difference? To take his mind from this, he allows his eye to fall on the grotesques and busts of famous men that look from the lunette frames, surrounded by scenes from the works of Virgil, Dante, Ovid, Statius and even

Lucretius. He follows the mythological scenes of Tritons and Nereids running along the base. Lucretius! His eye is drawn back again, why in the name of all that is holy would Signorelli honour a man who said that it was fear that made the gods? A man who tried to mix Epicurean with natural philosophy, and show how all life evolved by Fortuna's hand rather than that of the gods? Lucretius had his answer in Cicero's *Somnium Scipionis,* Dream of Scipio, if he had been listening.

'Aha, Alfonso, look you at this my pious and honourable friend.' Bembo has spotted the fresco of Lucretius, too, and begins to use the fresco to tease Cardinal Petrucci. The cardinal has been on his best behaviour. He no doubt knows that the bishop of Orvieto is a terrible gossip and passes everything back to the pope.

'"Happy is he who has discovered the causes of things and has cast beneath his feet all fears, unavoidable fate, and the din of the devouring Underworld."' Bembo quotes Lucretius from his didactic poem *De Rerum Natura,* 'On the Nature of Things'. His eyes are alight with mischief. 'Imagine if those Epicurean ideas took hold in Italy!" Without the pains of purgation, of the eternal flames, how then would you terrify and control us? Where then would you derive your prepends, stipends, your indulgence taxes?'

But Petrucci will not be drawn, saying rather that a pious man like Signor Pietro Bembo should have no fear about purgation, adding wryly, 'at least not from the church.'

'Oh, tush tush, my dear Cardinal,' Bembo chides. 'There is already talk of atheism in Italy, and more particularly, writing, too. As you know, I say my *Pater Nosters* to St Julian, read only the most religious writers of antiquity—Plato, Aeschylus, Virgil—that sort of thing. But there are others that grow cynical of the church, of religion in general. And before you scoff, Alfonso, remember that a shout in the mountains can bring down an avalanche. Have you not read Boccaccio's "Three Rings" in the *Decameron*? Or of Dante's friend Guido Calvacanti who tried to prove that God was not? Of course, God is not susceptible to proof or disproof. But we must be vigilant, a shout in the mountains, I say.'

Hugh does not hear the cardinal respond; his mind is away somewhere else. *No God!* he thinks. *What a glorious comfort for a man in my predicament. That for all my infamy, there would be no one to answer to, no final reckoning.* But he knows even this cold comfort to be mere wish fulfilment. That sort of thinking – the very idea of a cosmos evolving out of chaos; of there being no creation at all, only a sort of perpetual fall – yes, that sort of pessimism really did become possible during the demise of the republic when Lucretius lived, poor sod. He saw the best wine of that saner paganism, and the weightiest political creations of late antiquity all growing stale with exhaustion, with cynicism, a colossus going down under its own weight. Was it any wonder that under those circumstances men shook their despairing fists at the impotence of the gods? For surely if there had been gods behind the universe, then *that* moment would have been the time to step forward and support the crumbling edifice. They didn't reckon on a Galilean carpenter, of course, so they sank in hopeless despair. How else could it be possible for a body of otherwise sensible men to reverse a subconscious assumption in the soul? To give in to Fortuna, the bitch goddess of chaos, caprice? To accept life arising from matter? *Madre Dio!* It was the abnormality of the times that made atheism possible. *And Bembo is wrong, wrong even to joke about it. Atheism will never be seriously contemplated again, no matter how low Christendom sinks. No. As Roland says in the Chanson, even if the Christians are wrong, the rest are bores. The best story always wins, however uncomfortable it is.*

'The damnation of the wicked!' Cardinal Petrucci's exclamation interrupts Hugh's thoughts and brings him back with a fright. *What? Is he talking about me?* The cardinal is stroking parts of his goatee with his left hand and pointing out various segments of the fresco under which Hugh sits. 'I don't think I've seen the like anywhere in Italy. We must have Signorelli in Siena.'

'Why?' Bembo gibes. 'Are there many wicked there too?'

'I dare say fewer than Florence, but stop your endless teasing man. Look at those demons in flight, the powerful foreshortening. Fra Hugh,

Fra Hugh, wake up. You are something of an artist. Are these not extraordinary?'

'Yes indeed.' Hugh gazes at the multi-coloured demons, some in flight, some torturing their human prey while the Archangel Michael looks on from the right-hand corner. It is grizzly to behold—the tortured forms, twisted, mangled, contorted faces wracked with terror. Hugh knows those expressions; he has seen them, felt them, made them. He knows how far short even this painting falls in capturing the reality of souls and bodies in torment and death. But Petrucci will not let him remove his eyes, for he keeps pointing at this one and that one, always asking for Hugh's response. And then he points to the sinewy grey demon pulling at a garrotte around a woman's neck. 'And look at this fellow with the garrotte, I fancy the artist must have seen it done. Are they keen on that sort of thing in Cortona? I will ask the bishop. It's one of his benefices. And look at this one, a fiend biting his way into the skull of the wicked!' He points feverishly, almost like a child at a carnival.

With sudden rapidity Hugh feels his bile rising in an involuntary spasm from the pit of his own gut.

‘Look! There is another,’ says Petrucci. ‘Feeding on his very flesh. My, Signorelli has an eye for detail, does he not, Fra Hugh? Fra Hugh? Hugh!’

Hugh voids his stomach.

THE EPISCOPAL PALACE, ORVIETO

‘Hugh, my boy, how are you feeling now?’ An hour later, and back at the episcopal palace, Prior Battista is making a pastoral call.

‘Better.’ Hugh hunches in the window seat, gazing over the pantile rooftops to the imaginary freedom of the Umbrian hills. ‘How is the cardinal?’

‘I think most of your innards are wiped clean from the skirts of his robe, but he’s sending to Bologna for a new pair of silk slippers. He will survive.’ The prior takes the opposite seat. ‘In truth, my boy, they are saying that you were exorcized of a demon under the holy painting of Fra Angelico.’

‘An exorcism!’ Hugh groans. *Would to God it was that simple.*

‘Well.’ Battista raises his bony hands apologetically, saying ‘They do hold the Dominican’s work in very high regard around here, and one does hear of such things. Anyway, the main thing is that you’re feeling better now.’

Hugh stares across the campagna. All is *not* better now.

After a long silence the prior rests his hand on Hugh’s. ‘Hugh,’ he says softly, almost fatherly. ‘Hugh, what is this burden you carry? Can you speak of it to no man?’

Hugh instinctively draws his free hand across his stomach, shaking his head in reply. How can he speak of it? Is it not enough that God knows that he is a monster? Must the world know too?

The prior sighs, shaking his head sympathetically. ‘We must find you a confessor, Hugh, as de Blanchfort instructed, before you tear yourself apart.’

PALAZZO DEI PRIORI, PERUGIA 25TH OCTOBER

They've seen it all, the Perugians, whose city walls even predate the Romans. The party enters under a monumental Etruscan arch, modernised and renamed fifteen hundred years ago as the Arch of Augustus – probably by Octavian himself, after he besieged the city and conquered it. Hugh casts his eye about the ramparts and bulwarks. *No wonder Cesare Borgia garrisoned his last army here. Besieging it would be bloody – and bloody expensive.*

They settle into their quarters at the Palazzo dei Priori, hopefully for the last time before they resume the tour next spring. In a few weeks they will finally winter in Rome, but this evening they assemble opposite the palazzo in the Notaries Hall, in the centre of the proud city next the Duomo of San Lorenzo and the Fontana Maggiore, where women with stone jars and goat skins loiter and chatter. The winds beat on the twelve heavy Romanesque-arched windows. Curly brown leaves from ash and chestnut trees fly pass, along with swallows heading further south for the winter. This northerly wind they call the *tramontana*, and it bites.

The travellers are guests of the Bonfigli and Baglioni families. This preliminary audience is more a social introduction. Many have come just to see the two families represented in the same room.

Castiglione points to the lion and griffin on the palace façade, sculpted *intutto tondo* in bronze. 'They are rumoured to symbolise the two families,' the ambassador explains, 'locked in a century-old vendetta. But it is probably all nonsense. The lion was the symbol of the Guelph party to which they were both loyal throughout that tragic war. The other interpretation was no doubt circulated by one of the families to increase their fame.'

The young cardinal is not present. Hugh detects the livery of Petrucci's retainers among the throng of servants in the doorway, but no master. They whisper behind their hands. Something has excited them.

While he waits, Hugh casts his eye about the heavy arched hall, richly painted in geometric designs by Pietro Cavallini. His eye is drawn at first to the biblical scenes, then the coats of arms of the majors and captains of the city, and then to the representations of Aesop's fables. As he makes this final switch, something clicks in the deep recess of his being like a drawer opening. In it goes the word 'Aesop.' The drawer closes, and then he catches the whispers. What are they so nervous about? The whispers spread and presently Castiglione sidles up to where Hugh is standing with the prior.

'A rare treat, signoria, a rare treat.' The ambassador arranges his eating knife and scrip nervously about his belt. 'The serpent of Siena has come forth from his lair. Do snakes have lairs?'

'Of whom are you speaking?' But even as the words leave his own lips, Hugh knows the answer for all the hairs on the back of his neck stand up.

'Why, Pandolfo Petrucci, of course. The cardinal has gone with the Bonfigli's to escort him through the Porto Sant'Angelo.' The ambassador casts his eye nervously out of the window. 'It is very rare for him to leave Siena. The last time was when he and Baglioni met. They had just outwitted Cesare Borgia during Borgia's siege of Siena. Both dangerous men, though perhaps not as bad as some of their former friends.'

‘Really? How comforting.’ Hugh says.

‘Yes, of course. Gianpaolo Baglioni had incest with his sister, and only became lord of Perugia by murdering his cousins and nephews. It is almost safer to be an enemy than a family member.’

‘And his friends are worse?’

‘Oh, yes. His former allies against Cesare Borgia made him look like a saint. For example, Liverotto, Lord of Fermo, gave a banquet for his entire extended family and had them all murdered, including the kindly uncle – the previous Lord – who had adopted him when he was orphaned. The remaining two claimants were only infants. One he threw from a window himself; the other had his throat cut at his mother’s breast. So, you see.’

‘*Dio Mio!*’

‘Yes, I know. But he got his own throat cut by Borgia eventually.’

‘Borgia? Why does this man’s shadow rest everywhere?’

‘Yes, Cesare Borgia casts a very long shadow. But Petrucci is his equal in many ways. I am told that when Borgia besieged Siena, Petrucci and Gianpaolo, Baglioni left by mule through secret ways known only to himself. So that’s Petrucci, Hugh. He completely outwitted and outlived even the Borgias. He is fanatical about Siena, will do anything for her greatness, and his own, of course.’

‘But... but why has he come here?’ Hugh’s eye twitches.

‘They say it is about a marriage alliance, but that won’t be it. Excuse me.’ The ambassador goes to speak to his friend Bembo, whose face is visibly draining.

The prior leans in to Hugh. ‘If he asks for you, be on your guard. I’ve heard that in a five-minute interview, he’ll get more out of a man than God got out of Adam. Don’t show him your eggs.

‘What eggs?’

‘Exactly! That’s the spirit.’

It is a chill winter wind indeed that has brought the tyrant of Siena out from his strongholds. As the doors open to receive him, that wind seems to stiffen the bowels of every person in the room. Even the lute players miss their notes. One almost drops his instrument. No wonder, there is something in the face that would unman a garrison of Gascons.

Even as the page announces his party, the aged tyrant strides in ahead of his Bonfigli and Baglioni escorts. A tall man robed in red silks, in his late fifties, thick necked, barrel chested, a heavy Roman nose and broad, dimpled chin, his hard, greedy blue eyes dart about the room, unbalancing humours wherever they point. He wears no beret, showing off tight-cropped silver curls. His movements are deliberate, if somewhat impatient. He seems to be looking for someone, and acknowledges Castiglione with a nod, but it's not him. Then Bembo with a slight inclination of his head, but it's not him either.

His son, the young cardinal, appears demurely at his father's side and whispers something in his ear, at which the man's eyes come back to Castiglione, and then rest on Hugh. Hugh feels the dread in the pit of his gut, but he refuses to avert his gaze. He'll not be unmanned by some bloody Italian. He screws his fists, and returns the steady stare, refusing to bow his head when Petrucci inclines his slightly to the left. "So, I'm the reason," Hugh mutters to himself, while the names are being announced and more and more Bologna silks, taffeta, ridiculous turbans, and pink cheeks file into the room.

One of the Bonfigli stewards calls for refreshments for the illustrious guests, saying that after these entrees they will process back to the palazzo for dinner and dancing. Before long the guests have broken up into knots of gossip and the occasional nervous laughter. Bembo's shrill voice can be heard every now and then disclaiming to Colocci on a play they had been subjected to in Naples. 'A bad play saved by a bad performance, fitter for a harlequinade than a romance. Lovely scenery, but the actors kept getting in the way of it, and the music. The music! My dears, I've heard Italians falling down stairs with their lyres making better arrangements. I'm quite serious; those Aragonese maestros wouldn't get a job in a Venetian brothel.'

Colocci guffaws with effected laughter. 'And that's saying something, I can tell you!'

From his position by the window, Hugh sees that, between small conversations, Pandolfo Petrucci and one of the thick bearded Baglioni's are heading slowly their way. 'Who is the man in black with Petrucci?' Hugh asks the prior.

Prior Battista squints in the general direction but is subtle. 'I do not know. Ambassador?'

Castiglione turns to get a better look, still sniffing his wine. 'Gian Paolo Baglioni, would be lord of Perugia if he could. He was a commander under Cesare Borgia. A cruel man you would do well to avoid. As with Petrucci, under that hard exterior beats a heart of stone.'

A moment later Castiglione turns again, this time to bow before Petrucci and Baglioni, smiling as if he'd never said or thought anything ill of them. A true ambassador. 'Most illustrious signori, our most sanguine hopes are all met to see you in health.'

Petrucci observes Castiglione's bowing form as it might have been something on his shoe. 'What a silver tongue you have, ambassador. You should come work for me.'

'As ever, your lordship is too generous.' But by now Petrucci, with his thumbs hooked confidently through his belt at the hips, has ceased to listen, focusing his attention rather on Hugh. The ambassador begins to introduce the prior and then Hugh. But before he has finished Petrucci speaks over him.

'I will speak to the Englishman alone. Can he speak Toscana, or will French or Latin do?'

Hugh bows stiffly and replaces his beret with a quivering and sweaty hand.

'His Italian is excellent,' Castiglione says, still straightening.

But before he has finished the older man cuts in over him. 'Then let him speak for himself if he has a tongue.'

'I am …' Hugh's mouth is dryer than he realised. He gives a limp and apologetic cough. 'I would be honoured to talk with you.'

Petrucci leads toward the far doorway where there are few people, and where the musicians will cover what he says. Baglioni stands near with his arms folded and takes a step forward. Other men move nearer, men who entered after the main party, men that Hugh does not recognise. He instinctively removes his grandfather's ring and drops it in his scrip. If there's to be a fight and he comes off worse, he's told Wilf to take it home to his mother. He counts the men. Four, five, six, none chosen for their looks or sense of humour. Hugh slips his eating knife up his sleeve, inwardly cursing the fact that he allowed the prior to convince him not to offend his hosts by attending functions fully armed.

Petrucci turns. 'Signor, how fortuitous that we should meet here.' His skin grey and moist, he isn't smiling now. 'I expect you know the reason.'

'I expect I do.' Hugh draws his hands together.

Petrucci looks at him steadily. 'Then you will understand why I wanted to speak to you before you returned to Rome. Surely you know that if Julius gets his hands on that Borgia gold, you'll not see a *scudo* of it in Rhodes. I don't know what he has promised you, but that is the truth.'

'I'm sure His Holiness will do what is right.'

'Only when he has exhausted all the alternatives. His conscience stops at his purse. But if you deal with me, I am in a position to offer certain assurances that you will get a great part of what you are seeking.' Petrucci smiles again. It is not a pleasant sight but this is as much of the velvet glove that he can feign. 'But you will have to work with me, share what you know, *if—*' He lingers like a terrier at a rabbit hole 'If you do know anything.'

Petrucci holds out his hand, but Hugh keeps a steady gaze on his eyes. He's not going to tell this man that he has nothing to go on, for that would risk not finding out what Petrucci knows. And yet he will not answer too quickly either, for the more he looks at the man, the more he feels Petrucci in his own head, reading his every thought. The hand is still being offered. Hugh still ignores it. He feels Baglioni's stare from the side.

The other men. The hand. Those eyes.

He'd sooner try to outrun and outwit a Turkish flotilla than out-guess those eyes. He feels his heart drumming on the walls of his ribs. The hand is still there. 'I don't think am in a position to help you.'

'Perhaps we could help you *into* a position where you could.' The older man lowers his hand. 'I have always found people give me what I want.'

'Are you threatening me?'

'Just sympathising.'

'You think I fear death? I am Hugh Erpingham.' He'll not take threats from anyone. There is only one language these Italian's speak. If Petrucci gives even the slightest gesture towards his men, he'll have a knife in his heart before he can say 'filthy lucre'.

'There are many things worse than death.' Petrucci continues to stare straight at him, if anything, more animated by the scent of a fight. 'For example, I hear auguries say that Vendramin is coming after you.' He then leans further forward with a delicious look coming all over his face, 'In fact, I have heard that even the White Cardinal takes an interest in you.'

'The White Cardinal?'

'Yes, no one knows who he is for he deals with great subtlety. My own people cannot tell me; my own son does not even know; no one does. Maybe he is not even a cardinal though I think he must be. And maybe he calls himself white because, well, you know, not even the devil is as black as he is painted. But he has marked your card, as has Vendramin.'

'Really. And how do you know?'

A spark ignites in the older man's eyes. 'When you've survived as long as I have, it pays to have more than just the two ears God gave you.'

Petrucci glances at Hugh's hand held purposively near his other sleeve. 'You want to kill me. Fine. I understand; people have always wanted me dead, people greater than you—like Cesare Borgia, even my father-in-law Nicolo Borghese, my own brother Giacopo, but you won't know them anyway because I am still alive and they are...' He lingers, smirks and almost shrugs. 'And I now have what was theirs.'

'Except this Borgia gold.'

Again, the return to a passive smile, the stone eyes. 'I think you misunderstand me. How can I explain it to you? You, you are foreign. You English, Franks and Germans do not love your cities as we Italians do. I have observed this. It is shameful. I pity you. Siena was once the pride of all Italy, the greatest republic, a beacon of light among the nations sunk into monarchy and the machinations of eunuch prelates. In those days Florence was nothing, but then came the plague in the days of my great grandfather. Half the city perished. Fifty thousand souls. Fortuna struck us sore, but—' His eyes spark back to life, like the fire that you might imagine kindling in the heart of an ancient dragon. 'Fortuna favours the bold, and it is our destiny to rise again. My family's destiny to make the republic great again. My destiny. It is not Borgia gold. It is Piccolomini gold, Sienese gold. It was meant for the raising of the republic, not the papacy, so don't cast your chips in with Julius. The church's days of power are numbered. There is a new spirit abroad in Europe—the rebirth of the mercantile republics, the ancient city states. And Siena will be among the brightest stars. That is why I say, work with me; don't make me your enemy. Why would you do that? You may not fear death as I do not, but you fear failure. I know you do. I see it in your eyes. You and I are much alike; success, victory for us is more than absolution. I promise you by the stones of our Palazzo dei Singoria, that if you serve me in this matter, I will not send you back to Rhodes empty handed as Julius will. And after we've recovered the gold, you can do with Vendramin whatever you like. I'm sure a man like you has orders. I can't imagine your grand master sent you here to attend masques and masses and to tickle the ears of cardinals.'

'And you are sure that Vendramin is still alive? You have evidence?'

'Oh, I know he is alive, and exactly where he will be at Easter.' Again, the smile, distended canine teeth in evidence. 'Come to Siena, and I'll prove it to you. He comes each year, then disappears into thin air as Apollonius did before Domitian.'

'How is he there? What do you mean?'

'Ah, I will tell you. I will... Hmmm.' His eyes are greedy as a spaniel's. 'I will bear to you some of what I know, as a token of good faith, and then we shall have an understanding, no?' The hand comes up once more. The eyes widen. 'Yes?'

'Very well.' Hugh takes the hand, even as the pit of his stomach churns and all his humours broil. 'Tell me.'

Petrucci's eyes return to arrow slits. He draws closer. 'For these last five years since our Pius III passed so tragically away, every Easter morning on the Piccolomini altar in our duomo, there appears a gold bar with a word on it. The bishop divides the value between the poor, so they say it is a miracle. They sleep outside the night before. The poor even come from Florence on Good Friday – from Florence! They want Pius canonised.'

'And these five words, are they the same word?'

'No. So far they say "I - was - murdered - by", and that is all.' Petrucci examines his nails disinterestedly. 'The mob grow anxious for the final instalments, eager to avenge the saint.' Petrucci removes a hand from about his belt.

Hugh observes the beads of sweat on it. 'Could be awkward,' Hugh says.

'Not for me, I assure you.' Petrucci raises his grey eyes level with Hugh's. 'Of course, it is Vendramin. He and the pope loved all that ancient drama. And it is certainly the Borgia gold, for he's gone to no trouble to obscure the mark. It's revenge he's after, to destabilise the republic. But it won't work; we'll catch him this year.'

He is a good liar, Hugh thinks. 'Hide in the cathedral overnight presumably?'

Petrucci shakes his head. 'No, Pius's nephew Giovanni is the new bishop and needless to say, he is eager to keep these supernatural visitations free from secular interference. He will not cooperate with the signoria, so we have to employ other methods which as yet have yielded nothing.'

'You think Vendramin and the bishop are colluding?'

'Of course, I suspected as much, but upon questioning, the bishop denies it, and I have no reason to suspect that a man of the cloth would lie to me.' The smile. 'Neither can I explain how Vendramin can enter a secure building with two thousand people looking on. But I thought you, a man of his own order, might fare better. You know...' The smile again. 'Set a wolf to catch a wolf and so forth, or is it a thief? I can't remember.'

SAN SERVERO, PURUGIA

Next morning, after morning mass, Hugh is out walking near the church of San Severo. He feels and looks ill again. He has just spent an hour trying *not* to look at Raphael's altarpiece, showing the judgement seat of Christ. It is becoming quite a settled theme. Right now, though, the prior is at his elbow, looking worried. 'What did you promise him?'

'Petrucci?'

'Yes, Petrucci, of course, Petrucci. I wish you had sought my council before making any pledges, if indeed you did. Where there is money, you always find – Well, all I mean is that the man is not to be trusted.'

They round a corner at a point where they can see above the city walls and right across the plains to distant hilltop villages and towns. Hugh walks to a low wall where the cobbled street starts to descend to the gate. He leans, then sits on it. He has forgotten Petrucci for other things have impressed themselves overnight on his mind, distending his already swollen conscience. Christ sitting in judgement, even in the most pleasing hues rendered by Raphael, has done nothing to alleviate his abiding sense of horror and foreboding. He has hardly slept again, his darker thoughts like hornets buzzing in and out. In and out. The prior sits next to him, carefully avoiding the pigeon muck. 'Well?'

'Well,' Hugh echoes. 'Well, it appears that our friend from Siena knows more than we do, though perhaps he doesn't know it, so I agreed not to help Julius, which I can't in any event because I don't know anything, and –'

'Yes, and?'

'And that I would visit Siena before Easter. He says he has proof that Vendramin is alive, and that he knows where he'll be at Easter.'

'Well, well.' The prior removes his cap and runs his fingers through the remaining white strands. 'How very curious. And what did he promise you in return?'

'Not to be his enemy, which apparently is quite an offer in itself, and also a share in the gold when found.'

'Oh, I'm sure the maths of division will look more favourable in his eyes after one of you is dead.' The prior casts his eyes about, wrinkles his nose. 'It is a fast game you play, my boy, a fast game.'

'In the absence of other clues, my options are limited.' Hugh's attention is diverted to a particular hilltop village.

'Yes, yes, I know that, Hugh, but Petrucci? Siena? I'd rather make my bed in a brood of vipers.'

Hugh is not listening now, for he feels a strange numbness in his senses, like a hopeful humming from his insides to his fingers. 'What town is that, in the distance under the hills, with what looks like large walls, or fortifications, or something.'

The prior follows Hugh's finger, squints and then opens his eyes wide with delight. 'That, my boy, is Assisi, the town of the great saint.'

Almost before the words are from his lips Hugh can hear the words, 'You must visit us at Assisi', the words of the strange little monk from the island of Procida. 'I should like to visit there, after the party has broken up.'

'Well, I suppose we could delay our –

'Alone. I would like to go alone.'

'Oh.' Awkward pause. Hugh registers it only after several blank seconds.

'Don't be offended. I will meet you in Rome before the rains. You said I need to sort myself out.'

'Yes, I see, my boy. Well, perhaps you will find a confessor there.'

Hugh attempts humour. 'You don't feel the need to follow me?'

'No, my boy. A man's search for salvation is a deeply personal thing.'

Hugh smiles faintly. That seems to please the prior. 'And I won't even send spies to follow you if you don't want. What? You don't think I have orders to keep you out of trouble? I do, but as long as we are all together, I don't think the enemy from within will move, and we need him to. Go to Assisi. See who goes with you, and make sure your man, the fat one, has his cross bow ready.'

LETTER TO FLORENCE FROM PERUGIA, 26TH OCTOBER, 1508

Most noble Signor M,

I write with grave news, though you may already have heard it. Our illustrious patron has saddled forth to speak with a certain knight behind your back. Did you know of this? Did he tell you? I begin to wonder whether he has grown restless, and has dispensed with our services, and verily, that we shall receive no part of the spoils.

Though it is far from me to advise a man such as you, yet I would humbly suggest that you press your claim. Remind him that he would have nothing without you, and that he should leave matters in your most capable hands. We might appeal to his piety, maybe even his sense of family or civic honour, though they may not hold as much sway over him as one would like. I am confident you will know the right course.

He and the knight spoke for some time on the evening last, and the discourse seemed to be agreeable to our patron, and well it might if he can get what he wants without sharing it.

I write in the assurance that you will know what to do. For myself, I will stay close to the knight. You may send your reply to your people in Rome.

Incidentally, I have heard today that the banker Jakob Fugger is to be made a knight of the Holy Roman Empire. We may suppose that the emperor has done this so that he will be well furnished with capital to prosecute the war that is surely coming against Venice. He should succeed where he twice failed earlier this year. With Fugger's backing from the north and Chigi's from the south, I cannot see Venice surviving this final assault. It would not surprise me that Julius, in his hatred for Venice, would not even shrink from calling on the French to join his crusade to dismember the Venetian state. I would be obliged if you had any more information about this matter.

I am as ever, et cetera.

ON THE ROAD TO ASSISI, 28TH OCTOBER, 1508

The supposed great parting turns out not to be so great an occasion as might have been expected. They part from under the loggia on the south wall, outside the Duomo of San Francesco after high mass. Each claim to look forward to the recommencement of their visitation of the Italian courts in the spring, while inwardly hoping that it won't come to that. If war comes with Venice, which it will, then they might all have better things to be getting on with. It is here that Hugh announces that he will not be returning straightaway to Rome. The wind blows the water out of the Fountana Maggiore, where it runs down the elegant carving and causes the horses to whinny. Servants and retainers hasten to their masters with embossed leather riding boots and travelling furs. No one but Pietro Bembo seems interested in what Hugh is proposing.

'A pilgrimage is an excellent idea, *mio cavalliere*. Let me come with you, and let us go barefoot as the friars minor did of old.'

Hugh examines his cloak. 'You have sins to atone too, signor? You do surprise me.'

Castiglione, standing near, seems amused by Bembo the penitent. 'It suits you, Pietro. I will attend as far as Assisi as it is on route to Urbino.' He tucks the long *liripipes* of his petit chaperon into the folds of his head covering. 'Well, almost on my way, but it would be worth the diversion for your company, and the sight of your bare feet.'

Bembo quips that Castiglione had better hurry with his *liripipes* before the wind causes them to take someone's eyes out, and did he know of the mania in Dante's day in Florence when one man, or perhaps woman, wore a petit chaperon with *liripipes* made from a full nine yards of cloth?

Hugh does not observe the man, but rather thinks on the implications of this latest twist: Bembo. *It is Bembo? Or is it Castiglione? It would be unpleasant to have to kill either of them, though worse to wake up for the last time singing to the tune of their lyre string*.

One hour later, they are a mile down the road to Assisi. Bembo, true to his word walks ahead of the horses, his white feet and legs picking over the lime silts, pebbles and potholes. Hugh and Castiglione are only just behind, the latter making encouraging remarks, like, 'Bembo, you look like a starved stork. Give up and get back on your horse. You don't fool anyone.'

'It is easy for you to mock, Baldasarre. How can a good man like you understand the chains of guilt that hang around men like myself and Fra Hugh, who have fallen? People like you say that guilt is the guardian of goodness, but really it shows you know little of the torture. I suppose that it is fitting that we prodigals should be mocked by the righteous older brothers as we seek a path to return from our pigsties. It is just, I suppose.' He glances back at them as he says this. Even now Hugh does not know how much the poet is in earnest, and how much is pure effect.

The ambassador obviously decides it is the latter. 'Cease this false comparison, Pietro, and do not insult our noble guest. Are we not all alike sinners who receive the same sacraments? Now get back on your horse, or we'll not make Assisi tonight and be forced to stay in some infested inn.'

'Same sins? All sinners alike?' He turns back to the road, and walks round a large puddle. Bembo theatrically raises a finger, about to speak like some eastern sage. 'Isaiah says that "some men's sins are scarlet, going ahead of them to judgment." How can these men show penitence before a just God?'

'If he is just, Bembo, he would not start that celestial banquet of eternity without you, legs and all. For where else will good men find entertainment enough to last the ages?'

The poet harnesses his humiliation as part of the purgation, using it also to discourse to his companions, the servants and any passing, on the theological difficulties of self-mortification.

'When divines spoke of the whip of penance, I dare say no one doubted that they were likening penance to the scourge of the soul.' He stops to remove a thorn from his foot. 'But I suppose also, as with all ideas that degenerate in abnormal ages, that it was only a matter of time before it became more than mere metaphor. Perhaps I will have my horse after all.'

'Don't take any notice of him, Hugh,' Castiglione says, securing the fine teal-coloured *liripipe* that has come loose again in the wind. 'He always has a bout of piety when he is near Assisi.'

'How could I not? And don't tell me, Baldassare, that you do not feel it too, *nostro delectissimo familiare, uonomi qualificati, galantuomo*, for I know you remember. How could we not?'

'What?'

'Feel awe, hope, sublime hope, to be near where Francis walked, composed verse and gave us back the world. How could a man *not* have hope again in the city where the camel passed through the eye of the needle? If I ever collect an anthology of Italian poetry, then I will make sure that Francis' *Laudates Creaturarum* is preeminent. I mean it, I will. He is the first hero of our new *Humanista*, the morning star of our *renaissance*—mercer turned poet, poet turned knight, knight turned mystic, mystic turned saint. God, even that is poetic! See what I mean? When I walk in Assisi, I feel even I could be different, as if anything is possible in this a place of smaller men and bigger skies. I suppose you know my mother wanted me to take holy orders? Have you ever noticed that our ultimatum for love, life and liberty is in direct inversion to our chastity, poverty and obedience? But you must assume the former *a priori* in order to have the latter, in order to give them up.'

This they discuss among themselves, agreeing that there was not really any religious order suitable for the poet. Bembo starts sighing in his saddle about what a cursed creature man is. 'We cannot enjoy the beauties of holiness, nor the pleasures of sin in this world. It produces misery in this life, and grotesque allegory in literature, which is probably worse. Have you read Guillaume de Guileville's *Pilgrimage of the Soul,* Hugh? No? Good. Don't bother. He has his pilgrim show repentance by plucking out his eyes and placing them in his ears. It is repellant. Even here at Assisi, like a dead mouse in a loaf of bread, the devil has perverted Francis's true humility and repentance with his fouler counterfeits. Did I ever tell you about Jacopone da Todi? I dare say you've never heard of him. I know Baldasarre has.'

Hugh, who has said virtually nothing since they left the city gates, says that he has not. In fact, his mind is as busy as a mill grinding in tandem. Firstly, the matter under discussion, but then alternately this more tumultuous revelation, that he rides today next to his own Judas, maybe even two of them.

'There is no reason for you to have.'

Hugh comes to. 'Pardon?'

'Read Jacapone's poetry. I'm not boring you, am I?'

'No, I am just a little tired. Please continue. Who was he?'

'A lawyer from Todi whose wife died when a building collapsed on her at a wedding. When her body was recovered, she was found to be wearing a hair shirt under her party clothes. This was but a few decades after Francis' death. Jacapone spent some years on his own in contempt of the world *and himself.*' This last word Bembo emphasizes. 'And was so mad that he was not even admitted in the Franciscans at first. When they eventually did, he so stank out the dormitory that they threw him in the privy, where he composed *'Launda, O jubilo de core ....* and then the next part I cannot remember the Latin, maybe something like *che fai cantare damore.'* Read it, Baldasarre?'

'I confess I have. I was made to when I was at Padua University.'

'Not to my taste either. It has an acrid stench about it – more decomposition than composition. Jacapone claims he saw a vision of Christ, who unleashed the most beautiful of scents around the cesspit, but he – trying to outdo Diogenes of Corinth – only asked for another, more horrible hell in which to purge his sins. His followers – yes, he had some if you can believe it – claimed that after the cesspit, Jacopone always had about him a perpetual light. All bollocks. The incident sparked a whole movement of flagellation, starting up there in Perugia and spreading all over Italy. They erected gallows to keep it out of Milan and Naples. And good riddance. Mind you, I better be careful of what I say. I hear the Knights do not discourage that sort of purgation. Have you tried it, Hugh?'

'Pietro, *caro*!' Castiglione says. 'You go too far.'

Hugh glowers across the bridles and flapping manes at Bembo from under his hood. 'The answer, signor, is yes. I have *tried* the lash for five hundred and twenty three days, tried it until my back was one big wound, until I couldn't feel anything. The Turks did not spare me in purgation, but it did nothing to purge my sins, nothing to lighten the burden, ease the conscience.' Hugh's head sinks again. *What can I tell him? Him who's only defence is a sanguine wit. He can sneer, but he cannot laugh. I can do neither. Shall I tell him that I abhor myself far more than his Fra Jacopone ever could? That I loathe my guttural being? That I sometimes awake to find I am trying to rip the veins in my wrists out with my teeth? You can't make a sonnet or a neat rhyming couplet out of that, not even in good Toscana.*

Bembo looks back, his face ashen. 'Forgive me, I had quite forgotten. I mean, I did not – Forget that now; forgive my lack of tact.' After a moment's respite, though, Bembo is back. 'But you have only proved my point then, I think you will agree. Francis has been willing to embrace the world in honour of its Creator, the same world that Fra Jacopone rejected, fearing it got in the way of self-annihilation. Francis saw the creation as good, if fallen and filled with fallen men, and all one needed was self-abasement – smaller men, and larger skies and so forth –

unlike Fra Jacopone, who didn't care how bad the world got, the worse the better, because it meant more compensation to the saints. When the Franciscans split between the Relaxed and Spirituals, the Spirituals made party with the Colonnas. And when the castle of Palestrina was raised, Boniface VIII had Jacopone held in a dungeon for a number of years.'

'Ah', says Castiglione, ever the ambassador trying to insure concord. 'So, he got his – what did you call it – "more horrible hell", and Italy had peace. Now why don't we stop before the Ponte San Giovanni and get some wine and olives? I know a place with a fine view across the Tiber that keeps a good fire and sells very fine char-grilled trout and pike, I can recommend it.'

OSPEDALE SAN FRANCESCO, ASSISI, 28TH OCTOBER

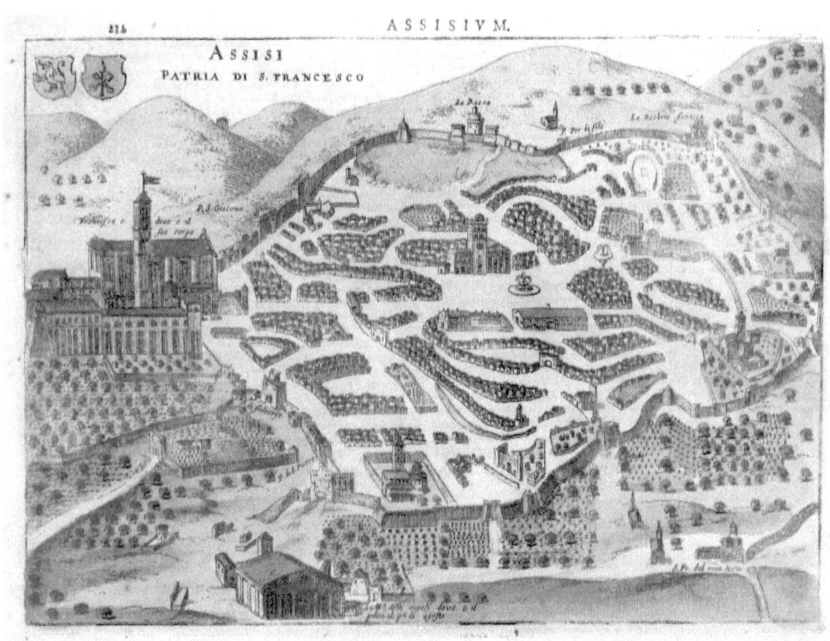

Enjoying the hospitality of an order that has renounced worldly riches is a gamble. They will share what they have, but if you stay with the *Spirituali* faction, that might be a share in watery herb broth. Aware of Bembo's new ascetic bent, Castiglione has led them to make enquiry with the Relaxed Franciscans. While the echoes of vespers waft through the corridors, Hugh and the others are simply but comfortably lodged in a cloistered hospital behind the basilica.

After supper, they attend compline in the basilica. It is cool, dark, and fragranced with incense and the prayers of pious men. Hugh stands in the nave, the others to his right. While the melancholic canticles and antiphons reverberate about the arches and inside his soul, Hugh marvels at Giotto's frescoes. It is too dim to get any more than glances at the clean lines, the robust forms, but it is enough to make him resolve to be up at first light to see them when the purest of the sun's rays will be pouring through the east window. He is near the fresco of Francis casting the devils out of Arezzo. Black beings crawl and fly from the rooftops, their mouths alive with the dark chatter than he knows so well. Augustine said that evil was *privatio boni* – the privation or absence of good; the negation of being; a derivative entity in business for itself; parasitic on creation. It is why Dante's Satan is so banal, such a non-character. *I know that, I understand. But to shake hands with a devil like Petrucci is to also know that evil is a power too. But who I am to catechise?* Hugh exhales quietly, and shudders. *Oh, to believe in miracles.*

After the doxology and procession of the friars, Castiglione asks, 'Well gentlemen, shall we retire to my quarters for some reading and refreshments? My men have been into town for provisions.'

'Very tempting, ambassador,' Hugh says, 'but there is somewhere I must go this evening. You go on without me. Perhaps I will join you later.'

Castiglione and Bembo leave via the steps to the lower basilica, saying they will venerate the saint's relics first. Hugh lingers in the stillness of the nave, where now only five or six widows kneel, whisper or walk about in their weeds. Hugh follows one such woman who processes along the frescoes with a candle, muttering *Ave*s to herself. She stops to mourn with the other devotees at the fresco depicting Francis's death. Women crowd the coffin, their faces lined in grief. One looks like Hugh's mother, another, his widowed aunt from Aylsham, the one who always reminded him, '*Momento mori*. Remember, you must die. Perhaps it will be this night.' Another breath, another shudder. It is not pain he fears, but what comes after. *Momento mori.*

When he has left what he thinks a decent amount of time, Hugh descends the steps to the lower basilica, then down again to the crypt where the lights are fewer, the air damper, the incense thicker. Voices murmur somewhere above him, footsteps of three men, the creaking of a door. Francis is tranquil beyond his grate. Three fat candles keep a vigil before the relics, but no one else is in sight. Hugh slowly removes the Colhona from its sheath and holds it tightly under his cloak. It is comfortingly weighty. His palms grease with anticipation. He'll not be caught wanting if his assailant comes at him from one of the many shadowy arches down here in the bowels of the earth. He nods toward the relics, to the knight-turned-mystic, promising inwardly to come back tomorrow if he is still alive.

He retraces his steps up to the lower basilica, keeping an ear out for that telltale echo of boot leather on the glazed tiles. Though he strains, he hears nothing. He makes a circuit of the lower basilica, walking quietly but deliberately into the side chapels even though he can barely see his own feet as he stumbles on the worn steps. At every corner he resists the urge to raise his left hand in defence. Saint Catherine, Saint Mary Magdalene, Saint Nicolas, side chapels to silent saints. Nothing.

He tries a door to the right of the altar. Locked. The only way is back up. He passes the altar and starts his ascent to the upper basilica. By the time he reaches the top he hears it, the echo of quiet steps. Someone has been waiting, unseen. He does not pause to listen, even though it is hard to be sure above the pounding of his heart. He passes up the middle of the nave without looking back, heading straight for the great east door, which is slightly ajar.

The widows have gone, scuttled away like black beetles before the advance of night. He hears the steps again. He will not look round. Let them come. *I am not afraid of any man living. I am Hugh Erpingham.* He speaks these words internally in between tight breaths and tightening muscles. When he turns to pass through the door, he chances a sideways glance and discerns an unstill shape among the shadows of the northern nave wall.

Outside, Hugh smells only night air, no scent of a hired thug or a pomandered gentleman waiting nearby. He slips into the night, turning right along outer covered walkways and down some stairs. The steps follow. Away from the church Hugh adjusts his cloak to the left, allowing his sword arm and de Blanchfort's blade some freedom in case of an ambush. There is no moon tonight. The clouds pass above, and the cawing of ravens can be heard. Myrtle and cypress trees toss and bow in the wind. Hugh heads down to the undercrofts where their horses were left earlier. He observes the silhouette of a caped figure with a large hat at the end of the cobbled track by the stables. An unnatural bulge protrudes from the cloak: a crossbow.

Hugh approaches in the shadows. When he is within ten yards the caped figure turns, raising the bow. 'Who's that? Is that you? Show yourself.'

'Yes, it's me.'

'Shit, you made me piss myself. Well, nearly.'

'All right, now point that somewhere else, before you do me an injury. Can you see him?'

'See who?'

'Quietly now. At the far end.'

Wilf strains his eyes back down the track. 'It's bloody dark; I can't see anything.'

'Never mind. He is there.' Hugh grabs Wilf by the cape. 'Let's go.'

They walk swiftly away toward another set of steps that lead down through a steep-sided olive grove toward the lower barns used by the friars for olive storage and oil production. This time they hear no steps following because of the wind casting about the brittle olive leaves. Hugh can feel the darkness here. It feels like home, that knife-edge place between the worlds of the living and dead.

Minutes pass.

The billowing of boughs, the bending of branches, the rushing by of clouds on their way to the Marches, to Urbino, Pescaro, then across the Adriatic toward the Turks. More olive leaves rush across the cobbles; more insects chitter and crackle in the dying litter of another season until the faintest step is heard in the shadows, the velvet tread of someone stepping toe first. A twig cracks, and Hugh makes out a shadowy figure sliding along the wall before disappearing into that part of the terrace where the darkness is most profound. Presently the figure emerges in the grey light further along the wall, moving like a cat. Hugh strains his eyes from his position in a small end window of a byre at the far end of the terrace. The shadow comes within fifty yards, then thirty. It is a man for sure. As he draws closer, the crickets become silent, and the air becomes thicker and thicker with imminence.

Hugh moves back from his window as the spy reaches the byre. He has left the lattice open on the ground with a rush light lit to attract his prey. It works. The spy approaches the window right under Hugh. Hugh steps on the ledge of the hayloft then jumps. Air rushes in his ears for just a moment before his full weight sends the spy to the hard stone of the threshing floor. The spy doesn't cry out or put up any resistance. He's out cold.

Hugh calls for Wilf, and they drag the body into the byre. Wilf lights a taper and holds it close. 'It's that gobshite Bembo, sneaking *dago.*'

While Hugh is still processing what this might mean, he has Wilf and Pico hood Bembo with a hessian sack, and tie him to a chair next to the olive press. 'Secure his hand on the press. It's time we ask our friend some questions.'

Two minutes later Bembo comes to with a sudden jolt. He gasps, as if his lungs are struggling for air under the hessian. 'What is this? Where am I? Who is holding my arm?'

'You are my guest, signor,' Hugh says calmly but coldly. 'My man is holding your hand in the trough of an olive press.'

'What? Hugh?' He pauses then cries out, 'Hugh, thank God. Unbind me.'

'Why were you following me, Pietro?'

'I, well, I was worried for you, I was –'

'You will tell me who you work for. In fact, you will tell me all you know about that for which I am seeking.'

'What? Are you mad, Hugh? I am not working for anyone. I've no idea what you are talking about. Come, enough foolery. Take this hood off.'

'I am not sure that you quite appreciate what is at stake here, and how far I am prepared to go to fulfill my commission.'

Bembo attempts a jocular grunt. 'Are you threatening me?'

'Just sympathizing.' He learnt that from Petrucci. Hugh nods to Pico who pushes the iron bar which rolls the huge wheel of stone.

Hugh's voice is casual. 'Is it Vendramin?'

'Look, Hugh, be sensible. I don't know what fanciful ideas are in your head, or what anyone has told you, but I know nothing of Vendramin or the gold, or anything.'

'Who mentioned gold?'

'You did.'

'No, I merely spoke of things that I seek.'

Silence, followed by the sound of swallowing.

'Are you going to hurt me?'

'Signor, I am probably going to kill you.' Hugh lingers on the word, observing the hessian head bow slightly in recognition. 'What? Do you think the world will miss a middling poet and literary critic? You have set yourself against the good of Christendom in opposing me, and do you expect to receive mere penance when finally caught? Ten *Pater Nosters* and five *Aves*? Should there not be hell to pay?'

Bembo gives a weak breath of laughter. 'I thought you liked my poetry.'

'Some of it.' Hugh steels himself. *Is this a ploy?*

Bembo sounds apologetic. 'Castiglione says it is too brittle, overly conscious of form, too little sentiment. Takes one to know one, I suppose.'

After a few moments of recollection Hugh says, 'Signor, if you can convince me how a man like yourself, a man of letters who has born witness to a world of noble feeling, can become a vassal of darkness, then I will let you live.' But even as Hugh says it, he does not believe there can be such an answer, or such a reason to extend mercy.

There pass yet more moments of silence before Bembo finally says in a slow, steady voice, 'That is very noble of you, Hugh, very noble. I wish that I could live so uprightly, so certainly as you do. In your world of clean lines, I surely could. But I cannot do all you ask. Yes, I will tell you what brought me to this state. That I will do gladly before you dispatch me to judgment, but as to divulging the monster that holds me in vassalage, I would not risk his vengeance on my extended family for a hundred lives. I would rather die at your hand.'

'You talk about it as if I were going to give you a good death, a clean Roman death. I mean to have that man's name and his city, and I will use this olive press to break every bone in your body to get it. And then worse things still, don't forget, *caro,* I know about pain.'

At this point Hugh gets Pico to push the stone wheel around the limestone trough. The very sound of grating and snapping twigs causes Bembo to cry out. Hugh calls a halt.

'Please don't make me, Hugh. For the love of God and the Virgin, don't make me.'

Hugh bends close. 'I need that name, and I will give you until tomorrow night to rethink your position.'

COURTYARD OF THE OSPEDALE SAN FRANCESCO, ASSISI, 29TH OCTOBER

'I am sure he meant you no slight, Baldasarre,' Hugh says, bright and crisp as this new day, 'but you know these poets are a strange breed. Perhaps his muse took him into the fields in the small hours so he might contemplate Saint Francis's birds, or compose verses to the sun.'

'I think not, my friend, I think not.' The ambassador smiles while adjusting his riding boots. 'Remember, I've known him too long.'

'Yes,' Hugh says meaningfully, gazing across the courtyard toward a line of penitent monks waiting outside the confessional. 'He often seems to be carrying some dark secret from his past. I saw you once refer to it privily when you were on the galley in the doldrums before we reached Ischia.'

'Ah.' Castiglione straightens and clicks his fingers for the horse to be brought. 'The *Bellum Intestinum*. Yes, he was cross with me for mentioning it. I didn't think anyone had noticed. He is very sensitive and private you know, behind that façade.'

'What could a man like that have to be so sensitive about?' Hugh speaks while pretending to be more interested in what is under the fingernails of his right hand. It doesn't work; an ambassador knows all the tricks.

'*Caro*, we all have our secrets. The sins of youth are many and various.' Castiglione mounts his mare, swinging his right leg over the leather saddle with grace. While arranging his reins, he adds, 'Perhaps it is as Polybius said, "There is no witness so dreadful, no accuser so terrible as the conscience that dwells in the heart of every man." Ask him, perhaps he will tell you. Arrivederci, caro.'

'Arrivederci.'

Touchez, ambassador. Don't worry, I will.

CONFESSION TIME

An hour later Hugh is walking near the house of the Franciscan Spirituals in the lower town. It is adjacent to the Ash Gate where the refuse is burnt and lepers pick over scraps. The order's three-story house is set into the town wall to the right of the gate. Incongruously, Hugh hears lute music drifting from an upper window on the miasmic vapours. He has sought this place out, without the escort of Wilf and Pico, who are still sleeping off the night's work.

He casts a weary but sharp eye about the street, half expecting to see the man he seeks. There are no shops here, no market, no one hawking their wares, for at this end of town there is no money, only the very poorest, those fallen into disrepute, or great debt, or leprosy, along with the Franciscan brothers, and those kind enough, or brave enough, to venture down the long and winding steps to give alms. Hugh tightens his gut, for the smell of unwashed humanity and voided bowels seems to attack him from every angle, sinking deep into his lungs. He steps past a sleeping drunkard, face down in his own vomit, and then again over the detritus that litters the path toward the gate. Still no sign.

Outside the gate lazar houses cluster on the outer town wall. Rubble, misshaped timbers and broken tiles, they are a tattered assemblage of all that the town has cast off, and in them dwell what the world has cast off. Hugh observes the hunched figures, half dead, picking over the rubble nearby like ragged crows. What lives are these? *Have they sinned more even than me to be thus?* And who would voluntarily choose this, *this* place and *this* life above all places and lives? The destitute serving the sick, the merely poor, or worse, the self-made indigent. For what are these brethren seeking absolution for by such lives? *Or what can they see that I cannot?* These ragged friars and these Poor Clares going about their work with scant bread, bandages and news of a better world. He casts a cynical eye about the place and recognizes the squat man he seeks, Fra Paolo Todesco.

Hugh approaches, careful to avoid contagion. He steps among them, unspotted, moving closer to the group of friars until Paolo finally sees him. At first his eyes betray shock, fear even, but soon after he approaches Hugh with an open hand. 'My foreign friend from the latrine! You actually came. I thought you would.' He glances toward the gate. 'Are you here in a private capacity or with the pope's people?'

'You knew about them?'

'All Italy knows of your coming, even us poor friars.' His doughy eyes turn sheepish, and he shrugs apologetically. 'That day on the island of Procida I could not but notice the scars on your wrists, and when I heard that the great English knight who had been killed by the Turks was once more alive and visiting the court on Ischia. I put two and two together.'

'I see, Fra Paolo, that you are not so simple as you claim.'

Paolo turns down his bottom lip. 'Then you will forgive my modesty.' He scratches the thick hair on the back of his neck, grinning and looking back toward the gate. 'So, you have not brought the entourage?'

'Just my own servants.'

'I see.'

Hugh adds, 'We are returning to Rome for the winter, and I was passing down from Perugia.'

Paolo takes Hugh's arm and murmurs confidentially, 'And you are still searching for treasure?'

Hugh does not answer at first, for he feels this little man, who by rights should be afraid, is once more actually mocking him. 'Indeed.'

Paolo's dark eyebrows rise with delight. 'Good, then you have come to the right place.' He casts his left hand about the shanties. 'For these poor are the treasures of Assisi, the meek who will inherit the earth.'

Hugh follows his hand with an indignant stare. He didn't come down here to be lectured, to have Sunday gospels quoted at him. But what has he come for? He hardly knows, so he nods stiffly but says nothing.

'Look, Fra Hugh. You don't mind my using your first name, we are all brothers, *petit frere, non*? Good. Well, you mustn't take this the wrong way, but I have someone I wanted you to meet, Fra Francesco i Bisognoso. He runs the work here among the lepers. That is him over there with Giacomo. Come, come.'

Hugh follows the little friar toward the left-hand side of one of the shanties, where an older Franciscan inspects the wounds of a yet more elderly leper. He touches the man.

'Ah, Fra Francesco, I have brought my friend, the English knight to meet you. Fra Hugh de Erpingham of Rhodes.'

'Honoured I'm sure,' Fra Francesco says, neither turning, nor bothering to look up at the stranger, but adding curtly, 'Hold this for me, would you?' He hands Hugh some postulant scraps of bandages that Hugh would not have taken for the smell, only he is wearing gloves, so he does.

Hugh observes the wizened, grey bearded face: the many lines with accompanying deep veins that speak of life out of doors, the two large moles near his left nostril, the white line on the bridge of the nose where it has been broken, perhaps more than once, the sharp eyes observing a singularly unpleasant and cankerous wound.

'It'll need washing and salve. Paolo, fetch me some wine to irrigate this wound, and some henbane to relieve poor Giacomo's pain. Yes, don't you worry my old friend, we'll pack it with honey and cobwebs too when we have cleaned it up, and next time you should come to us sooner. But we old men are so stubborn, so independent, no?'

Behind his veil, Giacomo chuckles and mumbles something incomprehensible to Hugh through toothless gums. Fra Francesco draws his head closer to the wounded foot and proceeds to adeptly remove cankerous skin and fragments of thorns from it, all the while speaking with Hugh. 'From Rhodes, are you? I suppose you still follow the Spaniard di Vigo's practice out there: cauterize wounds like this with boiling oil. Barbaric, unnecessary. Anyway, never mind that, what brings you here?'

'My commission is to unite the Italian states, and Europe against the Turks, for they are at present assembling an armada at the arsenals of Gallipoli.'

'Is that so?'

'Yes. I have seen it.'

'You have been to Gallipoli? In one of your ships? Hold still, Giacomo. I almost have it.'

'No, as a guest on one of theirs.'

'Ah, as a guest. I see. At the oars. Now we get nearer.' Fra Francesco draws closer still to the wound, screwing up his face to focus more clearly. ‘So, they have ships, and we must fight these ships, annihilate these infidels. I suppose you know Saint Francis was once a knight, a knight like you?

‘I have heard that.’

‘When leaving for a war he told his parents. “I will win fame and come back a great prince.” The prick.’

Hugh grunts. *What was the man’s point?*

‘Francis of the fine clothes, Francis the troubadour poet, Francis of the grand gestures, the lavish parties.’ The friar wipes his forehead with a coarse and soiled sleeve. ‘And you know, I suppose, that he was captured and chained by the Perugians as you were by the Saracens.’

‘I have heard that, too.’ Hugh hasn’t, but he hates these old men who know everything and go on and on.

‘Yes. Languished there, but it did not break him. He was a hard case for all his lavish clothes and verse. They say he even cheered his fellow prisoners, listened to those to whom God himself would not listen, so they say. But it was a sickness that finally broke him, sometime after his release. Sickness has broken many, Giacomo, but not you, eh, you old rascal?’ Again, some garble from the leper. ‘But God spared Francis through it, and he became God’s man. Never went fighting again. He went on crusade to the east but only to persuade the sultan to become a believer in the true God. Bet you never thought of that, did you? Better to make Christians than destroy Muslims. I know you, knight. You’re of the school of Pedro III of Aragon who sacked Menorca, shipped forty thousand peaceful Muslims in chains to the slave markets of North Africa. I can see it in your eyes. So much for turning the other cheek. And where is Paolo with that wine?’

Hugh glanced about and folded his arms in irritation. ‘I think, signor, that we shall just have to disagree on politics.’

‘Ah, yes, of course. You think people like Francis were too simple to understand politics perhaps? You are naïve because you are young, that’s your problem. But Francis was too skeptical to be a politician. That’s why he became a mystic. Ah, Paolo, there you are finally. I thought you'd never come. Let me have the wine. This young blood thinks we'd be more effective dabbling in the real world, in politics!'

'Not what I said,' Hugh murmurs.

The old friar turns his back to Hugh with a face twitching with sardonic mirth. 'You know something, signor, to those great practical men of his day Francis appeared no more than a thin, brown, skeleton leaf dancing before the wind; but in truth he *was* the wind, I tell you. Yes, he was the wind as history has shown.'

'That's not at all what I said.' Hugh hands the bandages to Paolo, who carries them away. The bastard is smiling again.

'It was implied,' Francesco says. 'Don't worry; as you can see, I'm not offended.'

Hugh is about to answer when the man turns to look at him. He is smiling too.

'So, you're here to rattle your lance, raise taxes. I bet Julius loves you. Anything else? Sit, sit.'

Hugh sits on a piece of limestone big enough to have been a corner stone. He gathers his cloak from touching the ground or straying too close to the leper and gazes momentarily across the wide valley. Paolo shouts over his shoulder while leaving, 'Yes, Fra Erpingham, from Asissi you can see the whole world.'

Before Hugh can reply he hears the gruff, accusing voice of the old friar. 'Anything else?'

'What?' What does he mean? Perhaps Paolo's been talking to him about our meeting in the latrine. 'Yes, as a matter of fact I am also here looking for someone.'

'Why?'

'To talk to him.'

'Is that all?'

'He has something I need, uh, we need.'

'I see, so more than talk to him. Yes, I see.' Francesco starts to pour the wine on the wound, and then to re-examine it as the red liquid runs out from the fissures of skin and tissue. 'Argh, sometimes we cannot see the source of infection until the wound is cleaned a little. Giacomo, you are a fool. This would have mortified if you had delayed coming to me any longer, foolish old man.' He speaks to Hugh. 'Do you know Aesop's fables?'

Immediately, at the word Aesop, a drawer opens in Hugh's mind. He remembers the geometric designs by Pietro Cavallini in Perugia from a few nights before, and the representations of Aesop's fables, that queer feeling he had, as indeed he has now, as if the name, or this meeting, were portentous. 'Aesop?' He repeats through a dry throat.

'Yes, Aesop. He says there was once a man who went out to the country telling all he met that he was going to hunt a lion. He tells the farmer, he tells the shepherd and so on, "Today, I am going to hunt a lion, yes, a lion." He is very proud, and they are very impressed by his courage. Until at last, he comes into the deep forest where he sees a woodcutter at work. "Hello, my friend" says the woodcutter, "and what are you doing so far from the town, down here in the darkest part of the woods?" "I am going to hunt a lion," the man says, to which the woodcutter replies, "Then you are in luck, for there is a lion just over there, in the next glade." At this news the hunter's face turns pale as a ghost. 'But I only wanted to hunt a lion; I didn't want to actually find one." It is an interesting story, no?'

'It is.' Hugh can feel his left eye beginning to twitch. The friar isn't watching him so he closes both and clenches his fists. 'And I suppose you are a woodcutter who knows where I might find a lion?'

'Hah, very good, signor, very good. Yes, perhaps I do work deep in the woods far away from safety. Perhaps I do.' Fra Francesco irrigates the wound again with more wine while he continues. 'And perhaps you search for someone like Isis searched for Osiris, when all the while he was dead. Have you thought of that? Then again, sometimes even our searches deceive us. Those earlier pagans never went to search the woods expecting to really meet a nymph, but merely in the hope of meeting one. There is a difference. But the darker sort of heathen did go to the deeper woods expecting to consort with demons, and did indeed find something, for Satan always keeps his appointments. Remember that, and even his promises if you must know. You say you are looking for one thing. Perhaps you are. Perhaps you don't know what you're looking for. I never met a mouse looking for a cat, you know. It might be something else entirely.'

'I see.' *Enough sophistry, please.* Hugh keeps his eyes and fists tight shut. 'But you still have not told me where I might find this lion. Are you a woodcutter or not?'

'Me? No, I'm a leper who binds the wounds of other lepers.' Francesco rests a broad hand on the leper's shoulder. 'But we can't bind wounds, Giacomo, if you don't show them. If you wrap them up in festering rags, they will canker as doth sin unconfessed.'

Hugh folds his arms. 'I haven't asked you for help.'

'Hah!' Francesco snaps back. 'And I already have quite enough lepers to see to. No one is forcing you.'

Hugh stands as if to go, but the friar, with a tone less familiar, more tender, and almost bordering on contrite, says, '*You* came to Assisi.'

'I was passing.'

'This is not the sort of place one passes, friend.'

Hugh pauses, and slowly sits back down. *Is this what the grace of God looks like? Shit. God help us all then. The magister, and de Blanchfort, even Prior Battista said he should find a good confessor. Bet they never imagined anything like this.* Hugh observes the lice in Giacomo's cloak. How at home they appear. *The things we carry! Why not? Why not this old friar?* A deep shudder runs through the very fabric of Hugh's inner being, as if his whole-body groans under a burden of lice in his soul.

Fra Francesco uses a stick, on Giacomo's wounded foot, to tease out the remaining splinters. He does not seem to be listening at all. Hugh does a roll call through the ranks of his excuses, his layers of defense. He reaches for words like Adam did his fig leaf, but nothing comes, only, 'I... I cannot sleep.'

'Something on your conscience perhaps.'

'Yes.'

'Some particular sin perhaps.'

Pause. 'Yes.'

‘And you want to confess, find forgiveness, rest, peace, whatever.’

Hugh cannot answer directly but murmurs an affirmation while curling his toes in his boots. He is not aware that his gloved right hand is rubbing at the scars on the left wrist, or of the shuddering in his right leg, or even the rapid blinking – all he can think of now is that cave, and the form of a man without breath.

‘Confess then.’ A moment passes with no answer. The friar changes tack. ‘When did this happen?’

‘Last year, I do not know the day.’ Hugh can hear the words, but it is as if someone else is speaking them.

‘When you were a guest of the Turks?’

‘Yes.’

‘Ah, I see, *ora et labora*. Pray and work.’ The old man pauses, looks to the ground pensively then adds, ‘And what did you do? Come man, what? Speak it out.’

‘I had been there for some months. In truth I do not know how long. Sometimes we were days, weeks at the oars, sometimes weeks in a cave under some citadel on the coast. They kept us like dogs, worse than dogs. There was another knight, an Almain. I did not know him, but he was of our order. A big man and strong, only newly captured. We were so weak, and when the guards brought food he would drive us away, beat us down. He would eat it all. We were starving to death.’

‘And you took vengeance?’ Francesco turns. Hugh nods. ‘What did you do?’

‘Some held his legs, some his arms. They were just peasants turned sailors; they obeyed my lead. We, all of us, were starving.’

‘What did *you* do Hugh?’

‘I, I took a wet garment and covered his face, kept my weight on him until the life went from him. I killed a nobleman from my order.’

‘Nobleman! What is aristocracy except a priesthood without a god. You killed a man made in God’s image! You murdered in cold blood; you killed a Christian, a man sworn to the same order as you, and you led other ignorant souls to do it with you. That is what you did. And is this your sin?’

'Yes, but no.'

'There is more to confess of this?'

'Hmm.' Hugh starts to twist his head left then right, then left again, as if he could shake something from his very mind. Eventually, he catches his head between his wrists and presses them deep into his temples. 'Help me, friar, for God will not. If it were only murder, I could face a respectable confessor on Rhodes. If it were only that, I could face God himself. Perhaps I could.'

He has Francesco's full attention now. The friar, who has been kneeling forward now eases back and straightens up. 'What then? What else is there to confess?'

Hugh, still clamping his head, starts to inhale noisily, and then to hiss like a pot under pressure. He shakes it left, then right. 'I cannot. I cannot.'

'What? You think a man should deserve to be forgiven before he can be? If it is deserved, it is not mercy. Can a man even deserve a sunset? Come now, confess to God.'

'God will not hear me. Why do you think I'm here? I am in torment.'

'You are English, aren't you? Do you not know your own poets? Your countryman Langland has written it well enough: "Hell has already been harrowed." God does not need your misery as payment. Now come, confess to God this thing.'

Hugh releases his head and stares at the friar with bloodshot eyes. 'I. Can. Not. Some sins cannot ever be pardoned. Don't you see? Don't you see?' In a moment he is on his feet and stumbling back into the town, staggering like a drunk. *It was a mistake to come here.*

THAT NIGHT

That night after vespers a creeping mist sits thick in the olive groves below the basilica. It is cold enough to freeze. Above it, the stars wander in their wide trackless path through the heavens. A good enough night for dirty business. Below, in the byre, with his hand under the olive press, Signor Bembo sobs like a baby, pleads like a true penitent.

Twenty-four hours hooded, without water have done their work. He is softening. In a fit of mercy Hugh has allowed his non-writing hand to be tried first, for the sake of his art. Wilf has the grim task of holding it to the stone with Hugh while Pico operates the bar, which pushes the stone closer and closer toward the poet's quivering digits. Hugh coolly advises him not to scrunch his fingers up into a fist to delay the fateful moment, but rather to spread them forth. 'Then they will not break in so many places, and one day may even be used again. If you survive.' The great stone rolls on with the sound of stray, dry olive twigs splintering under the tremendous weight.

In the end the man breaks down and confesses at the moment the stone first touches his flesh. The sack over his head, already soaked with sweat, shudders and cries aloud with heaving sobs. 'I will! I will tell you! Tell you everything, but please!' Sobs predominate. Steam rises from the sacking, caught by the light of the flickering olive oil lamps. 'Please no more, no more!'

'Who do you work for?' Hugh wastes no time. He stays Pico's hand for the moment, and grabs Bembo by the windpipe, shouting, 'Who?'

'Pandolfo Petrucci.'

Petrucci? If he had said the pope, Hugh would have believed it, after all it was Julius who assigned Bembo to come in the first place, but Petrucci? Why then did Petrucci come himself to Perugia and reveal his hand so publicly? He is not telling the whole truth. 'Why? For money?' The sack is silent. Hugh shakes it, and then says, 'No, it wouldn't be money with someone like you, signor. It is something he knows about you, some sin, some crime. It is for your blessed reputation, your immortal name, that you spy on me. Isn't it? You are being bribed, threatened, you implied as much last night.'

The sack angles up as if Bembo wants to cast a baleful eye at his tormentor. 'If I confess, it must be to you only, and you must swear not to tell.'

'I think you have misunderstood your position. A man on trial for his life cannot demand terms. Tell me quickly what I ask, or we shall *press* you for it.'

After a moment's hesitation, the sack sinks slowly. 'Very well. I will tell you and then you will know what brought me to this state. It was the god Amor.'

'Oh please!' Hugh slaps his thigh with a great guffaw.

'Is it so hard to believe? Perhaps it is. But I was once Love's man, Hugh, and it was my undoing. Too much Provencal poetry and Burgundian wine. God, it was like being chained to an idiot.'

'You a lover? The self-proclaimed Platonist, a son of Ovid after all? You are so full of surprises that I wonder you didn't find your character in Boccaccio's *Decameron*, just to put me off the scent.' Hugh gives Pico the nod, and he begins to roll the press.

'No, Hugh, wait! I swear every word is the truth.' A half-attempted laugh turns into to a parched cough. 'But now you mention it, Boccaccio has his abbess say, "It is impossible to defend oneself against the promptings of the flesh," and "Against the force of love all men, whether pages, princes, are equally helpless." Oh, how I remember it!' Bembo's speech is fast, frigid, almost hysterical in fear. 'I was not prepared for it. I was a fool; reckless, but not damnable, I think.' Cough, cough. Stupid, nervous laugh. 'You've read it all, haven't you, Hugh? In the *Decameron* a ghost returns from purgatory to say that such sexual peccadilloes don't count for much down there and even pious Dante has the *Fedele d'Amore* Paolo Malatesta only in the upper circles of Hell. So, I plead with you, signor –'

'Shut up with your endless prating, Bembo. It doesn't matter here. Now explain, or I'll send you lower, by God I will.'

'Five years ago, I enjoyed the patronage of the Duke of Ferrara, and more than just his patronage. His wife was a very persuasive –

'Lucrezia Borgia! You conducted a liaison with the pope's daughter under the roof of her husband!'

'God forgive me, yes, like Catullus and Lesbia. I was a madman.'

'Signor Bembo, I confess that I misjudged you entirely. I had you down for a melancholic, or at least an ascetic.' Hugh slaps Bembo's thigh again and let his hand rest there for a moment. 'But explain to me why this would drive you into a life of ruin. Surely a little gallantry in a poet is praiseworthy in this country?'

'Do not mock me, Hugh. I was hardly a knight devoting himself to a lady, more a Turk looking at a Circassian he could not afford. Was it Aristarchus who thought that our bodily passions contributed to melancholia? I think it was. I was a sane man once but then courtly romance and amorous intrigue undid me. God, she was a thorn under my skin, I tell you. The poetry I could handle, it was the prose I was unprepared for. She told her brother Cesare, and I only narrowly escaped being torn asunder by horses by her husband'

'Cesare blackmailed you? But he is dead.'

'No, it is another. Even worse.'

'I see, and how did the blackmailer find out?' Hugh won't use Petrucci's name because he is sure Bembo is lying.

The sack shakes woefully from side to side. 'I know not, but because of my talents, my access to various courts I was useful to him. It was I who escaped you in Rome, we came to abduct the navigator. Petrucci knew he was the only link. He had someone working for him at the priory that gave us information, left a side door open.'

'Do you know who?' No wonder the knights sent before him had no chance.

'No, I received my orders by letter.'

'And the man I killed?'

Slight pause. 'No one. A hired burglar. His name was Mario something.'

For a poet, he's a bad liar. 'Did you take the navigator, at the Domus Aurea?'

'What? No. I was there at table with you. You brought him *there?*'

'Never mind that now. What about his fellow conspirators, the other sailors who were killed? Was that you?'

'I'm no murderer, Hugh!'

'But you are a man stealer. Tell me what you know of those other sailors.'

‘The ship owner, the one that was crucified on his mast in Cittevechia, that was Petrucci’s people. The Sienese do things like that. The other sailor, I don’t know, perhaps that was Vendramin.’

‘And where is he?’

‘I don’t know, nor does Petrucci. If Vendramin really is dead, then his spectre haunts Petrucci, for he hates and fears him.’

‘And at Bracciano, was that you prowling the yard?’

‘No, I swear it! Besides, the duke himself says that he has evidence that people came in from outside. My orders were simply to stay near you, intercept your correspondence and report back to Siena.’

‘Very well, that is all the information I require for now.’

Bembo sounds relieved. ‘Really?’

‘Yes, but we must now ascertain its veracity. Pico, the stone please.’

Pico glances nervously across. Wilf holds Bembo tight as he writhes and screams for mercy. Wilf looks at Hugh, who looks at Pico, then down to the sack.

‘Please, Hugh, by the saints I swear it is true. Don’t hurt me. Have pity on me. It is true; I swear it!’

Hugh knows that it is not, for he knows lies and liars. But he cannot ignore the plea for mercy, remembering as he does now, Fra Francesco’s words that *mercy is not mercy if it is deserved*. Bembo does not deserve it, but then neither does he. So, what’s to do, as Wilf would say.

The grind of stone.

He glances in that split-second back to Pico’s ashen face. Would he make the boy a torturer?

The grinding. The mills of God. Francesco’s words.

No, he’ll let Bembo away, let mercy triumph over justice for once. He raises his hand to Pico, and the lad’s face breaks out in relief. Even Wilf smiles.

‘Forgive me, signor, but I had to be sure. I have my orders, too.’ Hugh removes the drenched sack to reveal the dripping poet beneath, skin white as tripe.

‘Oh, thank God, thank God.’

Wilf unbinds him so that he can take the drink that Hugh is offering him. He drains the earthenware goblet in a moment, and then another, before exclaiming again, 'Thank God.' Bembo runs trembling hands over his stubble, and then up to push the black hair backwards from his high forehead. All the while his eyes adjust, leaking water, and a vein throbbing on his right temple. 'I am in your debt, signor.'

Hugh mimics piety. 'We are all beggars at the gates of God's mercy.'

'And what now?' Bembo gestures with the shaking and empty goblet for more water.

Hugh pours it. 'We go on as before. You stick close to me, send back anything you find out, and help me when I go up to Siena for Easter as Petrucci's guest.'

'I see,' Bembo says, now biting his knuckle. 'Would to God that the old goat would die.'

'No need to trouble God.'

LETTER TO FLORENCE, 30TH OCTOBER

Most Gracious Signor M,

I write with news of a felicitous nature for you, though the turn of events was anything but for me. I was abducted two nights hence by the Englishman, and was treated sorely, and very ill, enduring torture worse than mere thumb-screws or drops of the strappado – which I know you will take into account when apportioning the reward for this hazardous enterprise.

Be assured though that he got nothing from me but such that I thought best, even though it was done so at great peril to my person. Your anonymity is secure, of course. Indeed, he now thinks that I work for our illustrious benefactor in Siena, which, in a manner, we do. And the Englishman tells me furthermore the reason for that gentleman's sudden appearance in Perugia, to wit, that he wants the Englishman to be his special guest for the Easter procession next spring. I can only conclude again that our benefactor is cutting us from the prey, and has information to trade with the knights. But do not worry; I think that I have the knight's confidence; he wants me to accompany and help him there. So, we shall see soon enough, firstly what the Englishman knows, and secondly, what Petrucci has kept from us.

I am now recovering from the rigors of my ordeal and am on my way to Rome to winter, where I will send further news when I have it.

Your servant, et cetera.

LETTER TO RHODES FROM ROME, 10TH DECEMBER

Most Illustrious Magister,

I write with momentous news.

His Holiness has, after the emperor's failure to subdue Venice last spring, turned to Louis XII with an offer of alliance. Furthermore, he has called for all Christian nations to join him in an expedition to strip Venice of her possessions. And so, this very day, the tenth of December in the year of our Lord, 1508, representatives of the papal states, France, the Holy Roman Empire and Ferdinand II of *Aragon formalized a solemn League against the Republic. I heard the imperial ambassador say that his master's forces would drive out the Venetians as one casts out last year's rushes, to which Signor Bembo says, 'What again?' It almost sparked a diplomatic incident, but the grand prior and I were in much mirth over it.*

I have seen the document with my own eyes, which is now being called The League of Cambrai, and I can confirm that it provides for the complete dismemberment of Venice's territory in Italy and for its partition among the signatories.

His Holiness seems pleased, and you will judge for yourself whether the inclusion of your own countrymen in the league, and thus the papal favour, will in time strengthen our cause or not. Preparations for the war go on apace here, and there can be no talk of defending Christendom against her joint enemy while they enjoy their internal squabbles. But perhaps when they are sated with Venetian spoils, they will be more willing to face the threat from the east.

On a less important note, I apprehended the spy that was in our party while in Assisi and have questioned him to my satisfaction. He claims to work for Petrucci of Siena, and I have allowed him to continue to do so, keeping him near me, for it is some peculiar comfort in this land to at least know who your enemies are.

I shall continue my progress of the courts, next spring, when the kings go out to war and will report back everything I think may be of use. Please find my accounts; I have kept on the mules over the winter at a good hire, for the muleteer tells me there won't be mules for love nor money in the spring when they go to war.

I am, as ever, et cetera.

LETTER TO THE ISLAND OF ISCHIA FROM HUGH, 11TH DECEMBER, 1508

Hugh pauses over the last page before sealing his letter. He has written more here about the state of his soul than he would dare utter with his lips. Perhaps he should consign it to the flames. He sighs, he lingers, and wrestles almost feverishly with it. Surely to send it shows a baseless hope, the last retreat of the villain and coward? His eyes dart about the room as if for an escape route and then alight one last time of the last page.

(Page Four of Hugh's letter)

...from my youth until this hour. But enough I have said. Let it be sufficient, and forgive my forwardness. Remember that my years have been spent in the barracks, the camp, and on-board ships where men have become insensible to all but the harshest criticism. With you, lady, I now see that my slightest whisper will suffice.

Let us therewith come to the religious verse you sent. It intrigues and vexes me in equal measure – perhaps for want of proper piety myself, or perhaps for want of that tender pity in religion which is the boast of your sex. 'Vex' is peradventure the wrong word, lady, for indeed I am ashamed all too often of a conscience seared by war and bloodshed. If I therefore seem a brute in my questioning, do all the more forgive. You write;

Though earthly tyrants with resistless brand,
Within, without my column smite alway,
In flames by night, in clouds of smoke by day
I see that other heaven-sent pillar stand

In these verses, you speak of your column. That is, if I understand aright, that you employ military language to describe the vicissitudes of the Colonna family, or is it your own self and interests? Is this correct? I suspect the former and shall infer thus. 'Batte la mia Colonna' will surely be taken this way by your countrymen at any rate. The allusion is strong, manly and worthy. I do not disdain it, though I would perhaps caution against the second canto.

Of God's high grace that I may not withstand
For so entranced am I, should I assay
From earthly love to turn, it still would stay
Within my heart and hold me with firm hand

Firstly, you employ the imagery of Sinai in relation to your family's enemies and thus confer on them, whoever they may be, the suggestion of divine judgement under the Levitical law? Or do I make this too complicated? Bembo says that I am always doing this. 'Stop looking for five legs on a sheep,' he says. I believe it is an expression in Tuscany. Well, perhaps I do.

Either way, I see you need it, so you can then extend the metaphor later on to show the divine favour toward your own family in terms similar. But here again – and not knowing what sorrow vexes you – I caution about claiming the sanctions of heaven for private advantage. If we can surmise anything about this God, surely it is that he is not a domestic one. Is it not by this slip that the whole world has gone mad? I judge not your particular case, of course, but warn you as a poet against a hubris that might be judged harshly hereafter.

But then you amaze me with hope with the lines, Dal natural amor, che fa soggiorno, Dentr'al mio cor, ben spesso richiamata. 'From earthly love to turn, it still would stay, Within my heart and hold me with firm hand.'

I encouraged you before to write only what you see, what you know by experience. Do I understand the words sufficiently? Do you mean you feel the divine love – that is, if you think me not impertinent – that you know this love by experience to be stronger and more constant than all the loves of this earth? If so then I marvel most truly, and feel my own deadness all the more palpably. Please explain this more fully in your next letter. I would know more. Does the duchess have similar sentiments in this regard? You give me hope, Lady. Sometimes I feel my heart is too big for my body. When I read those lines again, I feel great and pure things in the universe are trying to get into me. And yet I am unable to either take hold upon it or yet let it alight on me as a dove.

Me thinks that then a spell of peaceful rest
Is shown to me, the which I love to see.
I know not if my soul with fancies blest,
Deceives itself for its own good, while He
My generous Lord, without shows dark and drear
But flows with greater radiance clear

This too like a dullard I must understand. Do I perceive correctly that you see the outward face of providence towards you is dire, that heavens be of brass, and yet notwithstanding you feel his assurance within even so? 'Arde e lampeggia' would conjure to my mind a burning ardour. Is this what you mean, or is it peace and a gentle assurance? Your language appears so fixed, and has such fortitude that I wonder if I have understood correctly. Bembo is away in the country and the riders are leaving with the post for Rome in one hour.

Please write by return if you can, for these matters are of far more import than literary style to me. Forgive me if the latter part of this missive has been more interrogation than instruction.

My felicitations to your noble families and our friends at court.

Your servant, as ever, et cetera.

Part III - THE GODS OF WAR

BORGO SANT'ANGELO, ROME, 14TH JANUARY, 1509

It's the feast of Saint Paul the Hermit. The bells for compline sound thinly above the thunder and torrential downpour. It has rained solidly since Epiphany. The Tiber is fit to burst. Two houses have already been lost and eight souls with them.

Hugh and Bembo walk briskly in the colonnade on the Borgo Sant'Angelo after another evening of war talk with the pope at the fortress. Hugh is aware of Bembo's wary glances in his direction and his deferential tone when speaking. *He hasn't forgotten Assisi and neither have I. It's like being shackled to a wounded jackal that can recite in tersa rima like Petrarch, while all the time looking for your throat. Shit. I only keep him here because I – like an ass – want to believe in forgiveness, need to believe it.*

They are headed back to the Vatican stables for their mounts when Hugh spots someone backing under the same colonnade fifty feet in front of them, followed by men with lanterns. Their lamps show what he at first assumes to be a dusty vagabond, but as he nears, he recognizes the square forehead and rags of Michelangelo.

The largest of the toughs is taunting and pushing the artist against the wall, calling him 'a horse gelder and a slack-jawed *scapelino*.' The man is well dressed and armed, too. They all are, four, five, six of them.

Hugh says, 'Pietro, it seems Signor Buonarotti is in some difficulty.'

'And so will we all be if we interfere. The ringleader is the Florentine painter Torrigiano. Their quarrel is an old one, and he is not a man to meddle with.'

Hugh smiles, and removes his heavy outer cloak. 'You are saying that to goad me surely?'

'No, no! I mean it. He is an infamous fighter and *grand impassionato.* Humour him by all means, but do not risk offending him. It was he who disfigured Michelangelo's nose in the first place.'

'Did he now?'

'Hugh, what are you doing with your cloak?'

'I would do the same, and be ready to draw your swordif I were you.' Hugh walks three steps in front, listening to Bembo hiss behind him.

'Hugh? Hugh!'

When he is within twenty feet of the group, Hugh calls out. 'Signors, is there so little fun to be had in the eternal city that gentlemen must harass beggars?'

'What? Who's that?' The bulk of Torrigiano wheels to observe the newcomers. He squints for their lamps which are the only light.

Hugh observes the gaudy yellow silk in the man's slashed doublet stretched tightly across broad shoulders. 'I said, are you not afraid to catch something? Or worse, soil your fine clothing.'

Torrigiano casts his eyes about warily as if to assess the numbers. 'You wouldn't stop our little excitement, would you?'

'Excitement?' Hugh steps past the last column and into their pool of lantern light. 'Touch him again, and you'll find yourself on the wrong side of exciting, my friend.' Hugh tilts his beret towards Michelangelo slumped against the wall with a bleeding cheek, and then back to his foe folding his arms defiantly.

'What!' Torrigiano glances round at his friends, his heavy Roman nose flaring. 'Did you hear that, boys? This foreign joker and his skinny girlfriend are trying to pick a fight with us unprovoked. Think we should teach him a lesson in manners?'

'So be it. Manners it is.' Hugh is already drawing his sword. 'But if you have the balls for it, why not face me yourself and let our friends have the night off?' He lets the Colhona slide clear of the lining without noise. The blackened blade does not glint. *Poor bastard will have a hard time seeing this coming.*

The other toughs let out a whoop at the challenge, but quickly unbuckle their own blades when Bembo approaches them with his drawn.

Torrigiano nods grimly, then turns back to kick Michelangelo. 'You stay there. I'll cut you, too, when I have finished with him.'

Torrigiano removes his doublet. He draws a pricey Spanish cross hilt and levels it at Hugh, his square fists now visible. 'Who are you then, making yourself a nuisance?'

'Hugh de Erpingham, of England.' Hugh loosens his collar, and his neck muscles.

'England! And you've learnt how to use a sword and speak? I heard they all live in hovels and caves.' And with those words, not letting his adversary take a proper guard, Torrigiano lunges full length at Hugh's face.

Hugh has no time to parry. He weaves his head to let the blade past. Only after does he sidestep and parry to the right, deflecting Torrigiano's blade, kicking his arse as he does so. The toughs whoop again, this time uncertainly. But their attention is soon drawn away as Signor Bembo approaches and takes a relaxed fighting stance.

Hugh levels his blade. 'Manners, signor. A gentleman never seeks a cowardly advantage.'

Torrigiano curses and recovers quickly, lunging once, twice, stepping fast. The tap-tap of his horseman's boots echo off the alley walls. The thug moves boldly on the flags. His blade flashes orange in the light, up, across, back, forward, cut, thrust. All his tensile strength and agility deploy from the blade toward Hugh, who greets each new blow with stoic poise and minimal steps. The whistling of each cut pierces the noise of rain beyond the colonnade in one moment, and in the next is met with the clink or scrape of the Colhona. Hugh's body and feet move with economy but precision. He has spent years at this, eliminating unnecessary movement. He's like an aging sculptor who no longer feels the need to flesh out the details. At his best, between the lifting and resettling of the fog, Hugh fancies he can see everything as if from above, almost make time stand still, make space where there is none. He sees a blade coming even now. He knows to a pin's breadth how far it will go before Torrigiano will over balance. It whistles as the Italian slashes with rage. *Does he think he can dominate me with his sculptor's arm?* Never mind England, he should go to Germany; the Germans prize sweat above all else. But even strong men grow weary, and all swords become heavy with use.

Hugh waits for an overbalance, and then he extends his parry, allowing space to kick Torrigiano in the ribs, and send him crashing into a pillar on the colonnade. Torrigiano tries to raise his blade in defence, but Hugh slashes it savagely toward the pavement, then stamps on it, bending the blade out of shape. All this takes barely a flicker of the lights and no one has time to react as Hugh proceeds to ram the ringed hilt of his carrack sword into Torrigiano's once proud Roman nose.

Hugh steps back, leaving Torrigiano crumpled in his own saliva and blood. Hugh levels the blade at the others to warn them off and then back at his vanquished foe. 'And shall I – how did you put it? Ah, yes – *cut you*?'

Torrigiano's curly, black locks shake woefully, and he mumbles, 'No, please, no.'

'Shall I, Michelangelo?' Hugh turns to the artist, still panting, as he spits the words out.

The sculptor looks with horror from the ghastly specter of his longtime foe, back to the equally appalling sight of the red mist in his rescuer's eyes. He shakes his head, then looks away, undoubtedly wondering if the night could end anyway but in murder.

Hugh levels the blade once more, twisting it menacingly into Torrigiano's soiled silk chemise. His face and arm muscles knot with a rising rage. 'Shall I teach you a lesson, Signor Hard-case?'

'Please, no. Please, please.'

As they hear the raised voice of their leader, the other toughs back away from Bembo's blade, which has held three of theirs at bay with ease. For a moment they stand off, exhausted, and Bembo shouts back to Hugh, 'Leave him; let's go.'

Hugh's fast breathing begins to slacken, and something of a forced smile – like the smile of a madman – momentarily appears on his lips. 'Yes, I will leave you.' He raises Torrigiano's chin with his blade and says, 'But if you lay a finger on that man again, I will lose all patience.'

Bembo gathers the cloaks and helps Michelangelo along the road. Hugh, arranging his own cloak and looking on with disquiet, begins to follow. It was not primarily to rescue the artist that he fought. There were many less hazardous ways to do that. No, it was to lead Bembo into a position where Hugh could observe him. The outcome is unwelcome: Bembo is a first-rate swordsman.

CAPPELLA SISTINA, 2 AM, 15TH JANUARY, 1509

'I must confess, Hugh, I thought he'd be a bit more grateful. He's hardly said two civil words.' Bembo whispers to Hugh as a slump-shouldered Michelangelo fumbles with the keys to the Sistine Chapel. They won't oblige. Hugh and Bembo offered to escort the artist to his lodgings and now they discover Michelangelo was not going home after all. Instead, he has come here, to the chapel of Sixtus.

The artist starts to get agitated. 'I am all right. You can take your leave gentlemen. I can manage now.'

Hugh can see Michelangelo's eye blinking back tears . He knows how that feels.

'Perhaps I can help you with the keys,' Bembo proffers.

'No!' the artist almost shouts. He controls himself but is nonetheless brimming with rage. 'No. I can manage quite well. Quite well enough. Quite.' His hands shake and on this last word he breaks down, his shoulders shuddering and heaving in uncontrolled sobs of despair.

'Signor Buonarotti!' Hugh lays a comforting hand on his shoulder.

'Go. Please go. Leave me.'

'But why this distress? Torrigiano will trouble you no more.'

Michelangelo turns and with a mocking laugh, blurts out. 'Torrigiano! Do you think I fear him, that third-rate sculptor? No, tonight I thought he would finally end my misery and do me at least that favour.' His eyes plead with them in the torchlight.

Bembo at his most pious, says, 'Signor, you must not speak thus. To seek death is a mortal sin.'

Michelangelo says, 'Hah, seek death, seek death! And what does he do,' he nods at Hugh. 'I saw that look in your eye tonight, signor, and don't think I didn't. You court death like a bride, wear it like a livery. You dare God to take you, and so do I. So do I!'

Bembo's tone is even more pious. 'Signor!'

'Don't lecture me, signor. What would a poet know of hard work, eh? What would a literary critic know of an artist's despair, at any rate?' Michelangelo draws something out of his dusty doublet and brandishes it between grubby fingers. 'Poets, poets! I will read you a sonnet, signor. You can stick it in your anthology or anywhere else the sun doesn't shine! Here, here, here it is. I mean to send it tomorrow to my only friend Giovanni in Pistoia, but it might as well do you some good too. Hold the light up, will you?

I've already grown a goiter from this torture,
hunched up here like a cat in Lombardy
(or anywhere else where the stagnant water's poison).
My stomach's squashed under my chin, my beard's
pointing at heaven, my brain's crushed in a casket,
my breast twists like a harpy's. My brush,
above me all the time, dribbles paint
so my face makes a fine floor for droppings!

My haunches are grinding into my guts,
my poor arse strains to work as a counterweight,
every gesture I make is blind and aimless.
My skin hangs loose below me, my spine's
all knotted from folding over itself.
I'm bent taut as a bow Syrian.
Because I'm stuck like this, my thoughts
are crazy, perfidious tripe:
anyone shoots badly through a crooked blowpipe.
My painting is dead.
Defend it for me, Giovanni, protect my honor.
I am not in the right place – I am not a painter.'

'It gets points for honesty,' Bembo says quietly.

When he has finished squinting at the parchment, Michelangelo looks up, though not for approval. 'You want to enter here so you can see my work; to make sure that I will continue to bring glory to Florence, am I not right, Signor Bembo? You come to see that I will succeed, just like that ponce Raphael from Urbino comes to assure himself that I will fail, or at least so that he can copy from me. But what no one knows yet is that my failure here will be Florence's shame and my ruin.'

‘Failure?’ Bembo lowers the light.

‘Yes, failure. There, I’ve said it, and now you know. My work here is ruined, all of it, four months of it. I have failed. Let Raphael and Bramante clap their hands and thumb their noses at me.’

‘But tell me,’ Hugh says, taking the artist by the arm. ‘What has gone wrong? Your cartoons were so good.’ *Failure!* Hugh’s heart churns within him, not for Florence but the despair in Michelangelo’s eyes – it is like looking in the mirror. Petrucci himself seemed to know that the threat of failure stalked Hugh like a wraith.

‘Believe me, when God is set against a man, he likes to use the little things to remind us of our meaningless, insignificant lives. First my fellow artists fail me, now even the elements of nature conspire to ruin this work that was forced on me.’ He stuffs the parchment back into his tunic, and then holds up the key again. ‘Come I will show you what it is to be an enemy of God, though,’ and with this he glances at Hugh, ‘perhaps you know already.’

They ascend the scaffold to the vault via ladders and loose planks. Bembo comes last of all, removing his new gloves and cursing the dust. Everywhere their hand falls on crusted plaster and everywhere Hugh recognizes the clay smell he remembers from the pottery yards in Norwich.

Hugh notices a couch under the vault at the top of the last ladder. ‘You have been sleeping here?’

‘Just this week while this has been going on.’

‘The boy Michi?’

‘You know his name.’

‘Spoke to him last time.’

‘He brings the food up when he comes each day to mix and grind.’ He points absently toward a plank where some crusts and an earthenware jug stand. ‘Perhaps you would like some bread and wine. Certainly, I’ve no stomach for food.’

‘No, thank you.’ Hugh’s eyes strain to glimpse the flickers of fresco, which appear momentarily as the torch conjures them out of the shadows. 'But I would like to see the cause of this distress, see if there is anything to be done.'

'You can ask Noah.' Michelangelo moves the torch to light some charred wicks drooping out of olive oil-filled pots, and soon the mellow glow of five or six other lights illumine a vault not just glistening with monumental frescoed forms, but with something else: crystals. The more wicks are lit, the more they appeared, running along the junctures of different sections of work, sometimes just a thin crust, sometimes thick and white in great veils over the work. And there is mould too: black, green, brown, ominous, the fingers of decay and death eating into moist plaster. His adamantine Noah, collapsed in drunkenness and despondency has a great vein of crystal salts across his body.

Hugh gasps. 'Oh, *Dio Mio!*'

Bembo stops sniffing the wine. 'What has happened, *maestro?*'

'This north wind has fingers. This constant cold. Nothing dries here. I feel like poor Noah. I have survived the wrath of Julius thus far as he does God's but now –' He breaks off to slump his haunches onto a plank, and cast up his hands. 'Now, I think Noah's response is the only one left. Doesn't Ecclesiastes also say to give wine to those who have no hope?'

'Yes, signor, but it also says not to princes.' Hugh reaches into the sack of white lime next to the artist. 'And this is the lime, signor?'

Michelangelo shakes his head and waves his hand. 'Please, signor, you have saved me once tonight with your sword. That is enough.'

'No please.' Hugh has to find a way to help. *This man, this genius! They call me a hero because I have killed and made those alive like stone, but he has made stone live and breathe.* If Hugh had a morsel of decency left him by the devils, he would gladly lay down his life to have Michelangelo live and succeed.

'By your courtesy, let me speak a word to you. Peradventure as an ignorant fool, but let me speak. You see I have frescoed in a small way on Rhodes. The magister of my order, thought it would calm my humors.' He smiles. 'I have a tendency to be melancholic and phlegmatic.'

Bembo pours some wine. 'You don't say!'

'Pietro, would you not be better with water? You already had a skinful, and you're a long way up.'

'Hah, we Italians go straight from the breast to wine.' Bembo raises the clad cup. 'Water is for washing before mass. Besides, it's not every day that you see the secret work of Italy's greatest sculptor, or are insulted by him. *Salute!*'

Hugh turns back to Michelangelo, raising the lime dust in his fingers. 'This has a much denser consistency than the lime I have used there. Ours is lighter, more sandy. What is it?'

'Tavertine. It goes a tan colour when mixed with the *pozzolana,* volcanic ash.'

Hugh stretches up to the vault with a lamp to examine the powdery crust on the surface into which moisture has entered and formed the breeding ground for mould. He uses his thumb nail to scrape some of the salts away to see the plaster beneath before saying, 'I truly think that this lime is to blame and not the wrath of God –

'Who is usually busy punishing real sinners like Hugh and me,' Bembo adds taking another draft.

Hugh ignores him. 'It might be all right for the summer months, for spring even, but not the winter. It will take an age to dry here: damp, cold, no moving air in this vault even. Have you told the pope's people yet?'

Michelangelo shakes his head, speaking into his bib. 'How can I? On top of all the other difficulties that beset me in this cursed commission.'

'It's why they say no coward ever painted a fresco.' Bembo says, speaking into his cup.

'I think you should. It's not as bad as you think. The frescoes are still there. This can be cleaned; I'm sure of it. And if you don't want His Holiness to know right away, or Bramante, then get Maestro Sangallo to see it. He will know more than me. Help; that is what you need, not working here on your own. Get help cleaning these, and heating these miasmic vapours, and you—' Hugh lays a hand on the artist's arm. 'For God's sake go home, eat some proper food and get some proper sleep, or you'll be no use to anyone.'

THE GRAND PRIORY, ROME, JANUARY 21ST, 1509

'Special guests tonight?' Wilf is handing Hugh his finest doublet from the trunk, the burgundy velvet with intricate gold brocade.

'Same lot: cardinals, prelates, dukes, the pope, of course, and tonight also the banker Chigi, a powerful man with whom the magister wishes us to build ties. Gloves please.'

'Castel Angelo?'

'No, papal apartments tonight. The Holy Father wishes to show off his new apartments on the feast of Saint Agnes, only half finished, but he cannot wait. So, we dine in a building site but with all the best people.'

'It's almost every night. The pope must like you.'

'Is that hard to imagine?' Hugh tries to catch Wilf's eye with a smile. He knows he's been hard to live with these last months. Wilf doesn't respond. Hugh takes the gloves and tucks them into his belt. 'His Holiness keeps me close for his own reasons. Now that the bills roll in for his campaign against Venice – about a thousand ducats a day by my reckoning – he wants what Vendramin stole more than ever. And he is under the impression that I will, when I find Vendramin, which seems less and less likely, let him have first pick of the spoils – which is even *less* likely.'

Hugh sees Wilf arranging things in the trunk with the air of a martyr. 'And what's the matter with you tonight? Face like a smacked arse.'

Wilf smiles at the compliment, and Hugh sees it. Perhaps he remembers better times when the banter was more like this. Perhaps those times will come again. Wilf gives Hugh another approving nod and then returns to pushing down the tunics and cloaks in the trunk so that it will shut again. 'Just thinking what the lads will be doing back home.'

'On Rhodes?'

'No! Sod Rhodes. In Norfolk. We had some good crack on those long winter nights.'

'Do you miss it much?'

'Aye, sometimes. You?'

Hugh ponders a moment. Mother, Father, the dogs. Elizabeth, Kitty, Maud, little Cecil, the house, his old room, university friends, the land. Yes, he misses it. He has given up family and land for the kingdom's sake, *peregrinatio pro Christo.* But what has Wilf done it for? Poor sod. The vespers bell sounds hollow in the yard. 'Get Pico to fetch the mares, or we'll be late.'

STANZA APARTMENTS, VATICAN, ROME, JANUARY 21ST, 1509

The Papal Master of Ceremonies, Burchard collars Hugh before he ascends the flights of steps to the upper apartments in order to pass on Julius's particular intentions for the event. There is to be no talk tonight of the war against the recalcitrant sons of Saint Mark, not in front of the finer sort of ladies: the grander signore, *principesse, cognoscenti* and even a small number of the most select *cortegiane.* They have come to see the young miracle boy from Urbino, and, of course, show off their *belle figure*.

They are to dine in the great upper hall, yet un-frescoed but hung with lavish Flemish tapestries. He can smell the damp of washed lime, and something else: food. Canapes of San Giminato veal rolled in white bread, and other dainties like quail eggs are offered in the new apartments by boys in the papal livery. There is no one he knows or wants to speak to, so Hugh takes a handful and consciously eats them with the outer forms of elegance and not as a beggar. His fingers tremble. A canape falls. He casts his eye about. No one notices, or cares. *God! A year ago, fifty wraiths would have torn each other's eyes out for that morsel and look, even I am letting it go underfoot without thinking too much of it.*

He moves gingerly amidst the silken ladies and velvet gentlemen, feigning ease and contentment, and by a fluke falls into talking with Raphaello di Sanzio. The smooth skinned artist had been leaving one set of grand ladies and about to alight on another, as if they had been flowers and he a bee, when Hugh accidentally crosses his path. At first, Hugh goes to smile then move on, but then the young artist's deep brown eyes spark with recognition. 'But of course, you are Cavaliere Erpingham of Rhodes, no?'

'But of course, I am.'

'I have seen you often, signor, but not had the pleasure.'

Hugh takes his bow and observes the angelic countenance of the young man before him, who at that moment is descending also in a studied bow, his quite unbelievably orange silk sleeves flapping as he swings his arm. When Raphael is returning his beret and meticulously arranging the waves of his long, silky hair under it, and round his ears, Hugh gestures to the walls. 'I must congratulate you on your most exquisite work. You are very accommodating to us and His Holiness to allow this special audience. Not all artists would be so.'

'You mean Michelangelo, don't you? Ah, I thought so. You know he threw a scaffolding plank when His Holiness tried to inspect the work! I am told the Holy Father remarked to Bramante that he'd found it easier to master Perugia and Bologna than that one Florentine. None can deny his ability, but by my oath, he lives dangerously.'

Hugh moves to the side slightly and points up to the fresco over the door of the apartment. 'But tell me please, this fresco here?'

'It is the Mass of Bolsenna. The pontiff wished to be shown in place of his predecessor.'

'Yes, you have shown him well, but tell me, this suppliant in black below him, I recognize her.'

Raphael smiles as he follows Hugh's finger to the full lipped and rosy cheeked beauty in the bottom left-hand corner. 'Signor, you know Donna Felice?'

'Signora d'Orsini,' Hugh says, correcting the slight. He makes a conscious effort to look detached and adds, 'I had the pleasure of Gian Giordano's hospitality last autumn.'

Raphael takes Hugh's look and mention of the eccentric Orsini as a spur to impious humour. 'His Holiness wished to have his bastard in the picture for reasons best known to himself. He made me do it twice.

Said I had not captured her beauty enough the first time. So, I overdid it rather to pacify my lord.'

Hugh frowns. 'On the contrary, signor, you have failed to catch either her fair visage or the great inner light of her countenance.'

'Oh, each man has his own taste, but –' This last word trails absently from his lips, for Raphael has seen a different beauty enter on the far side of the room. 'Ah, but all men agree about *her*. Would you excuse me? Signora Ordeaschi beckons.'

He moves away sideways with an easy grace, revealing a party immediately to his rear, within easy earshot. Among them is Signora Felice. This could be awkward. The three women glower after the artist. For a moment she and Hugh stare intently into one another's eyes. She glows. Hugh averts his eyes by bowing to them, and she introduces her party which include the Duchess Elizabetta Montefeltro of Urbino, recently widowed, and her sharp-featured and sharp-witted lady in waiting Emilia Pia, whom he has already met at Bracciano.

After the introductions Hugh overhears Emilia remarking to Felice from behind her fan. 'Doesn't Signor Chigi's mistress, Francesca Ordeaschi, look well this evening? See how giddily she laughs. The poor thing must feel faint standing upright for so long. Upon my word she ought to have a sign made, *Publicitas Commoditato*.'

'The *querelle de femmes!*' It is Bembo's whisper at Hugh's shoulder. He too has snuck up from behind.

'Signor Bembo, *caro*.' The Duchess Elisabetta offers her hand to him. As he kisses the ring of his patron, Hugh

observes the woman that Castiglione had spoken so highly of. Cascading ringlets dark as wet oak, fall like tears around a broad forehead and the glinting, deep, brown eyes of a woman who observes and knows. When she has received Bembo's salutation, she smooths her black Bologna silks and says, 'We have missed you greatly these last weeks, particularly when we were given to understand you would winter with us. Daily we have expected you to brighten our firesides yet still you do not return. Shall we rent out your rooms? Poor Castiglione will be bereft with no one to tease him.'

'Yes indeed,' adds her lady in waiting, with a brief curtsy. 'Seeing that the pope will grant you no indulgence to marry your own good self, we begin to wonder whether you have taken a wife.'

Hugh observes that Donna Pia's *noli me tangere* is a mere girlish ruse. The mock indignation, the pinkness of cheek, the unmistakable meaning in her eyes. *Don't touch me*, indeed; she would have Bembo if he asked.

'Who me? Sacrifice the admiration of so many men, for the criticism of one woman? I do not think so. Women are a burden best left to Atlas. Brigands demand your money or your life, women demand both.'

'Why, Signor Bembo!' The duchess smiles. 'says who? Who claims such things?'

Donna Pia swipes at him with her fan. 'Bembo, God, and all the relevant authorities no doubt, as with everything else.'

Bembo bows. 'I know, I know. And with a little humility I would be perfect, but hardly even then suitable company for one woman for life.'

'Again!' Donna Pia blurts out with what appears a genuine exasperation. 'Here you exaggerate to deflect.'

'Do I? Do I verily?' Bembo says, now becoming confidential. 'Does not even Bernard of Clairaux say, "It is more difficult to live with a woman without danger than raise the dead." And besides, our dear – and very much married – friend Castiglione has told me, in the strictest confidence, when I enquired after his wife, "Bembo" he said, "I haven't spoken to her in years. I didn't like to interrupt." There now!'

Encouraged by their laughter, Bembo raises his hands in jollity and exclamation. 'Ah, I see you know Signora Castiglione, but did you know that among her other excellences she has an impediment in her speech. Yes, yes, indeed. Every now and then she must stop to breathe. The only thing that could deprive her of the last word is the echo. It is the truth, I say, it is!'

'Signor Bembo, for shame!' Donna Pia exclaims. 'Where do you get such stories. Surely it is from Bocaccio!'

'Madame please! It is all the truth.' Bembo says in mock disgust, now warming to his subject with relish. 'Why only last summer she was a long time at her closet before an important masque ball in Mantua, and he – our beloved ambassador – was very much afraid her lengthy preparations would make them both late, so he called by – to encourage her, you understand. She stood before the glass and said, "Oh my dear, I am really not sure whether this taffeta makes me look somewhat large and matronly?" Baldasarre, ever the diplomat answered, "Why, to be fair my dear, it is a very small closet!" I quote him word for word, I swear it, in confidence mind you! The dear woman has not only kept her figure, but added to it each year.'

'Signor, you are a wicked, wicked man!' Madonna Pia pokes him with her fan. 'If I were your wife, I would add Canterella to your wine.'

'And if I were your husband, dear lady, no doubt I would drink it.'

Madonna Pia is about to add another rejoinder, when Felice interrupts in a flurry of words. 'Do you agree, Signor Erpingham? Does a man not forsake something innate to his humanity when he forsakes the love of a woman?'

'Ah, Hugh,' Bembo cautions. 'Answer carefully!'

For a moment Hugh pauses and coughs into his fist. She is still looking at him. 'We have certainly been schooled to believe that romantic love is a natural and ennobling passion, but I cannot imagine myself trying to explain it thus to the ancients: Aristotle, Virgil or Saint Paul.'

'Well said. It is well said, a good dodge, Hugh, a good dodge. And she I deflect!' Bembo raises his wine cup to Hugh. 'Indeed, in ancient literature the tales are never about men and women falling in love, but of holy men going on pilgrimage, or to heaven, or to battle. A time of great loyalties –'

'And thus, also great betrayals,' Hugh adds with a knowing glance.

'Er, yes, indeed. Betrayals, too.' Bembo absorbs the words with a blink of the eyes but then recovers himself. 'Roland does not think of Alde on the battlefield but of his praise in pleasant France. The deepest emotion I can find is the mutual love of warriors who die together fighting against the odds.'

'And,' Hugh adds in a moment of epiphany, 'the love of a vassal for his lord.' Wilf's face is immediately before him—Wilf who took news of his birth to his father, who has been at his side these long years, put up with so much. Hugh has not recognized it until this moment because the idealized vassals of literature show such an open passion. But is not Wilf's stoic fidelity equal in substance?

'Correct me if I am wrong.' Emily Pia will not lose a point to Bembo, or any man. 'But surely the ancients acknowledged the felicity of a good marriage. Odysseus loved Penelope, did he not?'

'Ah, ah,' Bembo cautions. 'But only as he loves the rest of his home and possessions.'

'Hah,' she replies, looking to her lady for assistance. 'So speaks the great Bembo, a man not sufficiently ripe for marriage!'

'Or over-ripe, my lady,' Bembo says. 'For though Aristotle might grudgingly admit that the conjugal state may rise to the same level as a virtuous friendship between good men; yet for Plato the ladder between the human and divine loves is just that—*a ladder*. We ascend to the higher loves by leaving the lower loves on the rungs below. I do not say I agree with him, Duchess, only that this is the correct interpretation. Hugh, I think, will agree. Our Florentine Platonists like Ficino and Mirandola assume they can have both, but they are misreading Plato. Alas.' Bembo concludes, sighing with affectation. 'What can we unwedded creatures ever know of the conjugal state when we picket outside with our paper arguments. Surely, we should hold our tongues and let the gracious duchess speak, for all Italy reveres her gentle wisdom.'

Elisabetta nods graciously. 'I happen to know, signors that Politian once said to Ficino, "Among the works of the classics you seek for the true and I seek for the beautiful." To my own mind, I believe the unity is found only in Christ.'

'And in a good marriage, surely, my lady,' Emilia says. 'Do give Signor Bembo hope.'

'Perhaps. Yes. But what shall I tell you of the trials and bliss of marriage?' She extends one hand to her lady in waiting and the other over her stomach. 'I fear that if my own marriage will not convince you, then any words I offer will have little effect. If we have seen since the days of our ancestors, that their ruinous *romance of adultery* has become our romance of marriage, I for one cannot wish it reversed again. My years with His Grace the duke were not always easy, as you know, but they were good in the truest sense, and not contradictory as the philosophies we have inherited or dreamed up. But—' The duchess bows slightly. 'I know also that marriage and romance are not the only sources of good and beauty in this world so I will not say more before men of such learning.'

Twenty minutes later Hugh is seated at a window seat with Bembo standing obediently, though restlessly at his side. The shadow of the papal secretary falls on them. Angelo Colocci wavers for a moment before saying, 'Maestro Bembo, I passed your house yesterday.'

'Really? Thank you.'

'Oh,' Colocci jerks his equine head back in theatrical shock. 'Do I detect some coolness; that I am not welcome?'

'As welcome as anal warts, Angelo.'

'Very well, you may keep your little insults, and I, my information.' He turns a withering eye on Hugh. 'I wouldn't look so amused, Erpingham. A man with your list of enemies ought to be more discerning about the society he cultivates. If you would take my advice –'

'Ah, Master Secretary.' Bembo cuts across him quickly, but still looking steadily into the contents of his wine cup. 'You have delusions of adequacy, my friend. Is there a point to this conversation, to your existence even, or are you set on taking our time as well as our light?'

'Yes, I am here to tell you that His Holiness is coming, and that you should be ready in line to greet him, and, as a man who specializes in words, be ready to say something pleasant. If you are able to.'

Colocci leaves, joining the architect Donato Bramante near the entrance.

When he is gone Hugh remarks, 'Are your humors all right? You seemed – how shall I put it? – unnecessarily abrasive to our pigeon-chested friend.'

Bembo broods first into his wine, and then glances across in Colocci's direction. 'He's an arse.' He drains his cup and laughs cynically. 'He's a clerical whore; no better, no worse. What has he not done for money? Well-spoke Dante, of the Drearies who mill about inside the mouth of hell, whining wraiths "who lived without blame or praise as hateful to God as to his enemies." They live there now I tell you. See him there, sidling up to Bramante. And now look; they are joined by that cockscomb Agostino Chigi. Critic and patron of the arts, my hairy arse.'

This is said with such venom, Hugh replies, 'Now you do surprise me. I thought you would like a man who lavishes gifts on artists like your good self.'

'Not me. Raphael and his coterie, but not me. Look at them fawning over him. Both of them, worshipping the quicksand he walks in. And Chigi—the stupid person's idea of a clever person—look at him lapping it up. That is what money does for you, does to all of us, damn it.'

Hugh observes Bembo's meaning'I hear that he will leave for the war with Julius. Do you think it true?'

'*Se non vero e ben trovato*, if not true then well founded. Yes, to be sure of his investment. Besides, Fugger's bank has leant the emperor a hundred and seventy thousand ducats to wage war on Venice, so Julius doesn't want to turn up looking like a poor relation, and what is more—' Bembo's voice drops to a whisper. 'When it comes to money Chigi is no *manino*. He's Venetian after all! I heard my old friend the ambassador for Ferrara, say that Chigi's real reason for funding this war is to consolidate his own company's salt monopoly. Oh yes, don't look so surprised. Its only in war that one can lay waste provinces and literally hang the competition - two things generally frowned upon in peacetime.'

'I see,' Hugh says, trying in his head to follow the money and the motives. 'Alum.'

'Oh yes. Chigi has diversified from his father's banking practice. He has heavily invested in salt and alum. Lucrative but risky.' Bembo rubs his fingers together. 'My old patron, Duke Alfonso, is at loggerheads with the pope over salt monopolies in the papal territories. It's been going on for years. The duke's inroads into the Romagna and beyond, hurt Chigi, and my friend the ambassador believes that at some convenient time during this war, Julius and Chigi will do a little merger and acquisition. You know, consolidate their market holdings. I wouldn't put it past them, and after all, Ferrara is only really the size of a gnat's arse. It's just one step from Bologna on the way to *la Serenissisma.*'

'That is interesting, but I see the pope is entering. Come let us stand.'

An hour later, as the servants are clearing the table, Julius summons Hugh with the wisp of his fingers. When he arrives at the pope's side, Hugh is kept waiting by a bishop from Palma, who will not let the pontiff desist from hearing yet more tales about the depredations of Venice against them. But eventually Julius leans back in his chair, joins his fingers in a pyramid, and speaks to Hugh.

'It seems you cannot but attract attention wherever you go.'

'Holiness?'

'Emperor Maximilian will grant you an audience in Saint Gallen, or Kontanz or somewhere over the alps, so says his ambassador. Did you request this?'

'By no means.' Hugh hates trying to appear innocent. He feels the eyes of the pope bore into him, eyes that are doubtless off in a hundred directions and yet seem to him to be imagining the worst. Tonight, they seem jaundiced yellow and veined like a cobweb.

'I see.' Julius rolls his tongue about his mouth and teeth in order to clean them. 'The ambassador says that the emperor wishes to hear for himself about the situation in the Levant, and wants his bishops and princes to hear it too. That is what he says anyway.' Julius applies a thumbnail to his teeth and retrieves some celery. He examines the end of his nail. 'But he may have heard about that other matter. He's up to his eyes in debt. Tyrolean silver mines can't keep up with his madcap schemes. Be on your guard.'

'Yes, Holiness.'

'Take ship from Ostia to Avignon. Go round the alps. I will send people with you.'

'Thank you, Holiness.'

'Good. We will talk anon.'

Before Hugh leaves, a grateful Florentine, Guliano da Sangallo, whispers his thanks for helping a certain nameless fellow Florentine. 'We are cleaning the ceiling and, as you suspected, it was the travertine lime. His Holiness knows of it and is happy, or at least as happy as an impatient man can be. Perhaps we might repay your kindness with dinner?' The aged architect smiles warmly so that his weary eyes crease shut like a tortoise.

Hugh smiles too. Perhaps.

28TH JANUARY, 1509, VIA DEL BANCI, ROME.

'A *palmo* of velvet, signor? The best quality.'

Bustle, spices, smoke. The odours of washed and unwashed humanity. The rustle of silks, the clattering of ironware, the shouting of vendors.

'You, Signor Cavalliere! It's the feast of San Pietro Nolasco, a portentous day to buy.' A lean Genoan proffers a chemise in two open palms. 'Please, a new overshirt and doublet with six *palmi* of serge. Only six *carlini*. I can go a little lower if you order slippers. All for eight *carlini*? You will not find a better price in Rome.'

Even before the Avignon pope, or the councils of Basle and Constance, perhaps back even to the *insulae* of antiquity, Rome's financial district has been the best place to do all your shopping in one neighbourhood – a bijou Babylon. Older tenements from the time of Martin IV, are constantly being cleared, and modern apartment blocks are springing up all the way down to the Ponte Fabricio. The mercantile and clerical *arrivistes* take up their lodgings on the upper floors, but down on the ground floor the shops are quickly let to apothecaries, butchers, saddlers, shoemakers and cloth merchants. Hugh is not buying, and his companion the architect Guliano da Sangallo, who ought to be, isn't either.

'Surely a new cloak for signor?' A wool merchant pleads from behind his stall.

Sangallo examines for a moment his own inky sleeve, and worn elbow, and then remarks to Hugh, 'I always feel underdressed in Rome. It is one of the reasons I dine with Michelangelo when I am here. Yes, partly to feed him up, for I have learnt it is unwise to go into winters like these with so little on the bone. But also, because he is the only person I know who dresses worse than me. He makes me feel positively decadent!'

The merchant sees them pause to talk and takes encouragement. 'Signor, signor, try this! Try this! Smooth, fine, strong and durable—the best, signor.'

Sangallo places some seeing-spectacles on his nose in order to examine the weave. 'Ah yes, very fine.'

'You have looking-glasses,' Hugh says, and then feels rather stupid for stating the obvious.

'Yes, but I hardly need them. I wear them for important things like reading, and riding. Oh, and finding my horse.' He chuckles and pushes the cloth away.

The merchant proffers it again. 'It is the finest Worsted cloth, noble lord. From England.'

Hugh's ear pricks up at the word. Worstead is a village near his own family acres, near Aylsham. Its uncarded wool is rightly famous, but for a moment he feels taken out of time and back to the stalls of his boyhood days. He reaches out to let his fingers run over the grey cloth proffered by the merchant. The smell of wool; what worlds that unlocks! How small seem the concerns of a Norfolk lord, he thinks. Yes, but how right, how human the scale.

'I think this old coat will do for another winter, signor, even if I do not.' Sangallo brings Hugh away by the arm, fatherly. 'Come, Hugh. Signor Galli's house is not much further. Michelangelo will be there already, I should say. Jacopo Galli will not be there himself, but I stay here when in town. He is my banker, you know, and Cardinal Riario's, whose palazzo is just up here.'

As they move through the crowds into the side streets, Hugh attempts small talk. 'You do not keep a house in Rome yourself?'

'No, no. I did in the days when my work was here, before Signor Bramante's star rose, and even then, I was hardly there. In those days Julius had me everywhere building, his church San Pietro in Vincoli, his palace within the Castel Angelo and so on. I'm only down now because he wants my advice on the fortifications of Bologna.' He stops, sighs and casts a baleful eye about the Piazza Cancelleria, at Cardinal Riario's great palace. 'I used to think that my career would go from glory to glory, that I would finish in a blaze of Corinthian columns and celestial minarets.' He pauses to chuckle at himself, the loose skin of his neck shaking like a turkey. '*Omnia vanitas*! All is vanity. I never thought I would end as a military engineer. Tell me, Hugh, for you seem like a man who thinks about matters. Where did we pick up this idea that our careers, our buildings, our armies, artillery, our national coffers should grow *ad infinitum*? Unilinear growth seems like a sacred charge that has crept into all our calculations unawares, and unquestioned. It was not so in my boyhood, I fancy. No one talked about progress then.'

'Indeed.' Hugh steps over horse dung and does his best to sound old and disapproving. 'If I recall, the ancients saw it quite the other way round. That it was the shepherds with none of Socrates' *techne* that were, as mankind had once been, "living closer to the gods."'

'That is right. Yes, it is right.' The older man's eyes sparkle with remembrance of books half forgotten.

Hugh, encouraged, begins to warm to a favorite subject. 'Yes, back then they believed in a golden age where the maiden Virgo ruled, when men were content with their own borders, and war was not known among them. But during the silver age that followed she descended little among them from her lofty home on Olympus, except in sorrow. Until finally in the corrupt age of degradation, when men began to eat meat and use iron, she abandoned earth altogether to become a constellation. See how it all comes back to me. And how strange that we have not emphasised this strain of thought along with other aspects of the ancients' wisdom. I am old enough to have seen many benefits conferred upon the arts through this new learning but also some dangers, too. The belief that we and the world will, or even can, ripen toward perfection may itself be a greater snare than ten Borgias or ten thousand paupers.'

'A bishop from my country wrote, "The world hurries on and speeds towards its end, and because of men's sins, it must worsen day by day." Our Lord even, says as much; "Lawlessness will wax worse and prevail."' Seeing Sangallo frown a little, Hugh mumbles apologetically, 'I think our fathers were keener to emphasise past splendour than the present decline.'

'Ah.' Sangallo pats Hugh's shoulder, his smile returning. 'I knew I could talk to you about these things. I first remember their being talked of in earnest during my time with Lorenzo di Medici. *Il Magnifico* was a good man, and he had wonderful evenings in his *studiolo* with people like Pico Mirandola, Alberti and Ficino. All the boys. Even Michelangelo came to one or two, for he lived there, but long before his beard grew. We were young. Well, younger. We read Plato, Aristotle,

Livy, Manetti even. It was exciting. We talked as young men do – mostly piss and wind. But we felt free to explore the old world. We never thought this new learning, so called, would gather such a force, that these *Umanisti* in the emperor's territories would make it such a thing in itself. Some of them are as godless as Boccaccio and Farranata, and that is saying something. The foundation of Lorenzo's library was the Scriptures and the patristics. Even Pico, who was always prone to mysticism, came to his senses eventually. I remember him once saying to a sixteen-year-old Michelangelo, "Philosophy seeks truth, theology holds it, and religion possesses it." Or something very like it. I think it sound advice, do you not?'

'Yes, indeed.'

'Well, so you should. We old men have lived through times of great change. We have seen things. Tradition was valued then unlike today. A thinking man favoured Plato or Aristotle, but he loved Christ. And you could assume that a patrician was a Virgilian, or at least, a Horatian. But now, Hugh, now I sense a new spirit abroad. Oh, perhaps it is just my age but I fear this new prejudice for novelty, for progress, will isolate men's minds in their own times, cut off from the wisdom of former ages like an army severed from its other regiments on a long campaign. It bodes ill. But I see I am boring you. Forgive me.'

'Not at all, signor. I love to hear from your lips of these older times, these men of renown.'

'Ah, and now they are all dead—Pico, Lorenzo, old Bertoldo. Such good men, Hugh, so full of life and ideas. I wish you could have been there and met them. But they are gone now, all but me, and maybe old Botticelli.' He pauses and looks once more into the cobbles. 'And now I must strengthen the bastions of Bologna before I die, and not build a great basilica for Saint Peter as I had hoped. There are not enough cobbles on the path to the valley of humiliation. Pray God that I do not catch a slip on the way. Ah, but these are the ramblings of an old man, Hugh. I will leave you thinking that I am ungrateful when I am not. I have had the privilege of serving the Curia in many ways, for the glory of the church and of Florence. And not just Julius. Alexander before him had me construct the coffered ceiling for Santa Maria Maggiore. Have you seen it? I used volcanic ash, *pozzolana*. Came out better than anyone predicted, which is a good thing, or my neck might have felt the weight of my boots!'

'Yes, I am told that the Borgia pope overlaid it with gold from the New World. Was he as wicked as everyone said?'

'He was charming, actually. Very witty. That was what I remember most. That is the shock of it, Hugh. It is sobering and I often think on it. Philisophia tells Boethius that "wickedness is the reward of the wicked". Saint Paul says the same somewhere, and I believe it. I don't think Rodrigo Borgia, or his son, were any different from the inhabitants of Virgil's hell, who all "had purposed great deeds and got their own way". That gold from the new world? Some say it was wrong for the Spaniards to take it. Most say not. All I say is that it hurt the people from whom they took it, and I cannot but think that it will hurt us in Christendom in the spending of it. I do not mean the gilding of ceilings and altarpieces, though it has done much of that in Italy and Spain. I mean the way high finance now dominates everything, even the stars. It did us no good to have so much gold appear so quickly. It has made Christendom mad with avarice. Europe is now run, not from the palaces of worthy men, but from the counting houses of Antwerp, Seville, Naples and Venice. It bodes ill. My friend Jacopo Galli tells me things, keeps me abreast of these matters. He was a banker, you know, but I have already told you that. Look, here is his house. Give me your arm and help me up these steps. Why they are so steep, I don't know. Could they not recess them? If you want to see stairs, nice shallow stairs that virtually carry a man up them, then go the Palazzo Pitti in Florence, a brutish building for brutish times, but my, my, what stairs they have, they almost carry you.'

The residence of their absent host is a four-story townhouse in the piazza. It is part rusticated like the palazzos of the last generation and part iron-grilled fort to keep out Romans in high spirits, which seems now to be less regular than it was a decade ago. Galli's man leads them through a marble vestibule lined with prints and maps. They pass more doors and into a courtyard where Michelangelo is standing in front of a marble Bacchus, life size and highly polished.

'Greek?' Hugh says, after the general greetings.

Sangallo chuckles, and Michelangelo replies. 'My own work, the work of a younger man. What say you, Guliano? Ten, twelve years ago?'

'At least. You were a young coxcomb then, but sometimes I wish I could see that impish smile of yours again, my friend.' Sangallo watches Hugh run his fingers over the statue's hands, the cup, the grapes, the veins under the skin. 'Not bad for a ruddy-face lad fresh in the city, barely a whisker on his face.'

'Or *scudi* in my pocket!' Michelangelo adds, now smiling for the first time that Hugh has seen. 'The commission was for the great cardinal across the courtyard, and very glad of the work I was, too.'

'But why is it here?' Hugh stands back to admire the cheeky smile, the glacial idealism wrought in the marble. 'Was this man Galli given it as a gift from his employer?'

'Hah!' Sangallo laughs. 'Riario? Not likely.'

Michelangelo replies, 'He didn't like it, so Galli bought it, and I must say that it feels strange after so many years to see it again. Makes me grateful I think, that I am still here – grateful for all the work I did manage to do over these last years, I suppose.'

'I know, my boy, I know.' Sangallo cusps his arm about Michelangelo's shoulder. Hugh sees the tears in the younger man's eyes. 'They have not been easy years, but let us see this vault finished, then you can go back to the *pieta serena*. God will help you. Now come, come. I will freeze if I have to stand outside here any longer, let us find the fireside, eh?'

They have been conversing for nearly an hour before the subject of Hugh's travels is brought up. They are sitting in Jacopo Galli's upper *studiolo*, which reminds Hugh of his own family's solar at Erpingham Hall, which had always been a quiet place in the oldest part of the house, and a good place to lose yourself in a book. The thick beams are richly painted in geometric patterns and the walls are hung with tapestries and other hangings. Hugh and Michelangelo sit at a table covered by a richly embroidered rug, an inkhorn, many papers and folios. The old architect has pulled his chair up to the mouth of the fire, where thick olivewood logs glow and smoulder in rich plumes of fragrant smoke.

'These cold days get right into my lower legs. I feel them, cold as ice, and we've been here an hour. Anyway, anyway. Enough of my ailments, you say the emperor wishes to talk to you at Saint Gallen. Have you been there before? No? A beautiful area, the Bodensee, if you have not been to Italy, that is. But yes, beautiful, like a garden of Eden among the lands of the north. Around that vast lake they have vineyards, monasteries and farms as fine as anything we have even around Florence.'

'High praise indeed, signor.' Hugh winks at Michelangelo, who is not really listening.

Sangallo continues, 'And from there, where?'

'I'm not sure yet, but I have an appointment in Siena this Eastertide, so I will no doubt head south with the emperor's armies when he comes, or make my own way.'

'Siena.' Michelangelo sighs. 'I've not been there for a long time.'

'More work from your younger days, eh!' Sangallo adds.

'Yes, a commission for Cardinal Francesco Piccolomini.' As if Hugh might not know, he adds, 'Who later became pope, though only for eighteen days.'

'Yes, I know of it. What did he commission?'

'Oh, a number of statues, small ones, for an altarpiece dedicated to his uncle.'

'Fifteen,' Sangallo says.

'I didn't finish them all,' Michelangelo continues, a pinkness showing in the leathered skin above his beard.

'Four!' Sangallo snipes from his chair again.

'Yes, four. It was not an easy time.' Michelangelo's eyes are firmly fixed on the inkhorn.

'Not an easy time? You young people!' Sangallo roars a laugh, and turns back toward them. 'You signed a contract with the good cardinal to say you would take no new commissions for three years if I remember aright, and five hundred ducats was a goodly sum for a lad your age, and then you signed another with the Signoria of Florence seven days later to carve David.'

Eyes still on the inkhorn, Michelangelo rubs his nose. 'I know it was wrong, but I'd been watching that mouldering slab of marble for so long. It felt like destiny.'

'It's a good thing only divine geniuses do that sort of thing,' Sangallo concludes, settling back again in his chair. 'If we architects and engineers were like that, we'd be strung up, or find ourselves on the wrong end of a *strapado*.'

There is a long pause, with only the sound of Sangallo poking the coals with the tongs. Eventually Michelangelo sniffs and says, 'I did intend to return to Siena. In fact, it wasn't really my intention to leave. Only they were constructing the cardinal's new library at the time. It was built onto the nave of the duomo, and I went in to talk to the worker. I wasn't really looking where I was going, and fell into a hole. I sprained my wrist.'

'A hole?' Hugh says.

'Yes, it was a shaft that went down eighteen feet into the *bottini* tunnels under the city. I could have been seriously hurt. But as it was, I managed to hold onto the scaffold.'

'Tunnels?' Hugh leant forward trying not to look too interested. *Vendramin*.

'Yes, they are very common in these hilltop places like Orvieto. Siena relies on them for the public water supply, fountains, and so forth.' Michelangelo examines his right wrist, flexing it before his eyes. 'I was livid. It set me back weeks. Couldn't work, so I left for home to see my father and brothers, and then, well, then all that business with David started – I just knew it when I saw that slab of marble. It seemed to call to me.'

'And do you think it is still there?'

'The marble?'

'No, the hole?'

'I doubt it. They probably filled it in or capped it.'

'Probably.' *Vendramin*.

MARCH 6TH, 1509. THE MONASTIC ISLAND OF REICHENAU IN THE RHINE, NEAR KONSTANZ

'Welcome, honoured guests.' A weary Benedictine opens his arms in the courtyard outside the German abbey. 'Come, you are cold and wet. Welcome in the name of the Virgin and Saint Mark. I am Brother Santfrid,' he adds nervously. 'Come in, come in. We are most honoured.' It is the second watch of the night; no one is listening. They took a wrong turn and have taken hours longer to get here than expected.

The bedraggled party step forward without a second invitation. Amongst the sodden elect are Colocci, Bembo, the cardinals, Archbishop Ippolito d'Este and Hugh. Their own servants, retainers and affinity are unpacking the mules behind them, water running like alpine falls pour from their waxed hats and travelling cloaks. Their journey up from Avignon has been long and unpleasant: roads mired, horses lamed, everyone road-weary and rheumatic, some like Bembo, even feverish. The abbey serves them well; their cots are hard but free of wildlife. Hugh secures his own shutters and sees a gap in the clouds where the sleet has put a hard, bright polish on the stars. It might yet freeze, but even so, sleep comes readily.

Bembo doesn't attend the mass in honour of Saints Perpetua and Felicity later that day, but Hugh does. He has slept well, risen with the angelus bell and come alone to the abbey, drawn by the melancholic Latin chant of the monks. He crosses under the western portal into the simple nave with its sandstone columns and polychrome banded arches. *What is the lighter stone? Limestone probably.* Hugh inhales the incense, thick, peppery, sweet. The nave is full of villagers, mainly women who shuffle on the rushes and sniff their way closer to the altar. Perpetua and Felicity are popular with the women.

He advances to the back of the nave and lays a hand on the iron-red pillar, unfluted and roughhewn sandstone. He likes this early Romanesque simplicity. There is something pure and honest about it – young even, innocent. A pillar like this might be like the ones used at the military games in Carthage on the emperor's birthday when the Roman noblewoman Perpetua and her bond slave were slain. She refused the pleas of her father, and the cries of her babe in arms. She would not deny Christ, but rather died amongst slaves. Death, the great leveler. Christianity, the universal acid that ate up the old world, its gods, its philosophies.

Did they ever believe in Jupiter and Pan? Hugh wonders. *No, not really. Carthaginians were far too practical to be moral. Those Punic merchant princes, like modern Europe's, could never understand the spirit of the Scipios. Everything was material. Scudi per hour, as it is in our day. This new war is just the Fuggers' and the Chigi's money gambling on the despoliation of Venice. Their capital to gain a capital. He whose finance can leverage the most mercenaries, wins. Mercenary bands are purchased, as one purchases figs and dates. Apparently, the King of Naples once asked how the Florentines could possibly expect to resist him with their own soldiers. They told him: "fealty, honour, chivalry." What are they replaced with? Scudi, gilders and florins.*

Carthage will never understand Jerusalem. That said, even armies may march on florins, but they will not fight to the death for them, or at least, they will not go on fighting against hope. Could the emperor hire Christians to be eaten by lions for thirty scudi an hour? When sane men dream, it is not about how they can live, but why they do. Our drive for meaning makes mockery of all their calculations. No, Carthage will never understand Jerusalem. Perpetua knew that. She knew why. But do I?

He imagines the two women chained to the pillar. They have Felice's and Vittoria's faces. He imagines how he would rescue them. Many gladiators, Roman soldiers and wild beasts have fallen to his sword before he catches himself daydreaming and smiles. *Cockscomb.*

AN HOUR LATER AT LUNCH IN THE ABBOT'S LODGING

'I have heard that you are the scourge of every infidel.'

'*Se non vero e ben trovato.* If not true, then well founded.' Hugh smiles sardonically as he looks toward the grate. The fire smokes badly, but the smell of applewood is not unpleasant, it curls in the rafters under the tiles.

Brother Santfrid folds his hands inside thick woollen sleeves, saying as he does so, 'Did you know that our founder, Pirmin, came here first when fleeing the Saracens in Spain? He was greatly influenced by the Irish.'

Hugh nods, and tries to look interested. He hasn't eaten since yesterday, and so is consuming quantities of bread, quite happy to let Brother Santfrid do all the talking. The amiable monk, mid-fifties with rabbit teeth and no neck, rambles in Latin about the glories of their monastery. Hugh only half listens while his companions further up the table converse with the abbot. Bembo is within earshot, as ever, but not inclined for once to talk because of his headache and humors.

Santfrid makes exclamations every now and again in a Saxon dialect that Hugh cannot understand, and asks the questions for which he never waits for a reply. It is, as Hugh sees it, not because he is uninterested, but he does not wish to trouble his guests to answer. He phrases things so that a look suffices.

'Yes, yes, our school, our library and scriptorium are famous, eclipsed by Saint Gallen now. We are happy for them for we have always had a close prayer brotherhood since the earliest times. Many of the most educated men of these lands came here once and still do, for learning has flourished here since the Renaissance.'

Hugh repeats the word through his stuffed mouth, *'Renascentia?'*

Santfrid smiles so that the creases deeply furrow his bald forehead. 'You think maybe I mean this New Learning, these *Humanisti*. Italians, Italians.' Santfrid quietly dismisses them with his fingers, and whispers, 'They read a little Greek, a little Plato and it goes to their heads, like boys with strong wine. But here, on this little island we have drunk the oldest and best wines for centuries, since the reign of Charlemagne. Are you interested in learning? I see you are. English always are. Did you know that we have you Britons to thank for this place, for it was founded as a house of mixed rule, partly of Benedict, and partly of your Irish monk Columbanus. Not so long ago we had the best scriptorium and school of painting in Europe.'

'A monastery without books is like a fortress without weapons,' Hugh says between mouthfuls.

'Ah, you like Kempis. Good. Of course, our manuscripts were sought after and sent out to the world. Our abbots were permitted to wear dalmatic and pontifical sandals, reserved usually only for the bishops of Rome. What say you to that?'

Bembo stirs from the side and croaks, 'A rare marvel, brother.'

Brother Santfrid starts again. 'Pardon friend, I did not catch that; my hearing is not too good.'

'Want of practice perhaps?' Bembo says. Hugh raises an eyebrow at him.

'Ah, I speak too much; my nerves, you see.' Santfrid smiles sweetly. 'But let me fetch something for you. I can see that a fever is breaking. I will fetch an infusion.' With this Santfrid beetles off to the abbot's kitchen leaving the two men at table.

'He means no harm, Pietro, and we are his guests.'

‘These Alemani and their miserable weather. Oh, my head.’ Bembo massages his temples and stares through window glass made opaque by the constant rain. Hugh misses not having Prior Battista with him. And being this close to England brings on his own, somewhat unfamiliar melancholia. Hugh de Erpingham, the Norfolk nobleman, was a previous incarnation. To think of that man now, is like rereading a childhood book after many years and remembering the once familiar characters. Wilf has said little here, but Hugh knows he feels the call of home, too.

‘Here we are now.’ Brother Santfrid returns with a bowl of bread for Hugh, and a steaming cup for Bembo. ‘This, my friend, is an infusion of dried sage flowers with mint and honey. Sage was recommended by another of our famous abbots, Walafrid Strabo. “Effective powers and healing to drink,” he wrote in his *De Cultura Hortorum*. You know the name? No? Oh dear. He was the foremost poet of his age, and not just on theological themes – or natural philosophy. It will please you, Signor Bembo, to know that Walafrid recorded the dream of another of our monks, a brother Wetti, and his poem was an important precursor to your Dante Alighieri and his *Divina Comedia*.’

‘Ah, of course,’ Bembo straightens to receive his drink with something approaching a smile of apology. ‘The *Visio Wettini* is much talked about, but I have not read it.’

‘Perhaps I could have a brother bring it to your room this afternoon that you may read it in bed. It is finely illuminated. I am sure brother librarian would not mind – for a man, a scholar even, who is not well.’

‘Very good of you. Provided Hugh is not off somewhere doing something important, then bedrest and books sound like paradise.’

MARCH 7TH - FEAST OF SAINT THOMAS AQUINAS

‘Come, Bembo.’ Hugh throws his feather bolster toward the other bed. ‘Are you alive in there?’

Bembo groans under his covers. ‘Yes, in the sense that I cannot be legally buried. What time is it?’

'Breakfast, you sluggard. Get up, or you'll be late to meet the emperor.' Hugh prods the groaning form under the crumpled bedlinen with his boot.

Another groan. 'I can't be late if I don't show up. The riding is killing me.'

'Suit yourself.' Hugh opens the door and is about to descend to the refectory to break his fast. Bembo will show up, a chance to meet the Holy Roman Emperor is something to tell your grandchildren about.

He hears Bembo groaning and cursing under the sheets. 'This bed is so hard it makes some of those inns last week seem positively Burgundian.'

'Come on, man. Rouse yourself.' Hugh kicks his wooden bedpost.

'It's all right for you,' Bembo whines. 'You get a straight night's sleep. I remember youth well enough. When I was your age, I could get it up three times a night. But now I have to get up three times a night for the privy instead. When I turned forty, overnight I became my father, a positive martyr to his bladder. You wait, Hugh. Oh, what's the use. Yes, yes, I'm coming, you prick. Just wait for me, will you? It takes longer these days to wash my face. That's how I realised I was going bald.'

'Stop whining.' Hugh starts down the stairs.

'You wait,' Bembo calls after him. 'It'll come to you, too. Somewhere in your late thirties you will begin to fear growing old more than dying. *Dio mio*, my back is killing me.'

An hour later they are being rowed in the abbot's barge up river from the island in great state. Hugh observes the men at their oars as he sits on a cushion at the stern. His back twitches as if anticipating the lash. His humors unsettle; bile rises in his gut. The rattling of the rowlocks, the creaking of rope, and timber. The smell of pitch and pine. The slapping and lapping of calm waters on the hull as they approach the city. Hugh suppresses the irrational thoughts that bombard his mind at every sharp noise—thoughts that urge him to flee his cushion, throw himself overboard, escape before they fasten him to the oars. The bank is only a hundred yards away. *I could easily swim it.* Then what?

Hide in the reeds? Hide forever? He squeezes both eyes shut. Useless. It's useless. It is as close to hell by land as it is by sea.

Konstanz is a queen among cities, guarding the crystal waters of the Rhine as it flows from the Swabian Sea to give life to the northlands. Red roofed, square turreted, high, grey, stone walls – it's a place that expects to be sieged. After an hour the abbot's barge rounds the last corner onto the lake, which today is calm as a millpond. Forty miles long, the great lake is bounded by vineyards and orchards. Amidst these farmlands army encampments are interspersed like canvas infestations. Beyond them are great monastic cities like Bregenz and Saint Gallen – plantings of émigré Irish monks. And beyond that the Alps suggest themselves through jagged shapes in the mists to the south.

At Hugh's right, Brother Santfrid gives a running commentary of things needful and much that is not. He points to what looks like a headland to their left and says, 'Not a headland but actually the island of Mainau, where your former brothers, the Teutonic knights, had their castle. Do you intend to visit them? No matter.' He points to the other side of the boat to a large bastion opening straight onto a wharf. 'We will disembark here. That large dormered building to the left of the gate is the merchants' warehouse. It is the only place big enough for the emperor's coterie. It was where the great conclave was held in Pope Martin's Day. It's still called the *Konzilgebäude*. Watch your purses. The streets will be busy, and war brings all sorts out. And as to the soldiery in the encampments, they can laugh and spend now for most will never return.'

'You disapprove of this war?'

'Ah, well, what would I know. Besides, wars don't determine who's right, only who's left.' He's plucky for such a talker.

Twenty minutes later they are ushered to window seats in the merchant's hall. It is vast, low ceilinged, dark, with thick timbers and all about the throng of a court preparing for the long march to war. Hugh is not tall, but he can see Holy Roman Emperor Maximilian in his winter furs, sitting at the far end of a dais flanked by his advisors, knights and a tall cardinal in a crimson dalmatic. Hugh sits uneasily, ingesting the odors of malt and boot leather. The lake stretches beyond the window, but inside, all is business.

Santfrid talks to a young Augustinian in the next window bay who seems to know who is who. After a short conversation he flutters back to Hugh and Bembo to report: first the irrelevance that they had both been at the Erfurt University, 'which he called a beerhouse and a whore house', and then a list of illustrious persons at the other end of the hall.

'It appears we've come on accounts day. These austere gentlemen on the Kaiser's left are the upper German banker families. The old one in the blue is Jorg Baumgarten, something of an advisor. The others are the Weslers and Fuggers who have great shares in the Tyrolean copper and silver mines.'

'Ah,' Hugh says. 'Come to make sure their coin is being well invested.' The emperor is already indebted to them for a million gulden, but they look worried as men who have bet their own coats. Along with everyone else, they have heard the Venetians boast that they spent thirty-six million gold ducats in the last decade on wars against the emperor, the pope and the kings of France and Spain. Three hundred thousand ducats a month. Jacob Fugger worries that northern financial leverage will not suffice if the war drags out.

Hugh moves his eyes to the right. 'And tell me, who is the tall cardinal sitting to the emperor's right?'

'Cardinal Georges D'Amboise, who advises Louis XII.'

'Ah, yes, of course.'

Santfrid mistakes Hugh's look of recognition. 'You know this man? They say he virtually rules the kingdom of France.'

'His brother is the grandmaster of my order.' *What strange bedfellows wars doth make*, Hugh thinks. *Mind, even Pilate and Herod became friends on the day they murdered Christ.* Here too, inveterate enemies slouch uneasily on the same dais for the sacrifice and dismemberment of Venice.

They are interrupted by the court secretary, who has pushed his way through crowds of courtiers and now speaks imperiously through a bush-thick beard, '*Sie sind der Engländer, der Ritter?*'

Santfrid answers, '*Ja, er kann nicht sprechen Deutsch. Latein sprechen.*'

The secretary nods, saying now in Latin to Hugh, 'Come please. Just you. They will speak Latin for you.' Colocci, the cardinals, Bembo and the others sit back again. Hugh wonders if they are glad or insulted. Cardinal Petrucci, somewhat taciturn, says he doesn't see what all the formality signifies. 'For surely everyone knows the emperor's lands are little more than one more papal beneficium.'

Hugh removes his beret and bows so low that he can examine the stitching on his own boots. He is called to approach and so straightens carefully to give himself time to observe two of the most powerful men in Europe. The emperor's nose curls like a crumpled silk slipper, his lips curl down at the corners as one who expects to be disappointed. His eyes are intelligent, humane if careworn, and he seems genuinely pleased to have Hugh presented to him.

Kaiser Maximilian opens a long, heavy jaw. '*The* knight of Rhodes.' He leans forward on his elbows so that Hugh can see ensigns of empire carved into the headrest of the throne, and also the family escutcheon on the seat back. 'Come forward.' He speaks with a guttural attempt at English, which is more than anyone else has tried south of the channel. The emperor's raised arm reveals finely fluted and etched steel below the furs. He loves armour. It won't protect him from his bankers' ruinous interest, but it looks good. A large table is before them covered with maps and folios. Back into Latin, the emperor says, 'I speak many languages – one has to with a job like this, but that is all I can manage in English.'

Hugh nods uneasily and glances toward the bankers huddled in a group talking among themselves, and then across to Cardinal d'Amboise, seated and apparently reading a breve. 'Your majesty is most gracious.'

Cardinal d'Amboise speaks without looking up. 'I understand my brother has sent you with urgent news regarding the insolence of the infidel.' His gaze rises briefly, but then returns to his breve. His skin appears grey like marble, his tone as smooth and hard as porphyry. For most in the room, his face is the face of the very devil, but now, here, Hugh can see in the eyes, chin and nose the visage of his own master. *At some point,* he thinks, *we are all brothers*. Cains and Abels, Abels and Cains, all waiting to find out who is who.

'Eminence, your brother the grandmaster has sent me to inform all princes in Europe that they stand in gravest danger from the east, now more than ever. Even now the arsenals of Gallipoli and Constantinople are preparing a great fleet of invasion. These I have seen with my own eyes. With the leadership of His Holiness and your Imperial Majesty the threat can be countered.'

'Indeed, it must; *we* must.' Maximilian runs a searching finger along the fluting on his breastplate.

'And France surely. You will perhaps remember,' the cardinal interjects with a matronly tone. 'It was *we* Franks who countered the threat when the Moors overran Aquitaine, Narbonne, Provence. It was *our* heavy cavalry that repelled the Moslems, it was *our* ancestors.'

'Indeed,' the emperor says in a weary, mausoleum baritone. 'Indeed, and as it was in the days of Charles Martel, or Pipin and Charlemagne, so too it shall be in ours. For these *Christi nomines hostes, these* enemies of Christ, will not be happy until they have slaughtered their way through Europe and made it twice the hellhole as their own lands. We shall crush them, my good Cardinal, but first the Venetians, who have grown fat on their dealings with these devils. His Eminence agrees?'

His Eminence does. The despoiling of Venice and a crusade on the Turks is about the only thing d'Amboise agrees on with Julius, the man who beat him to the papal tiara. Hugh has heard the stories. Cardinal d'Amboise could have forced the conclave to accept him instead of Julius because he was then at the head of the unbeatable French army in Italy. But he was persuaded by friends that force was not necessary. They said that he should allow gentle persuasion to win him the place. The 'friends' were Julius' friends as it turned out. And from the look of him now, Hugh thinks, d'Amboise and 'soft persuasion' have not been on first name terms since. He has been heard to remark somewhat ungraciously to the Genoise ambassador, 'What do you expect? If we turn the election of the pope into a three-ring circus, is it surprising that often we end up with a dancing bear?'

'Tell me.' The emperor's ample, sagging chops move outwards into a smile. 'Is this the sword with which you slew a hundred Saracens?'

'Or was it a jawbone?' the cardinal adds, now looking up with a sort of sarcastic interest. 'I heard it was a jawbone.'

'No, Majesty. This was leant to me.' Hugh does not dignify the cardinal's mockery with even a glance. He has made whole ships red as charnel houses. If only it *had* been a mere hundred. He casts his eyes downward and holds back the tears.

'I see your modesty, sir knight. It is well. It is well.' Maximilian leans backward into his chair so that it and his harness straps creek and clink in unison. He begins to brush his smooth upper lip with the edge of his thumb, amused at something he is recollecting. 'I read in the new English prose account of Arthur that his knight Lancelot was both the "meekest man that ever ate in the hall among ladies", and "the sternest knight among his enemies". And that when he was lauded thus, he cried as if he had been a child beaten. What think you, Cardinal? The fiercest knight and the meekest courtier. A wolf on the field and a lamb in the palazzo. Not a mixture of the two, but both contrary traits *in extremis* within one man. To combine them thus is not a work of nature but a work of art, I fancy.'

'A work of Christian art if I may say so,' D'Amboise adds, who is now suddenly interested again.

They ask further questions about the state of affairs in the east, and before he is dismissed, Hugh tries to secure funds for arming a new fleet and better enforcements on Rhodes.

'I think you'll find that sort of request falling on hard ground, Fra Erpingham,' Kaiser Maximilian chides. 'We were given the impression that it was you knights who had inexhaustible wealth – what with your lucrative business of relieving the infidels of their ill-gotten gains. But with us?' The emperor breaks off with an eye to the Fugger's banking clerks to his left. 'Well, things might be different in a season or two.

Until then you must verily rest assured that we are obedient sons of the church. And as soon as matters are brought to a conclusion with Venice, you will find us ready to do our holy duty.'

'Yes, for God's sake,' Cardinal d'Amboise says with a weary sigh, 'tell my brother to be patient. Tell him that if he could perhaps restrain his knights from exacerbating the Turks by further pillage for a month or two, then we will organise relief of some sort. And don't feign surprise, Erpingham. Do you think we don't know that you knights are fourth-fifths of the problem in the current crisis? How else can you have your great glory, Fra Erpingham, if not for laying insult upon insult on the Sultan's head. No Samson, no angry Philistines. But don't go from here in a fit of self-pity, telling everyone that Christendom has turned its back on you. You shall have help, no doubt, but on our terms and in our good time. The pope shall have his *Cruciata* tax by midsummer direct to the apostolic camera; he need not send so many reminders.'

'Hah!' snorted the emperor. 'He'll have'em in Venetian ducats, *Deo volente.*'

Ah, thinks Hugh, as he bows out, *by midsummer, they will all be rich men. Deo volente.*

ONE HOUR LATER, THE EAST WHARF, KONSTANZ ON THE SWABIAN SEA

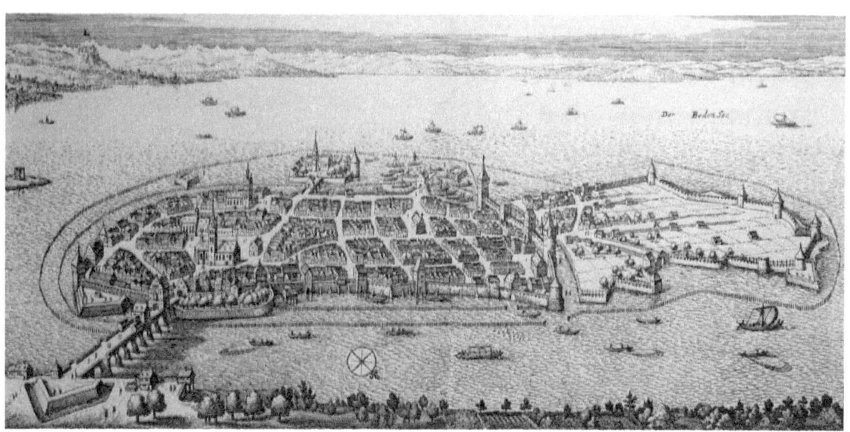

Back on the wharf after lunch, Hugh spots the Augustinian who Santfrid consulted with in the hall, standing at the end of the main pier, gazing across the still waters to the north. In an attempt to avoid the bombardment of questions from his own party, all eager to know what was said at the interview, Hugh slips from them and walks on the wet boards towards the friar. They stand shoulder to shoulder. They are of an age, both miles away in thought. Both angry young men.

The friar looks intently to the right, eyeballing something. Hugh follows his eyes toward a large fortified house on a small island; separated from the town and mainland by a clear channel ten feet wide.

The angelus bell clangs dull and forlorn over the little island. 'An Augustinian friary?' Hugh asks.

The friar smiles briefly and unconvincingly. 'No. It is a Dominican house. You are the knight from England?'

'From Rhodes.'

'Of course.' He returns his eyes toward the grey walls. 'Your Benedictine host told me about you.'

'Brother Santrid is a man of information.'

'Yes. He told me that a former abbot, the poet Walafrid, questioned the church's teaching on transubstantiation. I should like to visit Reichenau before I return, for it was once a place of great learning. Or so he tells me.'

'Or so, he tells everyone,' Hugh quips, adding, 'He told me that you teach theology at a university?'

'Yes, in Erfurt, north of here.'

'You must have studied hard.'

'It is not by studying and speculating that one becomes a theologian – or a knight, I suppose – but by living, indeed, by dying and being damned.'

'I did not get that impression from my lecturers at Cambridge.'

'Your university?'

'Yes.'

'How many years ago?'

'Five, six.'

'Me, too.' The friar's face widens at the memory, but constricts again. 'I was studying law at Erfurt, living a dissolute life like all students. They have this saying among the Franks: to drink like a German. Do you have this in England?'

'I have heard it once or twice.' *Thought it was a compliment.*

'I had been brought up a certain way. I pretended that it did not bother me, but one night in a thunderstorm, I was flung from my horse when a bolt landed near me. I was scared out of my wits, and cried out, "Saint Anne, help me. I shall become a monk." That was it; I just said it. We have a word *afechtung* but it is not so easy to translate into Latin. Maybe you have a word in English but I do not know. It means to be cut to the heart, to the very soul by the knowledge of sin. But that is not really all of it how can I say it? Because the knowledge of it within the understanding that Christ has already paid. You understand?'

Hugh is about to say he does, mainly from English politeness, but then he hesitates. The friar glances aside toward the lake out of embarrassment, but just as Hugh thinks he must change the subject the friar blurts out, 'but of course, you know the legend of this lake? Maybe you don't but I will tell it. One very cold winter long ago there was a man who lost his way in a great snow blizzard. He travelled many miles through snow drifts until his horse was almost dead. But then he saw the lights of a town. The watchman greeted him, all amazed. You have just ridden across the iced lake, he said. The traveller collapsed in horror at the danger he had passed through without knowing it. It is a true story they say, and maybe true for you and me too, eh? Anyway, two weeks later I bade farewell to my university friends. Two of them walked with me to the door at the friary in Erfurt. "This day you see me," I told them, "but after this, no more." My father was furious.'

'As was mine when I joined the knights.'

'Ah, so you know then, know how it feels. But "at the Day of Judgement we shall not be asked what we have read –"'

Hugh speaks the second part in unison with him, '"But what we have done."'

'So, you have our von Kempen on Rhodes?'

'Since I was a boy almost *The Imitation* was by my bedside. My mother made me read it every night. I could almost quote Book One off by heart at one stage. "I had rather feel contrition than be skilful in the definition thereof." Oh, those words.' Hugh breaks off and looks down at his feet – his clay feet. He did become skilful in 'the definition thereof' at Cambridge, but then went on to extinguish the voice of his accusing conscience, and thereby genuine contrition. 'Tell me, have you found rest for your conscience in the cloister?'

'Christ forgive me, but I find little relief in the rhythms of penance and absolution. My confessor despairs of me. I am regularly with him six hours at a time.' The friar turns once more to look at Hugh.

'Really?'

'He says I turn every fart into a sin, but I swear I do not.'

'I see.' *What do you say?* Hugh looks up at the eyes of this man who has, in all likelihood, been guilty of no more than youthful high spirits. Has not even *he* found absolution, rest for his conscience? One look into the man's eyes and Hugh can see he is serious.

'Some say, that conscience is no more than a child of tradition, of culture, but I begin to see that conscience is the vital spark of divinity within our fallen nature – the voice of God in the soul. Albertus Magnus of Cologne says that everything should be judged according to the testimony of our conscience. Everything! And no one calls *him* a melancholic. It is his pupil's feast day today; did you know that?'

'Saint Thomas Aquinas?'

'Yes, but I find in the scholastics a tendency to gloss over the terrors of the anxious conscience. Do not you?' The friar's hands are joined, and his right thumb rubs continuously and deeply on his left knuckle.

He's a serious lad, bit on the edge. I should know, I suppose.

'They proclaim "peace" where there is no peace', the monk says. 'They define a man by what he believes rather than what he is, as if he were a clock that just needed the right cogs in place. It is too simple; it is wrong. Have you read any of Johannes Tauler's sermons?'

'No.'

'You should. There are Latin translations, I believe. There is much among our mystical writings, what we call the German theology, that you would find helpful. Tauler speaks from *sapienta experimentalis*, human experience, not the dry dogma of the Thomists. Tauler gives me hope that there is a place of experienced forgiveness and release, which is all a man really wants in this world, is it not?'

It is a rhetorical question, but it does not seem so to Hugh. He see's the gruff visage of Fra Francesco before, and then himself walking away. *Tauler has given this friar hope as that Franciscan has given me hope, like a lone blade of grass in the desert rising at the scent of water.* His heart races, and his neck begins sweating profusely.

He changes the subject. 'I see that you still show an unusual interest in that island.'

'I have never seen it before. It is my first time here.' The friar leaves off his hands and folds his arms. 'Forgive me. I speak in riddles. That is where they held the Bohemian heretic Jan Huss before he was condemned to the flames by the Council of Konstanz, almost a hundred years ago. You have heard of him?'

'Yes.' *Name rings a bell, at least.*

'Huss was radicalised by your countryman John Wycliffe. His ideas tore a large swathe of Bohemia from the church and caused many wars.'

'Wycliffe was a controversial scholar.' Hugh rubs the back of his neck uneasily. 'I'd no idea we English were so influential.'

'Oh yes indeed, as our Colet and More now.'

'Truly. I had not idea.' It's about as politic as Hugh gets. He had heard Colet preach as an undergraduate, but had no idea that Wycliff's influence had spread so far. His great forebear Sir Thomas had Lollard tendencies, and of course, John of Gaunt's family, who shielded Wycliffe, was his neighbour in Aylesham. When the friar makes no response, Hugh thinks he might have offended, or worse been dull. 'These ideas must have been dangerous.'

'Well, of course,' the friar says, then nods seriously. 'Huss preached against indulgences, saying that men can obtain forgiveness of sins by true repentance, not money. He denounced the papacy as a den of adulterers and Simonists.' The friar strokes the back of his immaculately clipped tonsure. His jaw is resolute, face lean and tight as a bowstring. 'He also said that no pope or bishop had the right to take up the sword in the name of the Church; rather he should pray for his enemies and bless those that curse him.'

'Not a mandate for ecclesiastical preferment perhaps.'

'No. They sent for him here when the great council was convened, and King Sigismund gave him a guarantee of safe conduct. Wasn't worth a gnat's arse; they clapped him in irons over there.' He points to the castle-cum-friary. 'The Dominicans were very hospitable, apparently.'

The friar takes a deep breath and exhales like one with indigestion. 'And so, they tried him in the Munster there.' The friar gestures to the finely traced steeple piercing the skyline above the red roofs of the town. 'He said he would not recant doctrines he had never preached, but he would recant any part that they could prove from the scriptures. *Sola Scriptura*, that was Huss, men of his day were bloody minded you know. They led him through the streets naked apart from a high paper hat with the word *Haeresiarcha*, arch-heretic. And they burnt him with straw stacked to his chin. I confess to you that there was a time when I would have lit the first faggot. I say it to my shame. Anyway, they burnt him just over there.'

'When I was a boy, my father took me to watch a man burnt at the Lollard's pit in Norwich.' For a stricken moment Hugh shudders at the remembrance: charred fingers, beards aflame and lips bursting. When he can finally summon words again, they are faint. 'He had wanted a Bible in his own tongue. Not all speak Latin.'

'To coerce a Christian against his conscience is a terrible resort. It can never be otherwise. Never.' The friar folds his arms again. 'To kill a man is not to defend a doctrine; it is to kill a man. The last thing Huss said was that in a hundred years God would raise up those whose calls for reform would not be suppressed.'

'*Exsurgent enim defensorem domus ossa mea*, an avenger will arise from my bones,' Hugh says, trying lamely to impress the professor, while all the time a lump grows in his throat. Without being aware he had formulated the sentence, Hugh blurts out, 'Six years left then.'

The words seem to pierce the Augustinian like a bodkin between the joints. A creak on the planks alone breaks the silence that follows. Hugh turns to see Santfrid hurrying down the pier.

The friar nods with solemnity. 'Yes indeed. Six years. I heard that Pope Julius has issued the sale of indulgences for the rebuilding of Saint Peter's. I am told that the old basilica was not big enough for the tomb he plans for himself. You have come from Rome. Is it true?'

"I cannot say. People say many things in cities.'

"All I know is that more indulgences will strip the skin from the backs of my countrymen. It bodes ill. I will say no more.' He pauses. 'Could you go to the flames, knight? Frankly, I don't think I have the guts for it.'

The scuffle and shuffling on the boards grow louder as Santfrid approaches. 'Fra Hugh, there you are. Our boat has arrived.'

Hugh holds out a hand to the friar. 'I fear I must thank you for your conversation and bid you farewell, Friar…?'

'Friar Martin.' He smiles with the intensity of gaze that would unsettle a lesser man. 'Martin Luther.'

MARCH 12TH, JOURNEY SOUTH TO MILAN.

'If you don't think things can get any worse, it is because you lack imagination.' Bembo pulls his hood down, against the fifth shower of driving sleet of the morning. 'Spring my arse. What do they get in summer here, snow? I swear, I will never leave Urbino again!'

The sleet falls like icy curtains across the valley as they negotiate the road south to the San Bernadino Pass. They are still two days away, but already the Alps loom like the jaws of Hades. Every glance at them sets Hugh's humours out. Nevertheless, their guide says it can be done, and it will cut his journey to Milan by a third. The others have gone back the safe way - all except Bembo, who complains like a mule.

'I swear to you, Erpingham, that when I write up these expeditions, as His Holiness has commanded, I shall give myself all the best lines.'

'You have to survive first.' Hugh faces down, as he tries vainly to keep the water from running down his neck.

On their way towards Saint Gallen, they pass through the emperor's encampments, canvas cities of optimism and filth, sprawling into the fields on either side of the road. *Why don't German and Swiss fields have hedges or walls?* Soggy, flapping banners unfurl on poles at the outskirts of the camp, redolent with odours of wet wool and wood smoke. It is the only remotely pleasant smell here; beyond that, the lack of sanitation will be pervasive in nostrils, clothing, and hair. A minute later Hugh draws his scarf about his mouth and nose, thankful for the rain. Wilf curses at the rear, still calling them all "filthy dagos".

Contagion and pestilence follow an army like a sot runs after ale. Jail fever is already in evidence here, which can carry off more than battle or the drink. They pass the quarantine tent, hear the low moans. Bowels void continuously. Hugh imagines the poor sods supine, listless; delirious with raging fevers, head pains, red rashes and putrefying sores. The fever came from Spain, like other pestilences. Like the Borgias. The Swiss mercenaries are much in evidence, their pikes standing like forests about their tents. Maximilian's methods will be big guns, a monstrous weight of shot, and unstoppable Swiss pikes. Every prince in Europe is copying him. It's why these Schweitzer's are all rich men.

Movement is slow, for the road is clogged by the great stumbling tail of camp followers: tradesmen, tapsters, women and farriers. Sutlers hawk their wares from the backs of wagons blocking the road. It's boom time for them. Officers and vintners bark orders in the miserable rain and mud. They dream of warmer and dryer places, of drinking the Doge's best vintage in the Piazza San Marco, their feet dipped in the azure water of the Grand Canal.

Hugh spots a priest processing with a monstrance further up the field, surrounded by a band of monks and sodden soldiers. Some of the king's Swiss Guard, with scriven plumes in their helmets, and dripping brocade mantles, follow the monks. Also, a detachment of Gascon infantry. Everyone is devout when it comes to war. It is the feast of St. Gregory the Great today. Some say he was the last of the good popes. What would he have made of this: Christian preparing to fight Christian for filthy lucre's sake? Gregory is the patron saint of musicians. These, his heirs, have summoned the piper; now they must dance.

LETTER FROM SAINT GALLEN TO FLORENCE, MARCH 13TH, 1509.

Addressed to

Signor M, The Council of Ten, Palazzo Signoria, Florence.

Most Illustrious Signor,

Because I am in the emperor's territory and have no means of access to our usual courier, I fall back on our secondary method of communication as formally agreed. So please do not be angry.

I write in haste to give news of our progress from the far north, which we are now leaving over the San Bernardino Pass, toward Milan. Erpingham intends to meet with the maestro pittore, Leonardo of Vinci, for reasons I cannot get from him; only that it involves a promise he made to a lady.

So, he seems set on quitting the papal party, and crossing the alps alone. We will be in one of the first caravans to cross this spring; if you could call it spring. I advised against it, because of the danger, but the Englishman says he must be in Siena for Easter; I have therefore, stuck close to him as you commanded, even at the risk to my own life, for which I am sure you will not be slow to recompense me when the time comes.

Siena by Easter? What can this mean, but that he has some arrangement with our former benefactor, some vital piece of information Petrucci has kept from us. That we are betrayed? Or that some event will take place there this Easter? We must take council before then, and above all we must be ready for every eventuality.

The Englishman keeps his cards close, seemingly more interested in discussions about the arts, which of course I am happy to supply, but I know also that he would not hesitate to dispatch me the moment I hindered him. I live daily with this peril, and I am weary of travel. I have incurred great expense to ensure this reaches you before we arrive in Italy. This invoice for ten ducats will prove it. Please send any further instructions to our bank in Milan, with a further draw down of funds, for I am in need of new riding boots and by then doubtless my winter cloak will be blown to tatters.

The courier is ready to depart so I must desist from further entreaty,

Yours, et cetera.

16TH MARCH, CASTELLO SFORZA, MILAN.

Grey billowing clouds, strong winds, but no rain. No ice or snow either, thank God. Hugh breathes a sigh of palpable relief when he sees the spires. And Milan could make even Bembo forget the Alps. He's no mountain boy, nor is Hugh. They are sitting at meat in a sparse dining hall, on the south of the fortress, that seems to get more than its fair share of the wind. Fire belches smoke with the downdrafts that come twice or three times a minute. It curls into the vault in grey-blue plumes, twisting elegantly like Hugh's conspiratorial machinations, but then, like the smoke that dissipates, his thoughts pass into the ether. He feels he is approaching some ominous event, as if he is not only being stalked by his past but also by the future. He pensively divides his capon, glad at least not to be on the road. *The dead will always wait for you. Who said that?*

They are being royally entertained by George D'Amboise, nephew to the cardinal and his own grandmaster. He has been governor of the Duchy of Milan, seignory of Milan, and viceroy of Lombardy – amongst other laurels and epithets – these last five years since the French took the duchy from Ludovico, *Il Moro,* Sforza.

'Sforza!' Bembo says, when he hears Hugh mention him. 'All you need to know about the last incumbent was that he was a jumped up cordwainer-turned-tyrant seeking a fictitious lineage. But you didn't hear me say so.'

Hugh offers Bembo the bread basket. 'Really, *caro*. I always heard that it was he who gave Leonardo his real start as an artist.'

'Nonsense. He paid his dwarf more than Leonardo. Besides, he was first employed to arrange the duchess's plumbing. Think of that, her damn plumbing!'

Hugh isn't listening. He's thinking about his host. How strange; you don't see a d'Amboise for months, then two pop up in as many weeks. *I suppose it is what you get when the first minister of France sires nine sons; they become ubiquitous throughout European polity.*

The governor of Milan is keen to entertain them, keen to hear of his uncle on Rhodes, keener still to hear of his uncle the cardinal and the imminent arrival of the northern armies. But he is keenest of all – curiously enough – to see whether Bembo might affect a meeting between him and the Ferrarese poet Ariosto. *These Frenchies take in the chivalric and courtly love lyrics, with their mothers' milk.* D'Amboise has heard that Ariosto is barely supported by his vile patron, Ippolito D'Este, and might be persuaded to relocate to Milan. Bembo says that they just happened to have left the pious Cardinal d'Este on the other side of the Alps in Konstanz with the emperor.

D'Amboise looks surprised for a moment. 'Good. I hope he stays there and catches something.'

Bembo laughs guardedly, making sure no servants are listening in, and then says he will pass on the message to Ariosto either personally or through a friend. He immediately looks at Hugh who does not respond. Bembo is not sure he can go himself. To enter a duchy where he has bedded the duke's wife and only narrowly escaped with his parts is a risk. 'He is a truly great, but unacknowledged poet, my lord. But I have hopes for him and his noble soul. I have not discovered truly whether he is behind or ahead of the age. I suppose you know that it took sixty years or more after Giotto died for others to appreciate what he achieved. I will certainly pass on your invitation.'

After lunch, Hugh expresses a desire to visit Maestro da Vinci. D'Amboise nods with approval while he cleans his beard with the table cloth. He has not long let his beard grow after many years. He has forgotten how the grease gets everywhere. 'Da Vinci? Good, good. That is well. If you will not come hawking with us, then very well, visit his *bottega*. He is always to be found there. I will have you escorted by one of your own countrymen. Cremuel is an excellent fellow. Resourceful. Ask him if you need anything while you are here, supplies, victuals, you know. My usual supplier once told me there was no more Burgundy in all north Italy and that the court would have to do with Trebbiana. But Cremuel found us vintage Burgundy in the cellars of a local count within three days. He is indispensable.' D'Amboise nods to a clerk who speeds to the task.

Three minutes later the clerk returns, wheezing. 'The escort is here, my lord.'

'Very good.' D'Amboise rises from the table. 'Well, Hugh, I hope you can join us another day in the field. There is good game here abouts. Bembo says that you hunt like Diana.'

'He is full of compliments,' Hugh replies. 'You should be wary of his flatteries as I am.'

Bembo pats his heart forlornly, 'Unfair, Hugh! Unwarranted.'

Hugh removes his hat to give due homage. 'I will leave you to decide, my lord. I bid you *adeiu* until the evening.'

Hugh walks behind the broad-shouldered cockney man of business as they descend the stairwell to the lower gallery. The glimpse in the corridor upstairs was fleeting, but Hugh can already see from the hard, shifting eyes and the brevity of wit, that the man is shrewd. Hugh can't make out the clothes. The hose are worn thin at the calves and knees, the pantoffle shoes down at heel, but the black woollen cloak with silk trim covers all. It is as if a mercenary had just robbed a lawyer. His hands are like shovels, always clenched into fists, always held forward as if he were expecting to be set upon. *How old is he? Mid-twenties like me probably. Wouldn't fancy my chances against him without a sword*. Every few steps down, Cremuel, brushes the side of his nose with his thumb, then gives two sharp sniffs.

'You are a long way from home, Cremuel.' It is small talk.

'Further the better, sir, if you come from Putney.'

'London?'

'Is there another? God, I hope not. When they say round 'ere that Rome weren't built in a day, I tell'em, "Bleedin' right mate, that was Putney."' He gives a small skip when he reaches the corridor, so that his swagger meets the rhythm of his shoulders.

'Is that your real name? It sounds French.'

'Nah. Cromwell, my lord, Thomas Cromwell. Cremuel is just the way these Frenchies say it.'

'What's your trade?'

'All sorts, if you'll pardon the vagaries, sir. Came 'ere as a mercenary with the French. But soldiering is a mug's game. Can't really pay someone to die for you. Figures don't add up. So, I'm down 'ere seeing what's what; a bit of accounting, bit of victualing. The guvnor's a good man, but his quartermasters and sutlers are idiots. Too much *dolcevita*, this lot, and not enough speed. So, if you need anything, you or your friends, have your man come and see me. I'll sort you out, and see you don't get fleeced. Poor gov'nor, he's been ripped off left, right and centre.'

'So, you help him?' '

Where I can.' Cromwell thumbs his nose again, cranes his neck to the side, then skips back into step. 'The gov'nor thinks it's all honour and *noblesse oblige* and wotnot, but these Italians are all on the take. If you grew up where I did, you'd know that. There's always an angle with these people. So yeah, I'm 'elping, but I'm not obliged to be 'ere forever like. Not much chance for preferment really. The French look after their own; it's the way with them. Me, on the other hand, well, now I'm in Italy I'm sniffing about, putting my name around in the counting houses – seeing what's what. Met some decent lads from the Frescobaldi outfit in town. They're big in the Florence cloth guild. If they offer me something, I'll take it. As I see it, wool exports are the lifeblood of England and these blokes hold a few of the keys to the continental market. So yeah, if they offer a position, I might get stuck in, see what's what.'

'I wish you well, Master Cromwell. If keenness is the measure of your abilities, you will go far in a city like Florence, from what I've heard. Do you have any learning?'

'Not so much as you find in books, but I can read – like to read, whenever I can. And I'm good with figures, with bookkeeping and trade. Why, if you don't mind me asking?'

As he speaks, Hugh, is trying to imagine what a book like Castiglione's *Courtier* would do for a man like Cromwell. Up until now he had only thought of other *magnati* reading it. But in this new age of progress, perhaps even men of mean origin could change their stars. Cromwell's question brings him round with a start. 'Well, you seem like a man with an eye for detail, and quick wit,' Hugh says, returning his quizzical stare. 'And to be really useful – indispensable, is the way I think you put it – most great businesses, indeed any of the great houses need men of the law to advise them.'

'The law! It takes money and ease for that sort of study, my lord.'

'I thought you were making money here. Is that not what you said?'

'Suppose I am. A little perhaps. But I have expectations of more.' Cromwell glances at Hugh momentarily. as they round a bend in the corridor and begin another flight of steps down to a cloister below. 'You think I could make the bar then? Turn up at old Lincoln's Inn in a few years, and they'd take my money? You've got me thinking, sir, that you have.'

'Well, think on it, Master Cromwell. "A wise man will stand before kings," as the scriptures say.'

'That I certainly will, sir.' He says this as they round a final corner and enter a broad, blustery courtyard, flanked by stables and workshops. 'Just up these stairs, last door on the right. And remember, anything you need, have your man speak with me.' Cromwell tucks both thumbs into his belt and adds with full cockney verve, 'Don't forget—anything you need.'

Hugh nods his head slightly, and continues up the stairs.

IL MAESTRO DELLA BOTTEGA

Within the castle walls, which are formidable, Signor da Vinci enjoys his *bottega*, as any other man might enjoy his farm or his family. He is working on something for the governor, and he's not particularly interested in being disturbed. Not until, that is, he hears Duchess Constanza's name.

'*La Giraconda*?' Leonardo signals to the youth who is holding the door against Hugh to open it wider. Hugh then sees him, mid-fifties with long, well combed hair and a beard worthy of an Athenian stoic. The older man uses a right index finger to move the shoulder length hair behind his ear. His voice is thin, laced with the uncertainty that comes from deep wounds. Ones that only a father can bestow.

'I had the privilege of enjoying her hospitality on the Island of Ischia last year.' Hugh says apologetically. 'She knew I would be passing through Milan and asked me to inquire after her portrait.'

'And who are you?' Leonardo leaves the workbench where he has been working on a wax maquette of a prancing horse, and steps forward still holding his small, wooden tool.

Hugh steps in and casts his eyes about the shelves piled high with papers, designs, folios. Mathematical instruments lie on the table alongside pattern books, notebooks, wax blocks and carving tools. The stone floor is well swept, and a good fire blazes in the deep hearth near the desk. 'Fra Hugh Erpingham, knight of Rhodes.'

'Ah, the one who calls for a crusade to counter the Sultan's new ships. I have heard of you. I commend you on your grasp of our tongue.' Leonardo returns Hugh's bow, and after arranging his linen cuffs, motions toward a fireside chair. 'Did you know that Sultan Byazid wishes for me to build him a bridge from Stamboul to Galata, six hundred *braccia* long and high enough to let ships pass under it; perhaps seventy *braccia*. If I built him his bridge, perhaps he would not need a fleet.'

'Are you serious?' Hugh cannot tell. If anyone could do something like that, it would be the Sultan. He would think nothing of depopulating Armenia of Christians, to get himself a slave army. *Is he serious?* There is something playful, effeminate even, in the artist's eyes. With any other man he would have taken offence, only this is not any other man. Hugh would give his right arm, to draw and paint like this man, or rather his left arm. But he is aware as never before with men like Michelangelo and Leonardo, that he draws and paints merely as men did two hundred years ago. He is a relic; the world he is fighting for is a past thing, a dying thing; and *they* are – in some way incomprehensible to Hugh – forging a new future, new norms. It fills him simultaneously with pulse-raising curiosity and shivers of foreboding.

Leonardo waves his hand dismissively as he eases into a fireside seat. 'Yes, and no. He has not sent word recently, and I have been very busy. I offered to sort out the duomo here, too, but ah, so many things left undone. You will take some wine? Yes, Francesco, fetch cups and some olives. Francesco is one of my apprentices. A gentle youth with great promise. You are English?'

'Yes, I come from a small village in the county of Norfolk.'

'I, too, am from a small village, near the town of Vinci.' He points to a sketch hanging on a nail near Hugh. 'That is a sketch of the village, from the crags on a hillside opposite. I did it as a boy. I was supposed to be destroying eagles' nests for the shepherds, which I probably did as well, but…' He sighs. 'I keep it with me to remember, in all these my wanderings, my mother, my uncle– a good man. A kind man.'

'It is a fine sketch, signor. A fair village.'

'Ah,' Leonardo says with something of a wistful sigh. 'It is the sort of village where the population never grew.'

'Really?'

'Yes, really. Each time a woman got pregnant, someone left.' The older man smiles coyly so that his pointy nose flares slightly at the nostrils. It is a quip well-rehearsed, but too slight a bandage for such a deep wound.

'I see,' Hugh says, taking a cup from the young man. 'Your own father.'

'It is no secret.' Leonardo crosses his legs and straightens out the folds of the sleeveless woollen overcoat he is wearing. As he speaks, he examines the creases and picks at the spots of wax with his thumbnail. 'My father was a notary, a man of standing in Florence, my mother a peasant woman. So, there you have it. Things are as they are. Many have been in the same position. Ghiberti was a bastard too, but he rose above his beginnings. He became hungry for knowledge, and once said that *a man who learned many things will be a stranger nowhere. Even without money or friends, he will be a citizen of every country, able to disdain the vicissitudes of fortune.* I understand that now. And I cannot complain about my father really. He did not let us starve, and he got me an apprenticeship in Florence; but when you are born on the wrong side of the sheets, there are conventions, even in Italy. I could not go into my father's profession for example. No bastard is allowed to study Greek or Latin, so the knowledge I have gained is not from manuscripts – which are often unreliable in any case – but from experience, from experimentation. I try not to say this with bitterness, but I think many in our day make too much of the ancient texts. And not only in our day. Alberti studied those ancient arts but was not conquered by them as some were. The *umanisti* of his own day did not deceive him, prancing around with their scant Greek. He called them a stupid breed, and he was right, clad, as they were, wholly in another's clothes.'

Hugh glances nervously at the instruments. 'So, you agree with Aquinas, that the Book of Nature maybe studied independently of the Book of Grace.'

His eyes narrow as if under attack, though Hugh attempts not to look like an inquisitor – which is hard. People have told him, the provost at his college at Cambridge for one, and the rabbit-like curate from Aylsham for another; that he wears his hunger for truth rather too intensely for polite people. Ultimate questions make him edgy, and he always walks into them as if he had a knife in each hand. Hugh smiles amiably, trying not to show too many teeth.

'Well,' Leonardo speaks slowly, guardedly. 'You mean without the authority of the scriptures, the church?' He puckers his lips and sucks in. 'That is a question for theologians, my young friend. All I know is that knowledge has its origins in perceptions, in experience.' Leonardo takes some wine from Francesco's tray, and raises it to Hugh. 'Experience is the only mother of certainty.'

'But surely, all experience is derived from causation.'

'Yes, yes, but in order to understand the cause we must reverse the process; thus, my method has always been to consult experience that I may understand these causes. My science is the study of the things possible: possible to know, possible to achieve. Forgive me, but you don't look convinced, or is it the olives?'

Hugh throws an olive stone into the fire and re-crosses his legs. 'It is not that I doubt the usefulness of the method within limits," he says, "only unlike the saint, I come to doubt that man's reason did not fall with his other faculties in Eden.'

Hugh runs his tongue about his teeth, and looks into the embers under the iron grate. *Men construct an illusory world to validate their madness.* He's proved that much himself – he, Hugh de Erpingham, *le douteur et l'adorateur*, doubter and worshipper. Reason's large conscience has always been on our side. Lucifer, still thinks he is right, and doubtless has regiments of facts to prove it.

'I fear, signor, from what I have seen of mankind, that there are some who would like to build a new Lucretian world, free from the constraints of philosophy and theology.' Hugh glances at his hands. It is not meant as an accusation. A civilization that would frame their intellectual enquiry thus, would do so for one reason. You only ask questions like that, if you want a world without God. He should know. He has dreamt of such a world, longed for it, a world where he is not guilty, where death is extinction. A universe with limited liability, where finally there is a door marked 'exit'. For the ancients, sin, *hamartia,* was an unavoidable flaw, not a personal evil action. *Oh, blessed ignorance from which Christ woke us! And now awakened, can we ever sleep again?*

Leonardo moves his head back slightly, and lowers his cup. 'Even if that were true, it need not be such a bad place. Philosophers and theologians have often lied. Facts will not lie.'

'And swords do not kill.'

'Signor?'

'Perhaps that is unfair, but tell me, how do you know such an approach would not produce a system of morality that would, say—' Hugh glances at the sketch from the eagles' nest. 'Protect the nests of Vinci's eagles' eggs, but allow its, well, less wanted sons to be killed in their mothers' wombs.'

'Signor!' Leonardo wavers, his brows knitted. 'I need not answer you on this for such a world will never be.'

'Really? Infanticide was once part of normal life in the ancient times, and abortion is not unknown to us even now.' Hugh drains the cup and then quickly shakes his head with a sigh. 'Forgive me, Maestro, I grow melancholic with the season. I have much on my mind, and it rushes ahead of reason.'

'Do not apologise. I have kept many designs for war machines secret because I, too, came to know the evil of men.' Hugh understands from Leonardo's use of the plural that he means everyone, though perhaps not himself.

'I only came to pass on the duchess' compliments, and make enquiry.' He is aware of Francesco, at his shoulder. He turns to smile at the youth, perhaps the same age as his own brother Cecil, and gives him the cup. 'My thanks to you, Francesco. You are fortunate indeed to study here. If I had my time again…' Hugh breaks off, trying to dismiss the indulgent sentiment.

The youth is pink around the cheeks, shamefaced. 'Speak on, signor.'

'Perhaps it is with me as it is with your master; men hear stories about us, but they do not see all that there is to see. I have left undone many things I should have done, and done many others for which I seek forgiveness. I confess that my life has not been as I had hoped.' *An understatement.*

'Ah, *nessum maggior dolore, che ricordarsi del tempo felice, nella misera*. The poet Dante said it, "There is no greater pain than to remember a happy time when one is in misery." Come.' A light suddenly flickers in Leonardo's eyes. He springs to his feet. 'Come, please. I would like to show you something.'

He walks to a corner of the room next to a dry wall where fifteen or so canvases are stacked. Standing next to them is an easel with a small canvas facing away from them, for it faces the window's light. Leonardo plucks it from the easel and holds it up, so he and Hugh can see it.

Hugh stares at the face of a younger Constanza D'Avalos, wearing her thin Spanish veil. Her arms are crossed, her smile impish. He is not sure whether the eyes, though knowing, are not a little too passive, though he would certainly not say so in front of the *maestro pittore*. For one thing, Hugh is too much in awe that such a likeness is even achievable in paint at all. He mumbles, 'Exquisite.' And knows full well that in darkest England there is not even a word for a painted canvas yet, but there will be one day. What is happening here in Italy will see to it.

Leonardo is apologetic. ‘It is not finished. I don’t know if it ever will be. I came to paint this after a difficult time in my life, after I had been summoned to work for Duke Valentino.’

‘Borgia! You worked for Cesare Borgia?’

‘Yes, not a man you could say no to, believe me. I was to be his military engineer, cartographer. How eager I was to recommend myself and my great talents, and how much I had then to regret. It was not an easy time. I was there on his bloody tour from Imola to Frossombrone, Senigallia, San Quirico. Human life was nothing to Borgia. He had no conscience. I saw things, heard things that I could not unsee, unhear. That changes a man. I realised that I was not innocent. I had let myself, my powers, be party to that monster’s success. Something in me began to fray, to break apart. One day in the markets of San Lorenzo, I bought an entire cage of doves and set them free. I hardly remember doing it, which tells you the state I was in. It was about then,’ he raised his delicate hand to touch the canvas. ‘Then I met the Duchess Constanza, *la Giroconda.* She understood me. Women have such abilities with wounded men – I need not explain to you, for you have met her yourself. She is remarkable, is she not?’

‘Indeed, she is a remarkable woman.’

‘She asked for a portrait, a small one. I don’t think she really wanted one, only she knew my mind would rest amidst beauty. And that is what I painted, or have attempted to paint; the beauty and vivacity of one woman as if she herself were an antidote to all the evils of mankind. Dante had Beatrice; Petrarch, Laura; Saint Bernard, the Virgin; but I had Constanza D’Avalos to save me.’

‘Did she?’ Hugh blurts the words involuntarily like a drowning man taking in air.

Leonardo nods, but Hugh senses something mechanical in the smile, the eyes. *He does not really know.* Hugh does. He too remembers salvific moments with Felice and Vittoria, moments too brief where he was tempted as a unicorn to lay his head on a virgin’s lap. But alas, no. An accusing conscience may be distracted by beauty momentarily, like sweet nard on a putrid corpse, but that is all. Nothing wrong with the nard, but the gods of conscience are not so easily appeased.

Leonardo continues, 'This portrait became my study in beauty, my homage to truth. Painting, more than poetry, gives understanding of truth, signor. Poetry considers the mind, but painting considers the mind in motion.' He uses his left hand to run his fingers along the edge of the canvas. 'Painting is philosophy, a science representing works of nature.' Leonardo places the canvas frame back on the easel, and glances through the window across the courtyard. Shafts of morning light pierce the gaps in the clouds. They ignite water pouring from the gutters in a fierce white. For a moment it shines, then falls to earth.

'You are a young man, Fra Erpingham. You speak of sins, regrets. I often wonder if growing old well becomes the art of forgetting our unfulfilled visions, of seeing disappointment, not as an accuser, but rather, a less loved family member.'

Leonardo examines the backs of his hands where the freckles of old age have begun to appear. 'There was a time when I thought I would outshine all men; that I, Leonardo, would square the circle, find a unified field of knowledge, make the Arno navigable, make the largest bronze casting ever, even leave this earth and fly like an immortal god. The pride of Icarus!' He gives the faintest of chuckles. 'Many say, it is one of the arts hidden from men, but I do not think so. To fly free of this earth, to be lighter than air, has been in my heart since childhood. The memory of gulls flying above my crib is vivid, even now.'

'There is much in the world from which to fly.'

Francesco takes their cups and dishes into a back room, out of earshot.

Hugh changes tack. 'Signor, I know you are well connected in Florence. If I were looking for a man among the Council of Ten who would receive post under the initial M, who might that be?'

'The Council of Ten is Florence's Security Council. They say it is the Council of Liberty and Peace, but everyone calls it the council of war. A powerful group, my friend. Nicolo Machiavelli is its secretary. Perhaps it is he. I could send a letter of introduction with you if you would like, for I know him well. He was Florence's ambassador to Cesare Borgia's court, when I was in the duke's employ.'

'Was he now. And what manner of man is Signor Machiavelli?'

'Intelligent, witty – very witty, though a bit coarse – ambitious, a republican, a good servant of Florence.'

'Skilled in arms?'

'I don't think so. More the philosopher, poet; though active in his own way. It was he who first saw that Florence should have a trained militia, that to rely on Tuscan farmers with scythes and hoes was no answer to the threats of the modern age. Have you seen the size of these French canons?'

'Yes, and I expect that for the protection of Florence, Signor Machiavelli and his Council of Ten, exert great effort to obtain the latest weaponry.'

'Yes, I suppose.' Leonardo shoots Hugh a worried glance. 'I am sorry, Fra Erpingham, I do not take your meaning.'

'You hinted earlier that you have hidden many designs for weapons.'

'Yes, because of the evil of men.'

'Is Greek fire among them.'

'Greek fire!'

'Not so loud. Have you any knowledge of it?'

'No, and as I understand, it is one of the diabolic arts lost to men, thank God.'

'But has anyone spoken to you about it? Think carefully before you answer.'

'No. Why?'

'You are Italy's genius with war machines. Greek fire must be propelled by machines. So, I ask again: has anyone written or spoken to you about it, someone from Florence, or Siena even?'

'No, I am done with war and killing. I don't even eat meat nowadays.' Leonardo's eyes assume that chicken-like semblance common to most under an Erpingham interview. Leonardo finishes weakly, almost pleadingly, 'I swear it.'

Hugh eyeballs him for a quiet moment, nodding slightly and turning his bottom lip down in an approving smirch. *What am I going to do, turn the screws on one of the most famous painters in Europe?* That will not do. Besides, he might be telling the truth. Hugh is about to reply, when the door flies open and a young man about his own age, clad in a bright orange silk chemise under soggy, red, woollen doublet, barges into the room and dumps a dripping basket on the table. He speaks for show, ostensibly to Francesco, whom he calls by his surname 'Melzi', lingering on the last syllable in a malevolent way. 'Well, precious Melzeee, while you've been warming yourself with the great maestro, I have been wandering the streets like a drudge, probably ruined my chemise in that filthy rain.' He throws his beret down onto one of the fireside chairs, and flaps his long ringlets to shake off the excess water, before finally emptying the basket. 'Peppered bread, mushrooms, eels whose foul stench is in my clothes, smoked meat, wine, apricots, ricotta. I spent four *soldi* at the barber, though you wouldn't know with the rain, and six on eggs. *Six soldi for eggs!* It would pay us to get our own chickens.'

'Sallai, you recalcitrant devil, stop your infernal whining. We have company.' From behind him at the window, the anxious voice of *il maestro della bottega* rings forth.

'Who's this?' Sallai says.

'Forgive him, Fra Erpingham. For all we do for him, he still has no manners.'

Hugh smiles affably.

Sallai continues. 'One of D'Amboise' people, no, wait, don't tell me! He wears black. He's the new Spanish ambassador come to tempt us to move to Spain where it does not rain.'

'Silence fool. He is a knight of Rhodes who will mistake you for a Turk if you prattle on. He'll have the head from your shoulders. Ah, you have the ricotta, good. Perhaps we could interest you in a light luncheon, later, Fra Erpingham?'

Hugh bows graciously. 'Signor da Vinci, I have presumed on your time, and I am expected elsewhere in the palace this morning. Perhaps we will meet again before I leave.'

'Indeed, perhaps we will.'

Five minutes, later Hugh is pacing along a cloister, keeping dry and thinking. *Greek fire.* The cogs are turning. *Perhaps that is what they're all after, more than the gold. Yes, why not?* Whoever has the most powerful weapons, can have all the money they want. Greek fire might be the answer to these monstrous French canons, their omnipotent steel shot. Perhaps the only answer, if you haven't the technology or ducats to compete. Petrucci didn't mention it. *But why would he, to me of all people? If I lead him to Vendramin, he'll get both the gold and the weapon that will ensure Siena's rise.* He can think of at least one city, that the dragon Petrucci would like to shower with Greek Fire. And Florence? Bembo's blackmailer, if blackmail it really is, must be this Machiavelli. His intention? Same as Petrucci's.

My way forward? Interview this Machiavelli, help him unburden his conscience. Chastise where necessary. Then visit Siena, double-cross Petrucci, deal with Vendramin, get what I came for, and return to Rhodes. Hugh stops pacing and casts an eye heavenward, where there is no break in the unrelenting storm clouds. *A few months here and I am already thinking like an Italian.* There are thirty-three days before Easter. 'It is enough.'

'What is?'

Hugh jumps at the voice behind him. He turns to see Bembo appear from behind a column. 'Bembo. What?' He says with evident alarm.

'You were muttering something about it being enough.'

'I thought you had gone hawking.'

'I-er-I changed my mind. My humors are out today.' There is a slight pink in Bembo's cheek and wateriness in his eyes that puts Hugh on his guard. They are just below Leonardo's bottega window. Bembo has been listening. Hugh gathers his wits. *What did we talk about? Did I reveal anything? Damn, we talked about Machiavelli. He mustn't have reason or cause to send a message of warning to Florence. Time for a diversion.* Hugh says, 'Enough time to reach Siena for Easter; that is all.' They perambulate along the colonnade like two Athenians. 'I have paid a visit to Signor da Vinci.' Hugh glances at Bembo, who steps slightly in front.

'And did you find your conversation diverting?'

'Indeed, he is an industrious and ingenious fellow.'

'On what did you discourse?'

'Oh, this and that.'

'For example?' Bembo says this swallowing nervously.

'Oh, well, things like,' Hugh says casually, puffing out his cheeks, 'like the inherent difficulties with man's general desire to extrapolate norms from experience, experimentation, verification and so forth. And the dangers of applying such desires in the historical and spiritual spheres. Enough for you?'

'Oh,' Bembo says. 'I see.'

Hugh glances again at his companion and, perhaps, adversary. *He's not his usual self. I shall draw him, and make him feel all is well. No thoughts of Florence or betrayal. If it is this Machiavelli, he fears so much, then I'll come upon him unannounced like the pox. If I can't free myself, then by God, I will free Bembo from his tormenters.*

'Yes, come on, Bembo. Don't be a dullard. It's no fun teasing out these riddles with oneself. I say that if man's general desire to extrapolate norms from experience is problematic, then you say something like, "I suppose that the empirical approach would be valid if this world were only material." Then I say, "But of course, it is not." To which you reply –' Hugh pauses for Bembo to take the bait.

The poet blinks as he switches tracks, and then something of the old fire returns to his eyes. He kicks a pebble, straightens his shoulders and just as suddenly they are both kings once more, discussing the great mysteries of life and the cosmos. 'Yes, yes, Hugh, whatever you say. We have always wanted romance and true philosophy. And Christianity meets mythology's search for romance by being a story, and philosophy's search for truth by being a true story.'

'Indeed,' Hugh says, and then adds to stoke Bembo's fire further, 'And I don't think that it invalidates Signor da Vinci's quest for a valid field of knowledge, only that it can never be absolute or universal in a way that Aristotle thought it could be.'

'Of course, of course, Hugh. We are one in this. We agree. And Paul says as much in Corinthians: *the world through its wisdom knew not God.*'

'But if there is more, *caro*? If neither human reason, nor human instruments can avail us in the quest for a unified field of knowledge, what then?' Hugh stops at a corner of the arcade and glances meaningfully at Bembo, a man he has grown close to these last months. despite their troubles. In the pause that follows, Hugh feels a weighty grief in the possibility that he might be forced to kill Bembo. There are many possible scenarios where this could happen. But it is not the grief of personal betrayal. This he can bear, for he himself has betrayed mankind, and it is only just. It is the *peripeteia* of Aristotle and Greek tragedy, the great and just reversal of action and counter action. But if not this, then what? That he loves this man as a friend and brother? He, Hugh Erpingham, love? That is a new and fanciful thought to him. And would God make him choose between that love, and duty?

'If you ask me,' Bembo says, placing his hands on his hip, and gazing upward to the corbelled arches. 'Both reason and experience, must be the servants of a heart open to communication, not a masterful autonomy. If I want to understand the prose, and the poetry in this cosmos, then I must surrender and trust, and listen. I think this is what Augustine meant when he wrote *credo ut intelligam,* I believe, in order to understand. Natural philosophy might show Signor da Vinci the colour of my skin and eyes, but he cannot know the colour of my thoughts, not even if he cut up my head and dissected it – as I believe he has done to others—corpses, I mean. To know my thoughts, he would have to ask me. He must be open to my self-revelation. And there is the rub, I suppose. We seek the comfort of an impersonal knowledge that cannot be doubted, to secure ourselves from hurt, from risk perhaps, from disillusion –'

'From God,' Hugh adds almost involuntarily, then thinks, *why does it always come back to this?* 'Thank you, *caro*. It helps me arrange my thoughts to have you here, even if you are usually prating on about nothing in particular.' Hugh gives Bembo a friendly shove, and then moves to the edge of the arcade to glance up at the skies. The clouds are parting and the rain thinning. 'Come, the rains have abated. Let us visit the library.'

17TH MARCH, 1509. BELLA FIRENZE

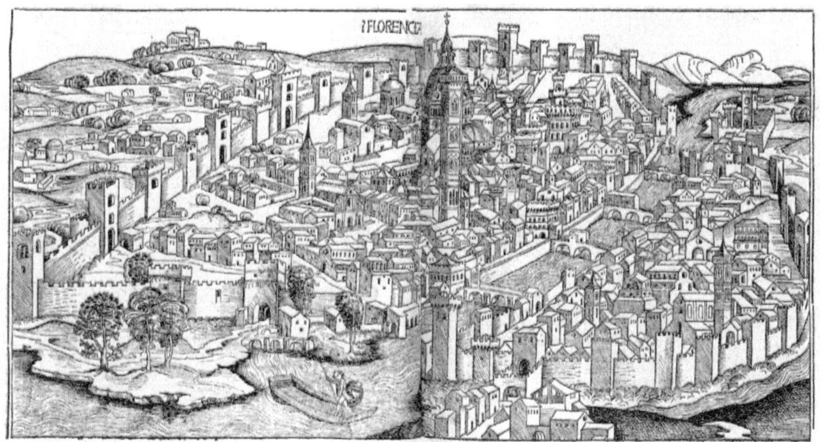

It is midmorning on the Corso di Porta Romana, as the group heads south out of Milan to Bologna, and thence to *bella Firenze*. Hugh hasn't told Bembo, that is where they are going; it wouldn't do to give the game away. The cobbles of Milan are cleansed by the spring rains, and in the lull between showers the streets throng with housewives and traders. The small cavalcade negotiates the people and puddles. Their mares ride shoulder to shoulder. Hugh talks to Bembo about his conversation with Maestro da Vinci from the day previous. He mentions the empiricism of Leonardo, giving his comments in the hopes of impressing the poet. But it is not working.

'Hmm.' 'Yes.' 'Oh, really.' Bembo fidgets furtively in his saddle and glances about the crowds, barely seeming to listen.

Hugh continues his virtual monologue. 'I did not say it to Signor Leonardo, but I am sure that the ancients exercised the critique of doubt on the basis of certain unmoveable tenets, so that in the act of doubting they did not doubt. I think it must be thus for *reason* to function at all. Da Vinci's distain for creeds and dogma – perhaps an honest doubt of a fatherless man – might in others, and in succeeding generations, conceal the arrogance it purposes to condemn.'

'Hmm,' Bembo says absently, glancing behind him.

'You cannot return to the harbour, or at least it is nigh impossible to return to the harbour, once you have let the ship of Christendom depart on that sort of compass bearing.'

'You might travel to some far away shores.'

'Perhaps, and yes, such a venture might test the creeds, but I think on the whole it would isolate the mind in its own age, clip its wings and leave it parochial, provincial, like a lone regiment cut off from the army, perhaps just when the battle was at its hottest.'

'Come on, Hugh.' Bembo suddenly comes to at last. 'A touch melodramatic! He's just one man expanding his field of enquiry.'

'Forgive me, but I speak of him in general, as if he were representative of what our generation might bequeath to the next. If we hand them, what I feel is a heretical imperative, we would thus compel them to refuse any anchorage but that of their own wills set before an abyss of limitless possibility.'

'They will be guided by reason, Hugh. Reason, as Aristotle was.'

'Ah, but surely you can see that reason is the rudder within the seas of tradition. It cannot function in a dry dock. Aristotle wrote within the tradition of the Greek polis. I simply do not believe we can work ourselves into a position independent of creeds, traditions, dogmas, as it were, without first inventing new ones. Facts are simply too theory laden.'

'Hugh, Hugh, always the *homme serieux*, always full of foreboding and woe. Maestro Da Vinci has already given the world many discoveries, many ingenious machines and who knows what else he and others like him shall discover?'

'It is not his machines, though they too may prove a scourge in the hands of wicked men, which he himself would tell you.' Here Hugh is thinking about the new herculean canon that spits forth a monstrous weight of shot, and indeed the Greek fire which he himself now seeks with unease. 'Yes, they indeed may be feared, but that is not what I meant. What I truly fear is that for another generation mere *techne*, as the Greeks had it, mere technical mastery over nature might not be a guiding ideal, but the only convincing model of truth. Already we are beset by the craving among some for the new, the novel –*rien plus ultra*. They claim it is its own justification. People are weak, Pietro. You and I know that; we have seen how easily they are beguiled.'

Bembo looks as if he is about to answer in defence, as if Hugh had laid an accusation on him, which was not the foremost of his intentions. But rather, the poet falls back again on the offensive weapons with which he is more familiar. He guffaws. '*Diomio*, Hugh. *Diomio*. The destruction of eagles' nests and the exposure of unwanted infants!' His face contorts with disgust, though it is all put on.

But there is no artifice in Hugh's sideways glance. Bembo *was* eavesdropping yesterday. For a moment Hugh entertains the real possibility that his trust in Bembo may be misplaced. *Could he still betray me, even after all this time?*

Bembo seems unaware of Hugh's stare and continues in high spirits 'Please tell me that you will never set down your metaphysical speculations in verse, Hugh. For if you do they will rank you with that Frankish Cistercian we have already spoken of. Do you remember? The odious *Pilgrimage of the Soul.*'

'It's not so bad. A bit heavy handed perhaps.'

'Heavy handed! So, you've actually read it? Good grief.'

'Yes,' Hugh mumbles, fiddling with his reins, patting the horse's flanks and casting his eye about a draper's shop so as not to show his irritation too openly. He had been in a good mood. He had forgotten the thing that stalked him. *Why, won't Bembo shut up? Why can't we just speak of philosophy in general? Why must he always slide some obscure literary crap like a bodkin under my ribs?*

'Ah.' Bembo's eyes twinkle with delight. 'You see yourself in de Guileville's pilgrim perhaps? Kidnapped, dragged in the mire, bound, beaten and left clinging to a rock in the midst of the sea.'

'Perhaps, but if so,' Hugh snaps, 'I would not want to speak of it further.'

'Yes, I see it all now,' says Bembo heedlessly. 'He too, was rescued by *Grace Dieu* and taken on board his ship of Religion.' Bembo slaps his thigh with delight. 'I wager you knights of Rhodes read it to each other on wintery nights.'

'Bembo.' Hugh growls, but Bembo seems hardly to hear under the torrent of thoughts spilling out. *Mother of God,* Hugh curses inwardly, *it is enough that he might well betray me again; must I be goaded too?*

'I always thought the poem should have ended after the rescue; but the poet shows the latter pilgrim, rough handled by Envy and her crew, who break all his limbs, which is more than the vices of the outer world ever did. And one must ask oneself, Hugh, is this you? Does this explain your misanthropy? That you were delivered from capture on the seas only to remain a prisoner still, of darker forces, your *culpa levis*, eh Hugh, eh? I only ask, for His Holiness wishes me to write about you. And you know me, Hugh, I wish to rescue the ordinary man from the enormous condescension of posterity. Are you de Guileville's pilgrim?'

'Bembo!' Hugh's snarl is lupine.

'Will you pluck out your eyes as the pilgrim did to block your ears against their voices?'

'*Bastardo*!' Hugh grabs Bembo's collar and shakes him violently. Bembo shrieks as he begins to fall from the saddle. But Hugh thrusts him briskly away, so that he regains his mount. The mare sidesteps against the pressure, and nearly rears. Hugh takes no notice as he takes the reins, but merely snarls. 'Do not speak of what you do not know.'

'Well, pardon me!' Bembo says, sarcastically, while arranging the collar of his sage blue doublet. But Hugh is already riding ahead. 'Come Hugh. I thought you were in jest. Hugh, come now, be reasonable. You know I would do nothing to offend you. Nothing to harm.'

Would you not?

Part IV - THE MERCY OF LIONS

20TH MARCH 1509. AN INN NORTH OF BARBERINO

'In truth I do not know who is more tragic in the tale: Troilus or Cressida.' Bembo is in the bed next to Hugh's at an inn. When he cannot sleep, he must talk out his burdens. 'You are Troilus, Hugh.'

'Go to sleep.' Hugh has been in a mood since losing his temper that morning.

'You are!' Bembo comes suddenly alive with impious verve. Tonight, they are talking about Chaucer's poem, not Chretein's or Boccaccio's, probably because Bembo thinks Hugh is more easily provoked to speech when defending his countrymen. 'Of course, you are Troilus—the embodiment of the courtly ideal. You say virtually nothing of interest, like Troilus. You're not so much ill drawn as an assumed type, the hero who suffers more than he acts. That is you, in a nutshell; I swear it on my honour.'

'What honour? Go to sleep, damn you.'

'Of course, Troilus is important. Every character has some role in art and in life. No one is entirely useless for they may at least serve as a bad example.'

'Bloody prating Italian! Will you shut up and go to sleep?' Hugh rolls to the wall and places the pillow over his head.

'So, if you're Troilus, who am I? Diomede the invader, the defiler? No, I know who that is. Perhaps Pandarus the faithful, resourceful uncle. I would like to think so, but no. I am not he, not really I don't think.' Bembo's voice trails away to a whisper. Silence reigns for several minutes. Hugh lets his breathing become regular and long. It is a full ten minutes before Bembo speaks again into the darkness. 'No, I am false Cressida, who yields herself to the invader *tamquam cadaver,* soul and body.'

Hugh's eyes are intently fixed on a spider weaving her web in the grey twilight. He hears Bembo stretching, the sheets twist. *Is he stretching his arms behind his head, or reaching for a blade?*

But Bembo is soon talking mechanically as if it were about someone else. 'Of course, she is tragic in the Aristotelian sense. Hugh, do you not agree? Not especially wicked or good. Poor Cressida. In another age she might have been a faithful wife, a virtuous woman. It is her betrayal, not her unchastity that makes her sin unpardonable. I see that now. Betrayal is always abhorrent. Dante knew it. It is why his Cassius, Brutus and Judas lie below Paolo and Francesca in *Purgatoria.* And do you know what it is? Hugh? Hugh?'

Hugh holds his breath. *What is he saying? Is this a confession? Or another trap? Perhaps he knows where I'm taking him? Perhaps he has sent word?* He releases the breath slowly, aware most horribly of his thumping heart and sweaty palms.

'Ah, sleep on and I will tell you. It is that poor, weak Cressida has no corresponding virtues to counteract her fear of being alone, of being forgotten.' Bembo gives a long and weary sigh. 'While Troilus is absent, she tries to be strong – we all try to be strong, you know. I mean, no one goes out of his way intentionally to be weak, to fail, to betray – but she fails. Do you know what it is to try and fail, Hugh? I don't suppose you do. And me? Ah, Poor Cressida. When Diomede comes, he breaks down her defences and becomes the answer. Those who worship strength and security, sooner or later embrace evil, me thinks. Don't you? "To Diomede, I will always be true," she now says. His sins become hers. And thus, easy is the descent into hell.' Bembo sighs like a man in pain. 'You still awake?'

Hugh gulps silently and breathes again. *Shit, he really is going to betray me. Of course, I'm awake. Chiba a fare con Tosco non vuole esser losco*; when you deal with a Tuscan you cannot afford to be one-eyed.

24THTH MARCH 1509. *BELLA FIRENZE*

Bembo rises in his stirrups and then twists awkwardly to gain a last glance of the road back to the north. 'Bologna is like Isabella d'Este, Duchess of Mantua: the only thing that ever makes it look reasonable is distance.' A week in the saddle does nothing for one's manners. Their haunches are raw as beefsteaks, and this is the nearest Bembo has got to humour all day. 'Come on. Hugh, smile. Florence is a wonderful place. Anyone who doesn't like it is either mad or sober. I can't believe you didn't tell me sooner that we were coming here. I could have sent messages to friends.'

Hugh does not smile, or reply. Bembo seems happy enough, but Hugh noted the alarm in the poet's eyes the moment he realised that they were making an unexpected visit to Florence. And the nearer they get, to what Bembo still calls *his city* – even though he is really a Venetian – the shriller and more nervous the humour. It bodes ill, and Hugh's hand is never far from his sword. He glances far down the road from Fiesole to Florence in case of ambush. The city stretches in the valley below, shaped like a spindle, narrow at the ends, broad in the middle, sixty towers rising from crenelated ramparts, perhaps more than two leagues around. She is the Pearl of the Arno, between the rarefied atmosphere of Arezzo and the heavy air of Pisa. The day is bright, but the wind is still in the east. Bembo calls it the *tramontano*, but spring is coming. Hugh glances back at Wilf in the cart with Pico. He's got orders to turn tail if there is trouble. If I'm to be crucified, we'll have one cross and not three. Wilf looks tired. It's been a lot of travelling for him these last six months, and he's not as young as he was. Pico looks just the same, but happier. Hugh watches the lad sitting on the baggage cart, flipping the coin Hugh gave him the day before. The *scudo* sparkles as it goes skyward, and Pico's face shines with all the joy of adolescence.

They avoided Bologna, staying at monasteries, inns, sometimes even stations. Bologna is the most northerly of the papal possessions, and Hugh did not want to be entangled with Julius and his army right before the war started. They saw the myriad patrician towers from a distance, and passed on happily. Each morning Wilf and Pico set off with the cart and other servants after breakfast. Hugh and Bembo overtook them for lunch, and then sped on to their next destination in time for Vespers, and victuals.

Today they are all together, the sun shines, and spring is in full bud as they leave the country behind. Today they enter Florence from the north, at the Fiesole gate.

Hugh rides to the front of the merchant wagons that line the road to the gate. The new soldiery, brainchild of Machiavelli, are delighted to see the papal seal that Hugh flashes at them. He gives his real name and knows that his adversary at the Council of Ten will probably have knowledge of it within the hour. He'll have to be quick if he wants any advantage.

When they are finally through the gate Hugh surveys the bustling street. 'Busy today. Is there some event?'

'The feast of the Archangel Gabriel. It will be busier further in.' Bembo pats the flanks of his horse with excitement.

'Are they always this noisy?'

Bembo laughs. 'It is a festival Hugh, a *carnivale*. These Florentines like to celebrate. Nine days a month we have holy days. Add that to Sundays and you can see why they are so happy; they only work every other day.'

'I see.' They enter the press of festival traffic, and the noise levels increase.

'Listen, Hugh, seeing we're here unexpectedly, I'll need to go on ahead to get us accommodation, tell people we're here.'

'No, you won't'

'What's that?'

'I said, *no,* you'll stay with me.'

'Don't be silly, man.' He pulls his horse slightly in front of Hugh's. 'I've been away from here for over a year. There are people I want to see, friends and so forth.' Bembo is about to say, "You can't stop me from going" when he catches the look in Hugh's eye! 'Well, of course, that can all wait, I suppose.'

They are silent for several minutes until Bembo points to the right, and says, 'The Dominican Convento di San Marco. It is where the prophet Savonarola was lector.'

'You believe he was a prophet?'

'He called for reform in the church. They burned him alive; I was there. Isn't that the mark of a true prophet—to be persecuted?'

'Perhaps, but he also said the Turks would be converted within the lifetime of his hearers. It has not happened.'

'Not yet, Hugh, but there is still time.'

Hugh grimaces and reins in his horse that has become skittish with the noise. He glances at Bembo and sees the beads of sweat on his temple. 'Did you see Michelangelo had a copy of Savonarola's sermons near his brushes in the Sistine Chapel?'

'Yes, and it doesn't surprise me. The Dominican casts a long shadow here. People are still divided about him; you have to be careful what you say. Though I did hear something amusing. Apparently, his grandfather was court physician to the d'Este family, in Ferrara, and gained a hearing for, amongst other remedies, he held that the generous imbibing of wine would aid longevity. He was, I say, popular, and a good man, no doubt, he was.'

Hugh is not laughing. Bembo leans awkwardly on his mount and points behind him. 'This used to be the Medici Palace, and up there is the university, which by the way, was the first, and for a while, the only university to teach Greek.' Bembo's eyes flit about nervously.

Is he looking for someone? Hugh's thoughts are interrupted by Bembo's shrill commentary.

'It took students from all over Europe. Among their professors were many great favourites of mine, Johannes Argyropoulos, Theodorus Gaza and Demetrius Chalcondylas – who, by the way, was the first to have Homer printed here.' He sighs with affectation. 'They work the students hard now, not like back in our day. We had it easier thanks to the carnivals, Midsummer Day, the sixty church holidays, Sundays and the autumn holidays. I can never say we were overworked. The students still wear the common black cloth, and still take their lectures in a great hall or studio, but on benches and not on straw like the other universities. The tradition in Florence is that when examinations are due the students ride on horseback, inviting their friends and familiars to attend the oral tests. If they pass, they can leave the studio to the sound of fifty trumpets. A nice touch, I always thought, and fitting. But they are expected to distribute wine and sweetmeats for the compliment, whether they pass or not. That's the price of an audience I suppose. *Panem et circenses,* bread and circuses.'

Above the tops of the pantile roofs and flags the vast russet-orange dome grows higher and more imposing with each minute. Thousands have gathered around a series of temporary festival scaffolds in the piazza. Each is fifty feet high and festooned with banners.

Bembo points up at the patrician towers that dot the skyline and shouts above the din, 'Our *Societa delle Torri*, our men of towers. You know, the merchant aristocrats who define everything as struggle and competition will have their great phalluses shoot up until the sun is blocked.'

'I thought you were all in favour, Bembo.'

Whether misunderstanding, or speaking his next thoughts without reference as he sometimes does, Bembo leans across his saddle again. 'These fellows in Florence differ vastly from the patricians of Venice. Venetians are more a clique of conspirators ruling a cringing populace through an invisible police state. And your Neapolitan noble is different again—more an idler to whom honour is an afterthought. The nobles of Papal States? Pastoral, agricultural, wouldn't soil their garments with trade. So, when you come here, there is a different atmosphere. I for one don't mind it.'

Hugh nods and lets Bembo ride a bit in front. Bembo acts nonchalant, but something is not right with him. Blithe, bordering hysterical. Hugh peels his eyes and hints for Wilf to do the same. It feels like Saturnalia: everywhere a succession of pageants, tournaments, spectacles and parades, musical revels, dances, jongleurs and acrobatic displays, knights and their ladies, heralds, standard bearers, fifers and trumpeters. Leading one and all are the bishops, cannons and choristers, bearing aloft the holy relics: a thorn from Christ's crown, a nail from the holy cross and the thumb of Saint John. Next a selection of the *Magnati* and *Grandi*, some wearing the much-coveted golden spurs of Florence only worn by four citizens at any one time. It seems to Hugh that the whole city and countryside must be there, regiment upon regiment of every profession represented in colourful livery.

Most notable are the guilds, each with their banners and emblems. They are, as Bembo gleefully points out, arranged in order of honour. The procession therefore is led by judges, lawyers and notaries, the *Arte dei Giudici e Notai*; followed by the wool, silk and cloth merchants, *Arte dei Lana; Por Santa Maria and Calimala*, these latter take their names from the streets where their warehouses are situated. Next come the *Arte del Cambio*, the bankers who bear the emblem of gold florins on a red ground. Dante, in all his travels to the underworld and above, never loses sight of the florin. 'There are only fifty banks in Florence,' Bembo shouts, 'there were many more a generation ago. They are, like the poor, always with us.' They continue down at the *Mercato Nuovo*, tables spread with green cloth, purse and ledger at the ready. These latter-day alchemists cannot only grow gold from base metals, but can also circulate it invisibly by letters of exchange. They are the real wonders of the age. They are the future, it is said.

After them come the *Arte dei Medici, Speziali e Merciai*, the guild of doctors, apothecaries and associated merchants who supply them. The seventh major guild to pass Hugh's bewildered eyes is the furriers, *Arte dei Vaccai e Pellicciai*, dealers and craftsmen of animal skins and fur.

And behind them come the minor guilds, the *minuto populo*: tanners, weavers, vintners, innkeepers, tailors, armourers, bakers, joiners, cooks, spinners, dyers, boatmen, beaters, peddlers, combers, all with banners; the *ciombi* with clogs from their wash houses; the stonemasons with aprons dusted white with the *pieta serena* marble dust, burly carpenters with their saw and axe emblem, the ruddy butchers with their black goat motif, the smiths with their pincers. The wool shearers and shoemakers are singing with deep voice, and at the head of the procession is the cross of *Santa Maria della Fiore*.

Bembo says the cloth guild have plenty to sing about. 'They can have raw and undressed cloths from Flanders, England and especially France, fulled, pressed, smoothed and cut any way you want. Their guild has warehouses and hostelries in Rouen, Caen, Provins, Montpellier, Avignon, Marseille, Toulon, and of course, Paris – which is only sixteen days from Florence.' They link arms and swagger as they process. Even some of the apprentices, sport doublets in scarlatto d'Oricello, which is the height of fashion at the moment. While Hugh is twisting round to check his back, he sees them: silk banners of ocean blue inset with embroidered lilies, carried by scores of children dressed in white tunics. Behind them the baptistery, Giotto's campanile, the polychrome banded marbles flashing their confidence, their brilliance, in the strong midday sun. People will always need wool. No wonder they look so happy.

A forty-foot wooden tower is erected in the piazza at the duomo. 'It is the tower of Saints Michael and Gabriel. Do you see the demons?' Bembo asks.

'Sometimes I think I see nothing else,' Hugh says.

'What's that?' Bembo shouts above the noise of the crowd.

'Nothing.' Hugh is all the while checking behind his back. No assassins, just swarms of apprentices, arm in arm, shouting, singing, stealing each other's caps.

'Demons! Up there on the tower,' Bembo shouts.

Hugh follows Bembo's stare to see men in hairy devil costumes scaling the towers where, in due time, they will be hurled by the archangels whose wings look like they might fall apart, even from this distance.

'Oh, I see, and I suppose they will attach ropes to their belts before they toss them off?'

'Yes. Would you like to watch them?'

'No. Lead on to the Palazzo della Signoria.'

'You have a meeting there?'

'Yes.'

'With whom?'

'You will see. Come on. Let's go before we can't move for this crowd.'

Five minutes later they are tethering the horses in the Piazza Vecchio, near Michelangelo's statue of David. Hugh doesn't have time to admire it. His hands are sweating, his heart racing. The great crenulated campanile thrusts upward into the heavens like a gigantic fist. Below it, in the Palazzo of the Signoria, within the corridors of power, lies his enemy – Machiavelli. Hugh glances up warily. Two bodies hang by their necks from the first-floor windows, black tongues, no eyes, probably beggarly pickpockets. He walks as casually as he can to where Wilf and Pico are waiting with the baggage cart. Wilf's hands are shaking as he ties the reins. Pico is still smiling, no one has told him. Hugh quickly removes his cloak and sword belt, handing them to Wilf who steadies his master's hand with his own. 'Nice day for sport, master.'

'Aye, Wilf, fair a day as any we've had this year.' Hugh glances back up at the town hall for a significant moment. 'Remember what I said.'

'Aye.' Wilf places the items next to him. 'Cap.'

'What?'

'Your beret, master; it has the knight's cross.'

'Oh yes. Almost forgot.' *Breathe. Breathe.* They swap caps. Bembo is shouting from the steps, asking what on earth is going on.

Wilf doesn't hear. 'Sure you don't want us in there?' he asks

'No, and if I'm not out, or haven't sent word within the hour, then get back to Norfolk and do something useful with your life. Take this waif with you. Get your sister to feed him up.'

'Aye, master.'

Hugh's throat wavers. 'You're a good man, Wilf.'

'Aye, and you're a bloody idiot. Should have stayed at home, all of us.'

'Yes, maybe.' Hugh glances around them pensively. 'See you in a few minutes.'

Hugh approaches Bembo on the steps, and reveals the dagger in his sleeve.

All that Bembo can say is, 'Oh.'

'That's right, Pietro *caro*, and don't believe that I don't know exactly where to stick it so that you will be in Hades long before you've finished your *Pater Noster*.' Hugh takes the other's arm, speaking quickly and quietly. 'Now, we are going to see the secretary of the Council of Ten. You will get us in; I will be your secretary. We will go together. Understood?

'Nicolo Machiavelli! Why him?'

'We'll find out when we get there. If you draw your sword, shout out, do anything to arouse suspicion, you will die.'

'Hugh, you're out of your mind. You can't be –'

'Go now.' He nudges Bembo to the top of the steps, following at his elbow. They pass a detachment of ten of the new militia with their constable as they enter under the first arch into the courtyard. The militia wears the uniforms Leonardo designed: white waistcoats under their iron breastplates, red and white stockings, white caps and leather shoes. All have swords. Some have lances, others the new *scoppietti*, a more portable, mechanical crossbow, cowardly weapon, unmanly, unknightly, thoroughly in keeping with the times. They ask questions; Bembo answers. The two pass through into the courtyard.

'Used to be able to just walk in here,' Bembo comments in a low voice. 'Now the place is crawling with this new militia. Really, you don't need the knife, my friend.'

They avoid the low fountain pool and the scores of notaries hovering under the balconies, talking in reverent voices. Hugh marks the exits, the position of the other militiamen who, thanks to Leonardo, are hard to miss. A soldier exits a door to the left still adjusting his harness. More voices come from behind that door: the guard room. The *Camera dell'arme* is a good place to find weapons if it comes to it. They pass the next arch which is flanked by soldiers with halberds and approach a high desk in the entrance.

A helpful clerk directs them to the *cancelleria* on the top floor. 'Up the stairs there, through the great hall, and follow the grand staircase to the top floor. The secretary's office is to your right. Just ask if you can't find it. Mind that might be hard today with the festival. Should I go with you?' The list of public officials is printed on a board behind the clerk's desk. In the Council of Ten there is only one member whose name begins with 'M'.

'No, no, thank you.' Bembo bows and leads the way to the stairs with Hugh at his shoulder.

'Very good, Pietro,' he whispers on the shallow stone steps. 'Keep it up and you might live out today.'

Bembo starts to remonstrate quietly to Hugh; but stops as four soldiers appear at the head of the stairs. Hugh observes them as they descend, their raven-haired leader, perhaps mid-thirties, carries the helmet of a captain. His cross-hilt is finely engraved, his face hardened, eyes cold, black, dead. Hugh knows the face of a man of blood; it's like looking in the glass. For a glacial moment their eyes connect, but then Hugh returns his gaze to Bembo who averts his eyes as they pass, even though the captain is now looking at him. Hugh focuses on looking down, and maintaining the demeaner of a servant. He must get to the secretary's office.

The soldiers pass without incident. Hugh shoots a glance at Bembo's stricken face – wide eyes darting feverishly in every direction. God, he seems more nervous than I am. As they clear the first flight of stairs, Hugh sees Bembo's left hand has left a sweat mark on the banister. They pass through the great hall where the public meetings are held, and out of the west doors to the final staircase.

'Hugh, will you listen to me?'

'No.'

You are making a huge mistake.'

'Keep going.'

'This man has nothing to do with the Borgia gold. Trust me.'

'Trust you?' Hugh tightens his grip and spits out with venom, 'No one trusts you more, *caro*. The fact that you are still breathing proves it. Now keep walking.'

'This is going to get me into a lot of trouble.'

'You're already in trouble, Pietro, and we're here to fix that one way or the other.'

'What do you mean?'

'Quit the pretence. I know that Petrucci is not your blackmailer.'

'I never said he was. It was you who drew that conclusion.'

'And you let me, in order to hide the identity of the real one.'

'And you think it's Machiavelli? You are mad. You don't know what you're doing, Hugh, or what you're involved with here.'

'Oh, believe me, I know more than you think. This blackmailer, this thorn in your side? You don't think it can be removed; it is too big, too powerful and your faith is small. And so, you act neither wisely, nor well, for you have lost hope of recovery. Trust me, Pietro; I know about these things, and though I have no wine to irrigate your wounds, nor hot irons to cauterise, yet still I have something as good as a surgeon's knife.'

'Oh *Dio Mio*! You're going to kill him, an innocent man!'

'Shush.' Hugh pushes him gently at the top step. 'I'm sure a Florentine politician may be many things, but innocent is not one of them. Now walk to that desk and speak well to this clerk.'

'Master Secretary does not like to be disturbed.' The clerk of the council is not quite as helpful as his counterpart downstairs. By the sorry excuse of a beard, the pallid-faced jobsworth has pockmarks up his neck and around a shrivelled chin that he thrusts aloof.

'Pardon?' Bembo for once is flustered.

'You may leave your name with me, and I –'

'Signor.' Hugh speaks demurely from behind. 'My master is the poet Pietro Bembo, pride of Toscana verse. He does not need an appointment to see his oldest and dearest friend.'

'Oh, I see. Signor Bembo, forgive me. I'll go and tell him.'

'No need, signor,' Hugh says, leading the poet awkwardly by the arm. 'This way is it.'

'The second door on your right,' the clerk calls after them.

They pass the first door, which appears to lead to a map room, and then the second, whose door is closed. Hugh knocks when Bembo hesitates and a lone voice calls from within, 'Enter.'

'What do I say?'

Hugh rests his hand on the door handle. 'I don't know. You're a writer; make something up.' He pushes the handle down and opens the door to a narrow room with two high windows facing north over Florence toward Fiesole. Eight desks are covered with papers, inkhorns, unbound books and broken reeds underfoot. At one of them sits a lean man around forty years of age, not nourished by anything you would call lunch.

'Yes?' He rises as they approach, his face genial, his hands running about his folios, his fingers spidery, precise, pale. 'Are you not the poet Pietro Bembo? But of course, you are, please take a seat, signor. What brings you here?'

Hugh closes and locks the door behind them. He observes the eyes of each man. *He's a good actor, Machiavelli. I wouldn't have thought they knew each other. Let's see how his skills hold up under pressure.*

'Well, I, er.' Bembo approaches on the tile floors with a bewildered expression.

'It's like this, signor.' Hugh strides up behind him, removes Bembo's sword with his right hand and shoves him to one side with the other. In a moment he is round Machiavelli's side of the desk, pinning him to the wall. 'I am Hugh Erpingham. It appears you've had me followed half way around Europe. Well now, I'm here so you can address your questions directly to me.'

'Had you followed?' Machiavelli's arms are raised, his eyes wide with abject terror and then anger. 'Are you mad? I know not of what you speak. Is this some Pisan plot, some conspiracy? For I know nothing of it.'

‘Really.’ Hugh tightens his grip on the beleaguered secretary’s collar, thrusting the blade close to his skin. ‘I intercept a letter from Bembo to *Signor M*, care of the Council of Ten, and you know nothing of it? I ask you one last time, spill what you know or I will spill your innards over this desk.’

‘Hugh, please!’ Bembo has recovered from being pushed over and is now standing ten feet away glancing to the door and back again.

‘Try anything now, Pietro, and he will die. Move away to the window. And you, signor, answer my question.’

‘I cannot, signor. I have received no such letter. I barely know this man.’

‘Liar. There is no one else on the council with M as an initial.’

‘I have no such arrangement, and if any abbreviation is used here, it is between intimates who call me Il Machia. I swear it is the truth. Besides this office is more than just the Council of Ten; it incorporates the justices and the militia.’

‘Lying horse gelder, it is you! You sought my life and ruined his; now you will pay.’

‘It is not I.’

‘On your feet. You will join those other two malefactors hanging outside.’

‘Please, signor, oh God, please, no.’

‘Hugh, stop this! For God’s sake, stop this!’ Bembo approaches with raised hands.

‘Get back, Bembo. I’ve warned you. If it’s not him, then confess who it is or he will die.’ Hugh presses the blade across the jugular vein. ‘Right here, right now!’

‘Please, Hugh! No, don’t.’

‘Three, two, one.’

‘It’s Michelotto. Do you hear me, you mad man? He is the blackmailer.’

‘Really.’ Hugh looks up and stays the blade. ‘Wasn’t so difficult, was it?’

'God help me. God help me. I shouldn't have said that.' Bembo starts pacing the tiles, rubbing his temples and breathing out like a man about to void his stomach.

Hugh lets Machiavelli fall back into his chair. The man has fouled his small clothes and is shaking like a leaf. 'Signor Machiavelli, who is this Michelotto?'

But the secretary is in too much shock to hear. 'Signor?'

Hugh strikes him across the cheek. 'Signor, look at me and tell me who this man is.'

Machiavelli rubs his cheeks and looks blankly at Hugh, speaking as one just waking. 'He was Borgia's lieutenant, his university friend, henchman.'

'Oh shit.' Bembo looks at the door, then the window. 'Oh shit, we've got to get away from here. Hugh, please, we've got to... shit.'

Hugh levels the knife in the secretary's face, 'But Borgia's lieutenant was the Catalan Don Michelle, the one they call the strangler.'

'They are the same man. He and Borgia were inseparable.'

'And why did he not fall with his master?'

'He did. In fact, we held him here in our dungeons before Julius transferred him to the Castel Sant'angelo.' Machiavelli massages his throat. 'Julius tortured him for months because he knew Borgia must have conspired to hide the papal treasures, but he never broke. A man like that wouldn't, you see. Not him.' The secretary's eye is also toward the door.

'Then what? Quickly.'

'Then I convinced Gonfaloniere Soderini, to hire Michelotto to raise up a strong militia in Florence as I had seen him do for Duke Valentino in the Romagna.'

'But he is Florence's enemy—a known murderer, who should have been tried and hung.'

'Great.' Bembo speaks as if to the ceiling. 'A moral lecture from you of all people. Hugh, we have got to get out of here quickly, for God's sake man.'

Machiavelli turns the rings on fingers that have not stopped shaking. 'You will forgive me, but as in politics, we choose effectiveness over moral consistency. I am sorry he has some vendetta against you, but for us he has given results against Pisa.'

'And you trust a man like this with an army? Suppose he had access to more ducats than the Chigis and Fuggers combined? Would he then still be your servant, or would he not rather turn on his former captors and tear them limb from limb?'

'You mean the missing papal treasures that Julius tortured him for?'

But Hugh isn't listening. He is looking at Bembo, and then to the door. 'The captain on the stairs! It's him, isn't it?'

Bembo's face is ashen. 'Hugh, you've got to get out of here. You don't know him.'

'No, but maybe I will today.' Even as Hugh speaks, they hear the unmistakable sounds of boots, barked orders and the clank of steel echoing back down the corridors and stairwells. Hugh casts his eye about the room as the steps grow louder. He runs and then jumps onto the window seat glancing out of the window. Wilf's cart is surrounded by soldiers, but Wilf he cannot see. *Shit*. There is a stone drainage ledge, half a foot wide, broken in places but a possibility for a man with no other hope – like him. He looks back at Bembo. 'Don't lose heart, Pietro, at least I know who the bastard is now, and where he is, which is half the battle.' Soldiers are now pounding on the door. Hugh puts his right leg through the window.

'Hugh, what are you doing?'

'Keep him talking, Pietro. You're good at that. I'm going this way.'

'Oh great, you're leaving me here, and what am I going to tell him?'

'Tell him I'm coming for him.' Hugh gets his second foot through and turns his body carefully into the wall.

'You're mad! You will fall to your death, you fool.'

With a sword hanging from his belt, Hugh pokes a less certain face back through the window one last time before edging along the ledge. 'Maybe. Fortuna is a woman. They say she favours men who are bold.'

Hugh inches east along the façade, grateful for each handhold. He makes the mistake of glancing down past his feet and nearly freezes for fear. It is work for a slim man. Wilf's belly would have forced him off. Hugh hopes they will not be too rough with him and Pico, poor lad. He gets into a rhythm, hand on hand, shuffle on shuffle. Parts of the stone ledge are already broken off. On two occasions, his weight sends great chunks of stone eighty feet to the street below. When he is thirty feet away from the window, both feet go at once, and he is left hanging with his heart beating out of his ribs. As he regains his foothold gingerly either side, he sees a soldier staring at him from the window he left, then shouting back to his companions.

Hugh looks left. Open windows. He starts double time, hand over hand. They will have to traverse the entire building to reach him because the double height council chamber is now between them. They will have to descend the stairs and come right round. He might have enough time to get in at the end. Or could he climb up to the roof? It would give him greater access for escape. He glances up, but the roof overhangs and handholds are uncertain. The far windows will do. They'll have to. He keeps up the rhythm until he is almost in reach of an open window. The sound of low voices, office talk. He looks in to see two clerks in black cloaks and crimson collars crowing over some folios. He swings his leg over and eases himself in.

'Excuse the interruption, signors. But if you call out, I will have recourse for this.' Both men freeze like rabbits as Hugh slides Bembo's sword from his belt. Hugh is breathing heavily. 'Stairs?' They point to the near door behind them. Hugh gets his bearings and then says, 'The council chamber?' They nod, drawing closer together and looking cautiously at the blade. 'Any other stairs? Quickly now.' They point to the far door. Again, Hugh can hear the familiar sound of boots to his right. Down the corridor toward the central council chamber. They are coming.

He runs to the left door and out into another office. The only door here is on his right. A corner office perhaps? He walks swiftly and quietly through the door to catch the direction of his enemy. They are behind in the room he has just left. He runs to the next door, through a smaller room where an old man is reading next to a bookshelf. A further door is opposite. He goes for it. Heart pounding, the voice of fear rising. *No stairs. You are trapped. Back to the galleys with you: shackles, chains, the lash, hunger.*

He pulls the door and enters a lobby area with stairs. *Thank God, a way out.* Two soldiers come through an opposite door. Hugh charges them just as two others come up the stairs. The first man has a sword drawn. Hugh parries it right exposing the man's left flank into which slides his dagger. The second man is directly behind him with his *scoppietto* already loaded with an iron dart. Hugh pushes the first man against him and rams his hilt into the second man's nose. Hugh wrestles the *scoppietto*. The soldier is still holding it when Hugh pulls the trigger toward the stairs where the bolt skewers the next rushing militiaman in the shoulder. He buckles.

Hugh charges again. *These men aren't soldiers. They've not long left Tuscan farms and herds. They'll wound, not kill.* The wounded man gets a kick, his companion a taste of Hugh's blade in the upper arm. In three moves, the last man is unarmed and head-butted back down the stairs with Hugh following hard upon him. Boots. Fists. Teeth. One flight, then another. He is at ground level.

He deals with two other soldiers before reaching the doorway to a broad courtyard. They scream so much he wishes now that he had killed them, for he can hear boots everywhere, and above them the voice of their captain.

Michelotto. Damn. Shit. Think. Think.

He keeps close to the walls in the shadows, peering into the courtyard, looking for a way out. It's not the courtyard where he came in. This one is bigger.

More boots.

And then he sees him, the Strangler himself, entering the courtyard, flanked by soldiers dragging Wilf and Pico by their hair. Behind them, Bembo, armed. *Bembo. Bastard.*

‘Signor Erpingham,’ the captain bellows, in a hoarse Catalan roar. ‘We have your friends. Please give yourself up. You are surrounded.’

Boots in the shadowy corridors to his left. Voices behind. And more boots. The echo of steps coming closer. Closing.

Hugh chances another glimpse into the courtyard. Wilf and Pico kneel in the middle. There are a score of *scoppietti* pointing at his doorway. They know where he is. *Breathe. Need time.* Wilf’s face has been knocked about a bit, but he’s still cursing like an Englishman, so he’s all right.

‘Come, signor. My soldiers surround you.’

Hugh shouts back from the shadows. ‘Are these the ones you trained? They fight like village women. Why don’t you come take me on yourself if you have the balls.’ It’s a bad card in a bad hand. Might have worked fifty years ago. The noises of soldiers in adjacent rooms and corridors cease in an instant as Michelotto’s bellicose laughter reverberates through the colonnade. ‘I need not waste my time on you when I have your friends.’

‘The fat one? Kill him if you want. He’s a lazy good-for-nothing. Mind you, I just let six of your men live when their lives were in my hand, so you could let them go and have me instead. Fair exchange?’

‘No exchange.’

‘Ah, spoken like a true Spaniard.’ If he’ll not make the exchange for honour, maybe for patriotism?

‘I don’t think you understand me, signor. You are hard of hearing, no? Let me give you some new ears.’

The briefest silence is followed by Wilf shouting, screaming in broad Norfolk English ‘No. NO. NO! ARGH!’ Hugh looks again. Four men restrain Wilf. Blood flows crimson from his head. Michelotto is holding a filleting knife in one hand and something bloody in the other. Wilf’s ear.

I’ll cut his black heart out, Hugh swears to God. *I’ll make him suffer.* His thoughts are cut short by a movement behind him. Two men come through the archway to his left—two of Michelotto’s lieutenants who were with Michelotto on the stairs. They swear at Hugh in Spanish and level their blades with swept hilts fanning out, wearing their bloodlust like wolves. *Good,* Hugh thinks. *Probably old friends of the captain. Let's see how they dance in Spain.*

The broader and older of the two lets the younger one attack first. He's fast and tall enough to lunge a great distance. Hugh parries four left then right but can see he's been forced toward a corner. The older man closes in to make any further maneuver impossible. Hugh must act. Wilf is still screaming. The fifth stroke is higher, toward his chest. This he catches with both sword and dagger, drawing the other's blade toward the wall. Holding it there with the dagger, Hugh frees his sword and slashes his opponent downwards onto his foremost leg cutting deep to the bone. Before he can scream, Hugh has yanked himself off the walls into his oncoming companion, with just enough time to avoid the blade. Hugh moves quickly into the open space, then straight back for the attack. The older man moves clear of his injured friend who is trying to stand. Hugh kicks over the injured man and approaches the other at speed, brushing his blade away with irresistible force. *Forward, forward. Thrust, cut, lunge. He hasn't long. This man is old-school, and he is out of shape.* Hugh catches his blade and draws it up high, closes and sticks the man in the gut with the knife. Not pretty, but effective.

'Signor, what is this noise? Have my men come upon you?' *The bastard is laughing.*

Hugh removes their weapons and moves toward the entrance, being careful to stay behind the pillar. 'They have, two of your lieutenants. Spaniards, who fought worse than the Tuscans.' Silence. 'I've kept them alive for bartering.' Silence. 'D'you hear, Captain, or do I need to send their ears out to you? Or their heads?'

'Qui està aquí?' It is Michelotto in his native Catalan tongue. He sounds annoyed, impatient, not overly moved.

The older soldier, propped against the wall clutching his bleeding stomach, confirms. *'És Fernández i Alonso. És com diu el capità. Perdó.'*

'Perdó, *Perdó! Fernández, Alonso, mostrar-se a si mateixos.* Let them show themselves to me, signor, then we will talk.'

Hugh catches another glimpse. Michelotto is talking to the men behind him. Wilf hisses like a bull. Pico is crying. Bembo is stone silent. *Judas, Bembo will pay for this.* Hugh turns his gaze to the wounded Spaniards who are looking more worried than they did before. 'You heard what he said. Come to the archway. Show yourselves. Or do you not speak Italian?'

They drag themselves unwillingly, at last linking arms to help each other as they near the opening. No sooner do they appear than the crack of ten or twenty crossbows smacks about the walls, followed immediately by the whistle of death piercing the heads and necks of Hugh's wounded Spaniards. Part of the shower glances with a flurry of sparks from the breastplates, but most hit where they were aimed—high. They fall backwards. The older Fernandez is instantly quiet. The younger Alonso thrashes with his legs in the blood, agony and despair.

Above the noise of Alonso's boots and belt scraping the pavement, Hugh hears the now familiar voice of their captain. 'You want to offer terms now, signor? Very well, let us barter. You come out unarmed or I will tighten my lyre string.'

What? What does he mean? Hugh looks again. Michelotto has it round Wilf's throat.

'Get away.' It's Wilf balling, then wheezing. 'Don't give in to the filthy dago bastards, master, argh. Get away. ARGH!'

No. NO, please God, not like this. 'STOP!' Hugh appears in the archway with his hands raised. 'Stop, I am coming out unarmed. Let him be.' He approaches the centre of the courtyard where he is put in irons. Michelotto releases Wilf who slumps forward clutching his throat and choking. The captain cleans the blood from the lyre string with his fingers.

He licks them as Hugh is brought close. 'The blood of an English pig, the taste of weakness, of failure.' He winds the string about its linchpin, placing it in the crimson doublet under his harness. 'Honour, chivalry, courtesy. It is no wonder you will not succeed in this world. Look at you, the knights of Rhodes, relics. Couldn't win a card game, let alone a war.'

'I demand to see Gonfaloniere Soderini. I insist we be afforded the rights of subjects of a sovereign state.'

'Listen to him, coming in here with his sword, threatening a council member, attacking her soldiers and now he wants diplomatic protection. Look around you, signor. The place is empty. I am your judge, jury and hangman. Now tell me about this boy here. What is his name. Pico? Yes, Pico, a nice name and a handsome youth. Bembo says you are fond of him. Perhaps he is like a son to you?' Michelotto angles Pico's head so that the lad is looking straight at Hugh, his face streaked with tears, his wide brown eyes pleading. 'Perhaps you play the backside game with him as our Signor da Vinci plays with his boys? Oh, do not look thus, signor. I am sure I never meant to insult the purity of a holy knight. But I will tell you something.'

'Leave him,' Hugh says. 'He is just a boy.' Bembo is looking down.

'Yes, I will tell you something. Last year you happened upon my sister's son in Rome. He too was like a son to me.'

'Michelotto!' Hugh strains at his chains but arms hold him. 'He's just a boy.'

But the captain carries forth with a cool venom, standing behind Pico and running his fingers though his curly locks. 'I don't suppose you remember, you brave, chivalrous hero of Rhodes.'

'Close your eyes, Pico.' Hugh shouts through a dry throat while the captain is still speaking. The lad is breathing hard. 'Say the prayers I taught you. Pico, say the prayers.'

'Yes, the brave knights –

Pico is squeezing his eyes shut, his lips moving fast between sharp breaths. Hugh can hear his faint 'Pater noster, qui es in coelis...'

'Don't do this, Michelotto, I beg you.'

'– Yes, you knights, for all your enemies are demons to be slain in Christ's name, but as I said, the boy you slew in Rome was like a son to me, and someone must pay for his death. Of course, that will be you when I have the information you have to give me but in the meantime. Oh, the fragility of young life.'

By this time Hugh and Wilf are saying their Pater Nosters along with the heaving sobs of the lad. He and Wilf do not stop as Pico's sobs turn briefly to gurgles and then to nothing. Hugh makes sure the boy's incredulous face can see him praying until his eyes finally drift and glaze. Wilf will not look. His eyes are closed as he bellows his prayer with gritted teeth and great, heaving tears. *'Dimitte nobis debita nostra, sicut et nos dimittimus debitoribus nostris.'*

Hugh sinks to his knees. *Forgive Michelotto? Monster. Villain. There should not be forgiveness for his ilk, just damnation. It is just. It is just.*

CATALAN REVENGE. TWENTY MINUTES LATER, UNDER THE PALAZZO DELLA SIGNORIA.

'This was my home once, this dungeon.' Michelotto is alone with Hugh now.

Hugh's arms are bound behind his back, and he is suspended from the ceiling-pulley by a rope attached to straps which slide behind his arms. He is naked, but they haven't begun the torture yet.

'I can tell you what is written on every stone, which one you should lick if you want moisture. I thought this cell would be the last thing

I'd ever see. I tell you something, knight: they should have killed me; it would have been better for them. Much better.' Michelotto leaves the wall and runs his hands along the stones as he walks the perimeter. Hugh counts thirty steps, expecting any moment a punch, a kick, a club to the head or back. 'You know, signor, this city always keeps a lion. The Lion of Florence, symbol of their pride, their fierceness. Arseholes. Or something or other. In the time of the historian Villani, it was recorded that a donkey kicked to death that lion. Can you believe that? It is true. They think I am here to serve their little republic, when I have led armies that made all Italy quake with fear. Right now, they think I am their donkey, their *manino*, to do their dirty work. Maybe I am. But signor, I will kick them all to death one day soon.'

Hugh looks up briefly to catch his enemy's eye. '*Quid viro forti suavius quam vindicta manu quere*; what could be more delightful for a strong man than to pursue a vendetta.'

'Oh, so you don't think I have cause? That I am not just?' Michelotto draws close to Hugh. 'You know what it is to have a dream, and then have it broken? To lose something like that? Maybe you do. Well, signor, Italy had a chance to be united, to be great, to be strong, but they chose to be divided and weak. Do you know how my people became united? How Aragon became great? It was through the bastard son of king Sancho. Yes, that's right. You have heard of him. Ramiro was a great man, signor. While his brothers were off fighting the Moors, wasting their time, he seized a great part of their inheritance and prospered as king. That is what Cesare and I would have done here among these weak, distracted Italians—unite Europe as Alexander united the ancient world.'

Hugh gives a half choke, half laugh, letting a long string of saliva and blood fall toward the straw.

Michelotto stops walking and holds his arms. He glares at Hugh for a moment then says, 'You know that we Catalans nearly ruled Byzantium, and we did rule Athens. What have you English done to match that? We Catalans are tough, not like these Italians who are always thinking of their bellies, their luxuries, their *dolce vita*. Europe could have been a great empire again with the duke as their emperor and pope, but no, these stupid Italians would not be led. So –'

The captain stops pacing and looks up to the high window, hands on hips. His face is shiny with sweat, and heavily pitted at the neck from the pox. 'A man is nothing without a great plan, a story, a vision – purpose. But see, I have a new purpose: I will. Kick. Them. To. Death. Yes, I will. I, Don Michelle, the last to remember, will make them all pay for what they did: the Roveres, Orsinis, Colonnas, Medicis. All of the old families who resisted progress, who betrayed Cesare, will fall to my sword. God! This republic, these idiots I must live amongst. They forget that their city only unified under a dictatorship. I swear to God, you never saw such a bunch of scoundrels and wastrels. The podesta, dear God, the bloody podesta, the *capitano del populo*, the Council of the People, the Council of Liberty, the Ten of the Balia, the Eight of the Guard – all lodging in the Palazzo Vecchio, all escorted about the city by my guards, all wearing their pink, violet and crimson Lucco gowns, all waited on by servants in green livery bearing the insignia of the commune. Get one of them, any of them, to show you around and they will show you without the slightest shame the walls hung with tapestries, the fine food, the fair linen, the silver plate and a monthly credit of three hundred gold florins. Shit, you would not believe what goes on above this ceiling: singers, musicians, buffoons, notaries to record every time the podesta passes wind, and a chancellor to attend to the correspondence when Gonfaloniere Soderini has forgotten how to sign his name. Six meetings are required to veto the smallest credit, to send a dying man to hospital, or to have the podesta's sixth secretary's wardrobe repaired. You have to live here to believe it. And they do not know how close their judgement comes.'

'With Tuscan peasants in uniforms. Optimistic.'

'Ya, ya, I know. Do you think I'm that stupid? An army is not built in a day. These Florentines are soft: bakers, wool carders, odd fish of every description. They own no horse and know nothing of the mastery of arms. And as regards chivalry, hah! They are trained in self-preservation and self-aggrandisement, not sacrifice. This is not *caballeria* but *cacaleria*.'

Michelotto stands before Hugh, hands on hips, looking into his eyes with lupine hunger. 'These soldiers are nothing yet. It is hard to train farmers. Their minds are already accustomed to weakness, to mercy. But soon they will give me their sons at fourteen years of age, thirteen, twelve even.'

'So, you intend to live a long time.'

'Hah! Longer than you, signor. And I will make them loyal to me, ruthless, efficient, fearless. I know how to bind men to me, signor, to my purpose – even a man like Bembo. And that is not all, for you – yes, you, signor – will tell me where I can find Vendramin, this gold, this Greek fire. First rule of war: secure finance. That is what Cesare always told me. "*Amigo*," he used to say, "do not forget what we learned at university in Padua: Philip of Macedon's first conquest was the Balkan gold mines." So, you see I have not forgotten. I will have that gold first. And later on, I will have twenty thousand, even thirty thousand, well trained soldiers with sufficient finance for new canon and a weapon like the fire that would set Italy ablaze. That is why you are still alive. I was prepared for you to go to Siena at Easter. I was prepared to let you live a little longer, but you have come here. You have, as they say, arrived at the judgement before your time. But it is no matter. You have seen what I do with my friends, so be under no illusions. I will have the information I seek from you even if I have to tease it out of your entrails.'

'You'll get nothing from me.' Hugh spits in his face and tries to head butt him to no avail.

Michelotto grabs Hugh by the ear and shakes his head. 'You think you are a hard case, signor? You think maybe you can endure suffering? That your back is the only back with scars? Let me tell you something, when they put Fra Savonarola on this very *strappado*, he broke long before his arms were wrenched from their sockets. Long, long before. And that was a man who scourged himself for fun. *Entendre?* Understand? So, you can spit and curse like a big man if you want, but I will have the information I need. You think that your cause is higher, superior to mine? That you have some holy commission, that God is on your side and you cannot be beaten perhaps? That the knights will reward you, rescue you? Or maybe it's this White Cardinal that you are working for all along? Maybe you think he will save you from me? He pays well enough for information about you, but he's not here now is he? So, in the end signor, you are nothing to anyone. Your life is nothing. Your cause, nothing, just one more filthy, money-grubbing maggot in an overstuffed shithole.' He shoves Hugh so that he spins on the rope with the walls passing around him, stones, blackness, the streaks of torches, the high light of the window. Hugh hears the door opening and Michelotto calling for Bembo. A few revolutions later Hugh catches a glimpse of Judas entering.

Then Michelotto catches Hugh again by the beard. 'Yes, it is Bembo, signor. Did you think he was your friend? Did you not think he would pay you back for leaving his head in a sack for a day, and threating to break his fingers on that olive press? Did you think maybe you would win him to your cause? Make a holy knight of him?'

'He told me that someone was blackmailing him.' Hugh looks toward Bembo who is arranging the ropes as he has been taught. Bembo does not look back, but under his pursed lips he sees the man's teeth are gritted.

'Did he? Well, maybe that is true, but did he also tell you about his great dream to have a university in Venice named after him to rival Bologna and Paris? Did he tell you that? Universities don't come cheap, do they, signor? Don't look so sad Bembo, virtue has never been as respectable as money. And if you, Erpingham, fell for that sob story, then more fool you. Bembo here knows the cost of getting things done in this world, and he is about to prove that to you. He will have his university and an illustrious name while you will be forgotten.' He motions upward with his eyes. 'All right, Bembo. Give him his first drop. Just a small one. Do the damage slowly.'

Bembo, still looking away, pulls the rope coming from the ceiling pulley. Hugh is raised another foot.

'More than that,' Michelotto says. 'That's better. Now let go. I said, now. Let him go.'

The ground rushes toward Hugh followed by the jerk, the creak of ropes, the tearing of sinew in his shoulders as his arms are yanked backwards. The pain, shouting through his shoulders, his back, his neck. He cries out and then breathes hard to dissipate the pain while tensing his muscles. *I've had worse. I've survived worse. Hold.*

'I told you it would hurt. Well, now we are going to do it again, each time a little higher. Or you can tell me what you and that snake Petrucci have planned this Easter in Siena. No? Send him again, Bembo. Go on, up with him.'

Hugh comes down again, and this time the celery crunch of ligament in his left shoulder is audible before ever he screams.

'Come now,' Michelotto says in mock sympathy, yanking his head upward by the hair. 'Petrucci: does he have the gold already? Has he found out where it is maybe, and needs your help? No? Maybe he knows where Vendramin is, or where he will be? Come, signor. Time runs out for you. Tell me, and I will make the pain go away, forever.'

Sweat stings his eyes, yet there are no tears to cleanse them. Hugh pants and hisses like a pot and finally says, 'No,' and then again, 'No. You'll get nothing from me.'

'Not at this moment, but I will. For when your arms are hanging off like a rag doll, then I will bring your fat English servant in here and cut him up slowly in front of you. Do you understand?'

'Tell him, Hugh.' Bembo's face is stricken with blackest guilt. 'For God's sake, just tell him.'

'Why bring God into it?' Hugh hisses. 'You'll get nothing from me.'

'Enough! Take him up again, higher. We have all day, all night. He will talk.'

As Bembo pulls the rope, there is a knock on the door.

'Who is it?' Michelotto barks. 'I said we should not be disturbed.'

'Secretary of the Council. Open immediately in the name of the republic.' Machiavelli steps into the dungeon. 'Ah captain, there you are.'

Other men in livery wait behind the secretary outside the door. 'The gonfalonier wishes to see you.'

'I am interrogating this man who is a threat to the republic. I cannot come immediately.'

'I will rephrase. Gonfalonier Soderini has returned from the *carnivale* to see that you have turned the courtyard outside his office into a charnel house and commands you to attend him immediately. The prisoner will wait.'

'He had better. And don't you talk to him. He must be left for me, or I will make my anger felt, secretary.' Michelotto stares coldly at Machiavelli for a moment, and then from Bembo to Hugh. 'We will resume shortly, Bembo.' He pushes past Machiavelli with Bembo following a step behind.

When they are at last alone, Machiavelli orders Hugh to be cut down. 'These men are gonfalonier's personal bodyguard. He has sent them to escort you and your man outside the city. The incident today was, how shall I say, unfortunate. The captain has become insolent of late, but he is not above the law. He will say that you forced his hand, that you brought the devil out of him, that most of the blood spilt was at your hand, which I think is true. You are to blame for this upheaval, these deaths. You should be punished. But as I say, Soderini doesn't want a diplomatic incident. He will deal with Don Michelle, and you had better say as little as possible to your magister, the pope or anyone else. Good God, what a day this has been.'

Minutes later Hugh is reunited with Wilf, the cart and horses. Head bandaged, Wilf is already seated in the driving position when Hugh arrives out of the side door to the north of the palazzo. The afternoon air is sweet to breathe, but the empty seat next to Wilf means the man cannot look at him. *Machiavelli is right; this was his fault. And poor Wilf too, disfigured for life. He didn't deserve that. I failed them both. It was my pride.*

'Come on, master. There's space up 'ere for you. Arms hurt?' Hugh winces as Wilf tries to help him. 'Don't worry; I can drive us. Just bloody glad to be out of this shithole alive.' He's putting a brave face on it. Wilf's hands tremble on the reins, dark with blood. Hugh lingers before sitting. This is Pico's seat. How often has he seen the lad asleep under Wilf's arm on it.

'Sorry, Wilf.'

'I know. Just get in, and let's be gone.'

Hugh slumps into the seat and then stares ahead blankly as some of the gonfalonier's bodyguard mount, and others assemble with halberds in formation around the wagon. Hugh shifts to remove something that he is sitting on. He can still use his fingers, but any shoulder movement is excruciating. It is Pico's half carved wooden horse and paring knife. He looks at them aghast. Someone will have to tell his mother. He slips the horse and knife inside his doublet just as the captain of the bodyguard gives the order to move off. He's an old soldier with a thick white beard, probably a friend of Soderini, or family member. Who else would you trust? He looks on Hugh from under bushy white eyebrows with deserved scorn. 'My orders are to take you back to the Fiesole gate. All right men, forward.'

Steel rims on worn ruts, the sharp clip of hooves, the smell of dish-water and dogs fouling. They take the streets to the east of the duomo so as not to be troubled by the crowds, whose tumult can be heard even from the Piazza della Signoria. The shade of the narrow streets makes the air cold. Cold and damp. No one speaks. Hugh looks at the black tufa paving slabs laid in diamond patterns and lets his body sway to the rhythm of the cart as it passes over them.

The noise intensifies as they draw level with the duomo. Hugh catches a glance at the dome down a side street, but then another sound —hoofbeats. A cavalcade moves at speed. He turns his neck stiffly to look behind, and at first sees nothing but the length of the street. The thumping increases. His pulse quickens.

'What is it?' Wilf says.

'My sword.'

Wilf reaches behind for the sword belt, and Hugh fumbles to buckle it on. Shoulders hurt like hell. 'Keep your pikestaff handy. I think Don Michelle is missing us already.'

'If I see that dago again, I'll make him taste it and hang the consequences. Can you fight, master?'

'I think so.' Hugh winces as he finally finds the hole for his buckle. 'Mainly with my feet and teeth though.'

He glances back again and sees the unmistakable flashes of white and red uniform as they approach. 'Captain, you should make ready. I think we have company.'

'Don't concern yourself.' The old captain swivels in his saddle. 'I have my orders.' He calls a halt on a street junction, and moves his horse to the rear where he can intercept the riders. Hugh is right. It is Michelotto, and as the thunder of hooves dissipates into a whinnying and clatter, it is Michelotto's voice alone that is heard.

'I have orders to return these prisoners. There is new information about them. Your orders are revoked.'

Hugh turns to see him, now red faced from the exertion, yes, but also from a leonine rage that was always barely concealed below the surface, the semi-permanent red mist that comes to dominate men of blood, insatiate and consuming. Bembo is not among them. *Good,* Hugh thinks, hoping he has gone to hang himself.

The captain of the bodyguard says, 'You have this in writing, or my master's seal?'

Michelotto speaks before he has even finished. 'The matter required upmost haste.'

'Really, then go and get one or the other, otherwise I am not free to disobey my orders.' He knows the Spaniard is lying, but it is impolite to say so in front of twenty subordinates.

The two eye each other. Michelotto smiles and nods. He agrees, yes, this is reasonable, he seems to be saying. His horse approaches the older man, asking to speak privately. Hugh sees the significant glance he gives his men, some whose *scoppietti* are already loaded. The captain of the bodyguard has no reason to feel alarmed. He is in Florence. They serve Florence, home of *giustizia*. Michelotto draws alongside, bends across to speak, but then takes hold of the older man's beard and slides a knife under his ribs.

The guards nearest who try to help their captain are pierced by the *scoppietti* bolts. The remaining horse and footmen engage each other as Michelotto dismounts and goes straight for Hugh.

This has happened so fast that Hugh barely has his Colhona clear of the scabbard when Michelotto appears at the side of the wagon with blade raised. Hugh catches his blade high, but the force sends splinters of pain into his whole torso. Hugh kicks out from his seat and hears the pleasing crunch of bone and cartilage in his enemy's nose. The Spaniard reels, his back hitting the street wall, but then he counterattacks with a great blood curdling cry, a blaze of heavy steel coming down again and again on Hugh.

Hugh's guard arm grows fatally weary. The next two blows will finish him off. He tries to kick again but to no avail. When the final blow comes, it is met not only with Hugh's blade, but also Wilf's pike-staff. The two of them parry Michelotto's blade to their left and down. Hugh kicks again and catches the man's upper arm, and he goes down against the wall. Hugh makes ready to pursue, but Wilf pulls him backward by the collar. The militia are winning; the bodyguards are mostly injured or slain, murders that will be apportioned to Hugh's account if he doesn't survive. His body hits the ground with a thud. Pain. 'What are you doing? Wilf, Wilf!'

'They're reloading them crossbows, master. We've gotta get away.' He helps Hugh onto his feet and, using a standing horse as cover, they disappear into the side street connecting them to the Piazza del Duomo. When they are most of the way down the hundred-yard *Via dei Servi*, Hugh looks back to see Michelotto with three others in pursuit.

'The crowd is our only hope,' he says as he sheathes his weapon with his right hand. He clasps his left to protect it from movement as he runs.

Wilf curses as they round the corner. The piazza is a mass of pressed bodies in their festive best. The grey and white northern flanks of the duomo loom high above them. Wilf wavers, but Hugh pushes past him. 'Come on. Get in as deep as we can and keep low.'

They move quickly, pushing politely but desperately forward. No one seems to mind. Italians don't have a word for queue. The crowd is generally moving in their direction, processing anticlockwise around the duomo because of the many attractions on wooden scaffolds. The one they had seen earlier, the devils cast out by Michael and Gabriel, is just one of seven towers on which mystery plays and pyrotechnics are replayed in a constant cycle. Hugh hears Michelotto shouting his way through behind. He doesn't turn, but stoops lower. He has half a mind to stay still, letting his adversaries pass. But he decides against this when he sees a priest with keys mounting the steps to a side door just beyond the north transept.

'Quick, Wilf! Over there,' he shouts above the noise of the crowd. 'The door! Lean on your pike like it's a staff. Quick! He's looking at us. Padre, padre!' Hugh mounts the steps three at a time. Wilf hobbles unconvincingly behind. The priest's eyes grow wide with alarm. Wilf's head bandage is red on one side, but Hugh pleads, 'Padre, padre, we are injured in the crowd. For the love of God and the virgin, have mercy on us. We must rest a while.' The priest's face softens almost instantly, and he moves aside to let them in. They pass into the cool, incense-rich marble interior. One or two people move about, but the place is not generally open today because of the crowds. Hugh looks behind to see whether they have been spotted. The priest is fumbling with the keys on the inside now. *Why won't he just lock the door? Come on, lock the damn thing.*

Hugh instinctively moves mouse-like toward the left. Along the wall thirty yards away is a small recessed door. He hates to run, to be hunted. Bile rises in his gut. But what can he do with his arm as it is? His left is aching like hell, even without exertion. He can hold a sword, but he wouldn't survive two bouts with a page, let alone this Catalan devil.

The priest turns the great key in the lock. Too late. Someone is banging on the door. 'Quick,' Hugh whispers to Wilf. 'It's them. To the other door.'

Wilf swings it open, and Hugh follows him inside. They are in a small stairwell with spiral stairs to the left and a small storage area to the right, stacked with trestle and board. Wilf props a board against the door.

'Won't hold them for long if they find out we're here, master.'

'Lean on it, Wilf, and it will hold a bit longer.'

'Very funny. What we gonna do?'

'You could start by putting my shoulder back in. Just push hard at my elbow when I say and don't blame me if I knock your teeth out.' With his back to the wall as ever, Hugh raises his arm with Wilf's help. But before he can count Wilf shoves hard on the elbow. Hugh crumples up with hissing and agony while Wilf edges away.

'Did I get it, did I?' Wilf says when the hissing subsides.

Hugh lets out a long breath. The pain has lessened considerably. 'Shhh, yes. Listen. They're coming this way.'

Soon boots and heavy breathing can be heard. Michelotto's muffled voice urges the intruders to check round the corner. Boot leather chaffs outside their own door. The handle turns. A shoulder's worth of force is applied. Harder. Wilf and Hugh maintain steady pressure on the board. *He'll think it's locked*. He does. The steps move away. Wilf is about to speak, but Hugh stills him with a finger.

After another few seconds Hugh whispers, 'I'll check upstairs, see if there is another way out in the clerestory. You hold the door here.'

He ascends the worn spiral treads, up and up, round and round until his head spins. Several minutes pass, and his legs begin to tremble. He needs water. Then a doorway, light, and a narrow cantilevered, circular walkway leading around the circumference of the vast dome. Directly opposite, about forty yards away is an identical doorway. Another way down? A mirror staircase or a way onto the roof?

Hugh chances a glance downward. Two soldiers run from the crossing in the direction of the door where he entered the stairwell. Their shouts echo too much up here to discern what they are saying. He leans on the iron railing to see more. He hears banging. The door. *Wilf!*

He starts back down the stairs, but he is less than half way when the shouts give way to footsteps. Wilf! They've got him. One set of footsteps seem nearer. They are light of step. Not Wilf. He needs a plan. *Get back to the walkway. Take up a defensible position.*

He starts back up, fighting hot tears. *Wilf, poor bastard. What am I going to do, with arms like these?* He comes near the upper doorway. Darkness shadows the space just to the left with room enough to hide while his enemy's eyes are drawn to the light of the door. Hugh darts in and tries to master his breathing. He holds the sword with two hands. Sweat stings his eyes. *Breathe.* He can possibly launch himself on the first man with his sword, and then see what happens. Not much of a plan. *Perhaps it will be the captain and that will be enough.*

Steps get louder. He can hear the enemy's breaths now above the thumping of his own heart. Steps slow as they arrive out of the darkness. The white and red uniform. Glint of steel. Tanned face, smell of sweat. The man looks to the light. *More fool you. Bastard. Here's for Wilf and Pico. One, two, three.* Hugh pushes off from his dark corners and drives the Colhona into the man's side. The soldier crumples against the opposite wall as the blade slides through his guts. Hugh's face is against his. The look of surprise, then fright, then abject horror. 'No, not me', that is all he says. It's not Michelotto. *Damn.* Hugh pulls away, withdraws the blade and lets the man collapse down the stairs.

The next soldier's face suddenly appears without a sound, sweaty and white. He is quick to step over the intestine of his comrade, spilled like tripe over the top two steps. He lunges with his sword at Hugh, who moves back through the door onto the walkway under the great dome. The soldier follows, and Hugh vainly tries to parry his blows. Now, even his right shoulder feels like a thousand knives have been driven into it. He can barely raise the sword.

They are a quarter way round the dome when Michelotto appears in the doorway and starts to run round the other way. *Shit, shit.* He means to cut him off from the far door, or any doorway ever again. If Hugh makes a full-on dash to the far door, it will expose his back to the first man's blade. Hugh blinks away the sweat, lunges to buy thinking time, and is parried well by the other. He cries out and watches the Colhona leave his hand and spin down into the void.

He turns and flies to the other door. Michelotto is coming. Hugh sees him level a *scoppietto* at him, hears the crack, the whistle. He twists his body but even so the bolt pierces his doublet under the right arm and lodges in his flesh. It is cold, but there is no pain. Hugh does not break pace. He will reach the doorway before his adversary. His eyes meet Michelotto's only thirty feet away, sword drawn, nose bloodied and swollen from Hugh's kick in the street. Just a few more steps. A few more. The other man pants at his back.

Hugh passes through the door, crashing his shoulder into the arch to help change direction. The pain almost paralyses his whole body for a moment. He sees steps to the right but nothing else. He is on them even as the thought processes, *I'm inside the dome; it must have an inner skin.* The stairs go up. *Shit.* There is no way down. No way out. He stumbles as the darkness overtakes him. He goes up, hands in front of him, ten steps, a small landing, then more steps, maybe forty. He stumbles again at the next landing. He feels the wooden supports among the brick.

Michelotto calls after him, panting. 'There is no way out, signor. Nowhere left to run from me now. Give yourself up, and we can talk.' The voice is getting closer. Hugh presses on. Another forty steps, a flat section, then more steps. On and on. Deeper into the darkness. He stops to listen. He cannot hear the enemy. *Have they removed their boots? Will they fall on him unexpectedly?*

Is this how I will meet my end? How I will pass ingloriously into history? Dying as a fool, a knife in the back, here in the dark with no one to close my eyes. No one to pray with me, no absolution. He cannot escape these thoughts as his hands brush the outer and inner skins of the dome on his left and right. *Is this why I was resurrected from the galleys, to putrefy like a mouse trapped in a partition; between the secular and sacred, in no man's land, a limbo of my own making?* He vaguely waves the blade of his dagger behind him with his right hand, and feels forward with his left. Up again. He is breathing rapidly in short, fast breaths, like a bloodhound. He feels for the crossbow bolt. It is a flesh wound, thank God. *What's that?* He hears breathing. The rustle of clothing. They are here! Hugh slides along the wall of the landing he is resting on. *Slowly, slowly.*

But then the wall is no longer there. He falls with a clatter onto steeper bricks steps that rise at right angles up the final, shallower section of the dome. Hugh can see light thirty yards above him. He heaves himself round and starts to climb. He is five or six steps up when he feels a hand on his boot, pulling him. No, it is two hands. The man has sheathed his weapon. Hugh lets himself be drawn back, falling suddenly onto his attacker, bearing down on him with both hands on his dagger. It pierces something soft below the man's face. He cries out as the two of them fall against the opposite wall. Hugh tastes the garlic of the other's breath.

It is not Michelotto. His breath stinks of wine. Hugh rolls away, off the body just as Michelotto's blade slices the ether, and plunges into the body of his injured comrade. The man's scream is high pitched as he is cut open at the chest. It is Hugh's only chance; he waits for the second slice then launches himself again, blade first.

But Michelotto is not there.

Hugh falls at the base of the brick steps. Fearing that dread slicing sound coming on him, he starts back up. Ten steps and Michelotto's breathing can then be heard, then a curse, and the odd scrape of the blade on the wall. There is no time to look back, no time for anything, just climb toward that light. What then? He must face him one way or the other. *Face him now while you have the height advantage,* Hugh thinks. *No, he'll see me coming. Just get to the door.* Ten more steps. Eight. Six. Four. One. Hugh staggers past the arch to his right into the blinding afternoon sun. *Now what?*

He is at the base of the lantern on a polished marble pavement four yards wide which surrounds the lantern tower. There is no railing, but thick, marble flying buttresses form a tight colonnade around the pavement. There is no other way up. The columns could provide a cover. Hugh goes for one, but when he sees the sheer drop, the crowd below like grains of sand, he moves back from the edge, heart in mouth. He watches the doorway, desperately seeking a plan.

Michelotto appears and sees him. Hugh retreats around the pavement. The captain gains his breath. 'You know, signor, you have caused me trouble today. Things are, as you say, complicated.' He points the blade at him. 'You and I must transact our business here quickly, for I have other work to do.'

They pass through one arch then another. Hugh has an idea. They pass another, he turns and runs round through the rest. He'll get back to the door and down the stairs. As he rounds the last arch, he comes face to face with the Spaniard's blade. He has doubled back.

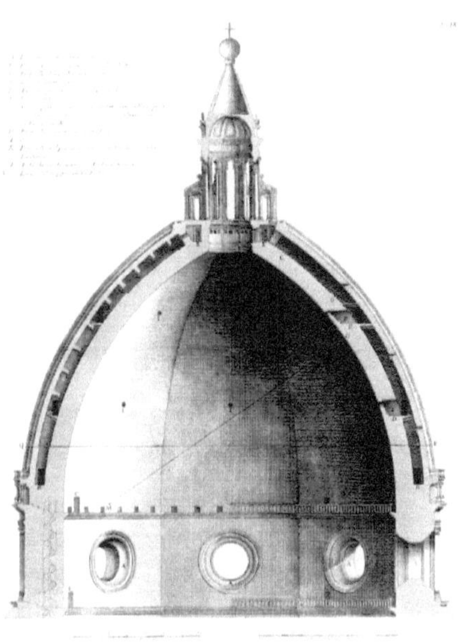

The blade comes at Hugh's chest. He twists and parries left with the dagger, but Michelotto is too quick. He grabs Hugh's doublet and head-butts him, crushing the cartilage in his nose and sending the tang of blood down his throat and on his lips. In the momentary disorientation all is over. The knife involuntarily slides from his fingers, bouncing over the edge and rattling down the roof tiles in higher and higher notes signalling the passing of hope.

Hugh tries to grab at his adversary, but his arms have no power. *Does it not say somewhere that the Lord breaketh the arms of the wicked*? So, this is how it ends, cold justice indeed, cruel but just.

Hugh can only hold Michelotto momentarily before his adversary mercilessly breaks the grip, landing blow after blow in his stomach. Hugh sinks and crumbles, retching bile and blood. He does not feel the foot in his face, but the next he knows Michelotto is behind him, yanking him up from the bloodied pavement. He tries to reach his hands back to grab at the man's face, but they will not go that far.

In the end, the lyre string goes round Hugh's throat with so little resistance that Michelotto laughs. 'They told me you were eight feet tall, that you could crush a Saracen's skull between your finger and thumb. The great Erpingham of Rhodes. How disappointing you are, signor. I thought you might be one of the great ones of the earth, like Cesare, but you are nothing. You will tell me now, what I want to know. Yes, you will, my friend. So just nod when you are ready to talk.'

He feels the string cut cold into his throat. He has nothing left. Maybe he should kick off from the side of the wall and take them both over the edge; go like Samson, taking his enemy with him. But Hugh cannot move his legs to the right position. All energy is exerted not to tense his neck muscles, to fight the garrotte from severing the skin. Even this is vain. His head is hissing, exploding. Eyes bursting. His lungs, his heart. His thoughts drift. *I cannot die like this, with things as they are. I could endure death if only annihilation followed, but if judgement should follow, as it must if this universe is just, then I will be damned. God, spare thou this wretch that I might find repentance.*

No answer.

His hand flails about the pavement looking for a weapon, anything, but he finds nothing but a silent heaven, a silent earth. Hugh draws his hands foetal-like toward his chest. He has no more breath. His right-hand brushes against something in his doublet—Pico's little paring knife. Small, but just right. He draws it out and slides it behind his right ear cutting his skin but severing the string. Blood flows to his brain. His lungs suck in great, groaning gasps of life.

Michelotto falls back on the pavement. He is on his feet in an instant, taking up his sword and stamping on Hugh's hand so that he releases the knife. Hugh collapses backward helplessly, clutching his neck. He receives a boot to the ribs and one to the head.

'So, maybe you will talk when I have opened up your chest and showed you your beating heart. It is possible; I have done it before. Let me show you.'

Michelotto steps round him and is about to plunge his blade downwards when a familiar voice sounds from the doorway. 'Captain.'

Michelotto turns. 'Bembo, you are a little late to help me.'

'I haven't come to help you, captain.'

'What? What do you mean?'

'Really, captain. Everyone is entitled to be stupid, but you abuse the privilege.'

Hugh cranes his head to see Bembo removing his cross hilt from the scabbard.

'You think you can stop me? You? For him?' Michelotto levels his blade at Bembo.

'For myself. I would not expect you to understand.'

'You could have stuck me from behind just now. You should have.'

'Not very chivalrous.' Bembo assumes a fighting stance, front leg shaky at the knee.

'Chivalrous! No one was watching.'

'Someone is always watching, you Catalan arsehole. That is precisely what I have come to understand.'

'Really, really. Well, let me tell you something: they'll certainly be watching when I toss your head and arms down there into the crowd.'

Hugh feels another boot to his head. For a moment he lies half insensible on the pavement observing sideways as Judas and Satan do battle.

Michelotto lets the blade tips touch. Bembo brushes it away, moves a step back and kisses the hilt. They are both right-handed, but Bembo has the disadvantage of having a wall to his right, allowing him less space for cutting. The pavement is not wide enough to circle, but each side steps right then left, back and then forth.

Come on Bembo. Come on man.

Blow for blow, parry for parry, slowly and surely Michelotto drives Bembo before him round the lantern. Hugh soon hears their grunts as they come round from behind him. Bembo draws level with Hugh. Michelotto double steps and uses the advantage of the open space to make a succession of brutal downward strokes on Bembo's arms. The cross hilt falls to the pavement near the edge. Micholotto holds his blade near Bembo's throat, snorting with the exhaustion 'You're a fool to cross me, Bembo. A fool. On your knees. Hands behind your back.'

Bembo kneels. His eyes meet Hugh's as he mouths a silent apology.

Hugh does not respond for he is at that very moment in an agony of his own. His own eyes involuntarily move to where his hand clutches his chest. He is removing the bolt slowly from the flesh under his arm. His cheeks smart as the barb tears.

Bembo looks to his sword, a yard to his left. All the while Michelotto gloats. 'Bembo, Bembo, you surprise me, I confess. I never thought a coward like you would have the guts to betray me. Did you make another deal with this English bastard? With Petrucci maybe?'

'With my conscience.' He hangs his head, looking once again to his cross-hilt.

Michelotto is scornful. 'Conscience, chivalry. Poets! I will never understand you Italians. But I will tell you something. The *dear* gonfalonier once told me that he comes up here often after high mass. He loves to be awed by the scale, does Soderini, thrills to it. He says it keeps him humble. The prig. The Florentines love of modesty is all hypocrisy, as much a lie as anything I ever heard.'

Michelotto rests the point of his blade on Bembo's chest next to his heart and twists it as he continues. 'You know why I come up here, Bembo? Do you want to know? Of course, you don't but I will tell you anyway. It is because when I am here, all I see is people like ants, milling around the church as they do today, aimless – useless. People like you, Bembo.' Michelotto repositions his hand slightly so that his palm is more behind the pommel. His upper lip raises to show his broken yellow teeth as he says, 'You really should have killed me when you had the chance.'

But just as Michelotto takes the final breath ready to plunge in the blade, Hugh lunges upwards and thrusts the crossbow bolt into his thigh just below the buttock, wheezing; 'Let's give him another chance then.'

The captain roars in agony, casting his head back. Hugh marshals his entire strength so as to scramble towards him, flailing, hissing. He wants to push the bastard over the edge, kill the devil, kill all evil, go over the edge himself, end it. End it all. But in the same instant Bembo brushes Michelotto's blade with a swift right hand and recovers his own with the other. Michelotto fends Hugh off and tries to realign his blade at Bembo, but it is too late. Bembo is up and thrusting his own blade under the captain's ribs; up and up through his lungs. Michelotto tries to move back and away from it, but Hugh holds his right leg until the job is done. It is a momentary and silent struggle. Three men gasping, shoving, hissing. Deeper and deeper. Eyes wider and wider. Then the groan. It is a mortal wound. Michelotto knows it. Hugh knows it, too, and releases his leg. This will be a slightly longer drop than he gave Hugh on the stapado. The Spaniard staggers to his right, overbalances, then falls like lightening into the abyss, crashing seconds later into Saint Michael's tower in the piazza and falling in three pieces to the street. Life imitating theatre, imitating life. Hugh stares after him for a long time, almost wistful.

The clatter of Bembo's sword brings him to. He turns to see the poet collapsing on the floor, shaking like a leaf. Bembo holds out a trembling hand. 'Forgive me. Please forgive me.'

For many moments, Hugh doesn't know how long, he does nothing and says nothing. His betrayer, at last. Eventually, Hugh takes the hand being offered and allows Bembo to help him into a sitting position against the lantern tower. Both are silent, apart from groans and gasps, as they stare south over the city, the Arno River, and the retreating sun which unwinds its golden spell of light and casts long cypress tree and poplar shadows across the Tuscan hills. Then tears from both men. After a few minutes silence Bembo looks at Hugh's neck. 'Are you badly injured?'

'Wilf?'

'He is all right. The door fell on him. Your neck looks bad. Let me see.'

'Better than Pico's.' Hugh brushes his hand away, then sighs. 'I'll survive.' He gently touches the wound. 'I'll have to wear a high collar. Anyway, thank you for – well, thank you.'

'What are you doing?'

'What does it look like? I'm putting my nose back.' Hugh tries to apply thumb pressure but without the adrenalin he struggles to make his arms cooperate.

'Let me,' Bembo says.

'Done it before?'

'I'm a quick learner,' He kneels in front of Hugh.

'Just place thumbs on either side, pull out, down, and then line it up.'

Bembo cradles Hugh's head. 'Pull down, out and line up.'

Hugh hisses as the cartilage pops. 'Is that it?'

'It is still a bit crooked.'

'Well do it again, harder.'

'Very well but I don't want to get it wrong and have it stuck that way for posterity. For the portraits, you know.'

'I wouldn't worry. It never stays in one place for long, and as for portraits – argh!' Hugh roars and pushes Bembo away with his remaining strength.

'That's it. Much better. Almost straight.' Bembo kneels back like a penitent, talking nervously. 'But seriously, there is a new young painter in Venice called Tiziano Vecelli who has painted Ariosto. They say he is the new marvel I think you should commission him if we are visiting Venice.'

'We? You still think you are travelling with me after this?'

'If you'll let me.' Bembo stares down toward his hands. Hugh knows that look but doesn't say anything. Bembo's shoulders shudder slightly. 'We never spoke after Assisi, not really. I wanted to tell you more, I wanted to believe you, that you could free me from this, but in the end, I was too afraid. The moment passed, and it was as easy just to go on as before.'

'All right, all right, you've said enough. I have forgotten.'

'What?' Bembo finds Hugh's eyes.

'I forgive you.'

'But...' Bembo swallows hard. 'Do not excuse me so easily. I am a dissolute man, Hugh. I belong in Dante's ninth circle; I am culpable of "treachery against those to whom I was bound by special ties". Who knows if I will not be frozen forever with Micholotto, in ice to my chest, as were Count Ugliano and Archbishop Ruggieri, the former feeding on the latter's brain as that infernal Spaniard has fed on mine.'

'Bembo, enough of theatrics. It's like a harlequinade. If I forgive you, can you not think God at least as merciful?' *Look who's preaching now.*

Bembo's eyes gape as does his mouth. 'Really?'

'Yes, now stop your prating. If you want to show repentance then look after Pico's mother. And help me up.'

When they are both standing, Bembo shows reticence to let go of Hugh's arm. He looks full at him. 'Thank you. I don't deserve this.'

Hugh winces as he speaks. 'A wise man told me once that if it is deserved, then it isn't mercy. I didn't believe him then.'

'And now?'

'Don't know. That's the truth. I just don't know. And anyway, its Gonfalonere who'll need to dishing out forgiveness. He's going to livid.'

Five minutes or more pass with the two slumped against the wall; their breathing slowing and minds taking in all that had just happened. And then slowly, like those emerging slowly from sleep, they begin again to hear the sounds of the street carnival and theatrics rising up from below.

Bembo exhales through blown lips and then, with dream like speech, lets his mind and mouth wander. 'There is a playwright of this city, Feo Belcari, from the days of Il Magnifico. Died some time ago. His *rappresentazioni* of the annunciation was awful; stiff, overbearingly didactic. But I will never forget the scene where Mercy and Peace plead for Adam's seed. Justice and Truth are not satisfied with even five thousand years penance. All sin is black as Hades, I know that, but I remember thinking, "*Dio Mio*, what shall become of *my* soul?" And that was while I was still quite a young man, before I had really stretched my wings in the business. And now, God help me, now this, this treachery of mine.'

'There are sins worse than treachery, Pietro. I would like to believe in such easy forgiveness as the Franciscans preach. But it's like you said before: if it sounds too good to be true, it probably is.'

'You English are as cynical as the Venetians. My father was Venetian, from Ravenna. But since I first came to Florence when I was fourteen, my heart has been Tuscan. There is an innocence in their faith here. That is why they have produced such great artists. Did you know that they keep a lion here?'

'Another lion story? I got one from Michelotto.'

'Don't tell me, the one that was kicked to death? I told him that, he always used to go on about it. But it's not that one. There was another time when the city's lion escaped due the negligence of the keeper. The beast, called Orlanduccio if I remember aright, attacked a young boy, holding him within his paws. Can you imagine that? How must that poor boy have felt, scratched but not mauled, still alive? I can understand it now. In fact, I have felt like that for these last months.'

'What happened?'

'Miraculously the beast allowed the child's mother to come near and snatch him back, not moving a muscle as she did so. She just took him, and he – the noble creature – allowed himself to be robbed of his prey. I don't mind telling you that I feel like that boy this evening. Seriously, that is how I feel now that I am free, that this is finally all over.'

'Over? Pietro, nothing is over yet. We're going to Siena after Vendramin. This has only just begun.'

LETTER TO RHODES FROM FLORENCE, 26TH MARCH

Most Illustrious Magnus Magister,

I pray God and the Virgin that all goes well with you, and that our work prospers.

I am currently convalescing in the monastery of Santa Croce on the edge of Florence, where the good Franciscans have shown me every kindness, and where their physician tells me I am to remain for three weeks. Their apothecary and physic have worked wonders on some wounds I received at the hand of Cesare Borgia's former lieutenant Don Michelle, also called, Michelotto. He was employed as bargello for the republic's militia, but was also secretly making plans of his own, to wit, to apprehend that which Vendramin hath and oppose anyone else on a like quest. He had been in a secret league with Pandolfo Petrucci, the tyrant of Siena along with the spy that I wrote about in my former dispatch. Michelotto is now dead, and the Florentine Signoria have shown me every civility for purging them of the Catalan's treacheries. So do not worry that this has caused any diplomatic difficulties. The secretary to the Council of Ten even quoted the words of King Edward to me. "Bon boisoigne fait qui de merde se deliver", it is good work to rid yourself of a turd. So, you can see that the republic is grateful to us, which may be of help in the future. You may also assure Prior de Blanchfort that his Portuguese sword has been put to very good use and is still with me.

My manservant was injured along with your servant, and is recovering here. But do not have fear for us for we English are terrific bleeders, and it keeps the wounds clean. Not so the local lad Pico that we brought from Rhodes. He was murdered by Michelotto. His effects are enclosed, along with money from an anonymous benefactor among our party here, who was much impressed by the lad's piety and courage. Please see that his mother gets these. He did not suffer long and he died confessed.

Petrucci then alone remains. We will travel before Easter to the center of his web—Siena. And we shall see how it goes with us there. I have some expectation of at last grappling with our enemy, Vendramin, but I confess to you, Magister, ofttimes doubts do haunt my waking hours that I shall ever apprehend this phantom. He seems to be everywhere yet nowhere. Always present in my thoughts yet without form. A spectre of my own fears perhaps. He has been the initiator, the first cause, the centre, like the unmoved mover of Aristotle. I know I can rely upon your prayers and the protection of the Holy Virgin.

With regards to the war, I hear that the King of France will depart soon from Milan for Venetian territory at the head of his army. Venice's offer to relinquish Faenza and Rimini has come too late. So, the war has begun. I understand that your brother, Cardinal d'Amboise, attends Louis in the field. I had the pleasure of delivering your message to him personally when I met the Emperor in Konstanz in March. I also enjoyed the hospitality of your nephew Charles, who is now governor of Milan. A courteous man of fine sentiment. He sends you his felicitations by me.

I hear that Venice hired Giulio Orsini and Renzo di Ceri as condottieri, laying aside sixteen thousand ducats with their bankers Agostino da Sandro and Bonvixi in Rome. But His Holiness took measures against this betrayal by employing the skill of his daughter, Signora Felice d'Orsini, who halted the financial transaction and negotiated with both the bankers and her wayward relatives, whom she has now reconciled to the pope.

I have met the Signora. She is a woman of considerable resource. The Venetians made the same offer to Bartolomeo d'Alviano and Nicolo di Pitigliano, transferring funds to them by means of their orator. This is all I have heard, and we shall no doubt see soon how these two do against France's formidable force. It is strange to me to sit as an observer during such conflicts, and I confess that having lived as we do in the jaws of the Turk, it fills me with shame to see how readily Christians war amongst themselves in this land.

I will write more when I have more, but for now I am glad to leave the north as the fog of war descends upon them. I shall write again from Siena or Rome.

Your servant, etc

SANTA CROCE, FOUR DAYS LATER. 28TH MARCH

Sweet cyclamen and the rhythm of crickets in the verdant borders are near bliss for Hugh. Plainchant echoes from the church. Sandals slap the cloister pavements. Hugh and Bembo sit in the shade of pines that spread like benevolent mushrooms over one end of a rectangular courtyard adjacent to the Basilica of Santa Croce. The day is warm enough to require shade, a welcome change for Hugh. The cold *tramontana* has been replaced by a gentle westerly breeze – sweet Zephyrus, bringer of spring. Both men breathe deeply for a moment as the air caresses their skin, warm like velvet. The dramatic events of the last days seem almost like a nightmare on this afternoon, like they never happened, or happened to someone else. Wilf scowls his regular morning scowl. He has survived, minus one ear. His face, like bad fat, is the only reminder of what passed—that and the crows picking at worms on Pico's grave.

The sight of Wilf, mutilated and grimly hunched over that grave, pouring mute tears out like water galls Hugh as no other eloquent elegy could. What was Pico to Wilf? The fatherless boy and the sonless man? What are a man's ears to him, or any part of the body that he carries about his whole life? Who can give a man his name but God? That his life has added to the measure of humanity's cup of misery is now a serious possibility. Perhaps that is why Hugh would have gladly gone over the edge and taken that devil Michelotto with him a week before. They were of a feather, alike in kind and perhaps even in degree. Both plummeting down under the gravitational pull of iniquity and consequence. God alone can judge these things.

A black cat stares out of the darkness under the bushes to Hugh's right. He feels a shudder. Easter will soon be upon them – and so too Siena. It makes moments like these all the more precious.

The good friars have set a table under the trees. These Franciscans are always just where you need them. Hugh's neck wound cankered the day after he arrived, and he sank in fever. In his delirium, he could have sworn that Fra Francesco from Assisi appeared at his bed in the infirmary and prayed for him. Fever does strange things to a man's mind, but Hugh is stronger now, strong enough to receive guests.

Guests and admirers. The table is neatly laid with Turkish forks. Picking his up, Bembo bemoans it as a Byzantine affectation. But he doesn't really care. Hugh can tell he just talks out of nervousness. *Perhaps he wants to know if he really has been forgiven.*

Bembo takes Hugh's silence as an excuse to regale him with the story. 'You know, we Venetians understand these matters because we have always been linked more closely with the east. I recall the story of Maria Argyropaolina, who married the doge's son in 1004 and caused a dire scandal by eating with a fork at the wedding reception. One priest who was present – a faultless logician, though I forget his name –exclaimed,

"God in his wisdom has provided man with natural forks – his fingers." And, let me tell you, she died two years later of plague, and it set tongues wagging like dogs' tails, I can tell you. But then again, perhaps the priest died too. There were many plagues in those days. It is not easy to read what should be from the mere fragments of what was.' Placing the fork deliberately on the table, he drums his fingers on it and glances toward the monastery outer gate. 'They are late, and I am hungry.'

But sitting here Hugh could almost forget the illustrious guests about to arrive. The secretary, Nicolo Machiavelli of the *Consiglio di Deci* has promised to bring guests to break bread with these new friends and saviours of the republic. It's a decent gesture but unnecessary. Hugh reclines and glances purposefully at Brunelleschi's small chapel at the far end of the courtyard. It was commissioned by the Pazzi family and built within the living memory of one of the oldest brothers at the friary. Six Corinthian columns and one central arch supporting a pan tiled loggia, and above that a cupola, shallow as a soup bowl. Nothing had ever been built like it before. Swallows dart to and from across their line of vision and both men breathe deeply.

'I don't know how it is for you, Pietro.' Hugh pauses to sigh. 'But looking at this chapel, I am filled with a sweet longing for something that I had forgotten so long ago, something I can barely grasp at. An aching.'

'Ah, yes. She is a gem, is she not?' Bembo is missing the point. He extends his legs further under the table and sighs. 'It was built in the days of the great chancellor Leonardo Bruni. Did you see the inscription on his tomb in there?' Bembo motions toward the southern wall of the basilica on their left. '"All history is in mourning."' They were great men who ruled Florence in those days.' Again, he pauses, this time letting a thumb caress his beard. 'They had an unshakeable belief that the city would be as Athens was in the times of Pericles. Is it any wonder that men like Brunelleschi built with such assurance at times like those?'

'Are you listening to me?' Hugh shifts the poultice on his neck to get a better look at his companion who has suddenly gotten up and is now pacing near the tree. Discoursing on the greatness of Florence always raises Bembo's humours.

'Yes, of course I am listening. You said that the building induces an aching desire in your soul, and I was about to say – before I was interrupted – that I think we all yearn for the greatness of Rome. *Poggio's lament* and so forth. I think it is deeply embedded in the mind of Europe. There. Is that enough of an answer for you?"

'No.' Hugh winces as the shake of his head stretches the wound in his neck. 'Shit. No, it does not. I think you misread it, as no doubt do your countrymen. I get that same pang of longing in other situations unconnected with architecture or Rome.'

'Like when?' Bembo folds his arms and leans against the tree trunk.

'Like when I read a sonnet, sometimes a quite ordinary one, or see a beautiful fresco, or even just smell the fresh *intonacco*. The song of a bird, the sound of a lyre, the scent of a rose, the face of a woman, or merely her laugh. The same desire wakened in many situations so I deduce that they point to something beyond themselves. Can you not see that?'

Bembo, the Platonist, begins to smile. 'You know, we Venetians have a saying, that a man with an education and character can become anything he wants, except of course, a great poet. But you, I think, yes, I mean it *caro*, you have the heart and the eyes of a poet beneath your armour and your wounds.'

The gate behind them opens as he speaks, and three gentlemen are escorted through by the porter. The echoes of their *bonhomie* reverberate along the colonnade on the southern side of the basilica's nave. The secretary Nicolo Machiavelli is at their head, cajoling and cracking jokes – almost a different man. Behind him follow an older man with two canes and long hair in the old style, and a younger man about Hugh's age dressed in trimmed, blacked Bologna silks. Bembo has already explained who they are. The older, the artist Sandro Botticelli, is dressed almost exactly as Hugh remembers Leonardo da Vinci in Milan. The tangerine silk sleeves protruding from the black velvet doublet look effeminate to Hugh, but then he remembers that these men grew up poor in an age when such luxuries were much sought after. Hugh did not know want as a youth, and yet he has plumbed its depths during his captivity, and so can empathise to some extent. Sixteen months had left its mark in him. How much more the formative years of childhood? He knows he is healing slowly, just as de Blanchfort said he would, yet he also senses even more strongly, a hollow place at his very core. No matter how full he may be in the future, there will always be a part of him that is hollow. Perhaps like Jacob, he has wrestled with God, has been touched in the hollow place of his thigh and will always limp.

The scuffing of boots on the gravel and the sound of laughter brings Hugh back to the present. He stands awkwardly, ready to receive the visitors. They are close enough now for him to see their faces better. Botticelli is still handsome with large eyes, open with feeling, a broad, manly jaw, noble in bearing. His sandy hair has turned a quarter grey and, in some places, white. Hugh guesses him to be over sixty. Certainly, his walking canes and hobble make him appear older, yet the eyes are alive enough.

The younger man, whose keen eyes observe Hugh even as he gives attention to Machiavelli, is Francesco Guicciardini, governor of Modena. He is only a few years older than Hugh and yet has already accumulated substantial experience as a servant of the republic and a man of letters. He is from one of Florence's most noble families, sent as their ambassador to Spain when only twenty. His black hair and beard are trimmed short, and he is dressed simply in a crème chemise under a subtle damask doublet. The chemise is slightly frilled on the neck and tied loosely.

All men doff their berets on approach and both groups bow with urbanity, Hug a little stiffly on account of his wounds. They make preliminary enquiries about Hugh's health, Pico's funeral, and various quips about Bembo's dashing blade and reckless heroism.

Botticelli sits first, going down with a groan. Hugh sits next to him with Guicciardini taking the other side. After more small talk and introductions, they are served cold meats and artichokes and sun-dried tomatoes in oil. Machiavelli, who has arranged everything, is keen to tell them that the white meat is indeed that large fowl that the Spaniards brought from the New World. While Botticelli is still sniffing it, the secretary squeezes in a dig at the uncouth English who first bought the birds from eastern traders and so called them 'turkeys'. The ambassador waits to see if Hugh is laughing before joining Machiavelli and Bembo in so doing. Hugh's smile is more wince of pain than genuine merriment, but it encourages Machiavelli, who is still understabably wary of Hugh, to declaim upon the sincere respect that Florence has for, what he called, the honest English.

'Indeed, we let your Sir John Hawkwood be Gonfaloniere of our forces with almost unlimited power precisely because we knew that unlike an Italian, he would not be devious enough to keep it.'

'He did well for us, and himself.' Botticelli mumbles though saggy jowls chewing heartily on the meat. 'They promised him an equestrian statue too, but eventually it was reduced to the painting of one by Uccello. A good fresco but I would have been pissed off if it had been me. Hmm, this stuff takes like chicken. Can't see what the fuss is about.'

In an uncharacteristically silent answer, Machiavelli revolves the platter and shows him a thigh bone. 'Big as dogs they are. One would feed my household for a month; yours, a whole year.'

They fall to eating, talking of the turn in the weather, the *Greco del Tufo* they are drinking, the gold from the New World and other things of no importance until most have each eaten their fill. Suddenly Machiavelli, exploiting a lull in the pleasantries, divulges the real purpose of the luncheon he has organised. All are there for a reason, except Botticelli who was invited by Giucciardini. Hugh sees it in the secretary's conduct —the careful licking of the lips, the furtive glances, the steady pushing away of the plate, the constant rearranging of his Turkish two-pronged fork, fingers rotating his glass goblet. Hugh notices it partly because he is sitting opposite and partly because Machiavelli behaves like a man about to pull a blade. All this in the moments before he finally moves his chair back and raises his hands as if to welcome his guests into some sacred confidence.

'It is no small conjunction in the heavenly bodies that we have the author of *The Asolani,* and you, Francesco, back in your native city.' He licks his lips as he snatches the conversation like a farmyard hen snatching straw from another. 'The city, I may add, in which you are among its brightest literary stars. I–er –' He presses delicate hands together as if in prayer, bows his head then raises it again. 'I have, as I am sure you know, published some verse in a small way when younger. In fact, there was a time when I would have dearly loved to be a poet.' Self-deprecating laugh. Small pause angling for encouragements from grateful readers. The others smile non-committally.

Only Botticelli raises his fork and nods before helping himself to some more meat. It's not every day an impecunious bachelor eats meat, even if he was once famous and sought after. 'Yes, I remember, that collection of *Carnvale* poems—a *pastorale* by you, some by Polition, some by Lorenzo and others.' He drops the meat on the table while trying to transfer it, swears and then says, 'I did the illustrations, I remember. Yours was dedicated to Lorenzo's son, I remember that too.' Adding amiably, 'You always were a little brown nose.'

'Indeed, I was, just as you were, you old prick. I wanted to be a poet. It's no crime. Not yet anyway.' Again, the theatrical sigh. 'However, the doors of preferment – so few to a man of modest birth – opened in a different direction for me, and so I studied law at Pisa, and became a servant of this noble republic in ways in which, of course, you know.' Again, the laugh. 'And I flatter myself that my service has been fruitful to her ennoblement and security. Along this road I have had a chance to observe the diverse machinery of governance from the courts of Duke Valentino and the emperor, to our great republics, and even the Holy See.'

Botticelli asks for the salt.

Machiavelli continues. 'And, and, and collating, as one does as a more or less objective observer, the little insights that have let some succeed and some fail. Added to that the extensive reading of the best books, as time allows.' Some more laughter. 'I begin to wonder whether it might not be a prudent literary project for me to set forth general principles for effective governance. I would dedicate, or even address, the book to Giuliano de Medici. Castiglione writes me that he wishes to do something similar for aspiring courtiers. And Paolo Cortesi for the cardinals –'

'But will you, Nicolo? Will you really?' It is Guicciardini who speaks from Hugh's left. He brings his fingers and an elegantly embroidered sleeve toward his brooding lips.

These two have some history, Hugh thinks.

Machiavelli is about to speak again, but Guicciardini, whose every gesture and word is marked by a gravitas born of birth and station, continues. 'Will you write of princes, will you? Be the one who instructs them? What will you do? Teach them from the scriptures? Quote them from four and twenty Sunday Gospels? Tell them to keep troth, uphold truth, love modesty, embrace humility, feed the poor, and lay down their lives for their subjects?'

Machiavelli is trying to laugh it off, hiding his mouth behind his hand and speaking slightly before his time. 'No, I was thinking of offering advice more practical, normative.'

'I thought so. More practical, more effective, for I know you of old. Take it from me, *caro*; when a theory presents itself to you as the only solution to a political problem, it is a sure sign that you have understood neither the theory nor the problem. Ideas aren't always responsible for the men who hold them but in your case I will make an exception.'

'Well, come now, Francesco! You and I have been in enough places, seen enough bad governance for three lifetimes. We've seen what works and what doesn't. Are you really saying it is impossible to posit the existence of normative laws—nay, to frame them—when men are doing so in virtually every other field of enquiry?'

'You want a value free, amoral philosophy of social and political power.' Guicciardini lays out the words like it was something that crossed his mind every other day.

'Yes. A true science uncluttered by superstition and self-defeating complexities. Not based on the ancients' writings, on some ossified authority, but based on the real world. Now. Here. The real world of experience. Real laws that never or rarely fail.'

'So, you do mean *amoral* then? Value free?'

'Yes.'

'I am cheered.' Hugh interrupts the conversation to which he was really only ever meant to be a witness . 'Yes, cheered by an optimism that can think such a place might exist in the universe.' It's not meant to sound as sarcastic as it does. *If there was a square inch left in the cosmos to hide from the fingers of moral law, damn him, I would have found by now.*

Giucciardini goes back to his dinner, saying, 'Yes, Nicolo, hear the English knight, and learn some sense.'

'Quite,' Bembo adds. 'And stop hogging the wine.'

'I know what I have seen.' Machiavelli rests his wrists on the table. 'A harsh world needs harsh truths, sometimes necessary evils, maybe even harsh rulers.'

Giucciardini responds. 'So, you would have tyrants like Duke Valentino perhaps.'

'No!' Machiavelli raises his hands. 'No.' He replaces his hands on the table, fingers fanned, spreading like ideas. 'Not exactly. But in some respects. I know of no better precepts to give a new prince than the ones derived from Borgia's actions.'

'You used to rail against his insolence, his tyranny.'

'No doubt I did and rightly so. He was our enemy when I was ambassador to his court in Imola. There were excesses. Of course, there were, but you cannot say that he did not bring stability to the Romagna. So yes, I say, harshness maybe used in extreme cases, a necessary evil, but of course, not the harshness of Severus whose cruelty was constant policy.'

'I see, I see.' Guicciardini gestures with his eating knife. 'But among the *necessary evils* – that, by the way, your new science would no doubt discover to be intractable laws – you would certainly not rule out tyrants, and perhaps even subjects fitted for oppression if need be?'

'Stop it, *gli amici*, stop it. But if people are not ready for democracy, what would you do? No private citizen who has read his history would not rather be Scipio than Caesar, or Phalaris than Timoleon. People will have rules or rulers. But without the rule of law there can be no stability, and thus no justice. You want the poor fed. Fine. It is justice that defends the poor and the innocent, justice that represses the rich and powerful, humbles the proud and bold, checks the rapacious and grasping, punishes the insolent, scatters the violent.'

This is a speech he has either done before or at least rehearsed. Machiavelli's delicate, insinuating fingers move from the table and flick upward each time justice is mentioned, as if he were releasing a butterfly. He continues, 'Justice generates equity in states, which is desirable for their maintenance. There was justice long ago, in a time when men were good and the gods dwelt on earth. But then vices grew and the gods returned to heaven. Empires that began in Ninus the Divine end in the effeminacy of Sardanapalus. *Valour begets ease, ease disorder.* It was ever thus and ever will be. The last to go was always justice, and with its going fell the great republics and kingdoms. Ever after justice has come sporadically to some city or other: Athens, Rome, and now Florence.'

'And Venice, Nicolo. And Venice!' Bembo is roused from the other bones he is picking over. His mouth is still full as he speaks, defending his birthplace. '*Summam imperii commendandam esse legibus non homini*. You find no surer rule, if there be one, than their doge bound by *buoni ordini*.'

'Venice, Venice.' Machiavelli wrinkles his nose. 'It is merely a case in point, like Athens and Sparta, insatiate, dissipated. You will live to see it. Venice should have stayed on her lagoon. If these are not her butchers now, others will come. But Florence, oh, Florence!' His eyes are now alight with an almost biblical fervour. 'With her, we have the chance for true renaissance. Just think of it friends! Where else might a wise people perfect a system of government? Where else, I say, but here in Florence? And when else, but now? Under such a government and educational system, just think what she might become among the firmament of stars, what heights her people might reach.'

'Come, Nicolo, come,' Giucciardini says wearily. 'You speak as if the only duty we owe is to posterity, to an ideal society in your own mind that might never come. Tell me: which of the old virtues might your new science trample down to achieve this new world? Which people will it command you to sacrifice for this unseen and yet undefined good? You want to make the signoria of Florence scriptwriters, when all the time they are cast as characters. And you too, Nicolo, cannot be the writer in a play in which you are a character. The two are incommensurate. In this cosmos we are adjectives, not nouns; and if you really want stability and justice, it would be better that you urge men toward the virtues of our religion rather than create a bastard philosophy to give them new ones.'

'Oh, come Francesco, you are only with us for two days and are you going to preach religious ideals at me like Savonarola?'

'I merely speak my mind. You think Italy is the world. But I have travelled to many countries and now bear the burden of a ruler. I know what I am speaking about. You want general laws? I tell you that man is a mad animal, full of a thousand errors, a thousand confusions, without taste, without delight, without stability. And the world's affairs depend upon so many accidents, and are so uncertain that the judgements made of them are often most fallacious. Anyone can see by experience, that almost always the opposite happens of what men, even wise men, have predicted. Do not you suffer the fate of those intelligent men not wise enough to conceal it. If you make peace or power, or stability even, as goods absolute, you watch it; there is little you will not justify in their acquisition, no small virtue you will not trample for their good.'

'Stop this pedantry! Are you now my mother? God, even Botticelli is nodding in agreement. See what you have done!'

'I am serious, Nicolo. You say you think you can delineate a value-free science, but to what end?'

'I have already said, for stability, for the prosperity of all.'

'Quite so, and can you not see that your philosophy has already assumed its own values: stability, prosperity, growth. That is hardly value free. What might a state sacrifice for growth? You and I know some very wicked men indeed who achieved these things for themselves to the ruin of their souls and many souls better than their own. Will you advise that we all join them in the lower circles? You want a predictive science? Then I say you are mad. And if you have brought me here looking for sponsors for this work then you will get no encouragement from me. Do not undertake it, I pray you. Give it up. Do not loose further the restraints on license that are already the scourge of our courts, dukedoms and republics. Rulers need no inducement to forsake the path of virtue for something easier. At every turn there is the coward's temptation to pragmatism, to expediency: the bribe, the broken oath, the weighted trial. The opposite of courage is not cowardice. Nine times out of ten it is conformity. So, I say, strengthen men and women with honest religion if you care, as I see you do. But do not devise some new, cracked, alchemist philosophy to cast a fig leaf on misdeeds that honest men have abhorred as sin since time began.'

'I see.' Machiavelli puckers his lips and casts his eyes toward his plate. 'And you, Signor Bembo. I suppose you are of the same opinion? That we should give up the search for a unified knowledge of these things.'

'I think, and I speak as a poet, not a public man.' Bembo's face is demure, yet laced with an amiable wit intended to ease Machiavelli's injured pride. 'Our quest for facts is at root noble, only overly ambitious, as Hugh says. You wish to be useful, to be remembered, *un uomino rispettato,* respected. That is not a bad thing. Only take Francesco's warning, for to be remembered only by the licentious as a feeder of their riot would be an ill epitaph, would it not? You were a poet once; why not again? As the poet you are free to describe life not as it is, but as it matters, to surpass mere facts with truth. What say you, Hugh?'

Hugh wipes the corner of his mouth with the table cloth. 'I am hesitant to speak as a guest in your city, signor, but I can say that we English agree with Cicero that monarchy, aristocracy and democracy *moderato permixtum tribus* – moderately, but thoroughly mixed – are more likely to balance their respective faults.'

'There, there, see!' Giucciardini claps his hands. 'There is realism, master secretary. If you wish for realism, hear the Englishman and be satisfied.'

'I see, I see, you are all against me. Well, perhaps I will write verse if I can ever find time. But life as secretary is –'

'Busy.' Botticelli completes his sentence. 'I am surprised you even have time for such leisurely lunches with so many anonymous accusations arriving daily in your little *bocca,* so many dangerous people to investigate and arrest.'

'Ah, alas Sandra *caro*, do not be bitter. All charges against you were dropped in the end.'

'A man's reputation is not so easily mended. Friends and clients do not forget.' Botticelli is pointing his laden fork at him.

Machiavelli eases back onto his seat. 'I am sorry for it. But I assure you that, imperfect though it is, the Council of Ten is as necessary now as it ever was.'

'I am sorry, friends,' Botticelli continues. 'But at my age you can see through the bullshit. And you needn't leer at me, master secretary. When you have leg ulcers like mine, the *strapado* holds little terror.'

The conversation does not recover much, after the silence and other small talk that follows. There is cautious conversation about democracy in general where Giucciardini upholds the point against Machiavelli that if democracy has any claim, it is not because of the goodness of men but the fall of man. Hugh notes with interest that Guicciardini does not think equality – a subject much discussed in Florence – is a good in itself, like wisdom or happiness, but more like medicine and clothes. 'We only want medicine when we are ill. No one wants it otherwise. And we only wear clothes for warmth or because we have lost our innocence. Equality's strength is that it is a defence against tyranny. Some might, even now, believe what Aristotle taught– that some men are only fit for slaves, but surely, we must face the possibility that even if that were so, the fall surely means that no men among us are fit to be masters. So, let democracy triumph if it will. Let men rejoice, either from the sense of just equality it promotes, or from an envious hatred of superiority. But let them also remember it's great, and perhaps only, benefit is as a medicine, not a wine. To take the idea further might lead to very strange conclusions. One tradition that I learned in Spain was that the people of Sobrarbe made their Aragonese kings swear an oath, saying, "We who are worth as much as you, take you to be our king provided that you preserve our laws." Something like that anyway.'

When the following conversation turns more to the politics of Spain, Hugh falls into a talk with Botticelli about Lorenzo whom the artist obviously remembers with more than the affection of a protégé. 'But you are here for a while, then let me escort you into town next week.' He motions toward the gate from which they entered. 'We could walk out together, talk, visit *her* grave.'

'Her grave?'

'Simonetta's. I have asked that when my time comes, which may be sooner than I would like, I be buried at her feet.'

A WEEK LATER. THE CHURCH OF THE OGNISSANTI, FLORENCE 4TH APRIL 1509

Tap, tap, tap. The smell of charcoal braziers, wax, oil and tallow.

Tap, tap, tap. All along the Via Porta Rossa down to the ancient Roman gates of the old city.

Tap, tap, tap. Tap, tap, tap. Hugh and Bembo walk side by side. Hugh is much improved by the administrations of the physics. As his strength returns, so does the looming dread of Siena. But today Hades can wait. Hugh is meeting up with Botticelli and soaking up the sights and sounds of the artisans at work.

Tap, tap, tap. Tap, tap, tap

A hundred hammers in the artisan's quarter, a hundred hunched backs, a hundred pairs of squinted eyes. Silver smiths, goldsmiths, gem-cutters. How many geniuses in the making? How many Brunelleschis? How many Ghibertis?

Bembo leans toward Hugh and says, 'I read somewhere that the earlier Burgundians would fine a man one hundred *soldi* if he killed a silversmith and two hundred for a goldsmith. Which shows how they valued the decorative arts, though they only set twelve *solidi* fine for a raped woman, or one whose hair has been cut off without cause, which always puzzled me. I mean, how can anyone prove they had no cause to cut a woman's hair off? If you had no cause to do it, surely, you'd have been doing something else, like writing a sonnet or cutting off your own hair.'

Bembo is prating again, but Hugh, in one of his melancholic tempers, merely grunts sparingly as they make their way through the crowds of Florentine hopefuls. Fame in the service of one's city became the newest of the virtues under the old civic humanism of Leonardo Bruni. Like the *arete* of the Greek city states, it was not so much to be good, but rather *good at* something, and preferably something that brought *la gloire* to Florence. The new virtues, like the new gods, put a yoke on men not easy to bear. Even the fashion of being clean shaven like a Greek Alexander or Apollo or one of Queen Eleanor's Provencal court, proved too much a burden. How many artisans, artists, *scapelinos*, musicians can no longer enjoy their work unless the bitch goddess Fortuna rewards them with fame? She is a cruel mistress, giving hope in her left hand to keep you her devotee, but with her right hand, misery and discontent.

Hugh and Bembo pass through the remains of the old Roman gates and onto the Via Parione, past the Palazzi Minerbetti and Bartolini Salimbeni. It's his first time out since the Michelotto affair. His wounds heal well, but away from the confines of the friary his hand is never far from the hilt. It's hard to imagine a man like Michelotto having friends, but the loyalty of soldiers is a primordial thing. Hugh's eyes dart back and forth to make sure they are not being watched or followed.

Here, amongst the open pots and stalls of street vendors, the Florentine apprentices steal time eating sugared rolls, or hot tripe. They gather in knots, talking ten to the dozen, a flurry of hands and mouths. Further back in the shops, just discernible, the humming, scraping, hammering of industry: instrument makers, designers of terracotta and wood mosaics, copyists, notaries, scriveners and manuscript illuminators. And beyond them, more tap-tapping of the typesetters, the creak of the printing press like the footsteps of modernity on the stair – squeezing new ideas onto paper, squeezing the purses of the copyists and illuminators. One sign reads, 'Signor Bernardo Cennini, first printer of manuscripts in this city. *Anno Domini* 1477.'

Bembo leans across. 'The Duke of Urbino told me that his father, the illustrious Frederigo would have been ashamed to own a printed book.'

Tap, tap, tap. Master Cennini's people are busy as squirrels.

'Of course, the duchess told me that he couldn't actually read. But you can sympathize if you're Italian: that sludgy, German gothic type, *Madre di Dio!* The characters look like overweight costermongers with inert bowels. It is little wonder this noble republic resisted the innovation for a decade longer than most of Italy.'

Five minutes later the two men are approaching the steps of the *Chiesa San Salvatori in Ognissanti*, the Church of All Saints Known and Unknown. On the church steps and in the small piazza that opens onto the Arno River, a cluster of friars mill in the sun. Hugh does not recognise their habits: robes and scapulars of white over ash grey tunics.

Bembo is happy to enlighten him upon request. 'They are an old mendicant order called the *Humiliati*, founded in the time of Saint Bernard, a century before the Franciscans.'

'I see, thank you,' Hugh says, signaling that the answer is sufficient and no further information is needed.

You have to be firm with Bembo who will write a book, let alone discourse, on the slightest provocation. 'I had an uncle join them once, and his wife join the sister order, where she looked after lepers in Rimini. The order was founded by some Lombardic nobles captured by Emperor Henry V after a rebellion. He exiled them to Germany where they adopted those grey woollen habits and took to ministering to the poor. The emperor was so impressed by their piety that he allowed them to return to Milan –

'Thank you.' *No lectures today please.*

'Yes, whereupon they introduced the improved methods of wool production that they had learned in Germany. It provided gainful employment for the poor and the profits were distributed to those in need.'

'Thank you, Pietro. Shall we go in?'

'Indeed, yes. Are we in a rush? Botticelli said to meet before Sext. I have not heard the Angelus bell.'

Hugh does not answer. They enter into the cool of the simple brick basilica. Sharp spring sun is reflecting off the white marble floors onto the gold altar piece, sending showers of light on the columns and walls. On approach Hugh sees a monumental Madonna enthroned in the centre. Her face is knowing, benign, human.

'By Giotto, a follower of Saint Francis,' Bembo whispers. 'See how the folds are defined by light and shade, not lines like Cimabue.'

Hugh walks to the altar and observes the brushwork closely, tempera on wood, still better than anything the English do even now, a hundred and fifty years later. Her chemise is so thin that breasts and even maybe nipples can be discerned. She is a woman. He averts his eyes, but then feels uncomfortable looking heavenward and so casts them on the pavement, examining the veins in the marble and comparing it to the rude rush floors of the English churches.

They are interrupted by the canes of Signor Botticelli on the marble. 'She was a wonder in her day. Compared to his master Cimabue, Giotto's style was a revolution.' The older man doffs his beret, his forehead beaded with sweat from the exertions of locomotion. He straightens, sniffs, then says, 'Perhaps it was then, but how soon everything begins to look old in this age of progress.' The brief smile is callow, cynical, pained even.

'Signor Alessandro.' Hugh bows and notices that the artist is wearing the same clothes, and shoes down at heel on both feet. His facial features, so pronounced and forlorn in the sepulchral gloom of the place, are unreadable. *Volto sciolto e pensiero stretto*, Hugh thinks, open countenance, closed thoughts. This man, of all men, has no reason to be cynical surely? Under Medici patronage he became the *de facto* leader of painting in the second half of the last century in Florence. One of the ten thousand smiled upon by Fortuna.

He sees Hugh staring, and then smiles the sort of smile children give before they are about to cry. 'I am not ungrateful though I can sound it when these moods come upon me. They say a clear conscience is the sure sign of a bad memory, but, sinner that I am, I do have good memories, signor. I cherish them now more than ever: they are like my second chance at a little happiness.But this bloody gout is a killer; wouldn't wish it on the bankers even. It was good of you to come here, humouring an old man.'

'Not at all,' Hugh says, and would have said more but the older man continues.

'I am tired, so very weary. I think an era can be said to end when its illusions are exhausted. Thought we would be young forever. Everything must be new these days, all must be change. It used to be a venerable thing to be old, but not now. I have lived too long, Signor Bembo, too long. I belong to the age of the old Florence, the Florence of the Medici. I look around me, and they are all dead: Bertoldo, Lorenzo, Guiliano, Ficino, Pico, Polition, Fillipo Lippi. They are just names nowadays, memories, but not to me. To me they were friends.' Botticelli shuffles toward the eastern transept, muttering again that he is not ungrateful, and no doubt expecting them to follow.

Hugh sees Bembo raise an eyebrow then roll his eyes. Hugh elbows him gently and follows the artist. They draw along either side of him and when he sees them near, he says again, 'No, I am not ungrateful. I had every advantage, trained by the Dominican Fra Fillipo Lippi. He watched Massaccio paint you know. Think of that—Massaccio!' A smile creeps on the old man's face, making his white and sandy moustache protrude outwards like a cat's whiskers. 'He was a wayward friar but a good man, and a good teacher. He let me train his son, Fillipino, not much younger than me, a very dear boy and a good painter. Dead now, like the rest. All gone. Last thing he painted was a deposition at Santissima Annunziata. All the workshops closed the day of his burial. He was well loved, you see. I don't think they will do the same for me.'

'Signor!' It is as sympathetic as Bembo gets.

'No, no, it is true; you need not lard me with sympathy. I have no commissions these days. Patrons would rather employ unknowns who imitate the new style than me. God alone knows why these cockscombs paint on such large canvases when a smaller one would hide their defects so much better. Then again, we Florentines always prefer an upstart with little talent and was modest about it. It is *cose all'italiana* - particularly Italian.'

He gives another long sigh and a weary shake of the mane. 'They say I have turned my back on the world, perhaps I just returned the compliment. But I am happy to paint the way I do. I am too old to become a Michelangelo or a Leonardo. I know them both very well. I completed my training in Verrocchio's *bottega* with Leonardo, though I did not have his inventiveness for all manner of other work that has made his star rise like it has. And I can still see that boy Michelangelo, in Lorenzo's sculpture garden before ever a whisker was on his cheek, pouring over the *Pieta Serena*, chisel in hand, old Bertoldo standing over him. Seems like yesterday. God, what days. Have you met him?'

'Yes,' Hugh says. 'We met him in the chapel of Sixtus where Julius has him painting the vault.'

'I have heard of it.' Botticelli pauses to chuckle, then continues his shuffling. 'Poor Michelangelo won't thank Julius for so many years away from his chisels. A man like that gets marble hunger you know. There was limestone dust in his nurse's milk; it's part of him. And Julius makes him paint the vault! Poor Michelangelo.'

'We also saw your work in Sixtus' chapel,' Hugh says, looking to bestow a compliment. The bitterness in this man reminds him of his own father's sleeve-worn disappointments. Life is cruel to those with melancholic humours, and there are few to understand these days in the business of life.

'I was your age when I did those, Fra Erpingham.'

'They are very fine.'

'Pah!' Botticelli casts his cane in a small, dismissive ark. 'Not my best, but I was richly rewarded for my labour by both Sixtus and

Lorenzo. My *Temptation of Christ* and *The Fate of Korah* were peace offerings really. Yes, peace offerings to bring the two of them back together after the break over the Pazzi conspiracy – to show Lorenzo as the penitent, though it was not him in the wrong. But that's the way it goes with popes; you have to grovel. I came back wealthy, or at least wealthy enough to do something I wanted. I wrote a commentary on the *Comedia* and illustrated it. My friends and fellow artists said I was mad to lower my art to that of the common printing press. But they are not laughing now. Printing will be the future whether we like it or not.' He stands back a moment with his hands on his hips and sighs uncomfortably as if not entirely happy to be in the right. 'I was so ambitious Hugh, so very ambitious. One thing age and infirmity do is let you know that the world will keep turning without you pushing it.'

He lays a hand on Hugh's shoulder and looks at him with a knowing eye and a wry smile. 'It is a sobering thought you know, that by the time Dante was my age, he'd been dead two years.'

He continues another few paces, and Hugh follows. They arrive at the side chapel of the Vespucci, and Botticelli points his cane toward frescoes above the altar: The Deposition of Christ and another under the round arch showing the Madonna cloaking a family of faithful Vespucci. 'By Ghirlandaio, and these faces, these Vespucci! I knew them all. We were neighbours. This one here.' He points towards an unbearded youth with long black curls. 'This is Amerigo Vespucci. He has sailed four times to the opposite side of the earth for the Spaniards, where the sun rises when it sets to us. They love him there, and he's a modest fellow – wants them to name the continent *Americus* after him. The prick. She married his cousin Marco, a very lucky man.'

'Who, Signor?' Hugh says.

'Who? Simonetta Vespucci, of course.' Bembo whispered reverentially. 'The most beautiful woman in Florence.'

'You, er, you painted her?' Hugh isn't sure what to say.

'Painted her?' Botticelli says, 'Sometimes I don't think I painted anything else.'

'Ah.'

The first time was when Giuliano de Medici asked me to paint her likeness on his shield for a joust that was to be held in the Piazza di Santa Croce. I painted her as *Pallas Athene* with a helmet with the inscription *La Sans Pareille.* Ah, I can see it now.' The old man points and waves his stick like an oversized paint brush as he sketches his memory into the incense-laden air. 'Simonetta was the Queen of the Tournament, escorted under a panoplied throne by eighteen members of the *jeunesse doree*, a Florentine society who took the part of the knights. In front and behind them were the heralds, standard bearers, fifers, trumpeters, pages, men-at-arms. Ah, I can see them like it was yesterday. We were young then. And there is no dishonour or shame in an Italian tournament, Signor Hugh, for they were not usually the bloody spectacle that they are in Germany, although I think it was on this occasion when Duke Federigo de Montefeltro lost his eye. But notwithstanding, it was a happy, happy day in my mind. Giuliano, still holding my shield, won that joust, but she won more; the hearts of every man in Florence. It was not just her face, you understand. Everyone loved her, not just Giuliano. Ficino often said to me, and it is written down somewhere in his books, the one on Socrates I think, that "love is the desire for beauty". Do you believe that, Signor Bembo?'

'There is something in it I think.' The poet approaches the frescos, squinting as he examines the departed Vespucci. *Momento mori*. 'My good friend Castiglione takes Ficino and Plato as models, saying that when a man contemplates beauty in a woman, he is really contemplating God.'

'Ah,' the older man rejoins. 'I too was of that mind long ago; a part of me still is. I think Petrarch and Dante were of that party too. Fra Savonarola taught that we should not tempt God. But I asked you, signor, and you have not answered.'

Bembo turns, smiles and bows gently. 'It is an old, old riddle, Maestro. I feel the contradictions running through my very centre. Nature and spirit have quarrelled in us. That is our problem – that is my problem.'

Ah, Hugh thinks, *Lucrezia Borgia.*

Bembo tries unsuccessfully to smile, then lets his face return to the façade of a scholar. 'In my life I have not answered it, but in my *Asolani* I attempt to solve it with a dose of Epicurean realism. It is not enough, I know that. But having lived under the patronage of so wise and so happily a married couple...'

'The Duke and Duchess of Urbino?' Botticelli adds.

'Indeed, having seen them, I am almost apt to hold my tongue and my pen.'

Hugh sees him smiling, but when he looks toward Signor Botticelli, Bembo is lost in thought, and muttering in old French, '*Je suis amor, le grandmaitre de dieux, je suis celui qui voient...*' Hugh listens attentively, translating the chanson in his head.

I am love, the grandmaster of the gods,
I am the one whom eyes see,
The one who governs the world,
Who first, outside the budding mass,
Gave light and split the chaos
And whereof was built this round machine.

When Bembo finishes and the last echoes of the words slide off the marble, the old man looks toward the tomb. 'She died a year after that joust, just twenty-three years old. Twenty-three, Hugh. I never married. Once, I dreamt I was married to someone else, woke up in a bed-sweat and walked the streets the rest of the night so that the dream would not return.'

Botticelli purses his lips and rearranges his feet in a vain attempt to keep his composure. He looks at Hugh, eyes welling with emotion. 'I gave my best years trying to contemplate pure love, Signor Hugh, to paint it – the best years. I made beauty greater than truth – the *only truth* perhaps. But we are fools to make gods of secondary things. Savonarola was right: we read too much Petrarch and too little scripture. But—' The old man swishes his stick like a switch, and sniffles a smile. 'When the real God arrives, then perhaps lesser planets can find their orbits too. And so, when I, as the poet says, have "cast off this gloomy prison", this *prigione scura, mio carcer terreno* – I want to be buried here.' He taps the marble under his feet with the cane. 'Yes, here at her feet. If God can make something so magnificent as that woman, then I will rest near her until the resurrection – even though the Dominicans may frown on me.'

Hugh says, 'Let us hope it will be many years, signor.'

'It is a nice thought.' He smiles a bashful smile from under a heavy, careworn brow. At this moment the angelus bell starts to sound, and the friars drift past for the midday office. Bembo suggests they take a stroll up river to the Ponte Vecchio where he knows a good place to eat.

'Yes, I think I might go that far, if you will bear with me. Have you seen the statue of Mars there yet?' Botticelli makes a move to go, and thinking out loud, adds, 'Or we might even join the brothers for repast at Santa Spirito across the river. They were ever hospitable to me, ever since the days of dear old Prior Bichillini. He let Michelangelo dissect corpses there you know. Yes, unbelievable. He is dead now, they all are.'

Back in the sunshine and looking across the cobbles toward the river, Botticelli is pointing to the *Ponte alla Carraja*, a worn stone bridge which he says collapsed two hundred years ago during a carnival.

'Dreadful, dreadful, my friends. Not just the *minuto populo* on the bridge itself, but the many actors below on pontoons who were dressed as devils from the underworld. And, hell it was that day, for all alike went down into the deeps under a mountain of stone. Terrible. Truly terrible.'

While Hugh is agreeing, he glances at Bembo, who seems not to have heard and is lost deep in his own thoughts.

Suddenly Bembo erupts with a croaky voice. 'Tell me please, for I must know, that is, I would like to know – for you mentioned his name just now. Signor, tell me about Savonarola, for I hear you were his disciple, indeed, that you added some of your own paintings to the Bonfire of Vanities.'

'If you like, signor, if you like. The early years of our short reformation were difficult ones.' The old man looks up for a moment with a stern face as if in warning. 'I was not one of his *piagioni*, his weepers, as they were called – Michelangelo's brother was, I think. But I listened. We all listened. And we all felt it, too, whether we wept or not. And none of those who were there even to this day talk about their part with pride, if they talk about it at all.'

Bembo is sullen in remembrance when he next speaks. 'They were the years when I was at university in Messina, in Padua, and at the Court of the D'Estes – in Ferrara, you know, where the Dominican came from. We heard so many wild things, things hard to hear. But I would hear from you, signor, if you would?' Bembo's arms are already folded as if ready for news that he might not want.

Botticelli pauses on his canes and looks out over the pan-tiled rooves toward the campanile of the Palazzo Vecchio and the brooding dome of the duomo. When he speaks, his voice is light pitched, ethereal – a man on the borders between remembrance and fantasy, the past that was and how he fashioned it. He is the man who remembers, not just the times, but himself in those times. 'I cannot explain it easily, you had to be there. I think Lorenzo understood in his own way, before the end. *Dio mio*, he was only your age, Signor Bembo, when he died. That it happened under the best of men, the most noble of rulers made it all the more poignant.'

'Did you know you were on the brink of a new republic?'

'No!' Botticelli looks askance. 'No. For us who were there – no – it was the dawning, rather, of a terrible realisation—that we had perhaps achieved the possibilities of civilisation in philosophy, art, letters and so forth, and yet in the next moment found that it was not enough. We were growing weary of beauty, of grace, urbanity, of knowledge, of pleasure – even as we pursued them. Delight, surprise, joy, it all melted before our eyes like spring snow. So, in our incredulity, our madness, we addicted ourselves to novelty, invention, mere progress. But still, we could make no discovery to recapture that mystical joy. Every new thing became old too quickly, and yet we had no power to make the old things new. We grew weary of horses and so painted centaurs. And finished with the wonder of neither. We wanted to paint life, not as it is—' Botticelli groans and raises two arthritic fists, canes and all, toward his chest. 'But as it mattered. In the end we could no more see a horse in its glory than a woman in hers – not truly. We came to the edge of the abyss. That is what I wanted to say to you, signor.'

'Signor, you become excited.' Hugh says, observing with alarm the veins throb in the older man's temples. 'Let me fetch you a stool.

'No, I mean it, I really believe we did. And Fra Savonarola alone called us back—like a lone voice in the wilderness—to deliver us from the tyranny of luxury, of ease, of excess, of sin, of ourselves. He spoke that hardest of gospels in our ears to throngs crammed by the thousand into the duomo. Yah, I know it is not popular now. Your generation thinks us mad. We were a little, I suppose. But I can still hear him now, see his eyes burn. Why did we worship princes like the Medici more than God? Were we not as weak and cowardly as the Israelites who craved a king in the days of Samuel? Had not he, Savonarola, come to call us to repentance, back to the real God? Could not God himself make a purified Florence great in the earth without the corruption of aristocracy – one man lording it over another? I say this having known and loved the best of them in Lorenzo, but I think even he, sensed the possibilities that pressed at our gates for admission. Imagine it, yes signors, just imagine it; a new and pure republic blossoming from the very navel of Italy. Florence would reform Europe – a second Rome.'

'And you believed him?' Hugh asks.

In the same instant, Bembo says, 'And you really did commit your work to the flames?'

'I did and would again. Would you not, Signor Bembo? Fra Hugh? Would you not bend your pen, your sword, your moral all to be part of a reformation of Christendom. I took some canvases, some folios containing sketches of Simonetta even, others brought masks, costumes from the pageants, oriental carvings, ivories, brooches, books of pagan content, hermetic texts. The Della Robbia monks brought terracottas, everyone was there. Yes, we believed him, though maybe some more for the glory of their city than justice for the poor. But how could we not? Israel stoned the prophets sent her; would we be like Israel? Savonarola had prophesied a new Cyrus would invade Italy to punish her, and then France came. He said France would scourge the Church, which would begin its renewal – a renewal that would spread East to conquer the Infidel and prepare the way for the Second Coming of Christ.'

'And France did come,' Bembo says glumly.

'Yes, France did come,' Botticelli repeats, his eyes now kindling something of that old fire and his fingers clenching into a fist. 'Then everyone believed the monk; we were all ready to acknowledge that, one and a half millennia after Christ, we were in the tribulation spoken of in the Book of Revelation. And who could deny that Satan had loosed the Antichrist and False Prophet on the earth.'

'Rodrigo Borgia?' Hugh says.

'The veryu same.' Botticelli nods solemnly. '*Pere et fils*. Cesare was at the head of an invincible army. When they slew Fra Savonarola and Fra Domenico, we believed even that was foretold in the eleventh of John— that they were the Two Witnesses. I wrote as much on my canvas of the nativity, which I painted at the time in my grief. They were days of sadness and oppression, more capes than cloaks were seen, more soldiers than citizens. People did not look or greet one another in the streets as in older, happier times. Informants were still rife; honest men were spied on by those who had the reputation for honesty. But in the end, Savonarola did not rise from death after three days as foretold. He was not one of the two witnesses from the book of Revelation after all.' Botticelli looks upward. 'So, in the end I do not know. In the end God chose not to be glorified by Florence, by our pious republic – skin deep though it was. But that doesn't mean the devil does not have a use for us. *Dio Mio*, what a city. In truth I don't know what to make of any of it these days. I am sorry signors, old men talk too much. They always do and now I know why.'

The three stand in a triangle for a moment, the younger two facing the elder. Hugh had been trying to imagine England under a similar reformation, fired by holy zeal to be another Zion – God's *almost* chosen people. Bembo perhaps is imagining himself reformed, alive with fervour. The poet turns his head toward the river, turbid, brown, and broiling interminably, like the hearts of mankind and the fortunes of nations. Without looking up from the river, he says, 'I am surprised you did not say more before the secretary last week.'

'Machiavelli? Do you think I have not? But you cannot wake a man who is only pretending to be asleep.' The old painter starts his slow shuffle toward lunch, calling after, 'Heaven understands hell, my friends, and understands her too well. But hell will never understand heaven. And if my years have taught us old Florentines anything, it's that in our present condition, we would find heaven an acquired taste.'

THAT EVENING IN THE CLOISTER AT SANTA CROCE, FLORENCE.

Hugh is sitting on a shallow, limestone bench with Bembo, stiff from the walk, slightly feverish again in body from the exertion but above all feverish in mind. Signor Botticelli has given him much to think on.

Was he right to talk thus? To deduce thus? Savonarola had not power enough to maintain his grip on the religious affections of the people. The people had not power enough to keep themselves in a state of fervour above a few years. They sacrificed their golden calf, some of it, and then burnt their Moses because he would neither let them enjoy the pleasures of Egypt nor lead them to Canaan – or even deliver them from Pharaoh. But that is not what Hugh wants to think about. *What is it?* His mind wanders, disorientated by words, impressions, images.

The compline bell sounds mournfully above the rooftops, yet the crows do not stir on the pan-tiles opposite where they sit. Feet shuffle on wooden stairs. Friars appear on the upper story of the cloister and process toward the stairs where others are already descending, appearing in the lower cloister. These all process in the same circular motion as if waiting for their brothers to join them before finally completing their journey to the choir stalls where they will fulfil their evening office.

That is it! Hugh thinks, that is it: circular versus linear. He turns to Bembo as the slap-slap of sandals on stone echo rhythmically off the milk-white vaults above him. 'Botticelli said something today –'

'What?' Bembo is brooding with his eyes shut and lips puckered, speaking without bothering to look. 'Him? Hardly stopped speaking.'

'No, it was something that touched me.'

'About the woman, Simonetta?' Bembo's eyes open, and he casts a wily glance Hugh's way.

'No. Well yes, that too, but it was something else. Something about their addiction to novelty killing their joy. Something about horses and centaurs, you remember.'

'Oh that. I'd rather given up by then. You know how old men go on. I should know myself as I'm more than half way there.'

Hugh ignores his comments and continues over him, grasping at threads and tying them off. 'You said something the other day, at that junction that would have taken us to Mantua. Do you remember? You were speaking about the sages and sophists of Asia and Cathay, that they saw history as a great circular flux.'

'I remember. What I was in fact saying, Hugh, if you were listening, is that the stories that reach us from those ancient lands miss a sense of development, of finale – they begin with a middle and end with a middle. They lack what I call the relentless necessity of what holds us to the page.'

'Exactly, and that is because we are taught that history is linear, that it has a climax.'

'Indeed.' Bembo moves his feet inwards as the friars pass them. 'And it creates the possibility for personal history, as Petrarch shows us; individual lives and actions become pregnant with meaning. You are not a mere instance of the class man, but a particular, unrepeatable creature who never existed before, nor will again. Under that ancient eastern view, which was in some measure present among the Greeks too, I think, *the new* was something to be feared, because it was an aberration of the natural, the eternal or archetypal.'

'And for us?' Hugh stretches out his stiff limbs now that the monks have passed. The wound from the crossbow bolt is healing with little cankour, but every now and again he gets cramps and pains there. *And us? Dear God. Surely, we must give account at the judgement.* Hugh savours the passing smell of sweat and incense. *Ah, that is us in a nutshell. Ora et Labora – work and prayer.*

'For us it could be welcomed, as could surprise. The only reality about the future that we can know is that it has not yet happened. We often overlook the importance of that fact, don't you think? Perhaps even you, friend? We, by our actions, may make it better.'

'Or worse.' Hugh adds, noticing now that even though the odour of sweat had been stronger, it had now passed leaving only that peppery hint of incense to adorn the stillness.

'Hmm, suppose.' Bembo affirms, 'The world may change and be better than it is now. You can create a real future in the present by what you do, or what you do not do. And that is the point whether you accept it or not.'

'Yes, yes, all right.' Hugh whispers so as not to disturb the friars, who have nearly disappeared from the cloister altogether. 'But an unfettered belief in progression in all areas proved disastrous to the people of this city. You can see that can't you'

'Yes, if you believe a bitter old man like Botticelli, who has more melancholia in his little finger than even you have in your whole thigh. What would you rather? Escape the future? For what? For fear of intemperance, excess, wrong paths? I can't recall who it was, but one of those sophists said that we should not attempt to accomplish anything in time, which is "only the dominion of tears. Do not search or journey, but sit, compose yourself by the river of life, meditate on the ceaseless and meaningless flow until you too become one with the Great Wheel, at peace with your own death and the death of all things in this sphere of corruption." Is that what you would rather? I think not. Hugh, Hugh?'

Hugh shudders and shades his eyes with his right hand.

Bembo, not the most demonstrative of Italians, places an uneasy hand on his shoulder. 'Are you quite well?'

Hugh removes his own hand and nods, saying in a hoarse whisper, 'Yes. But you forget the downside of a linear view of time.'

'What?'

'That we cannot mend the past; it is fixed forever. And ever. Set in eternal granite above the vast planes of time. Immutable.'

After an open-mouthed pause, Bembo, the sinner, says with the waver of uncertainty, and as if the weight of Hugh's words were an accusation against him alone. 'But we might seek absolution, and God may grant it, may he not?'

Hugh wipes his right eye which has begun to tremble. 'We may know it when the future arrives, but as you say, that future is not yet.' Hugh stands and straightens his stiff limbs, ready to follow his hosts. 'So, let us say our *Pater Nosters* and *Ave*s in the meantime.' *If that is all there is.*

16TH APRIL, SAN GIMIGNANO, THE HOUSE OF SIGNOR PAOLO CORTESI

Bembo has already remarked that intellectual blemishes, like facial ones, invariably grow worse with age. Hugh is now agreeing. They are sitting with their host in an upper loggia, looking out on the fields and patrician towers of their attentive host. Hugh's humours are out. He broods over his wine, nursing it a wound, along with black thoughts about his host, who will not shut up about himself. Signor Paolo takes Hugh's indifferent smile as an encouragement to rattle on. Even Bembo can hardly get a word in.

Great Neptune, Hugh sighs quietly. *Now not two but three great antique bores: Demosthenes, Cicero and Paolo Cortesi.* It's the sort of thing that can only be patiently borne by a corpse. It is not so much the affectation of his nasal tone, more the fact that he will not stop talking. *And how can he? He has nothing to say and so has no way of knowing when he has finished. When ideas fail, words are such good fillers.* Hugh finds he can only cope with the monologue by turning the endless flow of self-aggrandising data into a satirical elegy.

The late Signor Cortesi was a man of elegance, wit, refinement;
a man of Periclean modesty – and one who never met a digression

he did not like. Of late, a valued and much-admired patrician from the noble town of San Gimignano, Signor Cortesi was essentially a private man who wished his indifference to public praise to be universally acknowledged. Signor Cortesi had been apostolic secretary to many popes, including Rodriguez Borgia, whose cardinal sin was a preference *not* for Ciceronian Latin but the eclecticism of Polition and Ficino. (The fiend!)

Hugh is drifting, pleased with the diversion of his thoughts.

Signor Cortesi, *instrumentum regni, Capo Ufficio, Uomini rispettati* and most valued member of *onoreti societa, e gli amici degli amici,* departed this life on the sixteenth April, this year of our risen Lord, fifteen hundred and nine, when he was ingloriously pushed from his upper loggia by ungrateful foreign guests, and expired with sartorial elegance in the public square, the words of Cicero on his lips: *O tempora! O mores!*

Hugh is brought out from his meandering thoughts as Cortesi asks, 'Did you know that Saint Jerome once awoke in a frenzied sweat after having a dream that Christ had condemned him to hell for being more Ciceronian than Christian? Hardly the worst of his sins.'

Bembo says he remembers. Hugh shakes his head. Cortesi smiles so Hugh can see all his teeth, then he sighs wearily. 'And you a graduate of Cambridge University, too. I suppose you know that the great Erasmus of Rotterdam has been lecturing there but is even now journeying to Rome? Have you read his *Adagio*? Most diverting, though you will find many of the adages are taken straight from the Greek satirist Lucian.'

Hugh does not answer, so Cortesi continues. 'Bembo tells me you are a poet of sorts. Do you compose much? No? Well, it is hard for an active man to find the time, I suppose. That is why retirement suits me, why San Gimignano suits me; a man needs tranquillity to write.' Without waiting for encouragement or even acknowledgment Cortesi continues, 'Of course, perhaps you already know that I am writing a book called *The Cardinal.*'

He rolls the *r's* when he says the name *'De Cardina-r-r-r-lato'* with one hand raised like an orator as if he were at the speakers' roster in the senate. He explains that it will be a manual for the aspiring renaissance prelate-prince: what to read, what to build, which architrave or capital is *de rigeur* – all the important things. He says he has seen a good selection of palaces.

Bet he has, Hugh thinks. I imagine he was there to record the Borgia pope collecting them and dispossessing their former occupants – removing them permanently, so to speak, 'from the occasion of temptation to avorice.'

'The book,' Cortesi continues, somehow capitalizing the 'T' of the, so that it sounds like a very definite article. 'Will set the benchmark of good taste and decorum for all Europe.'

'You mean Western Europe,' Hugh says.

'What. Yes. Is there another?'

Lord help us, Hugh groans inwardly. Perhaps he supposes it will eclipse Gregory's *Liber Regulae Pastoralis* which has remained the bishops' handbook for centuries. Perhaps it will. *O tempora, O mores!*

'*The* book will be as Ovid's *Ovidium* was for the poets of his day. Bembo, you will like it. The cardinals and bishops of Europe will like it. I have traded his former Ciceronian Latin for something less callow, more –'

'Apuleian?' Bembo says, 'Our friend Castiglione is attempting something similar for the courtiers.'

Cortesi sniffs. He doesn't like to talk about other people's books and so carries on talking about his own as if he hasn't heard the remark. 'Every public man who has been honoured by great position, as I have, has a good book in his head, you know.'

He says it looking straight at Hugh, who wants to say 'best place for it' but refrains.

Bembo offers to read a draft. Hugh would rather have his teeth pulled out with farrier's tongs. He recommits himself to keeping a civil tone. After all he is a guest. But in the mood he's in, a hayrick with the pigs looks almost preferable for somewhere to sleep. Hugh sees Cortesi eyeing him narrowly.

Signor Cortesi says he has little time for the English poets, except 'Moral' Gower, whose tranquil and pellucid poetry is the nearest England has come to the best old French. 'I wonder, Fra Erpingham, whether you, yourself did not take some inspiration from Gower; you being a knight of Rhodes. For was it not in Gower's vision of knight errantry that his knight was "sometime in Prus, sometime in Rhodes" and the herald cries out "Valiant, valiant, lo, where he goeth!"?'

Hugh says that he could not discount the influence, but surely his host is too hard on the English verse. 'Have you not read Chaucer's *Parliament of Fools* or Langland's later works?

'You will forgive me, signor,' replies his host, 'but I have no stomach for the English or German tongue; always sounds like someone is farting when they speak. Here, we speak use Latin in church, French to curse, German for our horses and Italian for our lovers.' He makes the affected gesture with a limpid right hand. 'So you see, it leaves little room for other triffles which is why I hold these northern offerings in contempt.'

'But not, I should imagine,' says Hugh, 'that contempt which familiarity breeds.'

17TH APRIL, 1509 – SIENA, MIDMORNING IN THE PALAZZO PUBLICO

Hugh glances at the Bartolo's painting of Romulus and Remus on the wall of the second-floor antechamber to the *concistoro.* Impressive.

Bembo whispers into his left ear, 'Let that be a reminder, Hugh. Those two weren't the only ones to be suckled by a wolf. You're in Siena now, self-proclaimed heir to the eternal city.' Bembo coughs quietly then glances about the *antecapella* before concluding, 'They say that the earth is the Lord's and the fullness thereof, but Siena belongs to the Petrucci.'

They await the coming of the man himself—Pandolfo Petrucci, who at present is holding back-room talks in the *Sala del Mappamondo.* 'He'll be with the Council of Nine,' Bembo says. 'Their last meeting before Easter. It's how they do things here. Petrucci is *podesta*, and the Nine represent the people. They call it a limited republic, not quite as formal as Venice, or as ramshackle as Florence.'

'Limited republic with Petrucci in charge. Nice. Everyone is entitled to *his* opinion.'

'Yes, you've got it. I heard that Petrucci once said that he doesn't care how many people vote so long as he can control the nominations of the Nine.'

Hugh is still looking up somewhat dreamily for he is taken with the aptness of the image: be suckled by me and I will make you safe and prosperous. *Ploughing with the devil, indeed.* He starts a rather absent viewing of the other paintings in the room. Bartolo has painted the Roman civic virtues: Justice, Magnanimity, Strength, Prudence and Religion as historical figures significant in the foundation of Rome – Cato, Muzio Scevola, Scipione and others. *These paintings are probably already a hundred years old. Talk about being ahead of the times. Religion here already looks like the poor relation – some fruitless spinster aunt to Petrucci's puppet-polis. God's oath, there is more than one way for a man to forget his God and bury his conscience – these Sienese will smooth your way for you. Don't they brag that they were the first to site their town hall at the centre, and their duomo off on some back street? I know how that feels; easy at first. But you can never suppress one without getting something worse in the end. The crowd asked for Barabbas, and Judas got thirty pieces of silver, but it wasn't all they got.*

Hugh walks to his left, running his hand on the marble plinths below the frescoes. On either side of the great arch leading to the *Sala del Mappamondo*, stand two bodyguards with halberds and cross hilts. Their liveries are Petrucci, not Siena, a shield half topaz blue, half bright yellow with the join between them, a sharp zigzag. The sign is ubiquitous here, often with a black eagle in the corner, but no one is going to bother embroidering that on a soldier's surcoat. He comes near the bodyguards, casually observing their stance, muscle tone, eyes. Pointed iron helmets almost cover those eyes, in the manner of the Portuguese. Certainly the older one can handle himself. His hands bear the telltale white lines of a man who has survived numerous engagements. Hugh glances up above the arch and espies a map of Ancient Rome with the figures of Jupiter, Apollo, Pallas, Aristotle, Caesar and Pompey. Behind the doors he can hear Petrucci's voice. *Which does he think he is? Jupiter probably. It should be refreshing in an age of open atheism to see a civic leader still believing in at least one god. It has become something of a theme; the self-made man who worships his creator.*

The Nine are dismissed. Processing grey beards in black robes of office shuffle along the marble floors like so many choristers. A pale secretary summons Hugh and Bembo, with long, ephemeral fingers, leads them into the hall. It is the largest room in the palace, double height, with a coarse wooden ceiling and walls covered with frescoes of maps—places to trade, places to conquer.

'You're late. I was expecting you long before this. It is Easter tomorrow.' Petrucci's face is claret red, eyes weary and twitching slightly. A page removes his black cloak and smooths down the ermine hem. Other clerks are removing folios, papers, and inkhorns from the large oak desk behind where the podesta sits. Two guards close the doors behind them. Above Petrucci is Simone Martini's striking equestrian portrait of Guidoriccio da Fogliano at the Siege of Montemassi. The commander is cloaked in his yellow and black chequered tabard, embroidered with all the insignia of the da Fogliano family, his horse liveried in the same style. The heroic ruler.

Hugh checks automatically to his left, No exit. Only another enormous fresco by the same artist: the Madonna in glory. *Military glory endorsed by heavenly glory. How could Siena lose?*

'Pardon us, signor. I am Pietro Bembo, currently of Urbino.' Bembo bows. It doesn't do to mention Florence here. Hugh sees from behind that Bembo's hand is shaky. He is hoping, no doubt, that Michelotto never mentioned Bembo by name. 'One of our horses was lamed and so we spent a night in San Gimignano with Signor Cortesi.'

'Cortesi. Do I know him?' Petrucci raises his chin slightly so that the dimple in the centre of it seems more pronounced than ever by the play of morning light.

'Former apostolic secretary.' Bembo replaces his blue velvet beret uneasily, and arranges the white feather. 'I'm sure if you but visited the town you'd find him soon enough, signor. If you saw two people talking and one looked bored stiff, Cortesi would be the other one.'

'Oh, that Cortesi! Paolo! Ciceronian Latin! Of course.' Petrucci's face for a moment ignites into something almost humane. 'Yes, I know *him*. I spent a month down there one weekend. I'm surprised you didn't sell your horses and walk.'

It is an unexpectedly bright start to the business. But no sooner have the two men finished tittering then Hugh feels Petrucci's eyes rest once more upon him. He had been listening to the movements of the guards outside the door, and now he turns to observe the corner door behind Petrucci through which the clerks and page are dissolving. *They do not lock it. Through there; right, then right; stairs, exit.* With this ascertained, he is content to return Petrucci's iron stare and approach the table. 'Signor Petrucci.'

'I see Fra Erpingham is in health.'

'I am indeed. Thank you.' Hugh takes a chair and throws his beret onto the desk in front of him. 'Though the same cannot be said for your former ally.'

'Ah, Michelotto. I heard of his accident.' Petrucci sits forward slightly, and joins his fingers together. 'Yes, how are the mighty fallen?'

'Indeed, signor,' Hugh adds. 'One might say, *like lightning from heaven.*'

'Why, yes indeed, an unpleasant man, very coarse.' Petrucci angles his right hand slightly in order to examine his nails. 'I imagine even Florence will be better with one less Spaniard in it, or Catalan, whatever he was.' Petrucci looks up suddenly with a thin, lupin grin. 'But you are right Fra Hugh; Don Michelle and I did have a common cause in this present matter. But for all his claims, he proved himself ineffectual. At any rate, less effectual than you, Signor Erpingham. I am told you were less than half a day in Florence before the blood of countless soldiers and bodyguards were running in the palazzi and streets. You even throw the commander of their army off the duomo, and yet the signoria treat you as a saviour. I cannot work out whether you are blessed by the gods, or the devil's luck is with you.'

Hugh returns with a granite smile. What can he say? And the longer he is in Italy, the harder it becomes to answer. He was about to say *neither* and then something witty, but nothing comes. 'Perhaps tonight will tell. I presume you have made your usual arrangements to catch Vendramin.'

'Yes, and I am eager to know what you bring to the table, so to speak.'

'I understand you have tunnels under this city.'

'Yes.' Petrucci's brow furrows. 'But there is no way into the cathedral from the tunnels, I can assure you. Oh dear, I hope this is not the extent of your plan.'

'I should like to see a map of the tunnels, signor.'

'Very well,' Petrucci shouts orders to the clerks without bothering to turn his head. 'Lucca, bring the plans for the *bottini*.'

After a minute of rustling, the servant slides through the door without a sound, save the shifting of parchment. He unrolls the map, placing black stones on each corner, then leaves, trailing the smell of mildew.

Petrucci rests his fingers and thumbs on the table. 'These were still being dug when I was a boy. There are nearly twenty miles of them. Twenty miles! In a city little over a mile square. We Sienese are very great engineers, builders and artists as I am sure you know. Three hundred years we have been building the *bottini*. They capture and distribute water. Many houses have running water here. Not like Florence. In the old days Siena had eighty thousand people within her walls. We were one of the most important cities of trade in Europe. Florence was nothing then, but the plague came and two thirds died of it here - as I think I told you at our last meeting. Anyway, it has taken many generations to regain our strength. But—' He sighs again heavily, and raises his fingers off the table. 'I digress. These are the tunnels. What do you know that I do not?'

'Tell me about the vertical shafts that come up from the *bottini*.'

'The *smiragli*? There are many. They aerate the tunnels, and were used to extract material. If you see here—' Petrucci points to crosses on the plan. 'The fathers marked a red cross for a deep well – they can be sixty-foot underground – and a black one for a shallow one, sometimes only six feet below the street. Come, signor, you intrigue me.'

Hugh leans over the plan and points to the duomo. 'Where is the Piccolomini library?'

Petrucci goes to point but then stops. 'Ah.' He withdraws his hand and caresses his chin. 'It seems no one thought to update this plan. The library is here, attached to the nave. It is still shown as a courtyard on the plan and here.' He lets his finger fall on a black cross. 'Well, it appears you are right. Tell me, how did you come across this information?'

'Quite by accident, I will not bore you with the details.'

'Accident? I would say providence.' Petrucci reclines slowly in his chair, teasing a finger across his lips. 'If I didn't know better, I would say you were destined to meet this Vendramin – this man that everyone looks for and no one can find. Fra Erpingham, for the first time in a long time, I have hope.'

FOUR HOURS LATER AT THE FONTEBRANDA

Black clouds billow from the east like the sails of Turkish gokes. The vespers bell tolls mournfully from the austere, brick walls of San Domenico high above them. Crowds are already gathering at the duomo, sealed off by the archbishop since Good Friday. Poor sods will get a soaking. Afternoon is bringing evening, and evening, night.

Vendramin is already here. Hugh is sure. The sight of each man he passes in the street makes his heart race. Every open window, every moving curtain, every clink of steel or any loud noise. He is here. Perhaps he is already in the tunnels. *I would be. I would be holed up somewhere near, but also near a junction to give diverse options of escape.*

That is what Hugh told Petrucci. They examined the plans and discussed the operation. The *bottini* spread out under the city in the rough shape of an eagle in flight. Petrucci's men are doing a sweep of the head, wings and tail. Hugh chose the talons not just because they represented a smaller distance of tunnels but also because the Porta Fontebranda is the nearest gate to the duomo. It is a hunch.

The *bottini* feed two main fountains: the *Fonte Gaia* in the upper town, and the *Fontebranda* in the lower. The *Fontebranda* is the oldest, and has the sweetest water. The water pressure down here at the lowest part of town has enabled the functioning of mills, tanneries and dyers. That is where they are now. Hugh, Bembo, and Wilf stand before the three-pointed arches and crenulations. It looks more like a small castle than a fountain. Inside, under barrel vaults, the turquoise waters spill into three troughs. The highest is for drinking, the lower ones for washing, laundry and cattle. The water comes from small openings in the lower walls, cascading into the pools and sending out that nostalgic tinkling sound that makes all sane men remember how much they have forgotten of the wonder of childhood and the secrets of the world. In the far-right hand side, an iron gate to the tunnels is being opened by the fountain's keeper.

As they step under the right-hand arch, Bembo points to a house to their left. He talks incessantly when he is nervous. He is saying something about the great saint of the city, Catherine. She was born there, grew up a stone's throw from the fountain. No one is listening but Hugh. 'She was a dyer's daughter, refused to marry, received visions, tended the poor and made everyone obey God through her stubbornness, even dukes and popes. Is it any wonder Tuscan women are so strong minded?' Bembo adds, by way of afterthought, 'and I know for a fact that this fountain was referenced in Canto thirty of the Comedia, where Dante says he cannot imagine a more picturesque entrance to the underworld. Can't say I disagree, just wish we were somewhere else this evening.'

Wilf scowls at him. He is lighting the torches, face like a bulldog chewing a wasp. Tunnels are not for him, but he'll go anyway, muttering that he'll not leave his master alone with a treacherous dago. Hugh isn't listening. This is it. He knows what he has to do. He checks that his sword is secure, his dagger, his eating knife, the plan he sketched. He's constantly straightening and fiddling with his gloves, his fingers, his belt. Remoistening his throat, his lips. *This is it. What I have to do.*

He goes like Orpheus into the underworld. He will see soon enough whether the gods favour him, or if it is the demons who draw him here. He takes one glance over his shoulder, through the arches to the upper world. It might be his last remembrance of it, the world that defiled him and which he in turned defiled. Fat raindrops begin to dot the cobbles. One last breath. He turns back to face the abyss. In his mind he hears the old Friar's words in Assisi. "You murdered in cold blood; you killed a Christian, a man sworn to the same order as you, and you led other ignorant souls to do it with you. That is what you did. That is your sin?" Cold sweat runs down his neck. *That was not the half of it, but how could I speak more of it, to him a man of the church. And now look at me, bound to to commit further sin. Damned to repeat it all again and again. Pro Fide.*

THE BOTTINI OF SIENA. 10 MINUTES LATER

'Feels like I have been here a long-time master. Mortal cold it is.'

Wilf and Hugh are alone. Bembo is checking up a dead-end passage. The idea is to flush Vendramin toward the centre of the web. They stand on either side of a half-foot channel called the *gorello*. The sandstone walls are often moist to the touch. Part of the tunnel is brick-lined, the ceiling curved like a barrel vault, hence the name *bottini*, small barrel.

Wilf draws near to whisper. 'D'you hear that? Voices. I think it's none too clever you being down 'ere in the first place, but don't you think of disappearing off on your own. Ain't no one down 'ere what don't want to put a knife in your back. This Petrucci dago don't wanna share the goods with you any more than you do him. I bet his men have their orders to leave you down here if all goes according to plan. And this Vendramin old-boy ain't gonna spare you neither. He knows you've got orders, and he'll get the knife in first if he can. And Bembo! Wouldn't trust him for all his tears and fine promises. You let him off too easy, master. He's taking the piss. He knows he can still get what he wants if he keeps in with you, and when he sniffs that gold? Bumph. A cold knife in the belly for you, I don't wonder. So don't you go nowhere on your own.'

Hugh is nodding, and trying to listen ahead. 'What do you think we'll find up there Wilf?'

'Trouble, master, that I do know.'

To their left they hear the familiar scuffing of Bembo's boots, the glow of his torch like a halo on the walls. He looks pleased to be back. His sword is in hand.

'Everything all right, Pietro?'

'Yes, why wouldn't it be?'

'I thought I heard voices.'

'It was a rat.'

'A rat?'

'Yes, the size of a dog. I showed him my steel and quoted Orlando Furioso at him.'

'What?'

'The scene where Orlando meets the Saracen. He soon scarpered.'

'Not surprised.'

'What did he say, master?' Wilf looks ready for a fight.

'Nothing. Don't worry. I couldn't begin to explain. Let's go.'

They are traveling uphill under the *Via di Fontebranda*. Their next junction will be a right turn toward the duomo. Each has a white arm bandage, and the password *'Vedo nella Notte;* I see in the night'. It is the motto of the *contrada* just north of the *Campo Santo*. They are mostly cobblers and cordwainers in that part of the city, and their emblem is an owl. Why the owl? No one can remember, but the motto at least is apt for tonight.

Five minutes later they pass a vertical shaft. They can hear the thundering of heavy rain on the street some ten or more feet above them. Bembo points to the *gorello* where the water is now overflowing and soaking the soles of their boots. 'When it rains in Tuscany, it is not like England. I have heard in your country, Hugh, it rains a little for weeks. Years even. But here when it comes, it comes heavy and fast. Petrucci warned us about this. The water levels can rise quickly. May local men have been caught off guard and drowned.'

'Then let us get to the duomo quickly. Look! The junction is just up here.' Hugh sniffs, coughs. 'What is that awful smell? This place is as sulphurous as hell.'

No sooner are the words from his lips than Hugh sees a shadowy form fly across the opening of a junction twenty feet ahead. He discerns the lash of jagged yellow that he saw earlier in the Petrucci livery. He is still wondering whether he has really seen something and not imagined it, when the shouts of men echo indecipherably somewhere distant. His heart freezes. Vendramin.

He rushes forward, shouting, *'Vedo nella Notte.'* But there is no reply.

As he approaches the junction, a vast, warm, pitch-laden wind rushes past his face, hair, knuckles. The torches flap and dim, and then spring to life. Hugh nearly drops his, as an orange light ahead grows brighter and brighter, hot and howling.

'Down, Wilf!' Hugh throws himself face down into the *gorello*, submerging his head in the flood water. There is no time to look behind him. He feels the rush of heat on the back of his neck, sees a great flash of light to the left and right even through his closed eyes. In the next moment it is gone, and all is dark. The torches are extinguished.

Hugh hauls himself up. The smell of burnt hair invades his nostrils. Wilf and Bembo are spluttering, coughing and cursing. Flames still light the junction. The water is on fire and flowing toward them. 'Get up quick,' Hugh shouts to Bembo, then in English to Wilf. 'Get up, Wilf. There is Greek fire in the water. Get to the side.' Hugh pulls the dagger from his belt and with that, and the Colhona, he charges toward the junction.

'Master! Where are you going?' Wilf shouts after him.

'Vendramin went this way.' Hugh is at the junction, the flames licking his boots, but he keeps well to the side. It is like oil aflame, and the odours of tar and sulphur burn into the deep recesses of his throat, burning the nose, smarting the eyes. Thick, coarse, vitric death. *God, I can't breathe.* To the right, toward the cathedral is all belching flames and the distant shouting of Petrucci's men. To the left flames rise to chest height as far as the eye can see which is about thirty feet. Beyond that next bend, who knows? *Bastard. Cunning bastard.* Hugh punches the wall.

'Hugh, come on. We must get out of here.' Bembo is shouting, choking. His knuckles are burnt.

'He'll not get away again. I won't let him. You go back.' *He is the very devil, but damn me if I don't catch his tail.* Hugh wraps his wet cape about his body, his hands, and plunges forward toward the flames. He hears them screaming behind him as he rounds the bend and runs headlong into the furnace. His feet are on the far side of the channel, slipping on the oil fire under them. His boots are flaming, his knees scorch, his head spins. On, into the orange, the yellow, into hell's antechamber. His eyes squint, cinder dry. His retching mouth is raw.

Shit. It's killing me. I won't make it. Damnation.

On, through the gaping jaws of an ancient dragon, into its heart. He knows what he must do. His boots tap out a dance on the flaming stone, ten feet in, twenty, thirty. His right arm hits the wall. He's at the bend, but still fire, heat, billows of smoke, and now even steam as his clothes dry and catch fire.

On again.

He staggers from wall to wall, banging his right shoulder, then his left. Retching cough. His lungs scream for air but there is none. His knees buckle; the flames lick at his face. His eyebrows shrivel, yet still he struggles against the whisper of despair. The knife and sword grow hotter between his fingers. *Shit! The flames are under my cloak.*

Is there no end to this? He stumbles. *I am falling. I won't recover. God help me. Jesu, son of David, have pity on me.*

But even as he goes forward and down, the world grows black again. Black and cool. Water is all round him. *The waters of death are about my head. So cold.* Death is bliss. All the pain is forgotten for a moment. His legs, and his face are cold again.

His weapons chaff the ground as the delicious waters close over him. He is not dead, but rather plunged into some cistern or deeper channel. He surfaces, finds his feet, sees the flaming tunnel behind him and then turns.

The flames illumine a forty-by-twenty-foot chamber, four feet deep and filling fast from three other tunnels. A thousand roofs and a thousand streets are pouring water into the *bottini* and cisterns like these. A faint light gleams far inside the right-hand tunnel. He wades toward it, forcing the water away with his hips. He mounts steps, gallons of black water rushing over them every second. Water pushes at his shins as he enters the new tunnel. The light ahead is fading. Progress is slow against the current, but with every step Hugh's heart thumps with increasing violence. Vendramin is finally within his grasp. Fifty feet away, maybe less. *I will fall on this villain, this traitor, and he will not know I am the avenging angel. The judgment of God, you bastard. I'll be the death of you, you devil.*

Thirty yards on, the water is over his knees; sixty yards, to his waist. The light is more pronounced. He goes on for ten, maybe twenty minutes. The tunnel goes on and on. How far has he travelled? Under the earth time and distance mean little. And then, when he is beginning to think he's been imagining the light all along, that it is some damage done to his eyes by the fire, it happens. He rounds a bend and sees it up ahead—the light.

He sees him too, a shadow silhouetted by the lantern maybe forty feet away.

The ceiling is no more than six feet high here with no brickwork. Petrucci had told him that this happened when the engineers found harder rock layers to cut through. Sometimes they only managed a hole a yard high. Vendramin's iron lantern produces a faint ring of light on the pick-dented roof. Hugh is closer now. He can see Vendramin's cloak floating behind in the current.

He sheathes his sword. There will be no room for it here. This will be a knife job. *If he stops to rest I could have him in thirty seconds.*

The figure ahead turns to look behind. Hugh freezes against the wall. *Has he seen me?* The lantern is not bright. Hugh can make out the outline of a beard but not the face. The figure turns forward again.

Then all light goes. Vendramin must have hidden or extinguished the light. Hugh strains to hear above his heart. *Is Vendramin moving ahead, or coming back for me? Or waiting for me?*

Hugh glides forward, holding his dagger extended in one fist and his eating knife raised high in the other. No sound beyond the ripples of water on wet rock and the thumping of his heart.

Something brushes his leg. Hugh slashes wildly. His knuckles sweep over wet fur at water level. *Shit, a rat.* The creature scrabbles away from him. Another. Bigger. Yet another brushes his left leg. Hugh recoils against the wall. He can never smell a rat without the taste of their raw flesh coming to his mind, the crunching of their bone, the fluids. They are swimming in the opposite direction. *They're not stupid, these rats.*

He edges ahead, knife out front. Any second now. Hold steady. Air. Vapour. Blackness. Tremulous anticipation. He is not there. He has moved on without a sound. *I must go quicker.*

Hugh imagines that he is walking into a sword, a pike, a *scoppietto*. The crack and the whistle of a bolt might sound any moment. Anything could be in front. His breaths become sharp and irregular. He can smell the steam from his mouth: sulphur and brimstone. Hot steamy vapours burning his nostrils. Vendramin knows these tunnels. They could take you anywhere.

He's probably laughing at me, waiting to burn me up, devour me in flame.

On and on, the only guide is the wall, the only solid thing in this underworld.

Hugh's head grazes the ceiling. The water level rises to his chest. On and on, step, slide, step, slide. Blackness. Nothing. Soon there is but a foot between the water and ceiling.

More rats coming through. One climbs over his shoulder.

He can hear a cascade ahead. It echoes as if in a large chamber. The water is rising above his collarbone. He sheathes his eating knife and puts the dagger between his teeth. He pulls against the current, kicking off from the wall where he can. The current isn't strong, but even so his clothes and boots make swimming slow.

Ten feet, twenty. The ceiling scrapes his head. He hisses through clenched teeth. Thirty, forty. A few yards more. Suddenly the cascading sound vanishes. The water has risen to the ceiling up ahead. Hugh goes forward, mouth and nose upward like a carp. He takes three long breaths and then goes under, pulling with all his might. Pull, kick, pull, kick. *How much further?* His lungs are imploding. Kick, pull, kick, pull. He tries to rise, but bumps his head. Kick, pull, kick, pull. *Please God, please. Not now while I am so close.* Pull, pull.

He surfaces in another cistern chamber, but he cannot feel the ground. After the initial rising he starts to sink under the weight of his clothing and weapons. He comes up again, gasping with a pathetic cry. The dagger slips from his teeth and drops like a stone into the depths. And that is when he hears a voice somewhere out in front of him, above him, near him.

'For such a virtuous knight, you cry out like a man afraid to meet his maker.'

'Vendramin,' Hugh shouts, taking in water as he does so.

'People have called me that.' The voice seems composed, not breathless. It echoes, and what with that and the cascade, Hugh cannot locate the man. 'But you know, Hugh – you don't mind my calling you Hugh, do you? – we are, none of us, merely what men have called us. People say that you are an assassin, but I am not inclined to believe this.'

'Let me come to you, and I'll show you. Argh.' Hugh struggles to keep above the water.

'Ah, very good. But you should be more civil as we shall be together for a little while in this chamber, you and I. The tunnels are now blocked and the water rises.'

'You sound like you are standing. Are you on a ledge?'

'*That* I am not telling. You should have done better reconnaissance. Turning up here this morning was sloppy.'

'You saw me? Should have introduced yourself.'

'Hah, very good. I am glad the water has not dampened your humour. I was the soldier guarding Petrucci's door. And I confess, you did look ill for a man supposedly doing God's work.'

Hugh tries to remember the face of the devil, but he cannot. No one bothers to examine the face of a common soldier.

'I also noticed the scar on your neck. I expect Michelotto regretted doing that.'

'Where he is, regrets are all he has. Ugh.' Hugh strains again to keep his ears above the waterline. 'But I think you lie, signor. I was wearing a broad napkin round my neck. The scar was covered.'

'Yes, I know that but when you glanced up at the map in the doorway, I saw it.'

'You, ugh, ugh.' Hugh's heart stops. 'So, you really were the guard! Clever you.'

'The same. I like to call in at the palazzo when I am in town. You didn't look well, I must say, like a man burdened. Speaking of which, if you wish to survive here, I advise you to loosen "the weight that doth so easily encumber". Your weapons, for example. A man swimming with such impediments is as one trying to live with guilt. He sinks. Wouldn't you agree?'

'Speak for yourself.' Hugh knows he'll have to lose his sword belt and likely his boots too. He releases the buckle. It is a very mixed sensation he feels as it falls, and he rises. He still has his eating knife.

'Ah,' Vendramin says, 'but I am not the one swimming.'

'You betrayed your order,' Hugh shouts bitterly. 'You betrayed the church, for what? Some petty vendetta against Petrucci? A life of ease?' Hugh finds the wall behind him and starts to swim the perimeter, all the time using his ears to locate the voice.

'You presume great understanding.'

'Do not mock me, you devil.' Hugh thrashes his arms in rage and shouts out his months of pent-up anger. 'Our brothers, your own brothers in arms, to this day give their bodies as the shield of Europe, without a sufficient fleet, sufficient armaments, defences. Is their claim nothing to you? The claims of honour, your solemn vows, are they nothing?'

'They are not nothing, only not enough.'

'What?'

'Come, come man. Credit me a little. If I am to be a devil, let me at least be a clever devil. Think you nothing of the pope's claim? Of Petrucci's, or Michelotto's even? Yes, you think something of them, but more of your grandmaster's, your *confrères*. Am I right? Of course, I am right. You would trust him with these riches, this power? Greek fire would be the power of life and death on the seas. You think only of survival, but I think beyond—to the future. As we Venetians learnt long ago, power on the seas is power to control trade. The control of trade could eventually mean the control of the world. You put the claims of Rhodes above obedience to the church. That is your decision. I place another claim above both of them. And that is mine. Wherever that power falls, it will draw evil after it, so I will make sure that it is lost forever.'

'And the gold?'

'The gold was got with much blood from the New World. It shall not be used to spill yet more in the old. I have plans for it.'

'Vengeance against Petrucci?' Hugh reaches a corner after what he guesses is thirty feet. *Keep him talking. I am getting closer. He grows louder, the self-righteous prick. I'll have him soon.*

‘I am not telling you all my business, but I will tell you that it has nothing to do with that fox. I am here in memory of a friend, one who died in my arms.’

‘Pope Pius.’

‘Yes, and I did not promise him anything concerning his murderer. He was too holy a man for private vengeance. But I swore by the holy rood after he died that I would speed the ruin of Petrucci’s house for their many treacheries.’

‘The gold ingots in the duomo.’

‘Yes, though that is more a distraction while I weave my web over him. The young Borgia was right about Petrucci. He is a master deceiver. But I am a Venetian. And even men like him, or perhaps especially men like him, need ready credit. I have arranged for this. The Strozzis were sad to lose his custom, but my rates were better – or at least my alias bank was. I have the deeds to all his estates. He has great trade interests in shipping, *me again.* And everything was underwritten by his estates, with cross-bank guarantees so there will be nowhere to hide. He is over-extended, and business is about to turn bad. Soon he will be friendless and landless. While he was thinking about those ingots, about catching me one Easter, I became his banker, his business partner and soon his executioner.’

‘You think of everything.’ *He’s not far in front, maybe twenty feet.*

‘I do, but that is not what I have devoted myself to. I wanted you to know that. You particularly.’

‘And what is it then, this infernal scheme that you have sold yourself for?’

‘As I said before, I am not telling you all my business. That would give the game away. And I must warn you not to come too much closer either.’

‘Really, and why would I listen to you?’

‘Because soon you’ll notice a strong current about your feet and before you know it, you’ll be sucked down the main outflow tunnel toward the fort.’

Hugh is about to answer when he feels a tugging sensation around his boots. He swims backward when he touches the wall and feels his finger dragging irrevocably across the slimy stone. The steady scraping on his fingers tells him that his whole body has been moving in the general current. The tugging comes at his boots again, this time with more strength. The drag increases. And then without warning or fanfare his body starts going down. He cries out again and lashes out at the wall. There is nothing he can grasp on the wall. He thrashes his arms, trying to gain some leverage against the undertow.

'An iron ring is fixed to the wall directly above the tunnel.'

Hugh gulps water. "How do I know you're telling the truth?' he sputters. His arms, clad as they are with sodden clothes, ache under the strain. He can maintain his distance from the opening for the moment, but not forever.

'You will have to trust me.'

'And what if it is too high to reach?' Again, the surging waters fill his mouth and he splutters and gasps.

'The rings were put there by the maker of these tunnels for men exactly in your predicament. Or did you think that you're the first man to be trapped here? Reach high, and it will be there.'

'*Bastardo.*' Hugh hisses and spits. The enjoyment in Vendramin's voice seems like mockery. *He couldn't just kill me. No, he has to play these games of torture.* Hugh struggles with a water-slapping backstroke move which pulls on his shoulder wounds until he is all but spent. His sleeves flounder like the sails of a capsized ship.

'Suit yourself, but as the French say, *tous ne peut pas faire deux choses en même temps*. You can only swim or reach up. Not both.'

For a further minute Hugh gasps, fights, and struggles even though he knows his strength has gone. The undertow soon has his feet again. He kicks. Again, and again. Kick, kick. The current takes his boots and knees, drawing him face to face against the wall in that last second before it pulls him down.

Hugh claws at the wall, his nails scraping the mould. There is no iron ring, just as he thought. The head goes under, his legs are already in the tunnel below. His fingers continue to scrape lower and lower until his elbows and wrist are beneath the surface. It is the end. As water fills him, his last stupid thought is, *I was right; there was no ring.*

But then something clamps his wrist. A hand? Yes, a hand is pulling him back up: elbow, arm, head. He gasps and splutters. His ears unclog to Vendramin's voice. 'Foolish – stubborn – faithless man. You deserve to drown.'

Hugh gasps. He is being tugged up in jerks like a sack of potatoes.

'I – cannot – see – what – hope – there – is – for you.'

'Argh.'

'But here is the ring that you could have reached if you'd done so when I said instead of wasting your strength.'

'I don't understand. Why are you helping me?'

Vendramin grunts. 'Because I have seen you, *been you*. And as I said to you in Rome, I want to help you find what you're looking for.'

Hugh is still petulant, sullen, gasping. He grips the cold, iron ring tightly and splutters, 'You know what I'm looking for?'

'Yes, but apparently you do not, even though you wear your hunger like a wolf.' Vendramin sighs again, his voice gentle, almost familiar. 'Do you think you're the first man that ever sinned, that ever raised a fist against heaven? When I left off my studies at Padua to join the knights, I was too young to know what it would mean. I was an idealist, as no doubt you are, or were – for surely no one goes to live in the jaws of the Turk for mere sport. So, we became soldiers of the cross, you and I, a generation apart, two sons of thunder bringing down fire on the heads of the Samaritans. And all that in the name of one who said, "You know not what spirit you are of" and that we should love our enemies, turn the other cheek. The hospitallers started as physicians and ended as pirates, slave-traders, and murderers.'

'And you would leave Christ undefended?' Hugh gets a second hand on the ring, in order to ease the blood running from his right arm. His fingers strain on the hook, his shoulders scream and his boots are almost being sucked off by the water.

'Hah! You are a humorous man, signor – defend Christ! I'd no more defend a lion. Did he ever give you the impression that he needed your sword any more than he did Peter's?'

'Christendom then.'

'Let nations defend their borders. Let them pray for assistance even. But let them not confuse their kingdoms with *His*, or assume so willingly the mantle of his justice who have not known his mercy. You ask me why I will not return to Rhodes; this is my reason. You ask me why I will not hand over the gold or the Greek fire; this is my reason. You ask why it is that I help you, my assassin; this is my reason. You think maybe it is because I am old that I do all this, that soon I must meet my Maker, that perhaps this has made me soft in the head. But I tell you – though I think you know it – that every day we must face him—*Him*—whether we like it or not. This is the burden of being a man, the dignity he has bestowed on us—that we can never be nothing.'

'I suppose the navigator was the exception.' *Enough sophistry you prick*. 'You took him and made him disappear.'

'I released him. I swear it. I tried to help him disappear too, but I was not quick enough. He was captured for the information he had. The White Cardinal, certainly, and a clever devil at that. Yet one more enemy you have, my young friend. I do not know where he is, but I know that this cardinal has followed your trail with many spies. Young Cardinal Petrucci is one, which is why he attended your progress south then north. But he is not the chief spider, and he may not even know who it is. Whoever the White Cardinal is, he is a man of power who has lost his way, and he has marked your card because he thinks you will get to me. But he is wrong.'

'Don't be so sure, Vendramin,' Hugh says, less convincingly, 'I will find you yet.'

'I do not advise it. And if I hear that you yet seek me, then I might find you myself and teach you a lesson you will not forget quickly. Remember, my work here is bigger than you understand now. I will not let you thwart God's will out of ignorance. So, beware.'

'You beware. You have me *and* this White Cardinal to look out for now. You're your time is running out.'

'The White Cardinal! Italy is full of such men, which is why they will see not one *scudo* of the Borgia gold. Not one *scudo,* you hear. It shall not be the Borgia's or theirs, but God's.'

'And you wiped out Borgia light horse for it, two hundred of them!' *God, my shoulders.* Hugh reaches up with his left hand but almost goes under with the effort.

'I gave them fair warning. They were soldiers, not civilians. And I knew they had performed devastation against villages near Perugia. Their hands were not clean. And it is not just the gold, Hugh. If they had got the Greek fire, they would have laid waste whole fiefs and dukedoms. I acted as the situation demanded. The gold would be God's, not theirs.'

'I congratulate you. This new god is easily appeased if gold and Greek fire will suffice to stem his wrath. Would there was more of it about. Perhaps I could make up my potion with frankincense and myrrh, then call it a deal.'

'Hah! You are a still witty man, signor, but you don't fool me.'

Vendramin's knees crack, and he grunts as he stands. 'I have lived a long time, seen many winters, many wars and the sunsets of many dreams. Yes, I have. And I will tell you something: when men hear the accusing voice of conscience, they either go to God or to the devil. Or maybe they go mad. Mad in many different ways, of course, and many of them quite acceptable in the best society. And I don't just mean like Farranata and Boccaccio who said there was no God. I mean *other* ways.'

Hugh is weakening. 'I don't know what you're babbling about.'

'No, you don't, and that is your problem. But take courage. I do not think you are far now.'

Hugh hears the man's steps above him, moving to the right. 'What? What are you doing? Where are you going?'

'I have been here too long already. Though I am glad we have been able to talk, I do need to be elsewhere. The water is rising; soon you will be able to get up here. The tunnel to your right will lead you out to the Via Francesco. There is a well in the friary courtyard. If the rains abate, you can send someone back tomorrow for De Blanchfort's sword.'

'You know it?'

'I would know it anywhere. He saved my life with it during the great siege. When I saw you with it in Rome, I wondered why he gave it to you. Now I know.'

'Know what?'

'*Adieu*. You will find me anon among my own people.'

A GREAT WHILE BEFORE DAWN. EASTER MORNING, 18TH APRIL, 1509, PALAZZO PUBLICO, SIENA.

'And then you waited all night for the water to raise you to the walk-way. Interesting.' Petrucci paces the floor of the Sala del Mappa Mondo, behind the giant table of the council, unshaven, unslept. 'Signor, are you listening to me?'

'What?' Hugh is conscious of at least three of Petrucci's retainers standing behind his chair, all within striking distance. Even so, he feels very distant from the room and from his present situation. He blinks and tries to straighten his burnt knuckles. They hurt like hell. 'Pardon?'

'You seem somewhat absent for a man who just let his enemy escape.' The pitch torches and tallow tapers paint the Sienese tyrant in yellow, orange, red and deepest black. The hollows of his eyes are unseen. His words jab, probe, cut, sting. 'Let me rephrase this so you understand me. By your own admission and the testimony of your people, you disappear down a tunnel with Vendramin before the first watch and reappear at San Francesco after the second watch without him. You say you talked for some time about matters of a metaphysical nature, and then he bid you *adieu*. You struck no blow. And he let you go unharmed.'

'That is what I said.'

'You are his assassin, and he let you go.'

'He did.'

'No man.' Petrucci taps his knuckles on the table, with barely concealed rage. '*No man* lets his enemy go when he is within his grasp. He was within your grasp, and you were within his. And yet here you are. And what conclusion am I to draw? It is obvious that he indeed is not your enemy. That you have been, or at least are now, co-conspirators against this republic, against my person, against the authority of the church.'

'I am sure you know, signor, that in the dark it is difficult to separate friend from foe.'

'Oh, so now you are hinting that he is now your friend. Perhaps you think to mock me. Me—Pandolfo Petrucci. Let me tell you something: if you go to feed lions, signor, you make sure you don't run out of buns. Did they teach you that in England or on Rhodes? Did they? They should have.' Petrucci rams his knuckles into the desk, his words now growing in speed and volume. 'Perhaps he thinks to ingratiate himself with his old masters by striking a deal with you. Perhaps he is tired of wandering, of having no city. I don't know. I don't care. What I care about is the deal you had with me. We had an understanding. I help you. You help me. Of course, I knew your allegiance was spread thin, that the knights wanted something, that the pope wanted something, but I thought to myself, this is all true, but if I have him here in Siena, he will not betray me.' Petrucci slams a fist against his own chest. 'I said to myself, no one would be so stupid to think he could double cross me in my own city. No. One. Would. Be. That. Stupid!'

After some seconds with Petrucci's words ringing back and forth in the Sala, Hugh looks across the flames and says with indifference, 'I have told you the truth.'

'Oh, you have told me the truth. Very well, tell me how Vendramin is able to reach down from the ledge to pull you up and yet you could not climb up for many hours? Tell me that.'

'He climbed down a short way on a rope. I imagine that it hangs down usually. If your men go there, they can corroborate this.'

'Really. I am sure they will.'

'And they could retrieve my weapons.'

'Oh, they could, could they? But of course. Such an honour to help the great and holy knight of Rhodes, Hugh Erpingham, thief, truce-breaker. You think that your vows protect you from my vengeance, just because God is not so forward on the matter? Do you think you will even need your weapons after today or ever again? Do you? Good God. You amaze me.' Petrucci leans forward on his knuckles again. 'What are you doing? Are you smiling at me?'

'No, not really,' Hugh is caressing stubble where his eyebrows once were. He grimaces under the sensation, which must look to Petrucci like a smile. He smells the beeswax on the chair arms, and thinks of England – standing by his father's chair in the hall, about to be disciplined and sent to bed. It is a queer, restful feeling. He is quite serene for a man about to die. He is slightly amused at his own naivety, coming down here thinking Petrucci might be grateful. *Did they not stop Vendramin planting the gold ingot? Perhaps not. Maybe he got in earlier. Whatever is the case, I shouldn't have come here so vulnerable. I must be going soft.* Hugh sighs like a man with piles. His mind and body are almost so tired that he would welcome the sleep. 'Do you really think God is not forward to punish us?'

'What?'

'You said so just now. You said God is not forward in the matter.' *Isn't conscience enough torment?*

'God or Vendramin? You are not very subtle for a man who is out of chances. You want to talk theology at this hour, do you? Very well, let us do it on the way to the front balcony where my men will throw you into the Campo for the dogs. Then you can speak to God and find out for sure.'

Hugh does not resist the rough hands that bind him like iron and march him from his chair. Petrucci leads the way back into the *anticapella*, past the *consistorio* and toward the doors opening onto the piazza. His voice echoes in the vault as he talks. 'I learnt all I needed to learn about theology when I was a boy. We Sienese are quick learners. I had a friend once, a friend who became the pope when he was older. When he was a boy, he did not have many friends because he was slow, *stupido*, always caught up in ideals and dreams.'

'Francesco Piccolomini.' Hugh winces as the retainers scrape his raw knuckles on their harness straps. Burnt flesh, like toothache, has a pain peculiar to itself. Eight more men are behind them. Two others in front with Petrucci. Too many for a spent man. *My last walk.*

'Quite so. His father gave him the most beautiful Turkish dagger. The handle was gold, inlaid with gems – the loveliest thing you ever saw. His father always gave him things like this. He had so many things, he did not care for the knife. For Francesco it was all books and saints. No, he did not care for the dagger. But I did, you see. I wanted one, I cannot tell you how much. So, I prayed to God that my father would give me one like it, but I quickly found out God didn't work that way, nor did my father. So, I stole Francesco's knife and prayed for forgiveness instead. And that is what I have learnt.'

'That God is merciful.'

'Yes, why not? God is bound to forgive. It is his business. How else can it be where there is original sin? The scriptures confirm this. My confessor confirms this. So, everyone is happy. You ask if I think God is slow; I say, yes, he is. A grave mistake. Slowness in issuing justice destabilises the state. That is why someone like you must be made a swift example of. No vacuums, no uncertainties. Everyone knows where they are. Of course, we will say it was a terrible accident, you fell, but those who need to know will know. You don't screw with Siena. You don't screw with the Petruccis. The Petruccis strike first. I give orders and men obey. That is how I have learnt to survive in a world like this.'

'And if I am innocent?' Hugh sees the front retainers opening the balcony doors. Last doorway. The noise of a distant crowd chanting comes from the duomo. Petrucci is chuckling. Hugh is filled with a desire to see his mother, his sisters and little brother again. Last tiled floor.

'Ah, I wondered how long that would take.' Petrucci turns back and walks closer so that Hugh can smell the stale wine on his breath as he says, 'You are ready to plead.'

'No.'

'All men do eventually, even hard cases like you, signor.'

'I just asked the question, what if I am innocent?'

'You don't look innocent, and that is what counts.'

Hugh looks at Petrucci and almost smiles at the irony. *Can't really argue with that.* Petrucci raises his head in a self-righteous way, looking down on the condemned as if he were balancing his family tree on the end of his nose. 'Maybe you think we are playing games here, that this is just an elaborate ritual we have to extract confessions? I am surprised nobody warned you about me. Throw him over.'

'I'm surprised you don't want to know more of what he said about you.'

'Vendramin? Why should I care?'

'Because he is about to take everything from you. The shipping trade you invested in is about to go sour. In fact, it never went anywhere, the man you were dealing with fronted the company for Vendramin.'

'Liar!' Petrucci strikes Hugh across the face.

'And don't think your creditors will extend you anything else. They will probably be giving instructions to auction your estates as soon as the holiday is over.'

'Another word and I'll kill you myself.' Another blow.

Hugh's head reels. Blood enters his mouth. 'You should have stayed with the Strozzis, Pandolfo. They wouldn't have let you get so overcommitted. It looks like I'm not the only one here spread too thin.' The man's fear-ringed eyes quiver. He knows it is true. *Mene, Mene, Tekel, Upharsin.*

Bam. Knuckles across the cheek. 'Give me a sword. I'll run this bastard through where he stands.'

Hugh looks at the guards. 'You may as well give him your arms and your fancy epaulettes too. You'll be out of a job next week anyway.'

Petrucci takes a cross hilt from the retainer nearest the balcony door. And comes back for Hugh. 'Hold him steady while I gut this lying villain.'

Hugh is leaning toward his right so that the man who has that arm starts to compensate by pushing against him. He thinks Hugh is leaning away from the rushing certainty of the blade. How wrong can you be? At the last moment, still keeping his eyes on the mad intensity of Petrucci's face in the grey light of dawn, Hugh jerks violently back to the left. The retainer is unbalanced and drawn cross the oncoming blade. It pierces his chest. He shrieks, crumples, and releases Hugh's right arm. Hugh sticks his finger in the other man's eye, then shoves him at the guards behind, just in time to face another blow from Petrucci. The ruler lunges twice, and Hugh keeps his body away by moving back and to the side. He is edging toward the balcony. If there is escape, then it must be through there.

Petrucci growls like a caged beast. His teeth are bared. 'Get him! Get him you idiots.' The last man's gore drips from the waving tip of the sword. Hugh edges closer to the door. The guards there look uncertain. One of them starts to draw. Petrucci is fed up with cat and mouse and raises the blade to slash Hugh to ribbons from the side. Hugh charges him while the blade is raised.

They collide with a thud against the wall. Hugh knees him in the groin but doesn't bother to wrestle the blade. There is no time. The window guards are upon him. One has an arm round his neck. A mistake really. Hugh sinks his teeth into the man's wrist. Blood, sinew, bone. Crunch. Lots of blood and lots more shrieking. The Sienese, like all Italians, don't mind expressing emotion. The man won't try that again. Hugh is almost thrown toward the door as the beleaguered guard tries to shake him off. The second of the balcony door guards has only just drawn his sword.

Hugh rushes him and shoves him against the door. Through the door. Light. Air. Damp. The balcony is twenty feet long and six wide. *No way up or down. No time anyway. The flagpole!* It protrudes from the building at balcony level about ten feet from the end. Beyond that who knows? *At least I'll be beyond the reach of the swords, maybe halberds and lances too. One. Two. Three.* Hugh gathers speed along the tiles. The guards are at his feet. He'll get one chance. He springs onto the balustrade and with the same step continues across the void toward the pole. *Will it even hold my weight?*

The wood looks old, maybe rotten. His hands connect. He squeezes, even as the crackling of sundered wood hits his ears. It is rotten where the pole is inserted into the wall. His hair rushes in front of his face; his stomach passes into his mouth; the flag rushes upwards, and the ground forty feet away comes to meet him.

Idiot. I spared them the trouble. I threw myself off. Yet here I am clinging to the old oak like a credulous child, as if the shattered fragments could save me. A moment later he feels the fall arresting, a flexible tension slowing then stopping it. Rope creaks; the flags are still attached. He is about to thank God and Saint Catherine when his body slams against the coarse stonework of the palazzo and nearly knocks himself unconscious. His knuckles take another grazing. His knees bang so hard that he almost lets go with the pain.

He looks up to see Petrucci and the guards leaning over the balcony, but it's not him they are looking at. They point to the further edge of the campo. The noise of a crowd. Hugh turns his head. Thousands are coming down from the duomo after lauds. Thousands of torches make a stream of tangerine light amidst grey waking streets. Thousands of voices shout for Petrucci—murderer.

Hugh looks back to Petrucci. His face, eyes wide as eggs, mouth ajar with disbelief, shows that he recognizes a very different dawn than the one he expected.

They are coming for him. Vendramin got his ingot in after all, the sly devil. I - was - murdered – by – Pandolfo Petrucci, it read. The crowd are shouting his name.

Petrucci screams, 'What does this rabble want? Ungrateful vermin, sons of whores and horse gelders. The bishop is behind this, the filthy whoremonger. It is treason, that's what it is. Insurrection.'

'Master, we must away or they will trap us here.' The chief captain tugs at Petrucci's sleeve, but Petrucci shakes him off.

'Vile, ungrateful scum.'

Hugh, suspended as he is between heaven and earth, is a mere observer now. He is incidental, an angel allowed to see and record. Petrucci continues to pour forth on his countrymen words that you don't often hear in church. His great love of Siena in general seems not to stretch to Siena in particular. He thought they wouldn't mind what wolf suckled them as long as he made them rich, made Siena great. He was wrong. He presumed on them. He took them for fools and took God for a fool too.

'Keep me back from presumptuous sins lest I become guilty of great transgression.' The psalmist was no fool. Pandolfo Petrucci: the man who thought heaven too slow. *Oh, the irony! Wait till I tell Bembo.*

Petrucci bolts beyond view and as Hugh listens to the receding sounds of doors and bolts. From beneath him in the piazza, he hears a counter surge of the crowd battering down the doors of the palace. Wood is shattered, iron bars are sundered and, quick as that, Tertullian's words from *De Resurrectione* pass like a galloping horse across his mind, *'Quae portas adamantinas mortis at aeneas seras infererorum infregit.'* That image of Christ breaking the 'adamantine bolts of death and the iron bars of Hell' is, for him right now, a more wondrous vision than all his cherished hopes of one day seeing the holy sepulcher.

Hugh takes a deep breath and a stronger grip. He knows that, like this tide of Sienese beneath his feet, there shall one day be a flood of eternal justice that will sweep away all evil. *It is true, I feel it now.* He knows it should terrify him but somehow it does not. Somewhere, the poetry of providence has suffused with the very air. Through the cracks and obscurity of his usual confusion, and even the great terror of damnation; Hugh senses not just the beginning of a new story but also the promise that all stories will one day find a right end. This almost seems enough to him as he feels the last strength leaving his bruised, burnt and battered body. Letting go and falling would not be so bad perhaps.

It is enough that there might be a truer place in the universe for orphans like Pico and his mother; a place even for rogues like Wilf, or traitors like Bembo - even a way back for villains like him and Petrucci.

It is enough that there might be a God who is not like my father.

He is just thinking this when he hears his name shouted up from the passing crowds below.

'Hugh, Hugh!' It is Wilf, holding his own against the crowd and waving his cap like a madman. 'It's me! I found'ya, I found'ya. Stay there. I'll get a ladder, don't go nowhere.'

'Hardly likely to go anywhere, you idiot,' Hugh says, but the words do not carry. He smiles. *At least not with you always there, and you always have been.*

www.ingramcontent.com/pod-product-compliance
Lightning Source LLC
Chambersburg PA
CBHW020603310726
48979CB00008B/1328/J
9781739185091